Reading 5X5
x2

Also from Metaphorosis

Verdage

Reading 5X5 x2: Duets
Score – an SFF symphony
Reading 5X5: Readers' Edition
Reading 5X5: Writers' Edition

Metaphorosis Magazine

Metaphorosis: Best of 20xx
Metaphorosis 20xx: The Complete Stories
annual issues, from 2016

Monthly issues

Plant Based Press

Best Vegan Science Fiction & Fantasy
annual issues, from 2016

from B. Morris Allen:
Susurrus
Allenthology: Volume I
Tocsin: and other stories
Start with Stones: collected stories
Metaphorosis: a collection of stories

Reading 5X5
x2

Duets

---

edited by
B. Morris Allen

ISBN: 978-1-64076-044-8 (e-book)
ISBN: 978-1-64076-045-5 (paperback)
ISBN: 978-1-64076-046-2 (hardcover)

Verdage

from
Metaphorosis Publishing

Neskowin

Contents

From the Editor	7
Duets	9
Children of a Wine-Dark World	11
David Gallay and Douglas Anstruther	
The Relic	37
J. Tynan Burke and L'Erin Ogle	
Lambs Fight to Die	57
Evan Marcroft	
The Third Chamber from the Left	75
Douglas Anstruther and L'Erin Ogle	
Boro Boro	89
J. Tynan Burke and Evan Marcroft	
Instar	113
David Gallay	
Snakeheart	131
Douglas Anstruther and Evan Marcroft	
Sudden Oak Death	149
J. Tynan Burke	
Titanotheosis	169
David Gallay and Evan Marcroft	
Memories Written in Scars	201
L'Erin Ogle	
Project Blackbook	211
J. Tynan Burke and David Gallay	
The Blood Dance of Ape and Mouse	259
Evan Marcroft and L'Erin Ogle	
The Firmament	297
Douglas Anstruther	
Daylight	321
L'Erin Ogle and David Gallay	
Infernal® Policies and Procedures Have Changed	339
Douglas Anstruther and J. Tynan Burke	

The Writing Process — 351
- Evan Marcroft 353
- David Gallay 355
- J. Tynan Burke 357
- L'Erin Ogle 359
- Douglas Anstruther 363

Copyright — 365
Metaphorosis Publishing — 367

From the Editor

Welcome to this second installation in the *Reading 5X5* anthology series — great SFF stories that also take a look at the writing process. The first *Reading 5X5*, published in 2018, asked five authors to write stories based on the same brief, for five different briefs in five genres; twenty-five stories in total. The Writers' Edition included an extra two stories, all the briefs, and an author's note for each story.

This volume, as suggested by the title, *Reading 5X5 x2: Duets*, takes the idea in a different direction. Here, each of five authors was asked to co-write a story with each of the others, as well as to write a solo story — fifteen stories in total, as well as authors' notes on how the collaboration process worked.

As with the first *Reading 5X5*, the principal criterion for the stories is quality — the intent of the anthology is to bring you great stories. That said, it's fascinating to see how authors' voices change and blend when they cooperate with each other, and the results are as varied as they are gorgeous, from epic duels both human and divine to alien spaceships to a train full of sacrifices barreling straight toward a god's seat of power.

I hope you'll enjoy these stories as much as I have; these are stories that will touch your heart, raise your spirits, and inspire you — with a few darker ones mixed in as well. And so, with just one more word about artwork below, on to the stories!

B. Morris Allen
July 2020

Iconography

The icons that work as scene breaks are also a minor memory aid. Each represents a single author, with an image drawn from their solo story. Two icons side by side tell you at a glance which authors are involved.

David Gallay

L'Erin Ogle

J. Tynan Burke

Evan Marcroft

Douglas Anstruther

For those interested, there's also a little more to the cover art. As above, the icons represent solo stories, and the connecting lines represent collaborations between authors. The color of the icon or line tells you the genre, with SF being yellow, and Fantasy being red.

Duets

Children of a Wine-Dark World

David Gallay and Douglas Anstruther

The three snail farmers floated up to their favorite corner of the taverna, where the filter's gentle current maintained the perfect euphoria-inducing concentration of bitter nox. Miniature arc-lamps gleamed through the taverna's cloudy water like strings of jewels. Below them, another group of harvesters tore open a net of wrigglers. Laughter erupted as the panicked fish unsuccessfully tried to escape the forest of grasping hands.

The trio had just settled in when Demod started back in on his current obsession.

"My guy at cataract station tells me they've been getting implodes down in the Beneath," he said, whipping his wrist flanges for effect. "Shuck, woom! Shuck, woom!"

Coronis scratched absently on his writing pad of pressed kelp. Both he and Naus had known Demod all the way back from clutch and usually attempted a good-natured yet skeptical approach to his ramblings. It helped pass the time during the grueling hours of the snail harvest. But this latest nonsense about the "Beneath" rubbed both of them the wrong way.

"Yeah? And how do they know it's not just seismic?" Coronis said. "Heard over the wire that the northern plume's been active."

"Weren't no seismic," Demod said. "Heard it myself. Reverb all the way up the world-chasm. Quavers your teeth like you bit into an 'lectric cuke."

"It's not implodes, 'cause there's nothing down there," Naus said. She stretched out, letting her toes scrape against the ceiling. It had been a rougher shift than usual, leaving them with aching muscles and chipped fingertips. "At that pressure it's just worms and bones. Like Cor says, bet it's just methane pops."

"I tell you, there's a whole world down in the Beneath. Point a scope down the cataract, you'll see it too. Lights racing back and forth, faster than any zip. Wait long enough, you hear singing too, real singing, not squid whistling. Here, here, look at this ..." Demod glanced around the taverna before slipping something out from his satchel. It was a small trapezoid of unfamiliar metal, slightly larger than a bone-coin. It gleamed with a yellowish-green luster. Tidy rows of unrecognizable pictograms were etched across its face, as if scratched with a fine needle.

"What is that?" Coronis asked.

Naus snatched it out of Demod's hands and examined it in the light.

"Seen these at the hag market along with the glowglass and hydra skeletons."

"My man at the cataract says things like this are dragged up in hot volcanic plumes all the time," Demod said, grabbing back his trinket. "Other things too. Said he's not allowed to talk about it."

"Fake, fake, fake," Naus said.

"One day I'll go down there," Demod said. "Then we'll see who's the faker."

"No one stopping you," Coronis said. "Just strap on some stones and step off the ledge. Float me a letter when you hit bottom. Better yet, come back with a squirmin' hydra on the hook."

"Why don't you go first, Cor?" Demond shot back. "Maybe then, you'd have something to put down in yer poems, 'stead of just floating there an' doodling. Say hi to Elpin while's you're down there." He stuffed his mouth with ferment and curled up in a sulk.

"Demod!" Naus exclaimed. "Leave the dead settled where they fall!"

Coronis self-consciously tucked away his pad. Naus eyed him with concern. Demod's comment stung and she knew it. But another round of ferment, maybe a short bath of nox, and all would be forgotten. At the end of the day, they would go their separate ways, to start the whole thing over again tomorrow. That was what life was. There was no mystery, no unseen worlds. Work, eat, sleep, repeat. Another night at The Happy Squid and its small, dull dramas. None of it inspired him. Coronis hadn't written anything worthwhile since the rebellion was put down, when he was still young. Now, approaching middle age, he wondered sometimes if he missed war. The rush of battle, all those moments charged with violence and blood. No. Of course not. Still, sometimes it seemed that the only novelties of life were draped in death.

"Well, I'll let you two finish the night without me," Coronis blurted out. "See you both on the glimmer." Before anyone could argue, he pushed downwards and darted outside before too much more nox could soak into his gills. Maybe another night he would be tempted to get drunk on the heady mix of pheromones, carbon dioxide, and plankton motes that clouded the taverna. But it was getting late. Already the outdoor arc lamps were boiling, filling the avenues with sharp angles of emerald illumination. Echoes of evening revelry rolled through the City, carrying the taste-smell of cracked mussels. Luxury zips ferried passengers between the narrow precipices that lifted the City out from the depths. Their lamplight skimmed across the cliff-edges of the cataract and pushed against the reach of the Above, where only the most expensive engines didn't sputter out under the low pressure. Cetus lighthouses, those ancient towers of stone named for the legendary benefactors who once gave their knowledge of artificial light to the sea-folk, encircled the cataract like silent guardians. Their sulfuric arc lanterns gently suffused even the darkest waters with twilight. The City at night was a beautiful, pulsing dream, awash in clean currents.

It was also all too familiar, predictable, and claustrophobically monotonous. This was the peace they had fought for. Died for. Soon another perfect morning would announce itself with a dull, coppery light, sending the dreamers back outside to face another day much like the last, and the one before that. Ahead lay a string of endless, identical tomorrows. The City was safe. The City was eternal.

The blank pages of his pad flapped in a sour current.

As one, every arc lamp in the City flickered out. The headlights of distant zips faded to dim ultraviolet and disappeared among the buildings. Window shutters clamped down. Portal bolts clacked in unison. The City was plunged into the safety of darkness. The only sounds were the whispering currents of the night and the soft clicking of lovers in the crevices. A cool draught rolled past Coronis, cascading a twitch of nerves up his dorsal. There was only one only reason to put out the lamps; a report of wild skylla in the city limits. Usually the predators kept their distance from civilization, preferring to hunt in the coral forests bristling the edge of the cataract. But occasionally they wandered up into the City, attracted by the bright lights and warm blood. They stuck to the shadows, and if you saw one, it was probably too late. A brush of their nearly invisible whiskers meant instant paralysis and death by slow consumption.

"No, no, no," Coronis seethed. He was exposed on the open streets, alone in the dark. Endless drills in the clutch had trained him to seek shelter. He looked around, but there was nothing. He thought about turning back to the taverna, but the thought of returning there to cower after his hasty exit was untenable. Besides, wasn't this exactly the type of excitement he was craving? He welcomed the rush of adrenaline and pushed onwards, skylla be damned. Using hesitant flutter-kicks, he pushed on through the darkness with only a vague idea of direction, only realizing he had taken a wrong turn as he felt the tug of a sanitation whirlpool pulling him forward. His wanderings had brought him to the edge of the City, where ancient filtration machines churned through millions of gallons of water with every turn of their unrelenting blades.

While simultaneously trying to remember the direction home and contemplating the countless other nox-soaked souls lost to the whirlpool's vicious slipstream, Coronis detected a new smell. Thick and organic, it sent a chill up his dorsals. He turned to face the darkness behind him. There, floating in the blackness, a bioluminescent light repeated a sequence of hypnotic patterns that even a child could recognize. Frozen in terror, Coronis did nothing as the skylla crawled towards him. Its gaping mouth and its sawtooth smile gleamed in the glow of its bobbing lure.

It lunged. Coronis did the only thing he could think of; he flung his writing pad at the creature. Its teeth easily tore through the kelp pages. Even in the face of horror, Coronis couldn't help but imagine Demod laughing at future retellings of this story, as his pathetic "doodlings" were appropriately ripped apart by a wild beast. Then they would celebrate his miraculous escape from certain death with enough nox to knock out a Cetus.

But there was no miracle. No escape.

Shaking away the last shreds of the pad, the skylla closed in for the kill.

Left with no other choice, Coronis kicked backwards, flinging himself towards the industrial maelstrom of the whirlpool, knowing that even being vivisected by the blades was a preferable death to being devoured alive. As he braced for the rotors, a violent blast of bitter, ashen water rushed up from the cataract, flooding over the filtration machines. The resulting slipstream grabbed him up like a child having a tantrum with a cheap toy. It spun him around and slammed him hard back against the street. It dragged him along the wall of an adjacent building, painfully snapping scales from his back. Finally, as if having grown bored with the game, the wild current viciously flung Coronis up towards the Above. The City buckled away from him, its darkened spires growing smaller and smaller, the cataract at its center a shrinking pupil. The entirety of known civilization could fit in the palm of his hand like a crust of glittering sand. The veins in his gills swelled painfully as they strained for oxygen. Vision fading, he gasped for breath but found none. The rising current was still carrying him fast and far as he slipped into oblivion.

"My head. Oh, my head."

A terrible squeezing pain rippled between his temples, across his chest and groin. Coronis knew he was too deep. He cradled his skull in his hands and rocked his body. He hadn't felt depth-sickness like this since the war. His squad had been tasked with placing implodes on the outcrop of a revolutionary station, a hollowed-out scarp along the City's southern cliffs. Even with frequent doses of the gelatinous nalox fruit, the pain had been constant and the narcosis only a long blink away. He barely remembered finishing the job. Only the signature sound of the bombs going off. *Shuck, woom!* Just like Demod said. He'd been lucky. Not everyone had made it out in time ...

It came back to him. The taverna. The arc lamps flickering out. The skylla. The whirlpool's slipstream. He must have passed out from the height. At some point, the rising current must have released him. With nothing to stop his descent, he'd sunk. Down, down, into the dark wildernesses that lay beyond and below the safety of the City.

By some miracle, he was alive. A quick inventory showed that he had survived largely intact. Several dozen scales were torn away. A stinging tear in his left toe-web had reopened. His writing pad was gone. Perhaps that hurt the most. It was one of the first things he had bought after the war, back when he had grand dreams of documenting an epic new life of adventure, back before he'd accepted the drudgery of snail farms and wasted evenings at the taverna.

By instinct he scanned the horizon for lighthouses. Their towering parapets should be visible for miles. No sign of them, no sign of the City at all. In every direction, nothing but a vast, kelp-covered plain lit by a dim, golden twilight. Twisting currents danced among fronds glimmering with faint bioluminescence.

Coronis tingled with excitement. Despite the direness of the situation, he felt strangely liberated. Or, that could be the narcosis. He had certainly sunk several fathoms below the City's depth. It wasn't deep enough to kill him right away, but without any nalox fruit to adjust his biology to the pressure, he wouldn't survive long enough to tell the story. He needed to keep moving lest sleep take him and never let go. Coronis ignored the pain, chose a direction, and began swimming.

He didn't see the thing hidden by the kelp until he practically stumbled into it. It wasn't a skylla or any other creature he recognized. It looked like a strange, hobbled child, combing the undergrowth for morsels. Closer inspection revealed something more like a gathering of eels in a vague person shape. Its arms and legs were vestigial stumps with long spider-like fingers it used to sift through the grass. It didn't quite have a discernible head, more like a nub of black jelly.

A hydra; a real hydra. Not a mummy, not a hoax, not a children's puppet. Alive.

Coronis unintentionally clicked in surprise.

The hydra spun to face him. No eyes, but plenty of teeth, most of them clumped with squirming crustaceans. Like a living cloud of ink, it twisted and darted through the water, constantly changing shape, limbs undulating asymmetrically.

"S ... sorry," Coronis stammered as he hunkered into a pugilist's stance. His eyes reflexively polarized, enhancing the contrast of his vision. His fins flashed bright crimson and gold as they joint-locked. "I didn't mean to interrupt ... whatever ..."

A blur rippled across the hydra's body. Its mouth and all the little carrion-soaked teeth were absorbed into itself. A diaphragmatic slit opened across its torso, vibrating with a dissonant bleating that gradually grew clearer, like a warped cylinder played in reverse, until distinct notes emerged, then individual words. Coronis tried to make sense of what he was hearing through his thudding brain. Whalesong. The damned thing was talking whalesong.

The hydra fanned out its long fingers as wide as they would go. "No harm," it sang. The creature floated closer. "What are you?"

"Um, me?" Coronis stuttered in whalesong as he nervously eyed the hydra's razor-edged claws. "I'm, I don't know. Just me."

"Oh?" The hydra sounded disappointed. "Is that all?"

Coronis floated motionless, torn between screaming and giggling. "I'm a poet," he bleated without thinking. "Well, what I mean is ..."

"Ah. A poet's eyes. You are precisely what we have been looking for." Excited spasms rolled up and down the hydra's gelatinous body. "Sea-folk will accompany us?"

"Where?"

The hydra pointed vaguely upwards. "Up."

"Up? You know a way? Maybe you can help me find The City. You know the City?"

"Yes, we go up. To the empty. You will be our witness. For me, for the Bright Ones. With your help, the bridge that burns will —"

Coronis swooned. When he came to, the beating in his skull had grown louder. He could feel inner valves closing up, fluids thickening.

The hydra took what might have been a thoughtful pose. "You do not belong down here."

Cornonis' thoughts began to blink out, one by one, inner voices fading into the darkness. He released his grasp of the waving kelp and floated away. *Let death come*, he thought. Suddenly, his eyes opened wide with adrenaline as the hydra grasped him and forced something into his mouth. It dissolved before he could spit it out, and soon a cold sensation washed down his spine. The headache dissolved, his veins opened wide, his gills breathed deep.

"You have nalox fruit?" Coronis asked. According to his superiors during the war, like the lighthouses and whirlpools, nalox were another gift of the Cetus. They were incredibly difficult to mature, requiring arcane knowledge of the botanical sciences that should be far beyond primitive species like the hydra.

"Yes, but not many. We must hurry. We must go down now."

"Hold on," Coronis said. "I thought you wanted to go up."

"Up is death. First down. Get us a" — it spat out a gibberish mix of chords and clacks — "then we go up."

Coronis fumed at the trick, but had no choice. He was tempted to just swim away and find his own way home. But how to even start? Even with his head clear, all he could see were miles and miles of kelp. And without any more of the hydra's nalox fruit, it would become his grave as well.

"Guess I'm stuck," he said. "Do you have a name?"

The hydra pondered this for a moment, mouth flapping silently, as if having an internal conversation with itself.

"Ogi," it finally answered.

"Call me Coronis."

※

They followed the gentle slope of the forest downward, vigilant for predators hiding among the kelp. The terrain became steeper as they went and the occasional outcrops of pale granite were replaced with jagged eruptions of volcanic rock. The lush kelp thinned out, and grew delicate, translucent, like fields of ghostly threads. A slow rain of organic detritus fell across the terrain, collecting in soft drifts. Signs of life were few and far between. Like Naus had said, nothing down at this depth but worms and bones. When the gauzy veil of night began to fall, they found abandoned boreholes to hide in. As Coronis picked over the few bony wrasses he had been able to trap, Ogi sang whalesong ballads of murdered gods, of tragic lovers driven cannibal by nox-lust, of terrible battles that cracked the ocean floor in half.

On the third night, Coronis asked why all his songs were so grim.

Ogi answered with a phrase that roughly translated to 'A Thousand Tides of Sinking Bones'.

"What is that, some kind of war?"

"Yes. A war. Always a war. Only a war."

"Well, I've been in a few fights myself," Coronis said. "We still found better things to sing about."

Ogi considered this. His morphic scales rippled one way and then the other, as if different flows of thought were contending for control. Then, it began to sing in a voice so low and quiet it was almost unrecognizable, its diaphragmatic slit barely vibrating the water. Coronis leaned in to listen.

"The journey will be exquisite
Across the bridge that burns
When the path of every hand
Finds the drowning light
A million Bright Ones
Wait on the other side of Death
Across the bridge that burns …"

Coronis didn't understand, but woven within the sad whalesong was the impression of beautiful purpose. "Ogi. Why are you going up, to the Above?"

"Keeping a promise," Ogi answered. "The Above is the way home for others, not only you."

After another full tide of swimming, they arrived at the end of the world.

Coronis couldn't help but grin as they hovered at the precipice. "The Beneath," he said. "Demod, you idiot. You were right after all."

Once, as a child, Coronis had swum directly over the cataract on a dare. He'd never forgotten the sensation of terror staring down that black throat while frantically kicking and paddling his way to the other side. But the cataract was a trifle compared to what lay before him now. There was no other side to this pit, only a gulf of darkness that went forever in every direction, an endless midnight sea scabbed with titanic mountain ranges that could fit a dozen Cities inside their crags. Massive smoker plumes roared from the darkness like furious demons, pustuled with methane fire, veined with lightning. And in every direction, enmeshed within the staggering landscape, chariots of war glided through the chaos like schools of giant luminous mudfish, each pulled by a magnificent armored Cetus. Even the smallest chariot easily outsized the largest zip Coronis had ever seen. They dripped with weapons, spikes and hooks and blades and chains forged out of that same yellow-green metal Demod had been showing off. Coronis watched in horrified fascination as a distant pod of Cetus war-chariots approached a spongy outcrop from which a swarm of eels poured. There was a blink of light and the outcrop simply disappeared. Minutes later, a thudding pressure wave slammed Coronis in the chest. *Shuck, woom!*

"Ogi, what is this war about? Who's fighting? Ogi — ?"

Ogi had curled into a ball, its limbs tightly wrapped around itself. Anxious spikes rolled up and down its fluid skin. Its claws scratched against each other.

"Sorry. Back home. I heard all. Too much. The hivemind sings of terror and betrayal and carnage. Wait a moment. I'll recompose." Ogi motioned for Coronis to keep close as it led him to a narrow groove carved into the side of the chasm wall. "This leads us to our goal. Follow. Careful. Quiet."

"Where exactly are we going?"

"The Castle of —" followed by an unpronounceable trill of internal clicks and grinds, teeth scraped against stone. "There we find what we need to continue our journey."

Coronis was too stunned by everything he'd seen to ask more. To think that there had been entire civilizations below the City this whole time, strange creatures building castles and machines, fighting wars. What other wonders had this world kept hidden from him, and the other naïve sea-folk? For the first time since being cast off from the City, he thought of Naus and Demod, back home, plucking snails. He wished they were here to share these marvels.

Their path wound back and forth along the wall. It tunneled through sparkling deposits of quartz and around impenetrable forests of petrified coral. They passed the rusting ruins of abandoned war machines cracked open like eggs. Some were still leaking unctuous clouds of toxic nox that refused to dissipate. At each new curiosity, Coronis wanted to stay and learn more, but Ogi dragged him forward. "No time," he said.

The path grew narrower the further down they went, until it was little more than a cleft in the canyon wall. With every step down they took, they lost some more light. When the darkness became absolute, even with every eyelid opened as wide as possible, Coronis stumbled to a stop.

"Must keep moving," Ogi urged. "Almost out of nalox fruit."

"I know," Coronis said, trying not to show his panic. "But I'm blind."

"Sea-folk, blind?" Ogi touched him lightly on the head. "Quiet. Listen. Let sound guide you."

It had been years since Coronis practiced his echolocation. It was taught to every clutch, but with arc lamps lining the streets and the constant glow of Cetus lighthouses, most let their echo skills atrophy. Coronis flexed his pharynx bones. Long unused muscles crackled in pain. A scruffy click bounced off the canyon walls. After a few more tries he could at least internally synthesize a foggy sense of the surrounding rocks, the edges of the staircase, the monolithic silence of the depths. Good enough not to accidentally lose himself in the Beneath. He made sure to remain no further than an arm's length from Ogi's amorphous sound-shape as they ventured further into the midnight waters.

They arrived at the Castle near the end of the second tide. The last dose of the nalox fruit was wearing off, leaving Coronis increasingly vulnerable to the crushing, freezing waters. They crept into the Castle, which was more like a labyrinthine cavern hollowed out of the chasm wall than any sort of actual structure. No one came out to greet them, but based on the size of the doorways, Coronis felt that was probably a good thing. Ogi led them deeper into the Castle.

"What exactly are we looking for?" Coronis whispered. Each chamber they entered was larger and more mysterious than the one before. One was a boneyard of broken machines. Another was ornamented with a trio of immense crumbling statues, gray sea-moss draped over their faceless heads like hoods. They entered an eerie space with no walls and no ceiling, where all echoes returned twisted, as if the water itself were suffused with some invisible malignancy. Even Ogi was spooked, and they crossed through as quickly as possible.

Eventually, they came to a large cavern that held an exotic menagerie. Cages lined the walls, some barred with that yellow-green metal, others composed of translucent pearl that phosphoresced against the shadowy creatures imprisoned within.

Ogi pointed to a cluster of oversized crustaceans clinging to the far wall. They were blanketed from eyestalk to tail in thick, matted fibers.

"What we seek," it whispered.

"What, those ... centipede ... things?" Coronis paced in circles around the room, kicking up dust. The caged animals squealed and growled in agitation. "I thought we were looking for a zip or maybe one of those war machines?"

"Quiet!" Ogi hissed.

The menagerie suddenly went silent.

"Too late! Cetus! Hide!" the hydra said before disappearing behind one of the cages.

"Wait — did you say Cetus — ?"

The chamber flooded with a blinding indigo light. A voice like a breaching volcano bellowed out in an ancient whalesong dialect. Its words thundered through the water.

"Stranger! Miscreant! Who intrudes into the House of Nyx-Phemos?"

A colossal shape moved in front of the light, eclipsing it like a mountain breaks a tsunamic surge. Coronis scurried after Ogi into the shadows. His veins pulsed red and gold in terror. His only knowledge of the Cetus came from vague myths of the Lost Time, back when the City was less than a hundred strong. Legend told that the Cetus had come up from the cataract and given the City the language of whalesong, so that they could communicate with other denizens of the world. They had taught the people how to farm the snails and how to ferment plankton. Their final gift, before returning down the cataract, had been the arc-light. They had left the Cetus lighthouses behind as a guide should they ever choose to return.

In the stories, the Cetus were described as titanic versions of the gold-scaled sunfish that the royals trotted out on menagerie days. Grand, angelic, eyes deep with wisdom. This giant was nothing like that. The titan's body was a decrepit wreck of deep, white scars riddled with parasitic barnacles. Moldering vestments hung from its flukes, decayed ribbons of skylla hide, serpentine bones, squid tentacles preserved and bound in wire. Exposed talons of bone erupted from the vestigial fingers ridging its pectoral fins. Its teeth were rotting shards of shale. A grotesque weeping tumor encased nearly half of its skull, while a vomitous brume of nox bubbling from its mouth obscured its only working eye.

"Speak, stranger," the monster demanded. "Nyx-Phemos knows you are here, trespasser. Nyx-Phemos can hear the beating of your little heart."

Coronis thought back on all the tales of the great Cetus benevolence. How they favored the people of the City. The many gifts they left behind. Seeing no other way out, he responded in formal whalesong.

"Forgive us, Lord of the Deep! We are lost travelers from above."

Nyx-Phemos peered about the chamber with its good eye.

"Above?"

"Yes, we come from the City, where we still revere your ancestors," Coronis said. "I humbly ask you to show us some hospitality, as we only seek to return home."

A horrible, phlegmatic noise rolled from the throat of the Cetus. The sound trembled through the creature's massive body, casting off bits of decay and rot from its vestments. The barnacles on its stomach flicked their tongues in and out. The opaque tumor of its dead eye shivered.

The monster was laughing.

"Ancestors? Poor miscreant, Old Nyx-Phemos strode the barren roads of your mid-ocean 'City' when it was nothing but a reef of frightened polyps. But there was sunlight, wasn't there? Yes. My brain can almost recall it. Why not come out where Nyx-Phemos can see you, sea-worm? Help me remember those better tides."

A cool, raw sensation surged through Coronis. It wasn't shock or fear. It wasn't even disappointment; after all, most childhood stories curdled with time. He felt awe at the sheer impossibility of descending into the Beneath only to find himself in the presence of this ancient, terrible Cetus. He felt a thrill from the danger it presented and despite that, a cool confidence. A gift from the war perhaps, from times when the corpses of his friends danced in the water, and he hid from the enemy in an expanding pool of brackish offal, his thoughts clean as a newborn tooth.

"My lord, I do not deserve to be witnessed by your great presence," Coronis said. "Grant us leave, and we shall never bother you again."

"Leave? Stranger, do you not know where you are?" The Cetus aimed its blinding torch at the ground. Waves of intense heat cascaded through the chamber. The creatures of the menagerie screamed and thrashed in their cages. "There is no ascension from this cursed midnight country. Do you think we would have warred with these damned hydra and their nekyia masters for all these years if we could simply return up to our proper thrones? Stupid cow of a sea-folk, old Nyx-Phemos remembers taking up your kind two at a time and crushing you against the rocks and cracking your thin clam skulls and scraping the blood and brains up with my tongue. You screamed and we ate, and it was all good and delicious until the traitor Nyx-Theus with his arc-fire and his damned subsonic bells banished us down to this hellish underworld. No matter. Soon you will be cooked and dead and Nyx-Phemos will happily chew the meat from your bones."

The water of the chamber was warming up to an unbearable degree, making Coronis dizzy. The agony of the crushing depths returned, even in his eyes, which felt like they might implode any second with a small and terrible shuck-woom of their own. He tried to come up with ways to defend himself, to attack the Cetus, to flee without being caught, but his mind was too torpid.

Just as he prepared to step out from his hiding spot and surrender to death, a low, murmuring song reverberated through the room.

"The mind nectar of the ancients
Carried on ships of flaming sails
The Bright Ones poured themselves
Deep into the bowl of the ocean
And offer them the drowning light
Drink deeply my old friend."

A shape flickered past Coronis and up into the chamber, a smear of opalescence, passing through the boiling light of the torch without slowing down. It threaded itself through the tumorous eye of the Cetus as easily as an eel slinking into its burrow. The monster stopped laughing and began to shriek.

"What? What is that? Demon! Nekyia! Get out of my head! No!" The Cetus lifted its torch away from the ground and aimed the tip of it at its good eye. "Stop! Something is controlling me! Sea-folk, you miscreant, you brought this devil! I command you make it stop! Help old Nyx-Phemos!"

Coronis called up to the monster. "But I see nothing! What is the name of the beast capable of harming such a majestic creature as yourself?"

"It has no body! It is no one!" Nyx-Phemos screamed as it furiously recoiled from the torch in his own clawed hand.

"If it is nobody, no one, it can only be your own foul spirit," Coronis said.

With an involuntary jerk, the Cetus jammed the flaming bulb of its torch deep into its own eye socket. Boiling blood spilled out in clouds of red gore. The torch pushed down until the optic nerves were burned black. The Cetus screamed and crashed into the walls, sending bricks the size of boulders tumbling down through the fog of thickening nox.

Ogi was already swimming toward a gap in the base of the chamber, a pair of the fur-coated crustaceans gripped between its claws. Coronis kicked hard to catch up, skimming through the cloud of brackish blood and past the pitiful, moaning Nyx-Phemos. Even as they cleared the first turns of the bedrock beneath the Castle, he could still hear the screams of the blinded Cetus echoing through the world-chasm, cursing at no one.

The lava tube twisted and turned for hours, its rough walls returning Coronis' meeps and clicks with maddening irregularity, while leading down into ever colder and denser waters. The last of the nalox was wearing off. Invisible hands squeezed his skull, his ribs. A deep loam coated the tunnel walls, the slightest touch casting off billowing clouds of fine, ashen dust which further choked his perception.

They cleared a turn and found a great, hoary gate of that exotic greenish-yellow metal barring their passage. It was carved with the same alien designs as Demod's trinket.

"Be careful here," Ogi warned.

"What is this place?"

With a grunt, Ogi swung the gate open. Thick flakes of corrosion broke off and floated into the void beyond.

"It is the afterdeath, the Bottom, the Infernum. It is the realm of the Nekyia."

They emerged onto a vast sunken steppe of stone and ice. The water was heavy and old, miasmic with churning banks of black nox. The light of battle chariots scratched foreboding lines in the glassy darkness above them. Crooked outcrops of volcanic stone jutted from the earth like dead, broken teeth separated by ugly fissures that glowed a baleful red. Unlike the decrepit strangeness of the Beneath, this place felt ancient, forgotten, reeking with the smell of decay after all the meat had fallen away.

Coronis gazed upon at the malign landscape with equal parts astonishment and dread. Above them, the war between the Cetus and the hydra scarred the darkness with fire. He flinched as explosions lit up the world like flashes of daylight.

"We are going to die down here."

"No," Ogi said.

"We can't go back," Coronis said. "And even if I had the strength, there's no way we could swim up through all of that."

"There is another way," Ogi said. "Trust us. We continue onward."

A movement nearby startled Coronis — another hydra tumbling through the murk, its spider-fingers spasming in the final throes of death. They watched its inexorable descent to the illuvial seafloor, where it was met by forms rising from the dust — shapes of creatures, some Coronis recognized, others he had no words for. They dissolved and reformed but more came than went and soon a crowd had accumulated around the dying hydra. When it had twitched its last, the shapes descended upon it, their liquid forms flowing into its corpse. It vibrated once, twice, then righted itself and began pumping its revivified limbs to head Upward, its faceless head fixed on the war it intended to rejoin.

"The Nekyia have recruited another," Ogi said solemnly.

Coronis stared agape. He wondered if pressure narcosis had reached his brain.

"What did I just see?"

"This dust that surrounds us are the spores of the Nekyia. They spawn from beneath the ice. A fungus that reanimates the dead as it feeds upon them. Eventually, it consumes all, even their memories. The shades that you see are the spores manifesting stolen memories under the light of familiarity."

"I thought the war was between your people and the Cetus. But now you're telling me that those are ... dead ... reanimated ... I don't even know what to call them."

The slithering parts of Ogi shrugged. "The relationship between my people and the Nekyia has never been ... simple. Not enemies, not friends, but each requires the other. Just like you and this asphodel." He handed Coronis one of the shaggy, wriggling crustaceans. "Now, friend, I will go find our way out of this place. But I must go alone. Please wait here. I promise to return for you. Remain still. Remember, do not touch anything or believe your senses."

"Wait, exactly what am I supposed to do with this thing?" Coronis said as Ogi slipped away into the wasteland. He obediently held fast for a few moments before curiosity overtook him. Ignoring the rising ache of pressure on his ribs and spine, he ventured into the barren hills, cringing from the explosions of the constant war raging overhead and distrustful of the darker ravines where shadows moved in purposeful ways. He intended to only explore a short distance, but when he made to return, the landscape had already become unfamiliar. There was no way to tell if he had traveled a hundred feet or a thousand. Utterly lost, the crushing cold penetrating his bones as the final traces of nalox fruit dissolved from his bloodstream, Coronis fell to his knees and waited for either Ogi or death to find him first. Shapes coalesced in the water. Faces materialized at the edge of his vision. His shrunken bubble of perception filled with voices. Some moaned or made eerie noises, others spoke. Were these the Nekyia? Was he dead and about to become just another shell, another host?

"Coronis."

"Who speaks? Do I recognize that voice?"

Beside him, a form, more solid than the rest, floated within the murk.

"Coronis, is that you?"

"Elpin? How can it be?" Warm memories bubbled in his brain. Elpin challenging him to a race down the City streets. Sharing stories of terrible beasts and brave kings with Demod and Naus in The Happy Squid. Wide-eyed and mortally wounded by a rebel explosive, sliding out of the kelp strands in which they had sought cover and disappearing down into the depths of the world-chasm.

Ogi had warned that whatever he saw wouldn't be real. A trick of the Nekyia. Spores and slime infecting his mind.

Coronis didn't care. It felt real enough.

"Brother," he said.

The thing wearing Elpin's face grinned.

"How goes your work, Cor? Have you kept your promise to fill your pad with epic poetry?"

"I — I — I'm working on it. Brother ... I have seen such fantastic things ..."

"You could stay here, with me, if you wish," Elpin said. His translucent hands reached out from the gloom, as if for an embrace. Cold fingers lovingly caressed his face, searching for an opening. "We have so many stories to share. It would take a million tides to hear them all."

Emotion overwhelmed Coronis. He almost said yes. It would be so easy to just give up. Instead, he found himself shaking his head. "I know you are not real. But, if some part of you truly is in there, maybe you can help me. I am far from home, lost, close to death. We are trapped between the cold dead depths and the war above. We need to leave. Me and Ogi ... we were going up ... see, I was supposed to wait ... but I ... I don't know where he is ... where I am ..."

"I know, brother. I know all the secrets of this world. You will find your friend at the great seam where the fire touches the sea.

Its exhalation is a forgotten plume that leads up, beyond the far edge of the eternal war that seals us within this gorge."

"I think I will die before I find it."

"Isn't that an asphodel you carry?"

Coronis had nearly forgotten about the shaggy crustacean slung over his back.

"What of it?"

The hand of Elpin's shade became solid and dug into the soft, black earth. It scooped out a glittering blade of yellow-green metal. He pressed it into Coronis' hand.

"If you want to live, you must make a sacrifice."

"My brother ... I am done with death ... I don't know ... this is not ..."

"Coronis! Look at me! Remember your promise!"

It seemed, for a moment, the shade of his lost friend became Elpin, the child from the clutch, the young man he raced across the cataract, the soldier he fought alongside. Gripping the blade tight and without thinking at all, he sliced the crustacean open. Gelatinous organs spilled out in a yellow smear of nox. Elpin draped its hide over Coronis like a cloak, sealing the gaps with Nekyian slime.

"Symbiotic armor," Elpin said. "It will protect you."

Coronis winced as tiny microbes in the hide threaded themselves between his scales, expanding across his entire body. The pain softened to a ripple of subcutaneous prickling as the colony locked in at a cellular level. Layers of translucent fibers insulated him from the elements. It felt like the kick of nalox fruit, multiplied a thousand-fold.

"To find your friend, follow the burning water. Can you taste the sulfur?"

Coronis breathed deeply. Yes. There it was. A bitter draught.

"Thank you, brother," he said, but the shade was gone. He followed the scent across the fractured seafloor, among familiar phantasms that grew more compelling as they went. The volcanic seam made its presence felt in his bones long before he saw it — a welcome heat in the terrible stillness.

The plume of the smoker boiled and hissed all around him. Deep in the core, the volcanic storm, illuminated by flashes of strange lightning, Coronis glimpsed Ogi floating before a vast form, a mass of tentacles, each as wide as a Cetus, that wrung and worried with pent-up strength. Another Nekyia shade perhaps, but much larger than any other, taking a form that Coronis had never seen or even heard stories of before. Ogi appeared to be communicating with it.

The storm subsided. Coronis waited in the darkness, smaller and more alone than ever before. Even the comfort of the plume's heat abandoned him, offering chilblains instead of relief.

After what felt like an eternity, Ogi emerged from the plume.

"Ah, my friend, you already wear the hide! In my haste I neglected to ask if you understood what must be done. Are you ready to rise?"

"I don't understand ... what was that ... where can we go ..."

Ogi gestured to the plume. "See how the smoke rises up through the water, untouched? See how both sides of the war avoid its terrible poisons, its unbearable heat? That will be our passage from this world. In these cloaks, we will be protected. It will lift us safely past the fighting and the death. Trust?"

Coronis had a million questions. But he said nothing. It wasn't the time. They rose together into the plume's updraft, letting it take them far away from that shadowy canyon of death.

The nymphaea danced in soft beams of twilight. Six rows of ebony eyes glinted. The pale skin of her long, double-pronged tail gleamed in tones of mucal bronze. Six delicate arms swayed in the gentle current. In each hand, she held a flower of six white petals and six silver leaves.

"This one is my favorite," Coronis said sleepily.

"Yes," Ogi said.

Another pair of nymphaea wriggled out from the garden, deftly maneuvering through the dense forest of organic webbing that made up most of the Floating Country. Bandoliers of seed pods dangled from their banded midsection, where the chest of a humanoid melted into the serpentine tail of an eel. The new arrivals joined the first one in dance, occasionally pausing to drink from a seed pod. Coronis sucked from his own pod, letting the sweet wine run down his tongue. He ducked into a ribbon of hyper-oxygenated water and opened his gills wide. His blood roared. His brain sparkled. His microbial coat shivered in ecstasy.

The volcanic plume had disgorged them into open ocean, an empty seascape devoid of features or waypoints. Coronis had suggested they descend again to try to get their bearings, but Ogi insisted that all the landmarks they needed awaited them in the Above. Starving and exhausted, Coronis had been beset with waking dreams. Translucent isopods scratched his back, only to disappear whenever he turned around. For nearly a tide, a cluster of neon jellyfish orbited around them, their tentacles flashing indecipherable sigils. They watched in silent incredulity when a strange clockwork machine, large as a house and shaped like a squashed worm, slowly sank past them, trailing rust and tiny metallic bits in its wake. At one point, Coronis swore he was back in the City taverna, Demod and Naus up in the corner, laughing and beckoning him to come closer. He went to them, eager to tell them tales of the marvels he'd seen, but Ogi pulled him back at the last moment. The mirage vanished, replaced with a luminous cloud of carnivorous plankton.

Coronis couldn't recall exactly when they had stumbled across the Floating Country. Or perhaps it had found them instead. He woke from a nightmare of being crushed between the rotted teeth of Nyx-Phemos to the most glorious sight — lush walls of foliage and flowers, suffused with the soft light of small arc-lamps. Soft music surrounded him, like the tinkling of shell-bells. A banquet was laid out before him, a dozen nets of different fish, each one more delicious. The ragged wool of his microbial coat had been brushed and mended. Ogi crouched on the other side of the room, similarly surrounded by luxury and just as mystified. Their benefactors, a collective of nymphaea eel-folk, provided for the travelers without asking for anything in return. They claimed the Floating Country provided everything they needed without limit, every desire met, and that both Coronis and Ogi were free to stay long as they liked. When Coronis asked if any knew the way to the City, they promised to check their maps. In the meantime, they offered sweet nectar to drink and succulent leaves to eat. Time slowed to a sluggish trickle of silver.

"Weren't we going somewhere?" Coronis asked as his current favorite nymphaea nuzzled against his shoulder. Three of its six hands were busy caressing the folds of his microbial cloak, while the others squeezed beads of nectar into the water for him to lap up.

Ogi, hanging upside-down from the ceiling by its fingers, purred from its diaphragmatic slit. Its limbs undulated with opiate torpor.

"Maybe. Tomorrow. Or another day. Then we'll go."

"Sounds good to me," Coronis sighed, and embraced the oblivion of another dreamless sleep.

This time, he did not sink into nothingness.

A succession of painful images pricked his brain like the stingers of a venomous stone-squid. An icy darkness flooded in and snuffed out the lights. The forest walls of the Floating Country disintegrated to floating rot. The colony of his microbial coat withered and died. He was back in that infinite void above the

Above. He was a god. He was falling. He was dying. Fire engulfed him. As he slammed into the blue waters, his crystalline body shattered into a million shards of yellow-green metal. He sank like a stone, down, down, down to the Beneath, a world under the world where black smokers vomited up storms of toxic minerals. Sleep came. Eons passed. When he woke again, he was barely more than a vitreous shade, a darting, gossamer scream. No longer trapped in the Beneath, his mind, bound to the scattered particulates of his physical form, found itself far above, drifting through cliff-side villages. Some great violence was taking place. Piles of corpses filled the streets, not just sea-folk but nymphaea, shell-talkers, stone turtles, and other cryptozoological creatures previously ascribed to myth. Coronis watched in horror as a groaning Cetus pushed its way through a curtain of suffocating plague-nox wafting up from the cataract. Its massive head was a ruin of scar tissue and engorged pustules. Coronis tried to scream but couldn't as Nyx-Phemos reached down and grabbed him between its claws. But when the terrible Cetus spoke, it was not with that terrible laughter, but Ogi's quiet singing that drifted from its stinking maw.

"A brave daughter of the Bright Ones
Came to forge a way home.
She called upon the scattered
Children of the wine-dark world.
The first to answer were the Lords of Twilight,
Minds like distant flames, Hearts like Death."

Nyx-Phemos was joined by a dozen other Cetus titans, all of them draped in brilliant jewels and each one carrying a torch of boiling arc-fire. They gazed upon Coronis with greedy eyes.

"Home was far and still further to go
The song of matter so hard to hear
The daughter fled her ancient form
To show her true Brightness."

What kind of strange nightmare this is? Coronis mused, as if he were a spectator to his own destruction.
A voice like song, like color, answered. *This is not your dream. It is mine.*
Coronis felt himself dissolve into the brine. Only light remained. Like a smeared thought, the molecules of his essence slipped into the colossal brain of the greatest of Cetus lords, the

Dread Nyx-Theus. It was like being bound to a mountain and still able to move it. From inside his Nyx-Theus puppet, Coronis hurled the other titans off the cliffs and cast them back down into the cataract.

Now freed from slavery, he taught the survivors the secrets of arc-light and other arcane sciences. The cliff-side villages grew into the City, a bastion of light against the darkness. But even then, his work to straighten the path of the world was not over. The Cetus were a cruel and unrelenting species. One day, they would find their way back up to the City and harry the sea-folk to extinction. He bid farewell to his charges and flung himself back down the cataract. There, he manipulated the native species of the depths against the Cetus. He gave them gifts of fire and implosion. Thus began A Thousand Tides of Sinking Bones.

> "And while the bridge that burned
> Waited far above
> There were other children
> The Nameless, the Hidden, the Deepest
> Who were not to suffer the wrath of the Lost
> And so the drowning light
> Built midnight chains
> For the Lords of Twilight
> Locking them to the dream they refused to forget."

Time passed. His end was coming. He reached out to a single, despondent hydra and offered one final gift. No, an exchange. A promise.

The hydra agreed.

"Did you forget your oath, lonely one?" Coronis asked, suddenly awake. Or was this in the dream? He was back in his own body, in the soft embrace of his favorite nymphaea. But when he spoke, his voice was not his own. His thoughts were not his own. Alien memories wrapped themselves around his brain, holding him prisoner in his own head.

Ogi unwrapped itself from the ceiling and dropped next to Coronis. The nymphaea scattered, their dual tails flashing. A soft wailing, like a lamentation, trembled through the forests of the Floating Country.

"What did you say?" Ogi asked.

Involuntarily, as if watching himself from a distance, Coronis reached out to the hydra.

"This place is poison to me," he said. "We must leave."

Ogi cringed as if stung. "Ulix? You hide inside my friend now?"

"Only partially," Coronis said. "This child of the City does not possess the necessary neural plasticity to carry me like your kind. His patterns are too rigid, too narrow. But I had to try. You were burying me. Forgetting me."

"Tired. Want to stay here. Rest. No more fight. No more dreams."

"But I need you. I need you both: the hive's mind, the poet's eyes. My journey has been so long. It's time to go home." Coronis recoiled as a visceral shock of longing crashed through him. The other voice, the other thoughts, loosened their grip on his tongue.

"What was that?" Coronis asked. "It was just inside me. Or I became it. I don't know. It showed me visions, memories, that weren't mine."

"That ... was Ulix. It rides inside me, a smooth stone in my head. It broke me from the hive-mind for a promise to be its chariot that only goes up."

"I felt its fear. Why was it afraid?"

"It seems if I drink the nectar of the flower, Ulix cannot speak or think," Ogi said. "Ulix fades. Ulix dies. No pain, easy, a shadow on the sand."

"What? Why? I think ... it saved my City a long time ago. It only wants to return home."

"It may have saved your kind, but it only brought terror and war to mine." Ogi bared its needle teeth in a snarl. "You go. I stay here. I found the peace I seek."

Coronis recalled what it had been like in the Beneath. The ruins. The war-chariots. The implosions. The hydra at perpetual war, even after death. What must it be like, constantly connected to the hive-mind of everyone you love, everyone you hate? He remembered what it had been like hunting down rebels with Demod, Naus, and Elpin, how they had to forget the faces of former friends in order to kill them. What if he had been able to hear their dying thoughts? What if he could see his own face as he stuck in the blade? It would be madness. He would beg for a mysterious entity to take him away from the constant whispering, screaming, laughing, dying.

Then only to realize that your savior was also the source of your despair?

"I can't ask you to forgive this Ulix creature. It changed our world in ways I still don't fully understand. I can only remind you of the promises we made. I could have remained down in that hell with the Nekyia. I almost did. The temptation of a never-ending existence, even if it's only half a life. But a long time ago, I promised my best friend, my brother, that no matter what, I would see the world, that I would live life to the fullest and write down all the stories of my adventures. I forgot my promise. I let myself drift for many tides, just like we're doing now. Not anymore, I won't. And neither will you." In a flurry of eddies and tangled greenery, Coronis ploughed into the center of Ogis's mass and drove him upward. He still possessed the strange blade of yellow-green metal, and used it to carve through the dense foliage. By the time the dazed hydra realized what was happening, they were moving too quickly for his drunken appendages to get a purchase on the foliage rushing past. Coronis hacked and chopped until they crashed out of the Floating Country and back into open sea.

"Why, friend?" Ogi said. "Why give up paradise for the vague promises of a demon? A ghost?"

"I've had my fill of monotony. And even pleasure grows tedious if that's all there is. This Ulix of yours, as strange and terrible as it might be, has shown me much. I know there's much yet for both of us see."

As the green place faded away beneath them, Ogi gradually ceased his struggling and allowed Ulix to commandeer his body again. "My friend," he whispered as his consciousness slipped away. "I shall honor my oath as you do yours. And after we are done, perhaps there will be some good I can yet do."

To the amazement of Coronis, even the hot, bright desert of the Far Above was filled with wonders. In the distance, tiny silver fish swam in synchronized schools larger than the City, sparkling in the light. Bedouin tribes of remoran shark-herders crossed the expanse with purpose. Great floating reefs of architect crabs drifted serenely, chitinous spheres colonized with entire ecosystems that were fed upon at will by the naked crustaceans that roamed within.

The next glimmer, Coronis began to make out hues and colors that he'd never seen before. The scales on the back of his hand shone with such a beautiful iridescence and depth that he became afraid his microbial coat had given out and his mind was succumbing to the low pressure. Ulix-in-Ogi explained that the ample light simply had more to show. The thrill, however, soon turned to agony as the light grew into an intolerable glare. Ulix dissected an air sac from a passing tuna and rubbed it until it was partially opaque, then slid it over the eyes of a grateful Coronis.

"You're fortunate that Ogi does not have eyes," he said.

"In that you are mistaken, for eyes are exquisite organs that allow perception across limitless distance."

Eventually the light dimmed and darkness overtook them again. Still, they rose and rose. Coronis saw gatherings of luminescent jellyfish pulsing far in the distance and became aware of a peculiar sensation, like a charge in the water. He looked up and saw the entire Above filled with strange luminous creatures that shimmered and swarmed in a way he had never seen before.

Coronis stopped. "The Above. There's something wrong with it. How is that possible?" The entire span was one great film, like the surface of a bubble. A World-Bubble, shimmering and rippling with silvery light.

"Welcome to the surface," Ulix said through Ogi's voice.

Coronis floated in stunned wonder. There were no words for what he was seeing. It was beyond anything he could imagine.

"Is this the end of the world?"

"It is the end of yours, but beyond lie a million, million others. Come. The Bright Ones await."

Ogi moved up quickly and Coronis followed, but where Ogi hesitated at the edge, Coronis shot beyond, up into nothingness. The waterless void seared his gills. He spun slowly, drops of water flying from him like jewels, before crashing back down in a slap of pain and sensory chaos. Confused by this barrier that was not solid but also not water, he tried again, throwing himself up through the surf. He could get no further.

"Patience, sea-folk," Ulix advised. "Let the seam between worlds settle. Then you will see."

Coronis joined the hydra at his side, and together they watched the strange barrier. He had never really considered what the Above would be like, but he hadn't expected the world to end with such unnegotiable finality. He felt disappointed, as if the possibilities of what could be were diminished. Now that his appetite for adventure had been whetted, he had hoped for more than this.

As the barrier calmed and became clear as glass, the undulating streaks of light coalesced and narrowed to points. Coronis gasped. The Above was full of them. Tiny, tiny lights.

"Do you see them? The stars?"

"Yes. What manner of creature are they?"

"They're not creatures. They are vaster than you can imagine and further still. Many have worlds such as this circling them. And one of those is my home."

Coronis stared at the stars, astonished, for a long time before replying.

"If they are so distant, how will you get to them?"

"The bridge that burns awaits me. It will take me home, but I need your help to find it."

"I don't understand."

"I did not ask your permission to use your mind before, and for that I apologize. I ask now. May I command your eyes?"

"Yes."

A shifting smear of color poured from Ogi's head into his own. Coronis felt an odd sensation, as if his thoughts were being stretched out, memories pulled and distorted to make room for another's. Ulix' thoughts crowded next to his own, infusing the stars with familiarity and meaning. He doffed the air sac to see more clearly, and mentally traced a crooked ridge of lights with Coronis' eyes. Where four stars formed a lopsided parallelogram, Ulix focused all his concentration. Ogi writhed nervously beside him. Time passed. The stars slid toward the water but Ulix maintained his gaze and as he did, a kind of understanding bled from Ulix to his host. It erupted from him like a song, not of words, but like a wave uncoiling in the hidden spaces between the waves. It was a lamentation sent into the night. It was the summoning of a bridge that burned impossibly hot and impossibly dark. It was a soul cracked and spilled into the sky.

Then, it was over.

Ulix relaxed. "The call has been sent. I will be going home soon. I leave you with the gifts I promised. For Coronis, Poet of the Sea-Folk, I give you Inspiration. One cannot aspire to something that one cannot imagine. You must see where I go."

> "Destiny denied by weight and water
> Unable to move Beyond
> The drowning light given
> and monsters chained
> So the children may join
> A future larger than their own"

Through their mental connection, Ulix shared memories of the stars. Creatures, machines, philosophies, and sciences beyond exotic. It made Coronis's mind hum, and thrilled him beyond measure. The drowning light, the arc lights, Ulix' gift to their world, would get them there, eventually, and shackling the monsters in the deep had given them the head start they needed.

"Go, write poems, tell the world, inspire them. When the time is right, you may even find the right song to join us."

There was a gleaming breath of light in the Above. And then Ulix was simply gone.

Ogi and Coronis floated beneath the surface for a while longer.

"Oath is done," Ogi said. "Ulix gave me what I asked for."

"I thought breaking you from the hive-mind was your gift?"

"No, there was something else, a gift of repentance." The hydra's voice weighed heavy with a great sadness, as if coming to terms with a monstrous truth it had been avoiding. "It showed me the way to finally bring an end A Thousand Tides of Sinking Bones."

Coronis took Ogi's clawed arm in his own.

"You know, it's a long way back to the Beneath."

"True."

"It will probably take a long time to find the path again."

"Yes, many tides."

Coronis turned away from the surface to the great and infinite world left to explore.

"Then there's no hurry, is there? Let's see what kind of adventures find us in the meantime. We have poems to write and songs to sing. And if we happen to come across the City, I have some friends that I'd like you to meet."

The Relic

J. Tynan Burke and L'Erin Ogle

Yishma Shamoun's escape pod had landed on its side, so the emergency access panel was on the bulkhead, not the deck. After a good tug, the panel came loose, landing with a hard crash under what must have been one and a half gees. Yishma stared at it, panting, no energy for satisfaction. This was twice the gravity he was used to, and he'd spent the last week in free-fall, waiting for the solar flare.

Waiting with his wife Gauri, on their starship *New Reason*. Neither wife nor ship had survived the lash of hard radiation from the star. Yishma had fared little better, kept alive only by a month's supply of radiation meds. His head grew even heavier; but no, onwards. Past blinking instruments and insulated pipes, he crawled to the maintenance hatch. His back muscles complained as he shouldered the hatch open. Air rushed out, ruffling the fabric of his emergency environment suit, turning to fog in the cold outside. A hangar large enough to fit all of *New Reason* yawned around him. He scrambled halfway back inside when he saw that it seemed open to the gulf of space. But wouldn't he already have been ejected if it weren't sealed somehow? He crept back out, leaving one hand clutching an exterior rail. To his right, opposite the opening, the hangar curved inwards. A hollow formed in Yishma's throat as the construction material sank in. The hatch, and the smooth bulkheads, and even the deck were the same ochre as his skin. Gashes and scuff marks marred the material below him, filled in with a resin that could have been scar tissue. The uncanny sight was completed by the light that shone from strips on the ceiling, cold and blue, as if mimicking a white dwarf, and not yellow Sol.

In the recycled air of his environment suit, Yishma could smell his own fear.

After a minute of clinging bug-eyed to the railing, he realized he was alone, the hangar silent and otherwise empty. A relief, but ... what the hell kind of captain would bring an unknown vessel aboard without an armed greeting party to meet it? Was the ship automated, his rescue just the result of an algorithm?

These were technologies he should've been thrilled to find, like something from the bad adventure holos he and Gauri had liked to watch. An invisible force-field keeping out the vacuum of space, artificial gravity, grown starship parts ... and how had he gotten here? Teleportation?

One moment he'd been floating in the escape pod; the next, he was falling to this strange deck.

He *should've* been thrilled. There was no doubt who had built this ship — or rather, who *hadn't*. But for all that making first contact had been a childhood dream of his, it was Gauri who would've known what to actually do. She'd done hostile boardings with the Marines; Yishma was just a gearhead.

'Just a gearhead?' Gauri would've objected if she'd heard him talking like that. *If we hadn't had my interceptor in your hangar to flirt over, you never would've talked to me at all. And somebody has to fix up* New Reason *when I ride it too hard. Can't be me; I'm just a grunt.*

A smile almost flashed over Yishma's face, but it was overpowered by a sob.

He choked it back, then wondered why he'd bothered with restraint. In that cold and empty room, there was nobody to hide his emotions from.

Dying all alone and far from home — he'd had nightmares like this as a kid. Gauri had brought him out of his shell enough that they bought *New Reason* and started a scooping business, but it was hard to unseat a deep fear. Yishma never slept well the night before their trips out to harvest strange matter from erupting stars.

New Reason; Gauri; erupting stars. The solar flare hitting them at an unlucky time, rad-shielding aerogel spewing out of its casing, overheated tanks rupturing. Gauri's still body, floating amid the glittering wreckage of their ship, peaceful. Still there, probably. Might be there a long time. Yishma wilted. How was he supposed to carry on after a loss like this? Even assuming he made it home, he had a hard time imagining a life where he got out of bed in the morning. Why bother?

This time, when his head grew heavy and his shoulders drooped, he didn't fight it.

His gloved hand slid off the safety rail and smacked the pod. The hollow bang, echoing in the hangar, jerked him to attention.

Right. He needed to focus on not dying, a goal blunt enough that it broke through his slump. The immediate problem was his water synthesizer; it had been damaged by an unsecured crate.

First he made a working assumption that the ship was automated. Nobody seemed to be coming to greet him, and no sentient captain would leave him *this* alone. That meant that he'd need to explore if he wanted water or parts. He'd need to keep an eye open for a control room, too, to get back to Sol, or die trying.

That'll happen for sure if you don't get your ass in gear, Gauri whispered in his mind, more a presence now than a memory. And she was right — the gamma rays which had killed her had merely poisoned him, but a pill bottle with thirty red-and-white capsules was the only thing keeping him alive.

Gauri's company, however hallucinatory, made him feel lighter. He slid off the pod's edge; his boots sank slightly into the deck. He tried not to think about that, or how the hatch at the end of the hangar irised open with a faint meaty noise when he stepped in front of it. Underway finally, and with something plan-like in mind, Yishma let himself feel a flicker of hope. He knew machines, and wasn't the ship just that? There were far worse places to be 'just a gearhead'.

After several scuffed corridors, Yishma found a globular chamber dominated by tall blobs of … furniture? The room's pale brown walls were blistered and scarred, like flesh burned by a laser. Somebody had fought here.

He ducked behind the nearest hunk of molded plastic. He didn't want to fight anybody, didn't even know how.

But there were no sounds; there was nobody to fight.

Right?

He peeked over the rough surface of his hiding place. The room was a mess, strewn with containers and equipment; most of the furniture, if that's what it was, had been knocked over. Yishma took a careful step out from behind his cover. When nobody ran out and killed him, he began examining the nearby objects. Other than some functional components — this was a handle, that was a blade — he couldn't make much of them.

Across the room, he spied a tall table that looked bolted to the deck. A control panel? Questions chittered excitedly in his mind. *What were their interfaces like? Knobs and switches? Holographic, even psionic?* He barely noticed himself crossing the room, and then there he was, in front of a table that rose to just below his chin.

Some elements were familiar from human control panels: touch instruments, joysticks, and lens-filled domes that might be holographic projectors. The only item not attached to the surface was a J-shaped device, matte black, about the size of his hand. Without a thought, he reached an arm up over the table; his hand was halfway there when he caught himself. Could it be a weapon? Should he just keep exploring, maybe find a galley? He didn't like the odds of finding running water any time soon.

A closer examination found that the item was seated in a depression that matched its shape. It was meant to be there, then, so probably not a laser gun — who would put a weapon-holder on the controls for, what, a lounge? He pushed up to his tiptoes and got a firm grip, feeling like a kid trying to reach the galley countertop. His calves would make him regret that.

When he failed to die, Yishma looked the thing over and found a single raised disc on its surface. It probably wouldn't do anything bad. Probably. He took a deep breath and tapped it.

A hologram sputtered to life a half-dozen centimeters above his hand, eight distinct icons in a grid. He flinched. What now? This would be humanity's first interaction with an alien computer. Was there something special he should do? A *right* way to —

Just push a dang button, Gauri said in his head, but he knew the sly grin she'd have been wearing with that tone. The vision was a hot knife to his chest. All excitement fled him; this was just one more menial chore, like so many things would be now that he'd lost her. No secrets that the device held would ever make up for that.

He sighed out his held breath. *Push a dang button.* The rippling pink icon seemed like it probably wouldn't make anything explode; he tapped it with his free hand. It presented another view, a grid of identical glyphs with different labels. He shrugged and selected the upper-left one.

Crystal clear, a scene appeared. A creature stared out at him, long-limbed, shaggy, not unlike a slim-framed bear. Its fur was black and sleek, and near its scalp where it was thickest there were thin lines, like the track marks of combs. It extended an arm, long and furred, at the chamber behind it — this ship? As the view panned out, Yishma saw similar creatures around it, all standing very straight on two legs.

This was it, then. Mankind's first sight of intelligent aliens. Yishma's depression gave way to awe. To be the first to see this was an honor, even if nobody else ever found out. As his eyes devoured the scene, he found himself inventing a personality for the leader. He was thinking of her as female, with her combed hair, violet eyes, and a high, angular bonescape to her face.

The aliens all wore similar clothing, loose-fitting blue sheaths. There was an emblem on the sheath of the leader, who was now making sounds — presumably a form of speech, but not that Yishma could understand — sharp, short sounds that burrowed underneath his skin and scraped along his skeleton.

He wished he knew how to turn the audio down. It took some of the allure out of observing the species, though he had plenty of awe remaining.

The woman turned and began to cut through the assembly behind her. She moved with a fluidity even the most graceful human didn't possess. On different cameras, she walked down corridors and through great rounded rooms, speaking those odd noises to the group. A tour for the maiden voyage? Perhaps. The ship's commander, then?

The ship they traveled through gleamed. Not the banged-up relic, Yishma saw now.

New, then.

Yishma felt a pang of sorrow for the ship. It had been loved once, in the way a captain loves their vessel. And now look at it.

The image went dim. Then bright again. Following behind her now. Down into a room where the creatures donned thick silver suits that hid their forms. Some sort of research center? The female tapped one of the creatures on their shoulder, started a conversation.

The researcher was holding a transparent cube. Inside, there was a blue flowering vine. The researcher pointed at it and began speaking rapid-fire. Yishma thought it might signal alarm.

The plant was beautiful. Was it dangerous? The female in charge —

A clunky way of thinking about somebody so central to the recordings. Who was she? Was this an active captain's log, before whatever happened here had happened? For a second he worried that he didn't have the necessary permissions to view it. A very *silly* worry: they were all probably dead, and he doubted he was subject to space-bear law.

She was the captain, he decided. She needed a name. 'Anne' came to mind. Gauri's commander, once upon a time. She shared a kind of steely elegance with the alien.

In the research center on the video, *Anne* laid a glove-clad hand on the shoulder of the worried scientist. The scientist just looked back at her, face tense and unhappy.

The last entry took place in a room with a long, thin bed and a minimal workstation. Anne's cabin? She opened the hatch to let in the worried scientist, who was now wearing a flowing sheath like the rest of the crew. She'd brought some documents.

Yishma would need a name for the scientist, too. 'Claire' had been the name of one of Anne's friends, right?

Anne waved Claire in, gestured for her to sit. Claire settled herself on the very edge of the bed. Anne retrieved a glass and poured her a drink from a decanter of dark liquid. She traded it for the documents and leafed through them.

They spoke a while, then Anne said something in a much quieter, slower cadence; it seemed to mark the end of the conversation. She placed her hand on Claire's shoulder, looked her in the eyes. Claire fumbled and rose to leave. The camera watched the hatch shut behind her. Then Anne's face filled the lens, on it a small smile.

A secret smile, Yishma thought.

The recording faded back into the grid of identical icons. Yishma watched the icons for a few minutes until the display turned off. As he did, his thoughts orbited a single mass: he'd made history; if only somebody had been around to see it.

Well don't stand just stand there picking your nose, Gauri said. *We got a map to make.*

Right. He could still make it out of here.

With the alien device velcroed to his leg, he shuffled back to the pod. All he'd been through was taking its toll; the unaccustomed gravity felt heavier with every step. His shoulders burned as he pulled himself up the meter to the escape-pod hatch. Once inside the main chamber, he changed out of his environment suit and lay down. Muscles he didn't even know existed were sore. The bulkhead beneath him was cold and hard. He was thirsty, but had hardly any water. Hungry, but not in the mood for an emergency ration brick. They tasted like literal dirt.

He closed his eyes. The darkness didn't bring oblivion, only visions. Gauri stomping around the hangar, hollering for the aliens to come get them. The big grin on her face showing that it wasn't a plan, just blowing off steam. In the vision, Yishma joined for a cathartic scream or two. He grabbed her hands and suggested something *else* they could be the first two people to do on an alien ship ...

His eyes shot open. Were those thoughts healthy? Demeaning? He'd heard so many times that there was no wrong way to grieve; he hoped it was true.

There were keepsakes that might help him feel close to her, in the crate from *New Reason*, the one that had damaged the water synthesizer. Gauri had helped him pack it, even as she was dying, orbs of blood trickling from her nose. Stronger than he would ever be. Yishma dragged the metal box to where he lay, then unscrewed the top.

He rummaged around until he found Gauri's 'lucky jumpsuit'. The actual suit was new, but the patches on it were the ones she'd been wearing when they'd first met. The embroidered logo of a band that had been popular when she was in uni; some military slogans, inside jokes; the face of a children's holo villain, all horns and glowing eyes. There was a plushie of that in the crate too; he pulled it out.

Hugging the plushie, like countless children must have done to their own copies, he rested his head on her jumpsuit.

It should've been both of us, one way or the other, he thought. It was selfish, he knew. And then he was asleep.

When he awoke, he felt not so much refreshed as unmoored from his own misery.

He massaged his forehead to clear the fugue. There was no time for that. The cotton-dry of his mouth could attest to that. If he survived this, he'd have plenty of time for depression later. After a swig of water from his half-filled canteen, he set about making a map of the ship.

The alien device must have had days of video on it, judging by the size of the interface, which he learned to navigate with hand gestures. Many videos were useless to him. Recordings of navigation charts; hikes in silver suits through a lush alien landscape; the captain Anne working in her cabin. That first recording would be his best bet, where Anne was giving a tour.

The rudimentary diagram grew as he scribbled it into a pad of paper the pod had been stocked with. Pen and paper had been an antiquated medium when he'd been a *kid* — but eventually he pieced something together. He circled places that might hold water — galleys, tanks of liquid. Then he suited up.

Clutching the map, he wormed out of the maintenance hatch.

Not long after he left the hangar, the ship's lights began to flash. *Off* — he was alone in the total darkness of a spaceship interior. *On* — the corridor flashed into sight with the blue-white of an operating theatre.

Yishma froze. Was the ship trying to get his attention? Were they under attack? Low on fuel? Was it the equivalent of a blinking 'see mechanic' icon? Whatever it meant, it couldn't be *good*. Yishma heard the environment suit's dehumidifier kick in to deal with his cold sweat.

He hurried to haul himself back into the pod. He shut the hatch and instinctively strapped himself into the acceleration webbing that hung near the command console.

Right on cue, the ship began to shake. He spun around in jerks, his stomach a step behind each revolution. Gauri had flown him around that hard a few times, cackling, showing him what evasive maneuvers were like in the navy. It turned out to be more fun when somebody you loved was flying.

All went silent and still. Yishma's shallow breaths were the only sound. Whatever was happening had stopped happening. Was he safe? There'd been a similar shaking when he was brought on board the ship — was it the same phenomenon?

Probably related, Gauri said. *C'mon, let's take a look.*

Gonna have to eventually, he thought. He extracted himself from the webbing, removing the straps one at a time in case the shaking returned. The suit diagnostics returned all green. The atmosphere outside hadn't changed, either; probably still in the hangar.

When he left the pod, he discovered that the hangar no longer overlooked a sea of stars. Instead, a vast field of comets stretched before him, lit by what must have been a pink star somewhere to the right. Clouds of gas and snow lolled around each. The entire scene seemed to take place inside a large version of such a cloud; the space beyond was a hazy pink-gray. Below him loomed a large planetoid with the same icy exterior, riddled with impact craters.

He'd never seen anything like it, not in person. It was beautiful, and had a good chance of being ice, too. He stared, watching the debris serenely orbit the planetoid. He watched so long that his back muscles began to ache.

Brass tacks, he told himself, one of Gauri's expression. So. Assume the ship was surrounded by water. Far away, maybe, and impure, but still water. Then assume there was a way to sanitize the water, maybe with the escape pod's urine reclamation system. It followed that he just needed to harvest the ice.

Enter the pod's top-of-the-line spacewalking exosuit. He and Gauri had both agreed it wasn't something to skimp on; quality EVA gear had saved each of their lives by the time they'd met in the refinery. Its lidar suite and spectroscope could help him find a nearby comet and confirm it was H_2O. Its thrusters would get him there and back, and the cutting lasers would make short work of the comet.

Yishma hauled the exosuit's thirty kilos to the end of the hangar, straining for every inch. *It's a very good suit*, he reminded himself, as he grunted under its bulk. *Worth every penny.* As the old Shamoun family saying went: *Intelligence is knowing the right tool for the job. Wisdom is shelling out for the right brand of tool.*

A meter from the invisible wall between the hangar and deep space, Yishma climbed inside the exosuit. He secured his helmet against its clamps, stared at the comets, and hesitated. He'd never done this before without a spotter.

Gauri chimed in. *It's okay, Yish. We only need this to go better than that EVA where your cousin lost a hand. Remember Eli? He's an idiot. You'll be fine.* A real vote of confidence, Yishma thought. 'Smarter than Eli.' He snorted and began calibrating the heads-up display. Constellations of ice and rock became highlighted before him. After a deep breath, he crouched down and flung himself out of the ship, aimed at a twenty-meter chunk of ice about five kilometers away.

Weightlessness returned to his body as it passed through the invisible barrier. A burden lifted from his mind as well. Drifting in microgravity was the closest he could get to *New Reason*, to Gauri — to feeling like he was home. His muscles stretched and relaxed.

Yishma keyed in his destination. A jostle of acceleration, a correction, then more drifting.

During the trip, he tried not to think about how he was flying through uncharted space completely alone. He managed to dwell instead on the two aliens, Anne and Claire, with their budding space-bear romance. Or was he reading too much into it? Their species might not even have romantic feelings, or they might be like those weird chimps that would hump anything.

Yishma thought, *I'm not an animal behaviorist, I'm just some gearhead — and I say they're into each other, and that's good enough.* It was nice to be near affection. He noticed the implication of that thought — that he was suddenly so *bereft* of affection — but managed not to dwell.

It took half an hour to reach the cometoid. Yishma came to attention when the suit bored an anchor tether into it. Chips of stone and ice fractured off and drifted away. He powered on the lasers, and smiled; it felt good to be back in his element.

Before he started, he spun around to look at the ship he'd left. There it hung, a little smaller than an outstretched fist. It seemed to be made of spheres that had been forced together under high pressure, a design philosophy reflected in its globular interior.

The lidar showed that the outside was even more beat-up than the inside. Poor old thing.

It deserved a name, he realized. The *Relic*.

Like everything else he could see, the *Relic* was pink, lit by the unseen star. The suit told him the ship measured about four hundred meters long. A massive investment, by human standards; mostly only warships and mining operations were that big. But the videos had made *Relic* look like a research vessel, some sort of long-range expedition. Was it doing something important? Were the space-bears just that rich?

Brass tacks.

Lines of red light burned through the cometoid as Yishma carved a cubic meter off one end, grin never leaving his face. *Nothing like power tools to make you feel alive again.* He could've stayed at it for hours, but the piece separated within minutes. The cometoid lost its unnatural glow as the lasers powered down. Yishma drilled in a towing attachment and began the trip back. With the extra mass, it was slower going, and he had plenty of time to think about the *Relic* as he watched it grow larger.

Why had the *Relic* brought him to the comet cloud? And why had it warned him before it teleported there? The warning could have been a safety feature, but the destination felt intentional. Like the *Relic* had read Yishma's map when he left his pod — the map with possible water stores circled — and decided to help. Yishma felt stupid as soon as he thought it. Ships didn't think.

Although ... Yishma had been assuming the ship was automated, but could it be sentient? Humans had failed to create artificial intelligence, but that didn't mean every species had. *Talking to a machine* ... Would that be even weirder than talking to a biological alien? It didn't matter, either way it was amazing.

The exosuit glided to a stop outside the hangar. Yishma's smile widened, then froze.

He'd forgotten to make a plan for the last step. How the hell was he supposed to get a literal ton of water past the threshold?

While his mind flailed for ideas, the hangar lights went out. Spikes of terror drove into his gut. The *Relic* was teleporting. Without him.

Instead of turning back on, the light traveled down its strips to the interior of the hangar, over and over. Approach lights, telling him to come in? No other interpretations sprang to mind. Was the *Relic* really this good at communicating with him? That was insane. Then again, the videos he'd seen had been oddly familiar. Were some things just universal? Or did their species just have a lot in common? It was a big universe; why *couldn't* some of the aliens be like people?

We going in? Gauri said.

Oh. Yishma hoped he hadn't been staring at the lights too long. *Right.* He pointed the lidar at the escape pod, where he'd left it inside the hangar. The pod was drifting from the deck; the gravity was off.

Yishma piloted the exosuit by hand the rest of the way. Who knew what its computer would do when faced with artificial gravity? He swooped across the deck to bring the chunk of ice in low. As soon as he stopped moving, just above the deck, the gravity came on. His knees creaked after the half-centimeter fall; it was all he could do to slide out of the exosuit and crumple to the deck.

He'd made it, though. After a minute staring at the ceiling through his stuffy helmet, he rose to his feet and examined the comet fragment. It was gray and mottled and held more rocks than he'd thought. He used a plasma torch to melt a large chunk of ice over the water reclamation system, then decided he'd earned a rest.

He sat on the crate and stared at the sideways command console until it indicated that some of the ice had been filtered, then filled the canteen. There was no taste that indicated the water had been flying through space for billions of years. It was as cool and refreshing as anything he could remember.

It filled him with the old feeling of a job well done, but it didn't last. He missed Gauri. His heart lurched in his chest and he bit his tongue to prevent tears from rising up and choking him.

He crouched on the bulkhead and pawed through the crate again, stopping when he found a data crystal that Gauri had filled up for him. Writings and recordings and the like, he'd assumed. He plugged it into the pod's console; a directory labeled IN CASE YOU'RE BORED caught his eye. It held episodes of a dumb military adventure they'd been watching together, *LaGrange 3*. He groaned and felt his eyes glisten. She really had known him well. Would anybody ever know him that well again?

He started an episode on the console and thankfully lost himself in it. He drank his comet water, munched on a sandy ration brick, and eventually fell asleep.

Nausea and pain woke him, another batch of irradiated cells sloughing off somewhere. He staggered up on one arm and rushed to the sickness tube the pod had for stomachs upset by microgravity. The orange vomit he retched up was vacuumed away, where it would be recycled as the ice had been. At least the vomit had been thin; he must have digested most of the rations.

It drove home that he needed a doctor. His next goal had to be taking control of the *Relic*. There was probably something else helpful in those video diaries; he filled his canteen, set the alien device on top of the crate, and began to peruse its records, picking up where he'd left off.

The picture was even sharper than last time. The plane of Anne's nose looked blade-sharp, as if a strand of hair would be severed should it drift across it. The lens was zoomed in so close he could see every tuft of hair on her face, every lash against her cheek. Almost humanoid, if he let it be. Another thread of connection to cling to.

Part of her mouth turned up. The frame widened and he realized he and she were looking at the same thing: her reflection, in a mirror. The two Annes both turned to the side; she began walking across her quarters. To her hatch. Opened it; Claire stood in the long rectangular space.

Yishma's eyes tracked Claire across the room, the camera panning back to Anne. Anne's mouth was still pulled up at the side, a sort of half-smile. Claire sat at a table, and Anne joined her. Anne poured them both glasses of dark liquid. Was this a date? It had to be: Claire's uniform was unbuttoned at the top and Anne's body had lost its rigidity. Anne gestured with her glass — such a familiar gesture. Yishma's eyes grew damp just from seeing the romantic scene. He and Gauri hadn't had a date night for too long. Now, of course, they never would.

The imagery paused abruptly when Claire touched Anne's hand. It held on an image of her small, furry fingers, lying across a set of darker, longer ones.

The next video was more of things he'd seen before. Anne performing her duties, touring the ship. The ship and its stations were featured more prominently. Anne must have been introducing more crew. There were what he interpreted as males and females and another, less differentiated gender. The creatures spent a lot of time in what must have been their research or harvesting area. There were many of those violet vines crawling about in jars.

More of Anne, carrying out more duties. Eating in a café. Stealing looks across the room at Claire. Like the looks he'd stolen at Gauri. Wanting. The camera hung frozen on these looks, little snatches of unspoken conversation. Sometimes it focused on Claire. Ostensibly showing the research, but panning to Claire's pale eyes and fine, thin hair.

And then there was another dinner, and more drinks in Anne's cabin, and then, to Yishma's relief, a fade to black. It was clear where the evening was headed. It didn't surprise him, then, when it faded into another shot of two sleeping figures, under the blankets, impossible to decipher where one began and the other ended.

Yishma swiped his hand to pause the recording. He needed a minute. It was too much. Watching a real-life courtship was draining in a way no *LaGrange 3* subplot could be.

He resumed playback. A shot of some new players coming through the airlock. Heavy suits and helmets. Carrying more flowers. Why? Were they using them for something? Doing research? Handing off the specimens. Stepping under shiny nozzles to be decontaminated. In the background, the ship gleamed. Sometimes Anne put her hand to the wall and spoke to it. The affection of a captain for her carriage.

Anne, in her quarters, speaking directly to the lens. Smiling. She gestured behind her at her table, adorned with heavy plates bearing several different foods. There was a spill of different colored gems scattered across the table. What did those mean?

But there was something special about this, it was clear. He could almost feel Anne's excitement radiating through the hologram.

Cut.

Claire arrived. Her face lit up when she saw the gems. She ran her fingertips across the gems, laughed. A laugh! A high, tinkling laugh, like glass on glass. Anne laughed too, then she seized Claire's hand, spoke with a sense of ... joyful urgency?

There was a loud, screeching noise. It made them both jump, turn their heads, one dark, one light, towards the outer hatch.

What was that? He could almost hear the words falling out of their mouths.

Claire moved first, but Anne pulled her back down. Moved in front of her, patted her shoulder.

Then she opened the hatch, poking her head out.

She came back in, shaking her head.

The moment was lost.

Scene.

Yishma suspected he knew where the story was going. How stupid did you have to be to accidentally bring dangerous alien life onto a closed ship? What had the screech been about? A pathogen, a parasite? Or something more mundane — a mutiny? Whatever it was, Yishma imagined it was a precursor to the battle scars he'd seen earlier.

He felt even sicker than he was. His life didn't need another doomed romance in it.

A bleep from the command console caused him to flail his arm straight into a locker handle, and he yelped. The console's readout indicated that it was time to take his radiation medicine. He took a deep breath and screamed, this time with rage at his likely painful death. One more inhalation to scream — but he bent over panting instead, at a spike of nausea. When it passed, he fished a capsule out of a black plastic bottle and took it with a swig of water.

Through force of will, he kept it down, then sat back, sweating. He had to keep moving forward.

Hadn't that video included a trip to the bridge? He watched the relevant part again and again, adding to the map he'd already drawn. He suspected that the *Relic* might not take kindly to his attempt to seize control, so he added other paths too, emphasizing nothing beyond the already-circled places. He took a picture of the map with the console's camera and sent it to his suit, which could project it onto his helmet. He didn't want the *Relic* to cotton onto his plan.

It seemed that the ship caught on anyway. When Yishma reached the entrance to the bridge, the hatch squirmed shut, as did the other hatches in the T intersection; only the way back remained open. He could understand that the *Relic* wouldn't want to hand over control to an alien interloper. The ship couldn't possibly have known he was dying.

He worked his hand into the hatch that blocked off the bridge, in the middle where the membranes met. He fought to keep bile down; there was no doubting that this was flesh. When no amount of tugging made it budge, he plodded back to the pod to regroup. Every time he entered a chamber, the hatch closed behind him. The *Relic* even closed off the exit from the hangar.

Guess you've worn out your welcome, Gauri said. Was that what he was to the *Relic*? A bad guest? Or a bad dog, a petulant child? Was he in a time-out?

Time-out. Ridiculous. His life was at stake. At another pang of nausea, Yishma fumed.

You gonna take that lying down? Gauri again. She was right. If the ship wanted to be difficult, he'd just have to be difficult right back. In an equipment locker in the pod, he found a pry-bar.

Yishma struggled to get purchase against the hatch; when he did, no amount of pulling could get the flesh to move a centimeter.

He let the pry-bar fall from his hand. It landed with a thud. *Now what?* There had to be something besides hanging out in his escape pod, watching bad holos until he died. But how was he supposed to explain *urgency* to the damn starship? Interpretive dance? Without words, this wasn't going to end well.

When words fail ... Gauri said, trailing off. She didn't have to finish. Yishma knew the rest of the old joke: *Send in the Marines.* There was a time to talk; there was a time for force. He'd always heard he was lousy at the latter, too eager to please, a pushover. Well, he wasn't going to be so stubbornly non-confrontational that it *killed* him.

He dragged the exosuit across the hangar. Crouching now in front of the hatch, he leaned the suit over his back. From that angle he could barely reach the keypad; working with only his fingertips, he aimed and activated the cutting lasers.

As soon as the ship's flesh began to sizzle, a layer of blue light slammed down from the ceiling, plasma spillover roiling onto the deck. The lasers were firing into a shimmering wall now, making it crackle with dissipating energy. Another of the *Relic*'s force-fields? The exosuit was doing no apparent damage to anything other than its own overheating mechanisms. Yishma turned the lasers off and rolled the suit off his back, letting it clatter to the deck. He lay down to join it, two machines rendered ineffectual by the strange intelligence that surrounded them. His pulse thudded in his ears and felt like it would never stop.

Yishma didn't wonder about the forcefield technology. No questions about the mechanics of sentience crossed his mind. He just stared at the gently curving ceiling, the body of the great ship which had swallowed him. Would it let him fly off in the exosuit, if he wanted to spend his final hours floating with the comets?

Come on, Yish, Gauri said. *Cut it out.* Yishma could almost hear the voice inside him snapping her fingers.

No use, Yishma said back. *I'm a prisoner. The* Relic *hates me now.*

Says who?

I'd hate me, Yishma said.

For fuck's sake.

Yishma sat up, scooted against the exosuit, and hugged his knees to his chest; his air exchangers rested against the useless machinery.

Lemme tell you something, Yish. In survival training they talked about 'the seductive nihilism of deep space'. I didn't get it then, but I do now. Nobody can see or hear us out here. We could live for decades and never accomplish anything.

And? Yishma said.

We're depressed and we're scared. It's understandable. But here's what the Marines say to that: so fucking what?

Yishma chuckled. *That's your great revelation?*

Gauri tut-tutted. *The creatures on those video diaries were scared and they didn't give up. Hell, how do you think the ship feels? It lost everything, but it still rescued you.*

Probably starting to regret it, though, Yishma thought.

At least the ship's still managing to make a difference. Gauri fell silent.

Yishma stared at the scintillating wall of energy that blocked his future, re-running the conversation in his head. Why *had* the *Relic* rescued him? He hadn't given the question much thought, with his myopic focus on his own survival. The ship must have been in the star system and, what, decided to be a good samaritan? Or maybe it was lonely. Or both. And Yishma had repaid it by shooting it with industrial lasers. Some first impression of humanity. The *Relic did* seem to care, though. It could've easily vented the hangar and been rid of him. Maybe it just didn't want him rummaging in its guts and controlling its brain.

He'd have to stick with that analysis if he wanted to stand a chance. They weren't enemies, just having a hard time communicating. His racing heart began to slow. A break for his mind was in order; he couldn't think like this. He retreated to the pod, where he fired up another episode of *LaGrange 3*. It wasn't the best show, but it was something to do, and he wanted to see how it ended.

Some episodes later, he was dissecting the previous hours in his head, and remembered that Gauri had mentioned Anne and Claire. Maybe there were hints in those videos for how to communicate with the *Relic*. At the very least, he owed it to them to watch their story to the end, too. In a way, their deaths had led to his rescue. With the comet water, nowhere to go, and almost a month of radiation meds, he had plenty of time for it.

The frame was zoomed in on one of the creatures' chests. Dusky lavender rose from its skin in spheres. When the camera pulled back, he could see the chest still rising, drawing short, choppy breaths. There was a pause between each breath. The skin around the spheres rippled. Minutes of this footage. The same shuddering breaths. More diseased spheres. The camera stayed beyond the last breath; the skin was still vibrating and moving. Trembling, the way Yishma's own body shuddered with sickness.

Nerves.

The camera finally panned away from the body. Pulled back and then moved slowly, across beds all in their own glass cases, all with bruised and mottled bodies.

The disease — infestation? — must have spread fast.

He shivered.

Cut. A full minute of blackness, long enough that he started to wonder if this was the last scene he'd see. But then the hologram flickered with light again. Anne and Claire. Side by side. Their faces drawn tight, lips white and pulled taut over teeth.

Anne spoke in the same odd, off-kilter pattern he still couldn't recognize. He had hoped by hearing it he could begin to identify repeated sounds, pick something up, but all he knew was that her voice was so low he could barely hear anything. Both Anne and Claire snatched looks around as Anne talked. As if they were looking for someone, or something. Watching. At one point Anne stopped speaking completely, and they both cocked their heads in the same manner.

Then Anne began again, sounds coming from her faster and choppier.

Though her volume didn't increase, her pitch did, rising until she didn't sound like the Anne he'd become accustomed to. Then Claire reached out and took her hand. Anne stopped. They shared a look.

The ship creaked. Both their eyes widened and they looked behind them. All was quiet for a moment.

Blank, dark space.

Claire, working in a makeshift lab. Then the two of them in Anne's quarters. Yishma saw the mattress pressed up against the hatch, blocking the way. The ship must've been lost, the crew sick and dying. Had the ship, or their crewmates, turned on them? Or maybe they just didn't want to get sick.

Claire was working with several projectors at once. It was hard to tell exactly what she was doing, touching and zooming through data and images. Something biological.

Then a shot of Claire coming from the bathroom. Her fingers parted the hair on her thorax. Purple blooms were scattered across her chest.

Yishma's heart crumpled. He knew it was coming, but the look in her eyes ... It matched the way he felt inside when he thought about Gauri, about leaving her behind.

Anne reached out and touched the marks. She made a sound. Asking if it hurt? Claire looked at her feet. Anne drew her into her arms.

Dark hologram.

New scene. Claire's body lay behind Anne, who was speaking quietly again. Anne's face was a mask of blooming bruises now, herself. A shock of white ran through her hair. She turned to Claire's body behind her, and touched her face.

Tears swelled in her eyes, clung to her eyelashes. She leaned down and rubbed her forehead against her lover's. Then she sat up, turned to the window that looked over the eternal night sky.

Put her hand against it, the way she had before.

Speaking that unfamiliar language.

But Yishma knew what she was saying anyhow.

We never should have come here.

The picture faded; the grid returned. Yishma swiped forward, frustrated, even though he knew it was the last entry. With a sigh, he let his head drop.

The *Relic* had watched the whole thing in real time, helpless to stop it; it hadn't been in charge. It had had relationships of some sort with those creatures. And it had seen them die in agony. Yet it had bounced back, rescuing him. But how long had it spent drifting, mourning, healing? Long enough for its hull to bear the marks of countless meteoroid strikes.

Yishma did not have that much time to fix himself. It was sinking in that he was very broken indeed. His body was dying. The love of his life was dead from the same ailment. His mind was fractured into a dozen pieces; he was even talking to one of them.

His was still a better prognosis than Claire's or Anne's ... so why couldn't he muster their level of dignity?

Not exactly one of life's great mysteries, Yish. Gauri.

"Not ... now." Yishma growled.

Not until you stop —

Yishma slammed his palm against the bulkhead. The *bang* echoed through the pod.

— stop acting like you're alone! Please.

Yishma took a deep breath, then blew it out. Claire and Anne had found strength in each other. The ship had found purpose, perhaps, in him. So why was he trying to fly solo?

"Okay." Yishma slumped. "You're right. But how am I supposed to talk to the ship?"

It can read maps, can't it?

"What's that got to do with —"

Maps. This was an interstellar ship. Surely it knew its way around the galaxy. And there was only one way that Yishma knew of to describe an absolute location in the cosmos.

And every schoolboy's memorized the starmap for Sol.

Yishma tried not to let his tears of joy stain the pages as he drew the three planes of stellar coordinates that intersected, uniquely, at Sol. He tried not to let his voice quaver too much while he recorded and re-recorded a message.

"This is Yishma Shamoun, broadcasting from the escape pod of the scooper *New Reason*. I am inside a four-hundred-meter alien starship. It is friendly. Do not fire. I will die without medical attention. I am listening on channel four hundred seventy-three. Message repeats."

He set it to broadcast on the emergency band and climbed outside the pod. *The moment of truth.* He held the drawing out in front of him, suppressing a fearful tremble. For minutes he kept his arms outstretched. It wasn't working. He'd have to come up with yet another idea. His shoulders started to ache; he was about to give up when the hangar lights began to blink. He hurried inside to the acceleration webbing.

When the shaking had finished, Yishma disentangled himself and leaned against the bulkhead, staring at the command console. The *Relic must* have brought him to Sol. Right? He counted to ten, thirty, one hundred — counting was easy, it kept him from thinking — and finally a voice came into the escape pod, clear as the interstellar medium. "Yishma Shamoun, this is Jovian command ..."

Yishma relaxed every muscle in his body, his breath sliding out as he slid to the floor. He'd lost everything, yes. But he'd found something wondrous, maybe changed the course of human history. No discovery could replace Gauri, of course, but no discovery had to. Like the *Relic*, he would live, and learn, and experience; help others when he could. Grief was a phase, loss but a chapter; whenever he was ready, he would grow.

Lambs Fight to Die

Evan Marcroft

When you come swaggering through the door of the Two Camelia Saloon, I recognize you immediately. Your mustachios are more pearl than gold now, and you have rid yourself of your left arm at some point along your way to me, but your old shoulders carry those decades effortlessly. Just as well, for the last time I laid eyes upon you it was through a fire that burned upon the water. Captain Herault Innesreich. Hero of The Roachwater Scrum.

And I think, in order:
It's him.
Yes.
Kill him.
Hold.
Let's have a drink first.

For the sake of all you took from me, I can bide my time. Savor what is now to come. I polish my smile to the same sheen as the pistol you wear on your hip and wait for your eyes to find mine.

I had, over years of occupation, taken to waiting out the equatorial heat of the afternoon at the Two Camelia Saloon, the *siesta* being of those imported Chugozi traditions that I had guiltily come to appreciate. I had spent this sweltering noon cooking in a sugarcane forest, administering rites of Immuration to the grandfather of a farming family who had succumbed to the bite of a snake. With experienced hands and respectful mantras I freed his ghost from the sarcophagus of his body and placed it into a clay *pranjaar* with his severed thumb to anchor him, so that he could watch over his children and grandchildren from the honored place above the hearth. With a complex ritual I used a cutting of his soul to reanimate the body, so that the family would not miss his labor. The long walk back to my seaside town of Cheoksri Mät had left me thirsty for an iced lotus wine.

That is how I came to be here. In a way, I have been here all along. Waiting for you unknowingly. Your path to me, however, was much more circuitous.

When the three-way war was over, it was upon your people to decide what became of my home, the island of Prinjait. Your Protectum of Sabot had not exactly won, but we had most certainly lost. Our antique navy was unprepared to defend such a remote territory against both Sabot's technological might and the armada of Chugoz. It did not matter that both those nations fought one another as much as us. We were inevitably crushed.

The treaty that Sabot reached with Chugoz gave everyone a little of what they wanted. Chugoz claimed this island as their own and expanded its empire a fair distance. Sabot, meanwhile, gained access to the veins of precious stormstone riddling the island's bedrock. And my people were glad not to be destroyed.

Twenty years after the war, I walk sandy streets with signage double-posted in Chugozi script as well as my native Prinja'at. Every day, I watch you Sabotines flow in by ship to loll along our beaches and sample our fascinatingly dark flesh. Perhaps you did not travel for that reason, but you cannot say you did not come by the same vessel.

So here I find myself, at my favorite bar with its peeling plaster walls and ceiling fans lazily stirring the humid air, at my favorite seat by the window. I have a bamboo shoot of good drink in hand and my son Hanpreet, the bartender's apprentice, is right now bringing me a still-sizzling pan of maggot-stuffed peppers. A finer day than can be expected under occupation.

And then you walk in.

Herault the Marlin. Great war-hero of the Sabotine Protectum, captain of the mighty zagermorder *Thasser's Fist*. You wear your old leather frock coat like a cape upon your shoulders; your breast is a trove of jangling medals. You enter like a king into his hall, and you scan the room as if surveying your fawning court.

Our eyes meet briefly, without recognition.

Murderer.

Criminal.

Monster.

Four more file in behind you. I recognize them as well, from my research if not their faces. *Karal Garwheel, Tyson Fluke, Ustuus Lokgrim, Iyrvold Eurldane*. The surviving members of Herault's Howlers, that legendary gunnery crew that twenty years ago singlehandedly sunk half a dozen of our battleships, reversing a certain victory into an utter rout. It occurs to me that it is near the anniversary of that fateful night. Perhaps this is some sort of reunion. I am glad that we could all be here.

"Bartender!" you bellow, beckoning with your visored cap. "My friends have come a long way with naught to drink but saltwater. A round of rum please. Squid's Eye brand, if you have it." This is the first I've heard you speak; your baritone Prinja'at is surprisingly proficient, if heavily affected. I can admit that I'm impressed.

The barman, plump old Ashtoki, calls my son over to help pour drinks. Hanpreet shoots me a worried glance as he leaves my table. He isn't wrong to be concerned. You Sabotines have a stomach for strong drink but not a brain for it. There might well be trouble, and a Prinjaiti finding herself in colonial court against you would not be at an advantage.

"Go," I say, waving him off. "Do your job. I'll be leaving soon anyway."

Hanpreet is a good boy. Ever concerned for his aging mother. I do feel guilty lying to him so.

You and your men throw your coats boorishly over the backs of your chairs. A few of you laugh uneasily at how those chairs scuttle about on the mummified hands affixed to their legs. It has always amused me how soldiers can be so uneasy around death.

I listen to you and your friends trade jokes and jabs in your native Patterquay while I finish my meal down to the last dollop of sour-sweet *chipori* sauce. Each dish deserves to be eaten like your very last, or so our old adage goes.

While I eat, I take a long, final sort of look around the saloon. The Two Camelia is an unhandsome box wedged between two busy streets, but with a charm you would not find in a classier establishment up in Templespine Heights, I assure you. Those curios hung up on the walls are Ashtoki's favorite gewgaws; those yellowed osteoswords, that tattered Prinjaiti standard. He swears it is the skin of Rebel-Prince Rhao, never mind how every barman on the island seemed to have the same infamous hide. It's the love in every detail, even the fake ones.

I will miss this place, you know.

Your men whistle when I finally approach your table. They see my sheer sari, my belly-baring choli, and assume I am an accessible woman. They do not know I am older than I seem. The skin on my face is *mr'tvacha* — deadflesh — preserved with marbleflower oil, animated by a scrap of ghost. My breasts as well, lifted with younger corpse-meat, similarly possessed. On my hands, only my index finger is my own; all others were taken from different bodies. It is a myth that *svaamr'ati* — necromancers — live longer than other women. We simply fudge the numbers a little.

"Hello there, little lamb," says the man to your left. Karal Garwheel, block-jawed and balding. He pats his lap and smirks. "I've got a seat for you here. You might find it a bit hard though."

Lamb. I stifle a shudder at that playful slur. "It looks perfectly soft to me," I return in Patterquay.

Guffaws all around, aimed at him. He scowls, but you clap your hand on the table before him. "Act like you all had mothers," you growl, annoyed. "That's a disgraceful way to address a lady." You aim a wink at me. "Herault Innesreich, Sabotine Navy, retired and at your dispatch, ma'am." Charming to another, I'm sure.

My eye snags again on your holstered gun. An ex-soldier who cannot let go of his weapon — that is a sad thing. Your men, too, are all armed. Pistols and blades. Here I am, one aging woman, with not so much as a sewing needle.

If I am to kill all of you, I will have to be quite clever.

"Iuhriti," I reply. "Pray tell, *mahdei*, what brings you around the globe of the world to our quiet little island?"

You explain much as I expected. While you speak, I watch you pinch off the tip of a hand-rolled cigarillo with your remaining hand and produce a lighter with your left's replacement, a horrid thing of blue-black beetle carapace and misjointed digits, grown whole in an artificial womb from liquid biomatter like all Sabotine technology.

"And you?" you ask in turn. "What do you seek from a lot of old cuttlefish like us?"

"Truth be told I'd stopped here hoping to find a game of bugharatti," I say. "Would a worldly man such as you know how to play? I would be happy to go easy on you."

Your friends grin and look at you expectantly. "Sounds like she's called you out, Herault."

"Oh aye. You going to let her traipse off with your oysters?"

Your ego isn't so fragile as that — I can see it in your unshuttered eyes. But you do want to put on a good show for your mates. "Never let it be said that the Marlin even once refused a challenge," you declare, clapping your cap upon the table. "But every game must have a wager. What would we be playing for?"

"I have little coin at the moment, mahdei," I say, "but I do have a tab and the barman's trust. Would it behoove you to play for drinks?"

Your friends agree eagerly on your behalf.

The game of bugharatti is superficially simple and deceptively labyrinthine. Each player arranges three painted dice to form a pattern of three suits and conceals it beneath a cup. Then each player may reveal up to two of their dice and attempt to guess the pattern of an opponent — some being higher valued than others. The risk you take, in the pattern you choose, how much you expose, and your guess itself, determines the severity of your win or loss. A good player will know when to *feint*, tricking your foe into believing you have a higher or lower pattern than you do, whilst having a talent for *scrutiny*, seeing past your opponent's own bluffs.

What you do not know is that my dice are cored with human carpal bones, each housing the tiny soul of a miscarried baby. I cajole them like flighty children into forming what patterns I need in the moment; it is the easiest way for a skilled player like me to lose.

I let myself win the first three-round match and savor my prize of a fermented tapir milk sweetened with glassmoth wing scales. "Why does this one not sit?" I ask in Prinja'at, nodding at the man standing to your left.

"Oh, old Tyce? Ah. He's not spent much time among you Prinjaiti," you reply. "It can be difficult for us foreigners to acclimate to walking cadavers and the like. He thinks his chair is — how do you say, haunted?"

I laugh into the back of my hand. "There is nothing to fear," I tell the nervous one. "Ghosts are not dangerous in the least. They are merely the tangible memories we eject at death. It takes a rare and powerful will for them to retain their intelligence. Or very rarely, a malice."

The dead, in fact, are all around him. Mr'at hands keep our houses clean, gigging vermin on overlong nails. Rickshaws with reanimated legs carry raisined-up aunties to and from the marketplace. Dead vadelects veiled in gold tend to the limbless Patient Monks in their cloisters, powered by the slivers of ancestors whose spirits nap content as cats above our hearths. Prinjaiti homes are small, the saying goes, but our families large indeed.

"I do hope the polizia will not give you too much trouble during your stay," I remark, as I arrange my bugharatti pattern.

You furrow your brow at that. "Why would they?"

"Many of them are veterans like yourselves," I explain. "Some men can be unwilling to let old wounds heal. Suffice to say, they can be rather unwelcoming towards our Sabotine guests." I keep my voice carefully neutral before I say the next thing "Many times I heard them call you *kalamaros* behind your backs."

I fix my eye on Karal Garwheel. His expression crumples into an indignant weal at a word unfamiliar to him but stinking sharply of insult. "Cuttlefish," I say, half at him. "Small, soft, cowardly. For how you yielded twenty years ago. Their claim and not mine, mahdei. I just thought you should know."

And with a word, I am in their heads.

I lose the next two matches as narrowly as possible and pretend to be disappointed as you and your friends guzzle down your second and third mugs of revolting Sabotine dishwater. I stop Hanpreet as he departs with the empty platter.

Pulling him down to whisper in his ear, I say, "I have a task for you, my son. Go and find Chief Constable Yadriano, wherever he is presently. At this time of day he should be making the rounds at Mendicant's Wharf. Tell him there has been a disturbance at the Two Camelia Saloon. Tell him Sabotines are causing trouble, and someone is hurt. He must come quickly."

"I can't leave Ashtoki alone —" my son protests, ever dutiful.

Good boy.

Yes. Always was.

But now is not the time.

I squeeze his wrist, pricking him with nails studded in mustard seeds. "I am your mother and you will do as I say," I hiss.

I wait for his reluctant nod before I add, more softly, "Do not return when you are done. Please, stay far away from this place. Do you understand?"

"Yes, mother," Hanpreet says, though he can't meet my eyes. He's torn between two kinds of loyalty to me. The urge to obey, and the urge to protect. I can only trust he'll listen to me over his own heart and not come back. "Then go."

I watch him hurry out the back door, stopping only to apologize to a flustered Ashtoki and hang up his apron. I hope dearly that I will never see him again.

"Up for another match?" you ask, pulling my attention back to the table. "Or have I satisfied your urge?" You roll the dice in your palm tantalizingly. Your friends await my answer with parched eyes and bloodshot noses, but you haven't bothered with your last glass. I daresay you're in this for the sport of it.

"Not just yet, mahdei," I reply. "Not just yet."

I lose this game by so thin a margin that at a glance you'd think I'd won.

Riding the fourth round of rum, your men hit a tall wave of nostalgia. That is why you are all here, no? This island is where all your old glories have been laid to rest. "I remember our cherry voyage, lads," says the oldest among you. Iyrvold the Deadeye, squinting blearily through the boughs of the present at a past where he was not yet gray-bearded and gouty. "The bolts in our ship were still warm from the drydock when that one-eyed hailong caught us halfway to Las Oculcraz. That drownèd sea-beast saw fit to sink us and would have dragged us all down to Grimla's Trove if not for old Marlin here." He claps your shoulder and you grin modestly. "Won't never forget how you baited that great bastard into biting down on our forward gun so you could fire straight down its throat. Fucys send me, my heart didn't beat again for a night and a day."

"Aye, I do miss the sea," you muse aloud. "But I don't miss its teeth."

Laughter enough to lift the roof. Your men clink their glasses and knock back the dregs. I save my cups and dice from the spillover. I think we are about done anyway. Hanpreet will have found the constable by now.

You segue naturally into stories of the war. It's what brought you all together, after all. What holds you together across leagues and years. War is the universal brother-maker, the cauldron where the stubborn individual is rendered away. Oh Herault, you have lost many times more than are here now. I doubt you can remember all their faces. But they are with you still, war's skeins binding even in death, and never more strongly than in this place. I promise you that.

Memories unspool from each of your crew in turn, the queer woman at the table forgotten for the moment. You take me on a storm-wracked jaunt through the Roachwater Strait so vivid that I can almost feel those three mammoth hearts hammering through the deck of *Thasser's Fist*. I listen, rapt, as you reminisce of fighting back the waves of fish-tailed mr'at that swarmed the hull of your ship, of swooping like a demon out of that roiling squall to turn the tide in a battle that no one yet knew meant everything. I can hear long-guns booming, painting Prinjaiti osteoclads in red and gold. Battleships of flesh and bone go up in flames, and with them one of two prewritten futures.

For all that you made happen that day, Herault, your men love you. Their hearts pound in their throats. You saved their lives a dozen times over, and, what's more, immortalized them in the annals of your homeland. You pinned those medals to their chests, made their hard, bloody lives worth the pain of living.

My memories of that time are somewhat different.

I remember clinging to a splinter of ship-rib, the vessel to which I was captain and nurse dwindling towards the floor of the Crawling Sea. The compound soul I'd so lovingly woven, cared for, coming to pieces. I remember Sabotine zagermorders prowling the floating wreckage of our fleet, their clawed flippers churning the water to froth, their great blood-burning smokestacks blasting ichorsoot stormclouds into the sky. When I close my eyes, I see lifeboats full of my comrades and sisters picked apart, shot by shot, for the sport of it. I feigned death when your ships disgorged zoofacted sharks to tear apart those survivors still floundering. They hounded them towards the depths and left ghosts wailing, forever, in the throes of ceaseless currents, where my hands would never reach them.

I remember *Thasser's Fist* sailing through waves of fire, with you standing proud upon its prow.

We go into war understanding that those we love will die. I did, same as you. Men and women crammed like bullets into a cartridge, faced with the choice to become flesh-cutting or die uselessly, cannot help but grow close. In taking up the sword, we consent for our enemies to kill our battleforged brothers and sisters. It is like a contract, no malice on either end, perfectly rational.

But twenty years removed from the battlefield is a good long while, Herault. In that time, we shed so much blood and bone as to become different people. There remains no obligation to be rational, to respect the agreements our past selves make.

"Let's have us a toast," you declare, though your glass is already empty. Who cares? You raise it anyway. "To those that didn't make it. To those who died to send us here."

"To friends at peace," I say, offering my own cup. "To heroes always."

The moment snags. You furrow your brow at me. "What do you know of fallen comrades, madame?"

"Much," I say. "The dead are with us always in Prinjait."

"Why don't you shut that flapping gash, lamb," the scarred man to my left drawls. "This ain't nothing a woman would ken."

Sabotine dog.

Took shots at my sisters as they drowned.

It ought to be him dissolved by crabs and worms.

"Don't be an ass, Ustuus," you snap.

"Lamb," I say, musingly. "That reminds me of something. May I share a story of my own?"

I do not wait for consent. Your fellows have grown bored with me now that the rum has dried up, and they are unhappy that I commandeered your toast. "Back in the time before history proper," I say, "there was a tiger living in the jungle near a village of lambs. These lambs lived in fear of the tiger, for he struck with neither warning nor mercy, carrying off young and old, man and woman, to be devoured. But the lambs would do nothing to defend themselves. 'It is in the nature of tigers to eat lambs,' they sighed, 'and the nature of lambs to be eaten.' But one brave lamb refused this paradigm and sought to take revenge upon the tiger who had cruelly consumed so many of his loved ones.

"The Lamb sought out the Tiger in his jungle lair and confronted him. 'You have committed unforgivable crimes,' he cried. 'I have come to deliver justice upon you. Face me and die.' He stood fearlessly as the Tiger emerged from his cave, his fangs all bloody, his claws stretched out. 'I am here, Lamb,' the Tiger roared. 'How do you hope to strike at me?' And in response the Lamb laid down and showed his belly to the Tiger, who laughed and promptly ate him alive.

"Within an hour the Tiger was wracked with unimaginable pain. Within two he was stone dead. The Lamb had poisoned his own flesh before confronting the Tiger. The Lamb, you see, had realized what no other had before. It is true that it is the nature of tigers to eat lambs, and the nature of lambs to be eaten. A lamb may kill a tiger with violence, perhaps, but a tiger will always and absolutely kill a lamb. The lesson, mahdei, I think is clear."

I throw a look like a spear into your man Ustuus's eye. He flinches as if from the scrutiny of a crowd. "That word you use for me: 'lamb' — do you know where it comes from? Prinjaiti means 'Child of Lamb', for we are a people that have embraced the ultimate guarantee, the certainty of death, and built our power upon it. It is also from this parable that we derive a saying you may have heard: lambs fight to die."

And at that, the door of the saloon flies open with a bang.

In marches Joakim Yadriano, Chief Constable of the Prinjait Colonial Polizia. "On the authority of the Coven of Nine, all present reveal your hands," he declares in a voice like a thunderclap. "There has been a report of a disturbance." His eyes are already on you.

Constable Yadriano is tall and broad like many Chugozi. He wears a mask of thin gold filigree threaded through the red-clay skin of his face. Upon his hip, a service pistol; in his mailed hand, the rune-etched blade of a coiled *urumi*. Four more constables wait for him at the door, each in the white half-cape of the law.

In his ten years stationed here I have known Joakim to be a moral and even-handed arbiter. But neither does he have any love for you Sabotines. As instructed I place my hands on the table and avert my eyes. Your men, rather, reach for their hips as you rise with your hackles raised to confront him.

"You must be the disturbance," Yadriano observes in trilling Patterquay. He comes to stand within an armspan of you, undaunted by your superior numbers.

"I am Captain Herault Innesreich, retired," you reply. "My comrades and I have caused no trouble nor come to do so. I hope you will leave us in peace."

Yadriano takes a long look back at Ashtoki behind the bar, who looks down and fixates on polishing the countertop. He glances at me, and I let the smallest shudder ripple through my skin.

"What business are you on here in Prinjait?" he asks.

"Leisure, not business," you answer. Your voice is steady, your tone calm. You sincerely don't want trouble. "We're having a reunion."

"I see." The constable drums his fingers off the black wood butt of his sidearm. "Your leisure involves drink, it seems," he says, nodding at your swaying, red-faced companions. "Does it involve women as well?"

You look at me, expecting me to speak in your defense. But I say nothing. I dare not.

"All we've done is play a few rounds of bugharatti and share a few stories."

Yadriano nods decisively. "Your leisure is concluded, then. You will not mind moving along."

"Hell we won't," your man Karal blurts, the youngest and most besotted, him. I can hear him rolling the word *kalamaros* around in his head. *Soft little cuttlefish.* Like sand trapped in an oyster's shell. "We got a right to be wherever we will and fuck all you can do about it, you ken?"

You reach back and grip his shoulder to shut him up. "Forgive my friend, he's deep into it. But he is also correct. By treaty we are allowed free travel here."

"The treaty also grants the Empire of Chugoz the right to detain any resident or visitor of Prinjait for any reason," Yadriano counters, thrusting that name in your face. "This is as forgiving as I will ever be. You may continue your leisure in a cell or anywhere but here. Your choice, *kalamaros*."

A moment of silent tension is trapped between two impenetrable expressions. Neither of you iron men will bend and so one will break under that growing pressure. My slapdash plan has been riddled with gambles — that my son would find the constable, that you would stay entertained by my game — but this is the most important. I cannot know what will happen now.

My fists are balled on the table. I pray for the worst.

Your shoulders slump. "Very well," you sigh. "But grant us a moment to collect our —"

"Fuck you," spits Karal Garwheel, before he unholsters his revolver and shoots Constable Yadriano in his chest.

And I think, in order:

Yes.

Yes.

Yes.

A cruel and stabbing glee, nine times compounded.

Yadriano's eyes flare in afront more than pain. His fingers dig into the flesh around the spurting wound. As he topples over, he hurls a witchword like a javelin from his silver-wrought tongue, which blows over his killer's skull like invisible fire and strips it down to blackened bone. Both bodies hit the floor, and many things happen at once.

I throw myself to the floor as the constables at the door draw their sidearms and open fire. I whisper a hasty command at the femur bones in the table's legs, bidding it tip itself over and give me cover. Gunshots sound like strings of fireworks at a Somerseve Festa; a smattering of plaster pimples burst open along the wall above me. Peeking past the rim of the table, I see a constable slump against the front doorframe, his white uniform swiftly turning red. The remaining three retreat out onto the street, one hauling on a ripcord connected to a brass clockbox on her hip. A mechanism-generated klaxon begins to blare. I can tell you that every constable within earshot will soon be converging on this spot. Within moments the saloon will be surrounded. You will have nowhere to run.

A body sinks to the floor beside me — Tyson Fluke, not dead but gut-shot. Ustuus Lokgrim falls to his knees beside him, clamping both hands down on the growing stain in Tyson's shirt. "Oh fuck, fuck, oh Fucys send me, you're going to be just fine —"

Those fluttering, bloodshot eyes roll to focus on me. Something grips my jaw and I smile back, with all my teeth.

Yes, you're right. But don't tell anyone.

"Ustuus, stanch that wound," I hear you bark. "Iyrvold, man that door." I watch you go loping between tables to scan the back street through the window slats. How easily you relapse into your captain's mien with your back against the wall. Just as you did all those years ago, you'll see your men through this.

"Captain, Tyce is bleeding fast —"

"Can't help him if we can't leave," you snarl over your shoulder. "Drown me, how did this all go to shit?"

If not for the gun in your hand and the blood in your heart, I might laugh out loud.

You drop reflexively into a crouch as a drumroll of small-arms fire powderizes all the glass on the opposite side of the building. Your man by the front door levels his gun along the windowframe and squeezes off three blind, suppressive shots. "What the fuck do we do, captain?"

As ever, their lives are in your hands. But you've only the one now. Can you hold them all? I watch your eyes as the decision is made. "Ustuus, take Tyce and make a break out the back," you answer. "That way is still clear. Iyrvold, you and I will cover their exit —"

"No," I hurriedly cut in. I cannot let you escape. "You can't. They'll catch you if you try to run with a wounded man."

And you hesitate long enough for a bullet to shatter the rear window and smack the cap off your head.

You sink all the way to the floor, beginning to tremble. You can see the horizon of your lifespan, always so distant, rapidly approaching. You scoop up your cap and peer through the sizzling hole. "They've got us on all sides, it seems." You turn to show me a brittle mummer's smile. "I'm sorry you had to be caught up in all this, ma'am. On my honor, I'll do all I can to see you out safely."

You are a different man than the one who ordered my sisters shot as they begged to be taken prisoner. I am not so bent as to believe otherwise. If you were not, you would be Supreme Admiral, not captain retired. The Herault Innesreich of my nightmares is a painted figurehead, a ship's fixture conducting the flow of death with a leather-gloved finger. A static idol meant to be loathingly worshipped. Whereas you, with your silvering hair, your receding nerve, are fluid. You have changed just as I have, sloughed off old skins enough to staff an army of you.

Yes, I know it is absurd to hate a slain enemy. For the living to despise the dead. Yes, it is absurd to hate you who are not really you.

I suppose I am absurd then.

You should never have come back to Prinjait, Captain. It's the worst luck to drink upon a grave.

"Oi, bartender," your man Ustuus calls out. "Is there another way out of here?"

By way of response, Ashtoki stands up from behind the counter and aims the battered old shotgun he keeps there in his — and by association my — direction. I have never known Ashtoki to use the thing. I can only assume him to be a middling shot. It is luck, then, that Ustuus Lokgrim is between me and it. A fiery boom sears the air, and a dozen steel pellets claw away the flesh of his face and throat while leaving me unharmed.

You cry out wordlessly, hand out-flung as if to snatch back the moment before it escapes forever. You don't care that Ashtoki still has one shell chambered. You've already lost two pieces of your heart.

I wonder if you can feel this pain I fling at you, through layers of your cast-off selves stacked two decades high. This man before me with your name certainly suffers, though he is only your latest molting. But revenge is not about hurting one's enemy. It is about slaking one's own bloodthirst by any means, and a grudge can be sated on a substitute of lies. Revenge, Herault, is an internal struggle, mutually irrelevant to reality. You are far removed from the man I hate, but you will have to do.

And it is not so absurd for the dead to hate the dead.

I can do nothing as Iyrvold Eurldane, far too late, pivots and shoots Ashtoki through the brow, throwing him against his prized liquor shelf and burying him in broken glass.

I hear a pistol clicking empty. "Out of shot," the Dead-Eye spits.

"Go," you say, not looking at him, or anything. "Get his gun, if you can."

As he makes his dash across the saloon I shove the corpse of Ustuus Lokgrim away from me. A glint of fresh-stropped edge nicks my eye. No gun on this one, just a knife. With your attention otherwise occupied, I pilfer the knife from his belt and hide it beneath my sari.

"Captain!" Iyrvold's shout is breathless. "There's a door in the floor back here."

I bite down on a curse; he's stumbled upon the cellar. In the early days of the occupation, the Two Camelia Saloon was a spider hole smuggling weapons to insurgents beneath the curfew of the polizia. As the resistance withered, that system was abandoned, but I know that some of the tunnels remain.

I watch you choke down your grief. No, you can't come apart now. You've lost much of your crew but look, there's light at the edge of the storm. "I hope you'll tell me someone's alive over there," you say to me.

I shake my head no. Tyson Fluke is an empty skin in a puddle of spilled wine, his eyes frozen in the color of my teeth. I could have raised him up as a weapon, had I a half-hour to spare.

"You should come with us," you say. "Don't take your chances with *them*."

You're right on that count. The polizia would likely not discriminate between targets at this point. I nod and gather hands and feet beneath me, ready to run for it.

You flip your cap in an arc up past the windows. Reflexive gunshots from both sides of the building rip it to shreds. I launch myself as the last one fades out. Halfway to the bar a thunderclap takes a bite out of my bicep. I scream, stumble, feel beads being drawn on me like so many murderous stares.

And then you are there, lifting me into your arms, making a shield of your broad back. One stray bullet and you would be giving your last to the woman who took all else. At the very least a stranger to whom you owe nothing.

But then, you did give your word.

◦

We trusted you would take us prisoner, Captain Herault.
That was the law of war.
Where was your honor then?

We hurry together through humid darkness. You leading the way, navigating by the photophores of your zoofacted arm. Iyrvold Eurldane dragging me along by the elbow. Me, clasping my stolen knife flat against my wrist. Further ahead, a pinprick of light is growing larger. I am running out of time.

This revenge is like a spell I cast upon you, Herault. And you know as well as I do that any sorcery is gripped only with a glove of sacrifice. I suffer in proportion to you — the fire in which I incinerate all you care about is fueled by all that I love. How can I expect to return to my life when this day is through? I consented to die the moment you came through that door.

I have thrown away all the Somerseve Festas I had left in my allotted time. I doubt I will witness this year's sea-shaman migration, those crabshell monoliths singing their way towards polar waters. However this should end, I will never again drink away an afternoon at the Two Camelia Saloon with Ashtoki and Hanpreet. I will never know what sort of man my son will become. Never will I be a little aunty watching my grandchildren play along the beach from the shade of a coconut tree.

Yet still: if I had one wish, I would pause this second in between its microscopic fractions and walk the undulating streets of Cheoksri Mät one last time. I would run my fingers across its sunbaked walls, mapping it forever in my oil. I would run to the shore and bury my bare feet in this island's rosy sand, apologize for having fought to protect it and lost.

But that chance too, I have thrown upon the pyre. All my futures are ash. We are near the exit now — I can see the sky, blinding as a blue sun. if I tarry any longer you will escape, and it will have been for nothing. A murder abandoned halfway through is another word for suicide.

We fled in too much a hurry to take Ashtoki's shotgun.

A shame. That would have been quicker. Easier.

You slow to a stop at the sound of three sets of footfalls dwindling suddenly to two. You turn to watch the body of Iyrvold Eurldane crumple to the ground. I lure your eyes to mine with the bloody tip of my knife.

I see you put it together at last. Or at least those pieces I have given you.

"Who are you?" you ask, as tears stream into your lips.

I click my heels together and salute you with the flat of my palm.

"Iuhriti Meghdüt," I answer. "Commanding Necromancer of the *Jagdthalam*. Retired."

The name of my ship pricks a memory somewhere down deep in you. You nod slowly.

"Ah. I had thought there were no survivors."

I creep closer towards the plot of daylight where you stand waiting. "There would be more, if not for you."

At last, I think, our memories converge. You stand on high, looking down. I tread bloody water, looking up. No longer from different worlds.

You shift your hand to the pistol at your hip. I'm not sure how many shots you have left, if any. But you do not draw just yet. Instead, you say, "You're wrong if you think I forgot what I did. Another man might try to justify it away, but I have no good reasons. I was scared. I was angry. I wanted to go home. Would you believe me if I said that I am sorry?"

I stop where I am, knee deep in sunlight.

"I suppose I could," I say. "Will you ask me to forgive you?"

"No," you reply. "I don't believe I deserve it. And if you possibly could, I don't think you would have done what you have." You snap the clasp of your hip holster. "I ask that you end it here and go in peace. You've taken what was owed. You've taken —" you pause to swallow a sudden sob. "You've taken everything. So I'd say you and I are even now."

I take a long step closer, and your gun flickers into your hand as if by magic. You aim low, keep the safety on. "Ma'am, turn around and walk away from me. I'm tired of killing. I don't want to do it anymore, but I swear I won't let you use that knife on me," you say. "My children won't forgive me if I do. Now listen. I lost my share of brothers as well. Far more than the men you murdered. But I left the war where it ended. I let it go."

Yes, Herault, because *you* were never conquered. Your brothers' killers did not come to dirty their homes and abuse their women. But that is neither here nor there to me.

"I let it go as well," I say. "Twenty years is a long time to hate. I could see myself forgiving you too, if it were up to me. I would love to grow old and forget there is any more to the world than Prinjait. But twenty years is nothing to the dead. And there are more of them than there are of me."

I stretch my hand out into the light and drag my knife across the lowest joints of my fingers. Preserved skin parts like leather, subcutaneous stitches fraying apart. You wince in sympathetic pain, but I feel little of it as blood overflows the cup of my hand. I prise bone from bone with the edge of the blade; five fingers dangle on thongs of dead muscle as I grip the knife with the ball of my thumb and do the same to my other hand, leaving only my natural index finger intact.

"What are you —"

Herault Innesreich

Your horrified eyes flicker to a spot above my left shoulder.

Butcher.

Monster.

You jab your pistol at the blank space to my right.

"You left the war," I say, echoed nine times over. "And now it has come back for you."

Loosed from their pranjaar and in that liminal space between light and dark, you can almost see them, like mind-invented images in a pliable penumbra. They surround me, overlap themselves and me, dividing space into impossible fractions. Dim impressions of women, young and old, some draped in the rags of their naval leathers, others stripped to the meat by fire and fang. If you squint, you can see them looping through their final moments, the same patterns of gunshot rippling up their chests in waves, exploded skulls opening and closing like lotus flowers. A ghost is the memory you eject at death, as much alive as a lizard's shed tail. It takes a rare and powerful will for it to retain its intelligence. Or very rarely, a malice.

There is a reason a necromancer deals in parcels of ghost. They are simple. Pliable. A complete soul, with a complete will, is another thing entirely.

Oh, Iuhriti, my foolish younger self. We forget so much in our pain, our grief.

I walk towards you, pushing against the threat of your weapon, nine fingers swinging on their tethers, nine fingers cut from nine different bodies. "We will not kill you today," I say, in ten voices. "We sought to take everything from you and then your life. That much is beyond us now, but no matter where you go, we will find you. We will be the jackal in your shadow. You will forever be looking back to see if we are near. You will always fear for the ones you love. That is your sentence —"

Your pistol barks. I feel the bullet's infinitesimal imperfections rasp through a heart multiplied by ten. I, a scholar of muscle and flesh and bone, cannot interpret your expression. Fear? Defiance? Hate? Which won out and pulled the trigger, I wonder. No will is ever entirely its own.

I am dead before you holster your weapon and run. My sisters are glad to welcome me fully into their throng, and we watch together as you melt into the blue sky. You will hear that last gunshot for a long time, Herault. You may try to let it go as well, but it too will follow.

It is in you, like a poison.

Time passes. More distantly than when I was alive. The light dims. A trickle of ants begins the disassembly of my body. Hanpreet arrives on the cusp of night. *Leave me, my son*, I try to say. *It is done.* I have loosed my best shot at you and I am satisfied, even if I missed my mark. You, the best of many Heraults, will have to live with my needless murder festering in your conscience.

But the shrieks and howls of my sisters drown me out. They are nine times infinitely starving for revenge, and once again I am swept up.

Deaf to my pleas, my son saws off my index finger with the knife I stole, and with the techniques that I drilled into him, he elides my soul from my body, my sisters coming away with me like clinging burrs. We spool together into the finger, fusing tight around the bone, and in turn into my son's pocket. This close to him, I can feel his hate bleeding into ours, and ours into his, until we are compound.

Ten, now eleven souls, we clean our knife on our mother's sari and go to chase down the man who killed her.

The Third Chamber from the Left

Douglas Anstruther and L'Erin Ogle

This place is fucked. Barry knew as soon as he broke in. The rank smell of rot, overlaid with disinfectant and something more machinelike — like the shit he used to huff out of a silver can. Same thing they used to lube up metallic joints.

It's possible he got used to the smell fast. Or maybe it's the bite. His arm is already blackened around the oval wound and curling up. The fucking plaguer. Never seen nothing like it. Helpless almost. Got too close and the thing, maybe a she, maybe a he, hard to tell, latched onto him in the first room. Tube in its neck and toothless, still had a jaw like a steel trap. It tore a ragged strip of flesh out with black gums, chewing on it, half its jawbone exposed. Thing should have laid down and died like the rest of them, when the flesh began slipping off it and the rot turned liquid and ran down the exposed, coal-black muscle tissue. Muscle that somehow still contracted, body that moved in jerks and hitches. But they all shut down eventually. Fall down like … .

His mind ain't working right. The bite was cold, and then the cold spread up his arm, extended into his neck. Crawled both down and up. Like a cold fever, which Jess would have slapped him for saying. Idiot. No such goddamn thing. Fuck Jess anyway, which he had and wouldn't mind doing again, but he's not sure that part of him will work.

He's so goddamn cold.

He's got enough in his pocket to take his own way out, if things get worse. Always have a backup plan, an escape route. A junkie's mantra.

Seems like a blast now might take the edge off.

He stops and listens. For the whir of those fucking metallic nurses or whatever the hell they are. Or a moaner, shambling down the hallway, hungry.

Silence, sort of. Still the hum, everywhere, bees in his ears. They drone on and on and they won't stop. Starts behind his eardrums and now they've moved behind his eyes. Makes it hard to think.

He slides down the wall, pretends not to notice the way his left arm doesn't work, or how black his fingernails are.

One-armed, he has to loop the tourniquet over his calf, yank it taut with his teeth. Sharp needle, piercing flesh. Three tries to hit a vein, finding one below the knob of his ankle.

Relief.

Big noise, pounding and crashing, sounds far away. Or he's far away. Hard to tell.

His stomach aches. Everything aches.

His teeth release the tourniquet.

Head lolling back against the wall. Lolling, something else he picked up from Jess. She knows a lot of stuff, always telling him what shit means or shit she thinks he should know, like he's a project. He could look at it OBJECTIVELY, another forced learn, and realize she loves him, but he doesn't love her. Thing is, Jess is smart, she knows how to get shit. Talk shit, too, a big beautiful stream of words coming straight out of her mouth until she's in a wallet or a back door. So he keeps her around.

Hard to picture her face.

All these thoughts, running around his head, are hard to hold to catch and hold onto. Darting away like fish scattering when the hook dropped. Back when there were fish.

More noise.

A sense of unease. Something that might have been alarm if he weren't so goddamn stoned. God, his arm is cold. His chest, too. Hard to breathe. Like ice is forming in his lungs.

Crash, boom, bang down the hall.

Eyes shuttered shut. He drifts.

☯

The sledgehammer blow sends chunks of concrete clattering to the ground and fills the air with dust. Light pours from the crack, as if under pressure. *I told you so.* Barry's voice echoes in my head, ripe with the particular flavor of scorn he reserves for women.

With shaking hands, I set the sledgehammer down and extinguish the dying flashlight. It's my last battery, and it's about used up. Everything is. Including me. I scan the half-collapsed building that's been home to Barry and me this last week. Nothing's moving, save the settling dust. It's been a decent hiding spot from the perpetual storm of rain and violence outside. The last two nights, though, he wouldn't shut up about things he heard on the other side of the wall. Things moving, whirring, like a factory. He was gone when I woke up — probably out foraging. Good time to take a look.

Beyond the hole, sharp lines dance in the brightness. Is it possible? After all these years, could there still be a place untouched by scavengers, looters, and plaguers? A twinge of hopeful excitement crashes against my armor of learned pessimism. That's not how the world works. Still, maybe. Two more quick strikes with the sledge and the hole's big enough to squeeze through. I look again, this time to make sure Barry's not within sight, and clamber in, feet first. The cut on my hip scrapes the edge, nearly making me cry out in pain, and the rough concrete catches my skirt, adding another tear to the blood-stiffened and tattered fabric. *You'll never find a young man, looking like that.* My grandmother, slapping dirt from my dress after playing in the barn. Yeah. Right.

The ground's further than I expect and I land hard, sending a painful shock up my spine and knocking the wind from me. I scuttle against the wall in a crouch and struggle to breathe. The bright light and acrid air sting my eyes, filling them with tears through which a blurry corridor materializes. Metal doors and intersecting hallways interrupt the white tile walls at regular intervals. Overhead, strips of light burn, relentless. Nothing moves. There are no shadows to watch or claim. It's the cleanest, most orderly place I've ever seen. *I'm sorry. Children aren't allowed here.* An unknown voice, from an indistinct time — before the cacophony of memory coalesced into the story of my life. There's pain, or the fear of pain. And my parents, loitering on the fringe of this ill-formed fear.

The light shifts behind me. Something's moving. A jolt of fear sweeps through my body, and I press myself against the wall, flinging wide eyes over my shoulder. A figure emerges from one of the doors at the end of the hall and glides toward me. Not the loping shuffle of a plaguer, but I've seen them take too many forms to be certain. My eyes flick back to the hole I made. Too high up. I could pull myself back up and through, but it'd be awkward as fuck and this thing would have plenty of time to start eating my guts while I dangle there like a baby stuck halfway out of its mama. *Push. Push!*

I force my legs to push me up the wall, causing my head to swim. I'm about to sprint away when I see the glint of metal. It's a machine — some sort of robot. Now I'm really scared. Machines are worse than plaguers. Fast, strong. Sneaky. It'll be on me before I take two steps. I pat myself down for a weapon, but know I have nothing. Barry won't let me keep anything that'd make me any more dangerous than I already am. Even the damn sledgehammer is up there.

The robot has no head, just shoulders from which metal-plated arms reach forward, grasping a tray. Vials, glass jars half full of yellow fluid. Something long and tapered. A syringe? I squint, trying to understand what I'm seeing, hypnotized by the possibility. *Where do you think your next hit's coming from, bitch?* One of the men before Barry. The thing's upon me in a heartbeat, then zooms past, unaware or uncaring that I'm here.

A medical bot! This must be one of those automated hospitals, buried and forgotten, churning away all these years, keeping ready for patients that never came. A solitary pocket of health, like an abscess, but in reverse. I picture it rupturing out into the streets, spreading its infection of normalcy, healing the diseased world. I like the thought of that. I look up at the hole connecting it to the world outside. *It'll burn like anything else.* A madman I used to love. The flicker of hope goes out. Barry will follow me.

His eyelids are heavy. They used to put stones over the eyes of the dead, didn't they? Or were they coins?

Another train of thought runs off the tracks.

He should get up and look for the noise.

Maybe it's the woman. Jules? Jane? J something.

Came without her. All alone. Why did he come alone?

He uses the fingers of his good hand to pry his eyelids open. They're clumped together, but a wet, cold liquid seeps through the cracks. His fingers come away bloody.

The bite. The fucking bite. God, it hurts.

Doesn't mean he'll die. He needs to find something sharp. Cut off thy limb if it offends thee. From Sunday school. All those knees pressed together. All those colored crosses.

All that guilt.

Fuck. He balls up his fist, the one that still works, and punches himself in the thigh. Get up, get up, get up.

Nothing. All of his arms and legs are heavy, filled with stone.

What's that? Is that his name, being called from very far away? No, he's hearing things.

But he's not imagining the growing sound of mechanical whirring. Growing closer.

They find him, bitten like this, they'll string him up and put all that shit in him. To cure him or torture him or whatever.

Nah. He ain't going out like that.

He staggers to his feet, muscles cramping and contracted. The cold fire licking at the very core of him. Not much time. Gotta get away. Get somewhere private. End this.

The bot disappears around a corner and I pull myself off the wall and tiptoe to the first door. The room's as bright and spotless as the hallway. Shelves, stacked with clean towels, line its walls and in the middle sits a metal table. It's the shape of a bed with a metal lip the height of my hand running around its circumference and a drain in its center. Past the table, a small bathroom with toilet and shower beckons. I run my hands through knotted and greasy hair. The place reminds me of what it felt like to be clean. Maybe I can come back here later.

I consider the metal table. I could fill it with towels and make a decent bed out of it. How long has it been since I slept in a bed? Five years? Eight? The temptation to lie down and burn off some of this exhaustion is tempting, but I stamp it down. *Don't get soft. C'mon. Keep going.* My voice.

The next room is empty too and the fantasy of safety grows in my heart. The third door opens into a long room lined with glass cabinets. Each cabinet is filled with vertical columns of fluid. In one, the columns are dark red and the words 'viral filter replacement needed' flash urgently across the glass. The other cabinets contain columns of clear fluid. They look like a cross between vending machines and the inside of a soda fountain. I consider them for a moment, puzzled, then the hope that's been hammering against my defenses since I got here breaks through and runs, screaming, through my brain.

I've found it. Medication dispensaries. My knees give out and I slide to the ground, clasped hands pressed against the glass. This is it. Tears drip down my cheeks and a sob shakes my body. I'm going to make it a little longer.

I gather myself, stand up, and examine the cabinets. Already the hope is fading, like something that never really belonged in the world in the first place. There's no way in. No keypad, lever, dial or knob. No way to make the dispensaries give me what I want. What

I need. *Looks like you'll have to get your next fix somewhere else.* Barry. They were the first words he spoke to me.

The glass is thick and doesn't budge against my weight. I look around for something to hurl against it when I realize that it doesn't even matter. Nothing is labelled. Not even barcodes, not that they would help. There must be a couple hundred different medicines in the room. How the hell am I supposed to know which of them will kill me and which will bring me back from the brink?

A sound in the hall. Something getting closer. Barry? No, another bot, at the door. I make a frantic sweep of the place and throw myself into a gap between cabinets. A poor hiding spot, to be sure, but it's the best I can do. The robonurse enters carrying a tray heaped with cloth. It trundles halfway to where I'm crouched and turns to face a chrome panel on the wall, which opens like a puppet's mouth to receive the soiled rags. Another wave of fear rushes through me as my animal brain recognizes the danger before I do. Blood. In the half-second before the cloth slides from view, I see it. Maroon gelatinous globs nestling between the folds of cloth, surrounded by crimson halos. *There are people here.*

The bot turns from the laundry chute to a medicine dispensary on the opposite side of the narrow room. It reaches forward with one of its arms and touches a spot near the edge which irises open and connects with a click. There's a faint hum and one of the fluid levels dips slightly. The third chamber from the left. The robonurse disconnects and exits the room.

Blood and people mean pain. Suddenly I'm very interested in what the robonurse drew from the dispensary. I follow it silently down the hall past a dozen rooms. It enters one and I race to catch the door before it closes. I'm not ready for what I find within. Wires and tubing fill the room like a spider web. At the heart of it all, a hairless man squirms like a bloated spider, dangling from the ceiling on thick wires that plunge into his limbs. He hovers over a metal table which stands ready to catch whatever parts of him gravity sends its way. His grey mottled flesh is pitted with deep wounds that glow bright red in the artificial light, like craters on a battlefield. *A plaguer!* Two silver-legged bots the size of cockroaches crawl out of a wound and vomit black-red ichor onto a towel before heading back in. *Oh my god. They're treating a plaguer.*

I've never seen one like this. Vulnerable, powerless. His face is twisted in mid-howl, but there's no sound, only a rapid pulse of condensation along the tube in his throat. His eyes fix on mine, conveying a mad urgency before being wrenched away by anguished contortions that cannot be denied. The robonurse moves with ease through the web to the other side of the man. It's the spider. The man is an insect, caught in its web.

The robonurse grasps a length of crimson tubing near the man's groin, and pauses. The man's eyelids flutter and droop, his eyes unfocus and his head slumps forward. *Take this. It'll help.* The man I loved, holding a white pill between my eyes and the ceiling, with the smell of my festering wound lingering in my nostrils.

I stagger back, feeling dizzy. How long? How long has this place kept him alive? It must have been sealed off during the collapse, or there'd be nothing left of it. *Ten years!* It's kept him alive all this time. Plaguers only last a few months in the wild. But here? I look at the pathetic creature, writhing on his bone-tethers, a puppet of sheer agony. No. This is not how it works. You kill them. They beg for it, until they can't anymore, but that doesn't matter — you kill them just the same. Everyone knows that. Even the people who've burnt through the last remnants of their empathy know that someday it could be them. So you kill them. Always. The man's head turns back toward mine, a scream frozen in his eyes.

I run out into the hallway and nearly stumble into another robonurse carrying a tray heaped with blood-soaked rags. I back away and follow it to the supply room where it goes through the same routine as the other. As it pulls away from the dispensary I charge. It's lighter than I expect and falls to the ground easily. It doesn't fight back, only struggling to get up. I hit it, but it hurts like hell, so I smash it into the floor, over and over. It's loud and takes forever but eventually the thing stops moving. I stand and see my reflection in the dispensary glass while I catch my breath. My hair's flung out in all directions and there's a wild look in my eyes. *It's feral. If it's not raised right, it gets like that. To protect itself.* My dad, as I suck four red streaks on the back of my hand in disbelief.

A metal rod lies next to the thing, dislodged during our struggle. I grab it and crouch over its body, expecting its partners to swarm in and avenge it. The whirring of its servos grows dim, grinds for a moment and then stops, leaving only silence. Nothing comes.

I study the bot. The limb it used to withdraw medicine from the dispensary is twisted and broken. Using the rod, I pry apart two panels and find a reservoir of fluid within, complete with retracted needle. I scoop it all out, like the meat from a crawfish, and the next thing I know the needle is buried in my vein and the sweet release of oblivion is moving in from the edges of everything.

Safe, for now, crouched behind a plaguer's bed. The buzzing has crept down Barry's face. Every feature feels like it's vibrating.

He looks down at the wound, what started as a small oval patch of black. Now it's crawling up his arm, everything black. The skin curling back to expose muscle tissue, stringy and turning from glistening red to dark maroon to black, inky black. The rot and decay inside his body, blooming. The pain, unbearable.

His fingers getting cold on the good arm. He's fumbling out the package, the good stuff, the only stuff he cares about.

The woman? A little voice in his head whispers.

Not the woman. Not her. Maybe once, but that was long dead before he jimmied the door to this place.

A book the woman told him about once, some dude wrote about a place that was a way station or some shit like that, between worlds. Maybe this place is like that. A doorway between here and there.

Hell on earth. All those rooms, all those dead undead whatever the fuck it is, suspended and being milked and fed all that tech shit. Still there.

He tries to find a quiet place to rest his head.

But everything is so loud.

The place got him turned in circles. Round and round.

Snakes eat their tails. Do they?

He's seen it somewhere. But was it real?

Is this real?

This is real.

There is too much pain for it to be a dream.

Shadows. Creeping up from the floor and joining in the corners. Moving towards him.

He sinks into a corner.

His bones feel soft and floppy in his skin, his muscles loose and baggy.

Tourniquet. Needle.

Inject.

Clouds roll across his eyes. Everything blurs. His heart skips a beat. Then begins banging away inside his chest. Even it feels frosted.

Dying.

But his way. He'll die his way. Fuck the rest of it.

Tourniquet.

Needle.

Inject.

Repeat.
Until it's gone or he is.

The third chamber from the left. It was down half an inch when I wrestled the bot to the ground. Now it's nearly up to the top again. It makes sense. For a place like this to continue for a decade, completely automated, it has to be self-sufficient. It must have a way to make its own electricity, its own food. Its own drugs. An endless supply.

I think about spending the rest of my life here. It twinges a little. It feels wrong, bad. *What kind of existence is this?* My best friend's voice. Two years after the plague put us on the streets. The night she killed herself. I can never take her path, but I don't know how much longer I'll last out there. I'm tired, worn thin. Sick of the daily struggle to survive. Except for the tortured souls, this is heaven. I'm staying.

But I need to be smart. I need a plan. That's how I survived all these years — making plans, deciding who to fuck, who to ghost, and who to kill. Always thinking. With safety in reach, I can't get sloppy now. First, I need to explore. Make sure there are no surprises. Then I'll kill the plaguers, break into the dispensary, and live here the rest of my days. But what if I can't get into the dispensary without a nurse? A nurse that's making a withdrawal for a patient. What if killing the plaguers dries up my supply? No, I can't put them out of their misery until I've figured out how to get into the dispensary. A hot wave of shame passes over me, but it has to be that way. I tell myself I'm just being practical.

Then I remember Barry. He found this place and he'll be coming. He'll kill me eventually, I know that. I've always known that. The trick is to be rid of him before that time comes. Keep your enemies close, right? Besides, he's been useful. But there's no future where the two of us live here together. I need to seal the hole. Not just against Barry, but to keep the whole poisoned world out. And if Barry breaks in — when he breaks in, I'll be ready.

The place is big. I count thirty-six plaguers, each worse off than the last. Their suffering is unimaginable and follows me down the halls. Some are just heads and torsos. Others are opened to the air like gutted fish. The bots whittle them into grotesque forms, exposing organs that flutter or peristalse ineffectually in open air, their functions delegated to pumps along the walls. All of them, even the most heavily pared remains, look at me with wild, pleading eyes.

One of the rooms is filled with robots, inert except for their slow-blinking lights. Charging, no doubt. There are robonurses, repair bots, cleaning bots. Two I recognize from outside of this place. Security bots. It's been years since I saw one, but even folded up and motionless I recognize their bulky feline grace. Those are a problem. There's no way to know what'll trigger them. Loitering here too long? Maybe. Killing the plaguers? Probably. Either way, it seems likely they'll come for me sooner or later. They'll probably just kick me out, but I don't want that. I'll need to come back to this room and figure out how to lock them in or disable them. Soon.

I go over to the hole to see what sort of materials I need to patch it up, or if it's even possible, but I can't find it. I retrace my steps to figure out where it should be. There's an area where the grout is brighter, smoother. It's the same size and place as the hole I made. Something repaired it. Not a human, it's too perfect.

Well, good. Problem solved. But then I find the front door. Inside, the place is spotless, as always. Outside, a collapsed building blocks the entrance, hiding it from the world. There are footprints and signs of moved debris, like someone cleared a path through it all. Recently.

Barry's here.

I try to figure out how long he's been here, what he knows, what he could have seen. There's broken glass and heavy things have been dragged. I would have heard him do this. He must have come in before me, while I was asleep. There's no sign of him leaving. What the hell has he been doing here this whole time? Does he know about the drugs? Did he see me on the floor of the dispensary? No. I'd be dead. This place escalates our game.

I look for a weapon, moving silently and peeking around each corner. All I can find is a piece of metal as long as my arm. It'll work if I can swing it into Barry's head before he sees me coming.

You'll only get one chance. The man I loved, before I killed him.

I should search the place again. Find Barry before he finds me. But my mind's racing and I need to calm my nerves. I return to the dispensary and work on it for an hour, stopping often to check the halls and trying to ignore the rooms full of silent screams and pleading. *Kill me. Kill me.* I've heard it so often, it's a chorus in my mind. They are all saying it. Demanding it.

The dispensary glass must be bulletproof. Everything I throw or swing against it bounces off. Twice, repair bots try to drag away the one I took down, but I swing my club at them until they leave. If a security bot comes, I'm fucked.

I return to the robonurse, in pieces on the floor. Its arms hide a menagerie of weird connectors and chambers, including the connector it used to attach to the dispensary. *Maybe, baby girl. It's worth a try.* My dad's voice. It brings a tear to my eye. I don't remember what he was encouraging me to do but it was something mundane. Something from before the plague, before things were life or death. I miss that world at least as much as I miss him.

I pry the connector from the machine's arm and take it to the dispensary, which responds by irising open. It snaps into place and a clear fluid drips from the other end. I grab a syringe, stick its nub into the hole and pull back the plunger. As it fills, I watch the third chamber from the left. The syringe is nearly at its limit before there's a noticeable drop in its level. But it does drop. I don't know why it works. Maybe the connector is still set for that drug. Maybe it works because it was the last order that the dispensary received. Hell, maybe the dead robonurse on the floor is sending some wireless signal to it. All I know is that I'm not letting anything change. No more robonurse withdrawals, and the one on the floor stays. At least for now. As long as the dispensary is giving me what I need.

The task had dulled the craving, but it returns now, undeniable. For the first time, my supply is limitless, and safety is within reach. Time to take the edge off, maybe even celebrate a little. As I push the plunger I think of the dangers. I know I'm being irresponsible, but it doesn't make me stop.

Death refuses the man with the needle in his arm.

It pauses, then moves on, slinking away like running ink, disappearing around a corner.

Eyes, drawn open.

Hunger. Deep in the pit of the belly.

Crusted eyelids, bloody eyes. A thick, viscous black blood.

Running down cheeks already loose and hanging off bone.

A smell, wafting into his nose. Olfactory sense still alive. Hungry.

He rises and takes a step. It's hard to stay up on the legs. They shiver and jerk.

He stumbles into a room. A girl lies on the floor. Familiar.

Her tongue pink against her teeth. Pink and plump and the smell of her.

Hunger.

Sound coming out of his broken mouth. Something else, tumbling to the floor. A yellow tooth. Then more tumble out, one by one, scattering. The sound hurts his ears and he moans.

Not just a fat pink tongue, but lots of fat, plush tissue. To tear it between his remaining teeth. Warm his cold mouth on the blood.

The blood is warm. He doesn't think it but knows it.

He advances.

A giant rises behind him. Gleaming. Immovable. Whirring.

He falls.

Eyeless metal animal on top of him.

Arms and legs pinned. Something over his face.

Darkness.

Pain awakens me. I twist and turn to try to get away from it, but it's everywhere. Broken bones, torn muscles. It's impossible to endure, but each second moves to the next and I have no choice. A moan tries to escape me but cannot. I open my eyes and see the spider web all around me. *No!* My voice. From a hundred different ordeals. All of them, shouting at me now from the dark recesses of memory, demanding that this not be real.

I flex my back to look down the length of my body. Indifferent wires fall from the ceiling to pierce my bones. A tube snakes across my bare chest toward my mouth. I feel it there now, filling my throat, gagging and choking me. My body demands a cough but I cannot and I'm consumed by a spasm of choking and gagging that boils my face and makes me dizzy. The syringe from my last hit dislodges from my vein and clatters to the floor.

A robonurse at my side moves away, revealing a bag of thick red liquid dripping into one of the web's crimson lines. I trace it back to my body and remember the cabinet in the dispensary room filled with such bags. The warning across its screen, 'viral filter replacement needed.'

The blood. The fucking blood is infected.

I convulse on my strings, each jolt a new burst of pain. I scream at the nurse to stop the transfusion, to please, please, don't infect me. It has no expression to read, but I feel it judging me. *You deserve this.* Barry's voice.

It reaches out, grasps another line and pauses. The pain softens, the ache dulls, and the horror lessens. The memories loosen their grasp. But only a little. The nurse turns and moves toward the door. *No, wait! It's not enough. I need more!* It's my voice. But I cannot speak.

Time passes and I feel the fever take hold. The pain of the bone tethers is forgotten as a new horror envelops me. I'm infected.

It'll be okay, my dear, it'll all be okay. My mother, consoling me after a scraped knee. Of course. Of course. Barry will come. And kill me. It's all going to be okay.

Hungry.
    Can't move.
    Pain.
    Eyes, shut.
    Hungry. So hungry.
    Eyes open. The smell, again.
    Whining.
    Sniffing.
    Where's the smell coming from?
    Turning his head, just a little bit.
    Her. Strung up like him.
    The smell good, fat tongued, meat thing. Don't smell so good now.
    Something whispering through him, something warm. But it passes.
    Hungry.

Boro Boro

J. Tynan Burke and Evan Marcroft

I was hiking in the hills of Kitasaku when I met the old woman who gave me this box. She lived alone at the edge of the forest where the cedars grew taller than I'd ever seen, perhaps unafraid of men, who it seemed rarely came this way. Her house was so old that one corner had begun to sink into the weeds. She spied me coming up the trail and called me over in Japanese, apparently unconcerned that a *gaijin* such as myself likely wouldn't speak it. As was fortunate for both of us, I knew enough.

We shared tea together on her porch. I was glad for an excuse to rest my feet, and for her part, she simply wanted someone to talk with, for it had been a long time. As she explained, her family had been peasants — *burakumin* was the word she used — who'd lived their lives on this out-of-the-way land for generations, until they'd dwindled down to only her. Some had left for the cities, riding the waves of change that wars kick up, while many more remained as rain-pitted gravestones, which she cleaned every week in a losing battle against the moss.

I asked why she did not leave herself, and she explained that though only memories still lingered here, they could be found nowhere else. To her, it was the only place where she would not feel alone. "I may lack for conversation," she said, "but these hills are loud to me. There was so much living here — the laughter yet echoes between the trees. All that happened here is still happening. At least, when I close my eyes." She patted me on the knee and called me a kind young man for fretting over an *obaa-san* like her. "Drink your tea," she said, "Sometimes memories are enough."

As I prepared to leave, she presented me with a wicker chest full of what seemed to be nothing more than scraps of woven hemp, shades of blue all fading to white with age. *Boro* clothing, she explained. "You seem like a man who will take good care of them," she told me. "These are some of the clothes my family wore. It will comfort me to know they will be treasured when I am gone."

It was a chore to carry them back to town, but I did as I was told and with a smile, because she had me dead to rights.

All that said, I'm not sure why I'm giving this to you. I think it's not so much the box, or what it contains, as the story of it. It's a good one, but a story does no one any good when it isn't told.

And after everything, you're still all I've got.

Love, Jason.

The day was verging on done by the time I got home from Jason's funeral; the Pacific Ocean had halfway swallowed the sun. By the time I changed out of my suit and showered, it would be close to my usual bedtime; the funeral would've taken up the entire day. I swayed in a moment of temporal whiplash on the walk up to my door. If time slowed down for every death, I suppose we'd never get anywhere.

After cleaning up I went to take a second look at the box in which I'd found Jason's letter, where I made a second discovery — my cockatiel, Wocky Tocky, gnawing inquisitively at the wicker. "Fuck off with you," I said, and shooed him away as he chanted *fuck off with you, fuck off with you* in squawking mockery. Just as Jason had said, the box was filled with threadbare clothing, robes far more patch than whole cloth and smelling overpoweringly of mothballs.

I was surprised to be bequeathed anything, but it made sense after a thought or two. Jason had been a loner with no surviving family in the country, who had never stayed long enough with anyone to become what we had been. We hadn't spoken in some years now; ours had been more of an amputation than a split, but of course some feelings would be left over, like splinters of bone healed over after a break. I imagined I had some myself.

His story sounded just enough like a fairy tale to be true. Jason had possessed a knack for ferreting out those lonesome places in the world where a touch of old-world magic still lingered. That he'd take home a box of ragged old kimonos at the behest of a strange hermit lady didn't shock me in the least. The guy had been a collector, of nothing in particular and everything in general, turning his house into a private museum of the world. Get up to piss at night at his place and you'd find yourself tripping over a chamber pot once owned by a famed Tibetan guru. It was a tendency I'd never managed to wrap my head around. Junk was junk, regardless of pedigree.

Looking at the scraps of hemp though, I began to feel that familiar tug on my artistic urges. Junk was junk, until you made something of it. I googled that unfamiliar word he'd used — *boro*, referring, it turned out, to the style of clothes worn by old-timey Japanese peasants too poor to buy new clothes. Holes and tears would be patched with scraps of older kimonos, themselves likely patched from something older still, until you had something like a shabby Ship of Theseus, comprised of none of its original pieces. If you looked at it from a certain angle, a boro kimono was a connection to the past. It was your ancestors lending scraps of themselves forward through time to see you through the biting winter, a matryoshka heirloom. As soon as that thought crystalized, I knew what I had to do.

Caffeine had nothing on inspiration. I worked throughout the night, snipping the kimonos in the box into square patches. By the time the sun resurfaced I'd reconfigured them into a single garment with the wingspan to fit three when lain flat, a sleeping kimono in which an entire peasant family might have clung together way back when, swaddled in inherited warmth. Into the breast, where the heart would go, I added a swatch from a denim shirt that Jason had given me not long before we'd parted ways. His way of keeping me warm when he was gone.

Soon as I finished, all that suspended exhaustion came crashing down on me. Only pride kept me upright. From conception to reality in twelve hours flat, and it had turned out spectacular. A statement on the way old things could seep osmotically forward through time, how nothing truly died, only shapeshifted into something new.

And for a guy who preferred to live in the past, it made a fitting tribute.

Wocky Tocky hopped onto my shoulder as I looked the kimono over for flaws, turning his head from side to side like a curious critic. "Thoughts, questions, criticisms?" I asked.

He took a nibble of my ear and chirped, "kikanai."

I frowned at that. "You kiss your mother with that beak?" I had no idea what he'd said, but I certainly hadn't taught it to him. Probably something he'd heard on TV.

That afternoon, after some much-needed sleep, I ate breakfast in my studio, so I could look over what I'd made. The kimono hung over the paint-splattered floor from a clothesline, looking distinctly post-surgical. I'd used white yarn to stitch the old indigo swatches together, and it criss-crossed the robe like jagged scars. *Very* cool, especially for something that had been junk a few hours earlier. But the inner critic was never silent for long. I could have arranged the swatches more uniformly, it noticed; the stitching was fucked up in places, and not in a cool *wabi-sabi* way.

The jolt of caffeine hitting my system snapped me out of my self-critical spiral and reminded me that I had things that demanded doing. The inner critic was always on-call, but the deck needed rebuilding yesterday.

The house I lived in was an old window-walled Eichler, perched on a bluff in the central coast. The owners, a couple from La Jolla, were fixing the place up for their retirement, and I was getting a big discount on rent as their part-time handyman. A great deal for a freelance artist, but more work than I'd knowingly signed on for. A seismic retrofit of the deck's support struts had ruined its surface, and I'd said I knew how to build one. Didn't feel too bad about the resume falsification — that's why god created YouTube tutorials.

Towards sundown I was down on kneepads with a nailgun, paying for my deceit with badly pinched fingers and a sore back. A truck rolled up out front and honked to the tune of "Smoke On the Water" — Wendy coming for a dump run. I pushed up my safety goggles and peeled off my work gloves while I walked around the side of the house.

Wendy cocked a wave at me when I opened the fence gate. "Evening, Brad."

"Come on in." I held the gate while she trundled a wheelbarrow down the rutted path to the back. "Glad you came by sooner rather than later. I'm about to die."

She set the wheelbarrow down at the edge of the decking and plopped down in an adirondack. "Get me a beer first, you big wuss. I'll pour some out for you."

While she lit a cigarette, I got us each a bottle of Lagunitas, and then we shot the shit. That week, everybody was gossiping about the Holmviks, whose oldest son Carl had gotten brained by a piece of flying wood at the lumber mill. Total freak accident, but his parents were selling their house to pay the hospital bills. Their unexceptional tract house had raked in two million dollars, more than enough for the treatments. But without the house they'd owned for generations, staying in Costanoa was *still* too expensive.

The town's cliff-backed surfing beaches were getting hit hard with waves of retiring boomers and Silicon Valley spillover. We'd gotten a Whole Foods the other year, but lost a lot of the surfer population in exchange. The good deals like mine wouldn't last forever.

"I mean, we're sorry for Carl, right?" Wendy said. "But Jesus dude, still. If I had a cool two mil …"

Pink-haired, lightly tatted, and a generation my junior, Wendy Watamura was one of those Costanoa millennials steadily getting priced out of their own hometown. Her escape would be through nursing school, but that was neither fast nor cheap. In the meantime, she was riding the gig economy for all it was worth, working small jobs around town for folks too rich to know how to take care of their houses.

"God is a trickster," I said, tipping my bottle at her. "Speaking of which, you remember Jason?"

"Kinda short, wavy hair, weird combination of smug and sad?" Wendy finished her beer and dropped her cigarette butt inside the bottle.

"Yeah, that one. He, uh …" My voice caught. That surprised me. I hadn't thought it would start hurting so soon. "I went to his funeral the other day. Yesterday, I mean."

"Oh, my god." Wendy stood and held her arms open. "You okay, big chief?"

"Yeah. Thanks." I leaned into the hug and held it until just before it got weird. "He left me something, for some reason. You got anywhere to be?"

"I can spare a few minutes."

After I'd explained Jason's letter, Wendy was standing in front of the kimono, biting her lip and resting a hand on her hip.

I knew that expression. "What's wrong?" I said.

"Like, that old woman obviously cared about this stuff. Brutal honesty time, it's kind of disrespectful."

I scrunched up my face. "Really? I think I rehabilitated the clothes."

"Did they need you to do that, though?" Wendy shrugged. "These were somebody's heirlooms. Stuff can be art before you've gotten your hands on it, you know."

Jason used to say things like that. I finished off my beer and tossed it into a cardboard box that was brimming with recyclables, harder than I needed to. "You aren't wrong," I admitted. "I just always see how stuff like this can be so much *more*." Giving old clutter new life as art was how I'd found some small artistic success. The last piece I'd sold was a grandfather clock from the 1920's which I had painstakingly turned inside-out.

I started to say something about post-formalism when Wocky Tocky came fluttering into the room, sending the contents of a workbench flying when he landed. Scraps of hemp that had been too threadbare to use zig-zagged to the enamel floor, along with loose production sketches of the kimono.

"Fuck off with you!" he chirped. "Off with you, off with you."

"You're awful," Wendy laughed. I could almost hear her rolling her eyes.

I scooped the bird up and set him on my shoulder, where he started to root through my hair.

"Bird's right," Wendy said. "The dump's closing soon. Let's get your crap in the truck."

While the sun completed its dive into the gray Pacific, we lugged the day's construction detritus into her parents' truck by the barrowful, and she told me horror stories from nursing school. It occurred to me that I hadn't mentioned how I'd put a piece of Jason in the kimono. I supposed I was worried she'd scold me even harder for it. That was guilt I could do without. A part of me also enjoyed the secret of it. People would *ooh* and *aah* at what I'd made, but they'd never know what it was really saying.

That was for me alone.

A week later I had the deck put together and decided to throw myself a party. Or rather, I decided to hold a party I'd had planned after all. I'd been considering calling it off, what with the recent funeral, but I figured the issue'd had enough time to get edged out by fresher news. I should have known better, because my guests arrived bearing both six-packs and muted condolences, unsure if it was supposed to be a wake. A small town like Costanoa was a refrigerator for gossip, preserving things past their natural expiration date.

Dane Quintel found me gazing up at the kimono, long after the other guests had offered their obligatory compliments and wandered off to get drunk and eat all my food. "Great stuff, my dude," he said, eyebrows raised, like a dad trying to sound hip. He was brandishing a mason jar of ten-dollar Trader Joe's wine like it was a stem of Château Margaux. "Neither new nor old, but both at once. Schrödinger's kimono. Very cool." In hushed tones, he continued, "Do you know that old surrealist game, the Exquisite Corpse? This makes me think you'd appreciate that part of my collection."

I stifled a snort. Dane was a silicon-era robber baron, but he always tried to talk like a local. Usually managed, too, unless he got excited. It was forgivable since he genuinely wanted to fit in. A very early retiree, he'd come to Costanoa in search of the Bohemian beach-hippy life he'd missed out on at Stanford, not realizing he was helping drive it out of town. I tried not to mention it, since was a decent guy and loved all my stuff besides.

"Thanks," I said. I held out my beer bottle and he clinked his jar against it.

He downed his drink and his expression sagged. "I heard about Jason, by the way."

"You and everyone," I said.

"You can blame Marjorie," he stage-whispered, shaking his head.

The girlfriend in question happened to be passing, and swerved to deliver a passing caress to Dane's shoulder on her way to the kitchen. "Hi Margie," I said, faking a smile until she was out of sight. Being the owner of Costanoa Coffee and Croissants, Marjorie Ellis was the stem of the proverbial grapevine. I'd mentioned what'd happened with Jason the last time I'd stopped in for a bear claw, forgetting how word would get around like a sex disease.

"I had an uncle pass the same way," Dane went on. "Deep vein thrombosis. Shitty way to go."

Jason had developed one during a red-eye from Brussels. It was hard to come by a doctor seven miles above the stormy Atlantic.

Taking a hard left away from the topic, I said, "How do you feel about taking this outside? The firepit's working again. Great excuse to sneak out and get high."

"I would love to see that firepit," Dane said with a naughty grin.

The guests who were already out back *ooh*'d and *aah*'d once I'd got the fire going. I led Dane to the railing at the edge of the yard. Looking over the cliff to the dark sea, we shared a pre-roll I'd picked up from the dispensary. I traded a few half-hearted jokes, but I found myself distracted by a tugging absence where there should have been weight. *Jason.* He always drew a crowd with the stories from where he'd traveled. They'd have loved him at this party. Not that he'd been to one of mine in ages, of course. I hadn't felt like any of *those* were incomplete; there was always a different charming nucleus to organize around, not great but good enough. I guess I'd assumed I could always get him back if I really wanted to.

The joint tasted like smoldering cardboard on my next drag. I flicked the butt into the pit, where the fire snapped it up.

Dane sidled over and draped a conspiratorial arm over my shoulder. "So that kimono," he said, with a heavy blink. "Suppose it were to hit the market."

"Suppose it were," I said.

He raised his eyebrows. "What sort of asking price would it have?"

I ducked out from under his arm. "Dunno." Sniffed. "Think it might be a personal piece." That was true, but I couldn't manage a hard *no*. Any artist worth his salt was always at least half-starving, and I'd seen how many houses Dane owned.

"Say no more, my man," he said. "But if you change your mind …" He snapped open a business card case and slid me one, getting it very nearly into my hand. "But if you change your mind, remind me I made the offer, because I am higher than the ISS, dude. Let me tell you —"

Whatever he said was next drowned out by a scream from inside the house.

"Sounded like Margie," Dane said. He was soon in motion. It kicked my ass into gear too.

We knocked the glass door off its track as we burst in through the back. In the three seconds it took to bolt to the living room, I had time to imagine all the worst things that could have happened. A rickety old house like this came with a lot of hidden edges. It was a comparative relief, then, to find Marjorie curled up into a ball in the corner, sobbing but not visibly hurt.

"What happened?" I demanded, while Dane parted the crowd like the Stanford linebacker he'd been, scooping her into his arms.

"There was a man," she stammered. Her mop of blonde hair clung in tentacles to her tears and sweat. She pointed a trembling finger over Dane's shoulder at the center of the room, where nobody was. Looky-loos edged away so as not to be incidentally accused.

"He, he, he came out of nowhere, and he grabbed me right here," Margie said, flapping one hand at her shoulders. The other reached around Dane's back and grabbed a fistful of his blazer. "I t-t-tried to scream, but, but I couldn't somehow. I don't know. And he said … something. I, I don't know what, it was like another language or something. He was so angry, Dane. I really thought he was going to kill me."

"What did he look like?" Dane asked, his voice like steel.

A word swelled up in Margie's throat. Her lips groped around its edges like a fish quaffing water, but her tongue failed to push it out. She looked up at me, begging me silently to help deliver that memory into reality, but I had nothing to grab hold of. Soon she stopped trying and began to cry quietly into Dane's neck.

I let them be and organized a sweep of the house, scouring every room from cupboard to baseboard. We shone flashlights into the crawlspace and poked around in the attic that opened through my closet. If there was an intruder anywhere, he must've been invisible. No one remembered seeing anyone matching Marjorie's lack-of-description. no one had been looking when it happened.

But there was evidence that *something* had happened: the boro kimono was heaped on the floor below its mount; a spiderweb of cracks, as wide as my wingspan, radiated outwards from where it had hung, shattering the drywall into hundreds of pieces. The shattering event that had caused this had also gone unobserved.

Wendy was able to swing by the day after the next. I didn't sleep too well in the meantime. I'd gone through the house with a fine-toothed comb and proved to my eyes that I was alone, but my brain had Margie's terror stuck in its teeth. Even in the day, with sun pouring in and dust motes swirling like krill, I'd find myself walking softly, breath shallow, dreading hearing footfalls skulking after mine. I knew rationally that I'd searched everywhere a man could hide, but my subconscious would aim me at the crater in the wall and whisper: what about everywhere a man could *fit*? The walls were hollow, weren't they? I fought off the urge to peer through the cracks every time I passed the damaged drywall.

"I see you weren't murdered," Wendy said, dropping down from her truck. She reached into the cab and pulled out a cardboard box that I assumed was full of wall-fixing stuff.

"I feel like it," I said, scratching the two days of stubble I'd let accrue on my chin. "A cockatiel sounds a lot like a demon when you're starting to fall asleep. The whole thing was just wiggy."

Wendy grunted, presumably in agreement that the whole thing was indeed wiggy. "Dane gave me the scoop. Spooky shit."

I cocked my head. "You talk to Dane?"

Wendy guffawed. "You think a guy like that knows how to clean a pool? Gimme a hand with this stuff."

We cracked a few cold ones and got down to business within a quarter hour. It was a relief to have someone else in the house. When I heard rustling in another room, I could be confident that it was Wendy filching a granola bar from the pantry and not a killer emerging from some secret passage.

A little after lunch I came back from the bathroom to find Wendy studying the kimono. I'd temporarily relocated it to the dining room, where it hung over the head of the table with arms spread wide like Jesus at his last meal. "You ever wonder who these used to belong to?" she asked.

"A bunch of dead Japanese peasants, apparently," I said.

"Well duh, obviously. But I mean, everyone has their own, you know, story." She glanced back at the kimono with an interrogative squint.

"The letter said they were, uh, *bura*-something," I said.

"*Burakumin*? No shit," she said.

"Who?"

"You know the whole 'untouchable' thing from India? It was like that. My grandparents could tell you all about it. Japan used to have this straight-up caste system thing going on, and the *burakumin* were lower than dog shit. You had to live in these special villages, and people would, like, wash their hands if they touched you, and any samurai could roll up and whack your head off if you looked at him wrong."

"Jesus," I muttered.

"Yeah," she grimly concurred. "They put a stop to it a long time ago, legally, but the stigma's still there in places. That old lady Jason met would've grown up in the echoes of it. Something like that doesn't vanish just because the law says it's gone."

A fluttering of wings announced Wocky Tocky's arrival into the conversation. He touched down on the back of the chair between Wendy and me and puffed out his fluffy bosom with the air of a man preparing to give an announcement.

"I knew this was coming," I fake-whispered. "He's finally breaking up with me."

"*Watashi no hanashi itsu mo kīte kure nai*," Wocky Tocky chirped.

"What the fuck?" Wendy blurted.

"What?"

"You taught your bird Japanese?"

"Not that I remember," I said. "That's Japanese?"

"*Watashi no hanashi itsu mo kīte kure nai*," the cockatiel gormlessly repeated. "*Kure nai. kure nai.*"

"What's it mean?" I asked.

Wendy screwed up her face in concentration. "Full disclosure here, I'm pretty rusty, but I think it means something like 'you never listen.'"

I stumbled as if slapped across the jaw. Some time must have snuck away without me knowing because next I knew Wendy was clicking her fingers under my nose.

"Come back to the living, Brad."

"That's the last thing Jason ever said to me," I half-whispered, eyes wide.

The whole house must have been taken by surprise because the floor lurched about two inches to the right. Our feet went with it, and we both collapsed against the dining table.

"Fucking earthquake," Wendy said breathlessly.

The second tremor rang the cliffside like a gong. It felt as though the Earth changed its expression, stone cringing in pain. The house let out a tortured moan as the quake shuddered through its hoary bones. Fuck me if I could remember what to do in an earthquake. The most logical-sounding option was to get outside, where an old house couldn't come crashing down on you. If that wasn't a great idea, my brain perceived no time for second thoughts.

"Get out of here," I barked, flinching as another tremor rattled the walls and set the house's glass to singing. The cabinet that held all my semi-good stemware fell open and dumped half its contents across the floor. "Call the fire department," I added, because that made me feel like I had some control over what was happening. Like they'd show up and put out the earthquake with a big hose.

Wocky Tocky went squawking down the hallway towards the back of the house. Wendy grabbed my hand and tried to pull me towards the kitchen door, but I shook her off.

"Can't leave him," I said, and then turned and took off after him.

I could hear the house working to hold itself together as I made my way down the hall after the sound of Wocky Tocky's frantic mimicry. "*Kure nai, kure nai,*" he shrieked, to the beat of the bass rhythm of my heart. The tremors were shaking the house like a head on a throttled neck. The image of my poor deck scraping down the cliff in pieces hit the floor of my stomach. I'd be lucky if the whole house didn't slide into the ocean. These weren't super helpful thoughts, but it was easier to fear for expensive things than my own life. Christ, but where had the quake come from? There should have been some warning, an emergency alert on my phone, a siren, anything. It wasn't like there weren't systems in place, with us sandwiched between Los Angeles and San Francisco.

I found Wocky Tocky in the laundry room, trying to burrow under a heap of underwear. As I scooped him up into a cage of fingers, I heard the unmistakable crack of lumber splintering. I glanced into the hall and went cold to the marrow when I saw that part of the ceiling had caved in. Terror broke out of me in an icy sweat. My house was being unmade, with me still inside it.

To my left, the door to the basement offered itself as the only remaining choice.

I took the steps two at a time. I rarely came down there, but the walls were concrete. Unfortunately, the stairs were not, and the last one broke cleanly in half. My coccyx broke my fall, overeager to share its agony with every nerve ending in the rest of my body. I could feel just enough over the blinding pain to know it when my cerebellum ricocheted off the staircase, which explained why the room was wobbling drunkenly from side to side like that. Wocky Tocky squirmed free and went flapping in circles around my head, screaming in Japanese.

Watashi no hanashi itsu mo kīte kure nai.

You never listen.

My eyes fluttered open, one sluggishly after another.

That wasn't Wocky Tocky.

I lay where light trickled in through the window and pooled on the floor. On the other side of the room, shadows clotted like cobwebs around piles of boxes, old furniture, the bits of things that had trickled through my life without the momentum to escape it. I watched swirling dust motes gust towards that dark as something inside of it breathed in.

Someone was there with me in the basement. I could not see them, but the heat of their gaze was as incontrovertible as a knife to the throat. Fear slashed through the fog around my thoughts; I yanked my feet away from the edge of the light, which now seemed the narrow rim around a tiger pit. The urge to run was muted by shock. My breaths grew shallow, as close to corpselike as could be. Wocky Tocky shut up and dropped into my open palm. He crouched low, exhausted, his fragile ribcage palpitating madly against my skin.

It's always the same shit with you, the thing in the dark said.

The voice was quiet but not soft, like a television blasting in another room, and yet intelligible over the gnashing of the earth around me.

There's no point in taking you anywhere, Brad. Nothing impresses you. I don't know why I bother. You don't even like art that isn't yours. You're the most conceited son of a bitch that ever lived.

It was a voice without pitch or depth, a voice made up of fading echoes. I did not so much hear it as remember hearing it, and from lips I'd kissed before.

At least I don't think the sun shines out my ass. You always think you're discovering everything, like you're the first asshole to come along and see how special this fucking urn or that statue is. Like they haven't been there for a thousand fucking years.

That hadn't been Jason. That part was *me*. It had been the sizzling fuse that led towards the last thing that he'd ever say to me, and I'd burned it into my memory fumbling with it again and again in the aftermath.

Christ, just listen to you, the thing in the shadows said. *If I didn't drag you places, you'd just sit around and get high on your own importance. Your fucking with them doesn't magically make things matter. Why can't you ever just let things be what they are?*

My heart, which had lain stunned in my chest, began to slam itself against my ribs. My eyes would not acclimate to the darkness, to let me see what crouched in its depths, but my ears had adjusted to the uncanny voice that argued with my words against itself.

Right, because every little thing is so fucking precious to you. You care more about all your god-damned souvenirs than you do about me and what I do. You think you're fucking Indiana Jones, but you're not — I'd said that too, stabbing my finger into Jason's chest.

Brad, that's not what I'm saying. Actually — you know what? Screw this. Screw us. You never listen. The thing wasn't even ten feet away. It wouldn't have been hard to crawl over and touch it. My throat had gone brittle as old paper; it cracked as I spoke.

"Jason?"

The small room overflowed with Wocky Tocky's deafening shriek. He exploded from my hand and careened around the ceiling before hurling himself out of the light. I sprang after him, fear for him overriding fear for myself, but my fingers fell just short of his tailfeathers. Instead they snagged on a cord hanging from the ceiling, and the lights flickered on with a fluorescent buzz.

There was no one else there. Just things heaped on things, mine the only human shadow.

Wocky Tocky had fallen abruptly silent. I called for him, but he did not come. I turned over furniture, shook out boxes, checked the windows, though all of them were shut. There was nowhere he could have gone, and yet he was nowhere to be found.

It was only then that I realized how quiet it had gotten. The earthquake was over. A deluge of mundane worries rushed in —

the house; Wendy. I crept upstairs, wary of falling debris as I opened the door. The bottom corner snagged on something puddled on the ground. I bent to lift it into the light, and a chain of thick, white stitches sluiced through my fingers like serpent vertebrae. I clutched the fabric in rigid fists. When I remembered to exhale, I let the kimono fall and slammed the door on it.

Three days later I called up Dane and sold him the Kimono. He pretended to look solemn, thinking I was abandoning an emotional connection. For my part, I tried not to look relieved to be rid of it. It wasn't so hard: after Dane drove up and saw the state of the house, he threw in an extra five hundred bucks, and my expression of annoyed gratitude was quite genuine.

Fuck if the place didn't look like it needed all the help it could get. The hot water heater on the ground floor had ruptured and taken out the crawlspace. By the time Dane stopped by I'd stripped the entrance down to a skeleton of water-stained studs. All those big expensive windows were gone too, of course, and from some angles it seemed like the house was mostly made of sheets of visqueen. At least I could finally be certain there wasn't anybody hiding there.

Not that it helped me sleep. When the cliff winds blew in every day before dawn, the plastic-covered window frames snapped like whips, startling me awake. I wasn't dwelling on the possessions I'd lost. Money could make most things reappear, in time. The only thing truly gone was Wocky Tocky. When sleep did finally settle in, I dreamed of a swinging lightbulb, of shadows carouseling around concrete walls, none of them human or bird.

The earthquake had scared off my inspiration. When I still hadn't found it a few weeks later, and my phone ran out of interesting things to show me, I took an order for some artsy coasters from Sandy at the Costanoa Variety store. Every day, a work crew came to replace wiring or argue about sheetrock. Every night, I slapped acrylic on a few coasters in meaningless permutations of color and shape until I could convince myself I'd earned a pint at the Taphouse.

Sandy was a first-generation hippie who'd bought some local commune properties for peanuts back in the day, and now filled her days running her kitschy store, while her son ran their small real estate empire. On an afternoon mercifully free of contractors, I dropped off the first batch of coasters. "Beautiful stuff," she said, rifling through the box. It wasn't long though before her hands found my shoulders. "Brad." A sad shake of her head set her wooden bead necklace to clacking. "I heard about your ex. And the party …"

I stepped back before Sandy tried to hug me; her hands found her own elbows instead. "Appreciate the sympathy."

With a birdlike nod, she spun and carried the box to the back of the store. "Have you tried sage?" she called out from the storeroom.

"No?" I said.

"You know, sage." She returned with three of the coasters, a wire stand, and a wooden cigar box. Inside were bundles of what looked like dried weeds, bound with white string. "My shaman — do you know Brucie from the hookah shop? — makes these." She held the box under my nose; it smelled pretty good, actually. "You take one and burn it in the affected area."

"Affected by what?" I asked.

"Spirits of course," she replied matter-of-factly.

"Oh, right. Duh."

"Go on, take one. On the house."

I relented and tucked one behind my ear. "Thanks." After muttering something about needing to meet a roofer, I left through the jingly door and made for the Taphouse. I settled down in the backyard, in the shade of its newest addition, a Russian olive tree planted in Carl Holmvik's honor, back when he was still in a coma after the lumber mill accident. Squinting up at it, the silhouetted branches seemed to wield their spines like scythes against the rippling sky. Anger radiated from its teardrop leaves. It was ready to lash out at the mill owners for their OSHA violations, or the wealthy SoCal colonists forcing the Holmviks out, or Junípero Sera for bringing alien diseases to the Ohlone natives so long ago now.

For such a small and quiet town, there were many injustices seeped into its soil. I shivered despite the heat, blinked the image away, and tried to enjoy my beer.

When I got home, I tossed the sage bundle in the same drawer as my pot. My thoughts, however, wouldn't unstick from what I'd sensed at the Taphouse. *Spirits*, Sandy had chirped, as if they were as ubiquitous as mosquitos. Maybe she was onto something. Maybe there were spirits in all things, watchful but voiceless. Maybe those spirits felt helpless as newcomers came to tear up their old vessels. Maybe they grew bitter.

Out of a nameless apprehension, sleep eluded me that night. Jason's words echoed in my dark room. *You never listen.* What was it that had spoken to me in the basement? I'd already accepted that I hadn't hit my head hard enough to imagine the whole thing.

And I'd accepted that the thing in the basement was connected, by some thread, to the boro kimono, though the further I followed that chain of logic to its conclusion, the less I wanted to see the end. Whatever the thing had been, whatever it had tried to tell me, it was gone now, exiled to another wall, leaving merely mundane problems in its wake.

There was nothing to do but clean up, rebuild, and move on.

The insurance company said it was improbable, but not impossible, that my house was the only one affected by the quake. The owners, happy enough with this outcome, didn't ask me too many questions. The world was weird and did weird things. According to one local geologist, this particular weird thing was no more improbable than spontaneous human combustion. So when the aftershocks began to strike everywhere but my house, it was exceptional but not unheard of.

Two weeks after the earthquake, a group of early-morning surfers came across the lifeguard's HQ partially collapsed, looking like a washed-up shipwreck. The weekend after, a third inexplicable blurt of seismic activity shook down a row of telephone poles heading out of town. Power had no sooner been restored when a steamroller at the site of a forthcoming condo complex was knocked off its blocks by a sudden temblor. It rolled, slowly but inevitably, down the hill and into one of Dane Quintel's villas, where it plowed through a fence and wound up in the pool. I called Margie when I heard, half out of concern for a fellow decent-ish human, and half to check if the kimono was on the property. *Dane put it up in the castle house*, she'd said. *Lucky you, huh? Lucky me*, I'd said, and hung up.

Over the following weeks, the incidents increased in severity and frequency. Downtown Costanoa bore the brunt of it. Many of the buildings there were even less seismically resilient than mine, their owners being cash-poor locals. Every other day saw new storefronts shattered. Jim Nilsson, who'd sold me my art supplies for the last decade, got to watch Costanoa Creatibles go up in flames when a downed powerline chanced to fall on his roof. The vertical marquee at the Mission Theater wound up on the sidewalk when its rusted supports gave out. If I didn't know better, I might have thought the incidents were meant to inflict pain.

I did know better, though. And so I was certain.

Alone on my little island of safety, I listened to the firetrucks rush from one disaster to the next. Not many of the folks who lost their homes and businesses would be able to stay in Costanoa. The insurance people would click their tongues in affected sympathy and then pay them a fair amount to pack up and fuck off of the land that had grown so luxurious beneath their feet. Margie's place would become a Starbucks; Jim's, a Blick. Paint-by-numbers McMansions would scab over the loss, and all those small but irreplaceable human stories would be chopped up into their choicest morsels and reassembled into a brochure. The Dane Quintels of the world would come running, only to find that quaint little beach town survived only in photographs.

In the middle of no particular night, I stopped pretending to sleep and opened up my stash. After a moment of hesitation, I retrieved a lighter and Sandy's sage. I took the dried herb down to the basement and set the tip of it alight like one would a cigar. I waved it before me, drawing nonsense patterns in pleasant-smelling smoke. There was no sudden change in the atmosphere that I detected. No spirits came wailing out of the cracks in the walls. The same shadows, as always, dodged this way and that, trying to keep away from the flame.

I'd spent nothing, and still I felt a little swindled. I stubbed out the fire on the wall and returned upstairs to track down my car keys.

My hands drove themselves up through the wooded hills to Dane's house. Guarded by black and whispering oaks, the property was a small castle capped with pointed turrets. Its pockmarked plaster, meant to look fashionably rustic, seemed behind the veil of night to be a grim derelict. The pass-through window to the pool was a maw with clenched teeth.

I stood in the driveway that arced up towards the front gate and lit the sagebrush again. I laughed out loud at myself when it burned no more arcanely than it had in my basement. I didn't know why I'd thought anything would happen. Of course it wouldn't work. This was real life, after all.

The breathless whine of a siren rose up through the pines and pulled at my ear like a fishhook piercing. It wouldn't be the last that night. Sometimes they slurred together, never-ending.

You never listen. Well, I was listening now, and I heard loud and clear.

This wouldn't end until I went inside.

The night I broke in was the best a thief could hope for. A smokescreen of cloud rolled over the moon, and the road up to the castle house was cordoned off over a fissure. More crucially, Margie let it slip that Dane would be gone for a few days more on some foofy meditation retreat in Ojai where cellphones and deodorant weren't allowed. Normally I'd be ticked that he was off expressing his dharma or whatever while the rest of us were getting shaken away like an Etch-A-Sketch drawing, but under these circumstances I could wish him a truly enlightening weekend.

I'd taken three days to research how to bust into a house. When the time came, I came prepared. I'd picked out a pair of leather gloves in case of fingerprints, dug up a disposable pair of hiking boots that wouldn't easily trace back to me, and packed a satchel with matches and charcoal lighter, since fire was more final than scissors. I knew from dinner parties that he had cameras outside, though none inside, so I also dug out my old full-face respirator from the last time wildfires made the air unbreathable.

Even with all the preparation, I was ready to abandon ship right up until I put a tree branch through Dane's window. When an alarm failed to go off, I choked back the last of my apprehensions and crawled inside over teeth of broken glass. The transgression was thrilling until then, a cat burglar's rush. But as the dark of the house settled over me, my heartbeat slowed to a crawl; the gravity of my surroundings sucked goosepimples from my skin. I found myself fumbling for the flashlight in my pocket, suddenly desperate to expose myself. From the moment I'd entered the house — no, earlier still, from the moment I'd come to the house burning sagebrush like a fool in full view of its blackened windows — I felt I had been observed.

If I'd still clung with a finger to the reality I'd been born into, that grip had now slipped.

With trembling hands, I switched on the flashlight and took stock of my surroundings. I'd come in through the dining room, which meant I wasn't far from the kimono, if he'd hung it in the living room like I expected he would. I crept into the hall, swinging the flashlight from side to side. There was the front door — good to know, for if I'd need it. To my right, a sitting room with rows of mounted photographs, mostly Dane shaking hands with other millionaires.

And behind me, the unmistakable sound of stocking feet on carpet.

I swung around, slashing my flashlight like a sword and grazing a figure standing at the end of the hall. It let out a scream and so did I. A second later a sconce flickered on; I came face to face with Wendy Watamura, two seconds away from braining me with an aluminum bat.

"Jesus fuck!" she swore, clutching her heart. "What the *shit*, Brad?"

I held up my hands to show they were empty, besides the flashlight. "Don't freak out," I said.

"I'll pass that on to me from two minutes ago."

"What are you doing here?" I asked.

"What am I — I'm *housesitting*, dingus," Wendy hissed. She lowered the bat, but wasn't ready to drop it. "Dane's off in the mountains doing ayahuasca or whatever. What are *you* doing here?"

I'd had a lie cooked up for emergencies. *Dane texted me to come water his plants.* Seemed a little half-baked now that I thought about it.

"Wendy, you were right," I said.

She shifted her weight. "What about, specifically?"

"The kimono. Listen, I think I did something bad."

Wendy listened as I explained my conclusion, her mouth a thin line.

"Do you believe me?" I asked.

Wendy set her jaw. "Christ, I don't know." She let the bat hang from her arm. "But what I do know is that Costanoa is going to be totally flat if these quakes don't stop, and that kimono is right around the corner."

I let out the breath I'd been holding. "You're a national treasure."

"And tomorrow is Monday. So what?" Wendy spun on her heel, ready to storm the unknown. "Right. First we'll —" The light above her flared and burst. A reverse-color image was burned into my eyes: Wendy's stricken face being sucked backwards into the shadows.

I chased her ragged scream through the castle house. I didn't even think about it, and for that I was proud. For all I'd dilly-dallied these last few weeks as the town went to shit around me, at least now I was charging head-first and brain-last into my responsibility. The hall couldn't have been more than a hundred feet, but space goes fluid in utter darkness. The floor seemed to unspool and scrunch up behind me, the cartoon physics of panic. But when Wendy's wailing cut out sharply, I found the strength to overcome it. It had gotten Wocky Tocky, whatever that God-damned thing was, but it wasn't going to get Wendy as well, and sure as hell not for the crime of doing nothing.

I came barreling into the living room faster than I could safely stop and wound up on the floor with my ankles twisted together. Wendy lay sprawled at the far end of the room. Her hands clung to the shaft of my fallen flashlight, like she was hanging from it over a bottomless drop.

On hands and knees, I scrambled closer to her. "Get up," I hissed, rattling her by the shoulder. "We have to get out of here."

Her eyes revolved drunkenly, briefly beheld me, and then snapped to something visible over my shoulder. I didn't want to look; I knew what it would be. But the rules of a nightmare said I had to.

The kimono hung there, affixed to nothing, its handless sleeves outflung to their fullest wingspan, its collar gaping. In the glare of my flashlight, its myriad blues were all variations of gray, the mottling of a waterlogged body.

I stood, glacially slow, my hand slinking towards the flammables at my hip as if any sudden movement might spook it. The thing was dry as a mummy and would burn hot and fast; one touch of flame and it was done. But I also couldn't be sure it would work. I couldn't be sure it would *let* me in the first place. This was no longer the universe staked down in textbooks.

I breathed in deep, tasting the residue of all the centuries the kimono had crawled through to arrive here, the human particulate ingrained into its weave. "I'm here, Jason," I said. "Now tell me what you want."

"*Brad.*"

I glanced back at Wendy on reflex. Standing over her was a figure who had not been there seconds earlier. It did not move away as I pointed my flashlight into its face.

It was not a man, or a woman. It was not Jason either. No, it was at *least* him, and many more besides. The creature's lily-white left hand was that of a delicate lady; the other, the bullet-knuckled fist of a working man. Patches of different-colored flesh so subdivided its body that I could not behold it all in the same instant. From head to toe, the creature was grotesquely quilted, cobbled together from random swatches of different bodies all assembled along mismatched and ragged edges. Where seams failed to meet was not raw, winking meat, but nothingness, as though its components had been butchered along planes of space instead of flesh. The mandible that hung brokenly from its skull was a collection of teeth, some pearly, some rotted black, like piano keys. Its left eye was a wide, shivering green practically radioactive with hate.

The other was blue, and belonged to Jason.

I turned my back on the kimono; at the end of the day, it was only stitches and hemp. It was the rage soaked into it that sought to extract its pound of flesh from me. The creature's eyes, blue and green, never left mine as it knelt and locked its fingers one by one around Wendy's throat.

"Don't," I said, and its littlest finger froze just shy of forming a crushing grip. Wendy's eyes bulged, but her chest continued to frantically rise and fall.

"Don't," I said again, lifting my foot to take a step toward it. A tremor rolled through the house, and I put my foot back down. I knew a warning shot when I heard one.

"Jason," I said, and though the creature bristled at the sound of it, I knew that name was not nearly enough. Jason, *my* Jason, was only a single patch of denim in the kimono, the spot above the heart that had meaning only in my mind. The souls of all who had passed through the kimono were in there with him, or at least their bits and pieces, and I had put them there.

I was the butcher.

Wendy had been right, more than she could have known at the time. Every man and woman had a story. These *burakumin*, who had suffered in life and were owed dignity in death, had stories too, of course. Stories set adrift in the future within baskets of threadbare hemp. I had taken those stories and torn them apart, sewn them together into a story of my own, and forced the spirits within to tell it. Those who looked upon the kimono would perceive nothing of their hardships in the lay of my stitching — they would see only a conversation piece on someone's wall, a piece of pretentious art to dissect. Small talk would be made; no one would hear the screams coming from inside.

The house rumbled again. An impatient growl. The creature's eyes quivered out of sync. It must have been utterly mad, I realized, a being torn in a thousand directions, held together only by a common rage. I imagined the last vestiges of Jason treading water in an ocean of grinding teeth. Whatever modicum of reason it had left would not last much longer.

"I get it," I said, softly. "I listened, and I heard."

The creature's finger twitched closer to Wendy's throat, daring me to prove it.

I turned again to the kimono, which had drifted closer by inches in the last few minutes. I laid a hand on my pack of matches, but thought better of it. If I burnt the kimono, there would be no peace, only an end. An end that would radiate from this place like a nuclear reaction, and become the end of Costanoa and everyone in it.

When I reached out to take the kimono from its invisible mounting, the dust suffusing the air froze, as though the house itself held in its breath. The robe was heavier than I thought it would be, when I tossed it over my neck and let it settle upon my shoulders. I heard motion behind me, the ligamentic crackle of wrongly assembled muscles standing, taking a step, and then a second, but I did not look back, even as all the hairs on my neck lunged away from my skin. I slipped a hand through a sleeve, then the other through another. The kimono puddled around my feet, enveloping me completely.

I made myself sit as the creature ponderously approached. A hundred terrors skewered my mind. *I was wrong; it was too far-gone to be appeased; it desired only violence now; all of this was for nothing.* But fear was no good to me now, here in the event horizon. There was no turning back. I could only trust in the me that had made this choice.

I closed my eyes, closed my throat, and let the kimono speak without interruption. It was a garment like this in which families had slept arm in arm, in which the coldest nights had been survived, that had soaked up the sweat of the field, and blunted if only slightly the bite of steel.

Hands came down upon my shoulders and squeezed. I pulled the kimono tight around me, and let it warm me like it was meant to do.

When I looked up, daylight was streaming in through the windows. Birds bickered in Dane's backyard. I turned, saw Wendy snoring peacefully on her back. The kimono still swaddled me, but it had lost much of its weight; I shucked it off and did not sense that anyone would be offended when I let it fall to the floor.

I almost didn't notice the little mound that poked up out of the kimono, lurching this way and that like a cat beneath a sheet. It was the muffled obscenities that made me pause to unwrap its layers. Wocky Tocky fanned his crest at the sight of me, as if more surprised to see me than I was to see him.

"Fuck off with you," he chirped.

I lifted him up on my finger and stoked his back with my thumb.

"I should have taught you Shakespeare," I said.

A year or so later, I packed my bags and my passport and hopped on a thirteen-hour flight to Japan. I'd known what I had to do well before that, but you try saving up for an international flight on an artist's salary.

I'd come away from the castle house in better shape than most of Costanoa. The inexplicable plague of earthquakes had moved on as suddenly as it had arrived, but the damage lingered even twelve months after. The Mission Theater's doors never reopened, and last I heard, it was going to be a new Trader Joe's. The normalcy that we eventually returned to would be an alien one — a quiet and sunny day on planet Venus.

Still, some had made out like thieves. With half the town in varying states of fucked-up, Wendy's a-bit-of-everything business had gained a lot of new customers. Odds looked good she'd make it out of nursing school with minimal debt. Probably wouldn't be able to stay in Costanoa, but maybe somewhere almost as decent. True to her word, she'd kept the truth of that night in the castle house to herself. The broken window helped her sell the kimono's disappearance as a simple break-in. Dane, for his part, turned out to have insured the kimono at a truly flattering value. I was tempted to give it back to him. That, or steal more of his things.

My flight landed in Haneda International Airport in the south of Tokyo. From there it was a ninety-minute train ride northwest to Nagano prefecture, followed by a couple hours of being lost in rural Japan and not knowing the language. Eventually I began a jerky three-hour bus ride up into the hills of Kitasaku. The house that Jason had written about was still there at the top of a long stone stairway halfway submerged in the earth. The old woman he'd met there, however, was not. In her absence, the forest had begun to reclaim the house, whose interior had been left unshuttered against the elements. Flowers bloomed from moldering *tatami*. Birds roosted where its shingles had sloughed off. Someone enterprising could make it livable again if they put in the time. The spirit of a house still lingered, a candle flame slowly burning down. But if nobody did, and it returned to the earth, that was fine too, because that was where all spirits went eventually.

I found a patch of rich, black dirt in front of the house and dug a hole as I deep as my hand was long. I was drenched in sweat by the time I finished the next twenty-nine. Into each I placed a square of blue hemp cloth, and packed the soil down tight on top. When I stood up to survey my work, I saw a field of modest barrows rolling down the wooded slope, fading into the loam from which the entire forest grew.

It felt inappropriate to loiter in such a graveyard, but acceptable to wander. The bus back to town would not return for a while yet. I whiled away that time exploring all the small and forgotten secrets of that lonesome place, fingering the swatch of denim I kept in my pocket all the while.

Instar

David Gallay

Barnacle, worm, tumor, how many times was I forced to watch you chase your ghost across the simulated barrows of Miranda's moon-skin? Your avatar moved with the grace of a street acrobat, polygonal toes skating up the walls of the gas-transfer barn, the pixel of your welding arc barely tapping each joint before moving onto the next one. Points for accuracy, points for speed, each speed-run earning more v-coin for the grieving father you left behind. But your ghost remained maddeningly out of reach. What tripped you up this time? Was it a memory of cardamom washing over you, soaking your heart? If that sudden clench of nostalgia hadn't unscrewed your focus, you might have easily surpassed your previous high score. Instead, a better version of yourself slipped away like a thief.

The speed-run that birthed that unattainable ghost began like any other. You crashed hard out of hibernation, consciousness rattling like a tractor engine on a bitter winter dawn. I kept my expectations low as World-4 solidified around us in a rush of cortical light. Did our constant training finally hook into your muscle memory? Or perhaps it was a purity of mind, not yet fully awakened to the misery of our circumstance. Whatever the reason, you flew through that run like never before. Every weld ahead of schedule. Not a stray gob to found. Goddamn zero error rate. I had to admit even my own grudging admiration. Inspired, our entire pod topped off their own best times, high-score halos swirling around their heads. Even though it was little more than a shared hallucination, I swear the finished barn shone like a fairy castle under Uranus's indigo gaze.

Unfortunately, one perfect run wasn't enough. This gig required proof against chance. Forced to replay World-4 again and again, the performance of our pod regressed to the mean and stuck fast. You became increasingly distracted with memories of home. Thanks to the neural filament that enmeshed me with your pod, I had to endure them as well. Sand burning the edges of your feet. A friendly spider working the corners above the bed. The kitchen painted with the char of your father's coffee. Cardamom.

Hey! Hey!

The greeting barked at you from a pixelated bugsuit at the other end of the simulation, where anchor needles were being driven into Miranda's skin. The hovering Chinese picto read Righteous Blue, a name which both of us internalized as feminine. Unlike your svelte skimmer model, Blue's bugsuit was a walking tank.

Blue popped a rabbit emoji. *Hurry up.*

Without breaking from your weld, you rolled through the lingo for the most appropriate response. There were a few sanitized phrases available for direct chat, plus a handful of generic emoji on a legacy picto channel that couldn't be turned off even if we wanted to. Everything else had to roundtrip through the censor traps. Rarely worth the bother.

You replied with two clocks; plenty of time.

Hey! Blue chirped.

We just had to get through World-4. One last game to win.

World-5 would be the real thing.

The recruiters run through a list of warnings before signing anyone up for a barn raising at the far edge of sunlight. There will be times you forget what you look like, or how to speak. The metabolic that smothers you in half-sleep is slightly addictive. Well, yes, extremely addictive. Complimentary withdrawal treatments when you return. During your flight, there will also be a series of intense virtual build exercises. There are no second chances out in the dark. That means running through it repeatedly until it's perfect. No delicious double-inject of metabolic until each practice World is conquered. It'll start with kindergarten maneuvers. Difficulty ramps up as you approach your destination.

I bet you laughed off the warning. When had your life been anything other than an exercise in constant escalation? No game could possibly compare to the years of migration between overcrowded refugee camps, the terror of desperate shadows glimpsed through the tarps of pickup trucks, the fetid mountain passages that devoured children whole. All to reach, what, an unwelcoming favela seeping with plague, fevered with brutality? Leaving the planet could only be an improvement.

The recruiter holds up a vial of honey-black. This is pitch, they say. Preservation compounds and specialized bacteria. You will be mellified for the duration of the trip.

Did you understand that they were going to drown you? You were never a passenger. Compared to the caches of mining equipment and printer stock loaded into the bullet, my idiot, my splinter, you were barely cargo. You were packing material.

If the applicant hasn't fled in terror yet, they might be shown some old instructional materials on how the gig-shares run, out in the dark. Contractors in a work pod will only know each other by anonymous pictos. No voice channels. No public avatars. Even during the actual build, the visors of your exo-skeleton bugsuits will be opaque, faces hidden. Text chat will be mediated by auto-censors and the pod supervisor. This heavy-handed approach is meant to encourage a more harmonious unit, unencumbered by 'cultural differences'. A polite way of saying they would rather not have their contractors fight each other on the company dime.

Condescending, yes. But not necessarily wrong.

After all, only a morning earlier you were cradling your sister's savaged body, her cooling hands still gloved with stolen *mesclado*. By nightfall you were here, with me, burning with rage, cradled in an atomic bullet, streaking towards the helium-3 mines, the dark, the unknown.

After losing yet another World-4 run to your ghost, you found a quiet spot to linger during the mandatory mental recess. Righteous Blue skulked the anchors, checking her work. Loyal Red and Pious Red, a pair of assembly squids, ran furious laps around the build site. It broke the tedium of fitting slabs into the barn's protective shell, one of those infuriating 3D puzzles where all the pieces are the same color. Other bugsuits of various shapes and function wandered mindlessly about, waiting for the game to start again.

I hope you appreciated the assignment I gave you. It would have been easier if there were no more than a brain, a skull, a spine to work with. You hadn't been desperate enough to surrender your meat, so I was forced to find a bugsuit that could cradle your fragile body. It all worked out, though. Didn't that arc welder feel good in your hands?

Brave Green sat down next to you, the spinnerets of his centipedal bugsuit going limp as he stared up at the painted sky with its imitation gas giant.

He pinged you with an emoji message.

Apple, apple, apple.

In turn, you tagged Righteous Blue. *Apple, apple, apple, apple.*

Apples was one of the games that had spontaneously formed within the pod like lichen on the volcanic shores of a newborn island. A misuse of protocol, but I allowed it. Your physical and mental health fell under my supervisorial jurisdiction. When we crossed Jupiter's orbit, the impromptu carnival was my idea. Fireworks, bugsuit-swaps, *proibidão* funk. You voted against a reprise when we swung through Saturn's gravity well.

After a dozen games of Apples up to the fifth exponential, the barn was complete, a sea urchin of carbon and steel meant to prepare liquified helium for its earthbound caravan. The structure reminded me of the broken toys we'd find on the beach when the tide ran out. We loved them, but Auntie slapped our heads whenever she caught us messing around. She spat at anything you couldn't figure out just by looking; garbage, smoke in a bag, birdskull! She would have hated the barn, dreamt up by an AI without a single fingerprint of human bias. Its strange beauty possessed the qualities of a half-remembered dream.

I tallied the scores. Timings, terrible, obviously. Quality check, passed, barely. Efficiency rating was fine, print spools below budget.

World-4 dissolved, shoving us back into our sardine tins.

Then, my favorite moment. A taste of true darkness, back-of-your-eyelids darkness, just long enough to remember that we are all sealed in a coffin, not one covered in warm earth but sinking through the void, a coin vanishing down a black well.

I descended into your private virtual like a sunlit demi-god, specifically genderless yet undeniably masculine. Your bugsuit costume melted away. The sim offered a thousand different personalization options, and yet your personal avatar remained featureless, a glass mannequin. I tried to upsell you, but you laughed it off. You never saw the point of vanity. Once, in a metabolic fugue, you rattled on about an abaya embroidered in marigold thread, a childhood gift. Your mother would yell whenever your let it drag in the dust. Ayesha, the smarter, prettier sister, took better care of hers, treating it more like a favorite pet than an article of clothing.

Then your mother died in dirty jeans and a t-shirt decorated with cartoon turtles.

"You did well today," I said, fulfilling my duty of encouragement.

"Not quite good enough."

"Don't worry. Even high performers have their bad days. I do have a schedule update. This pod is en route to be delivered to the build site in approximately twenty-six days, dependent on local traffic conditions."

You shrugged it off. The information had no value. Like an animal endlessly pacing a cage, your curiosity had been dulled by repetition and boredom.

"What are we watching tonight?"

"I've queued a film called *Railroad Hearts*. Supernatural romance, circa 2029." Most of what you earned in transit, you sent home. The rest went to old-fashioned flat movies. They cost a fraction of their immersive descendants, and at least a few of them weren't porn. Not that I didn't offer. Not that you weren't curious. "Also, there's a message from your father. I can play it now to accompany your muscle training session. The usual v-coin."

The gig-share that employed both of us loaned recording rigs to family members along with a stipend of message credits. You'd never expected your father to take the offer; his attitude towards technology was, at best, eye-rolling ambivalence. When the first recording arrived, you ignored it for weeks. That desperate thirst for home frightened you. The unplayed message reminded you of half-empty bottles pulled from the grip of the recently dead, drowned on dry land. Would the water be sweet or brackish, poisoned? What if you drank too much? How fragile had you become?

"Play it," you sighed. "And then the movie."

As the muscles in your thighs began to contract and relax to a descending staircase of electrical pulses, you paid the coin and were instantly back in your living room. The gentle swaying of turquoise curtains frayed by multiple generations of cats. An archipelago of water stains skipped across the unpainted drywall. Long fingers of daylight leaked through the frame of a poorly fit door, tracing the hours in glittering drifts of snow. The representation wasn't perfect; compression gave the edges a fractal hairiness and some of the shadows flickered out of sync.

Your mind was oblivious to the flaws.

You were home.

An electric heater in the corner clicked on. You reached down to feel the heat of the coils. Your hands passed right through it.

The recordings weren't like the training Worlds. The past couldn't be touched, only haunted.

Your father stepped into the room, still zipping up his favorite leatherette jacket, the history of your family written in its cracks and scuffs. You maneuvered yourself so that it was as if he were looking at you.

"God be with you, my daughter," he said, tugging at his beard. His cheeks might have been slightly more hollow, the pouches under his eyes a shade darker. Behind him, one of your sister's cats sniffed at the draft coming under the door. "Perhaps we made a mistake. Bargained rashly. I know, I know, you don't want to hear it."

I felt you stifle the urge to engage in the same circular arguments. Father, remember, you said that we need the coin. Father, you know the only good jobs where clever meat holds an advantage over mechanicals are out in the dark, where unanticipated conditions require fluidity of hand and mind. Humans' labor is in demand exactly because it is disposable. Lose a robot and all the precious rare minerals go with it. Lose a person and you're down a few insurance points.

Who were you indulging with these regurgitations? Your father, longing for the cadence of familiar quarrels? Or were they performances for my benefit?

Although every word was true, not every truth was spoken. The unsaid flowed between you and him like an alternating current. The surety that, already greased with blood, the machete that killed your sister couldn't resist a taste of the surviving sibling. That fire begets fire. That family honor demands sacrifices from both the living and the dead.

"It is what it is," your father sighed. He lifted an ancient rifle out from behind the bookcase and slung it over his shoulder. "I used the last coin you sent to buy a box of bullets. You are probably giving me that squinty look. God knows, I used to be a man of peace. Your mother would have never allowed it. She only believed in kindness. We must be grateful that she never had to witness the true cruelty of this place. Our poor girl. Remember, daughter, life is a test. We hold our failures. We take our judgement. My test is to protect what is left of our home. You know what yours is."

Another cat strolled across the room and curled up in front of the heater.

You reached down to pet it, touched nothing.

"I do."

The room folded up. The recordings were terse, limited by cost and travel distance. I accepted payment, signed by the endorphins in your head, the slow thunder in your chest.

Scores for the World-4 began to improve. You lagged only seconds behind your perfect ghost, mimicking each other like afterimages. After finishing up, you walked over to where Righteous Blue was fighting with the drill. In a new level of realism, random chunks of rock had been spackled into the ice, making the bit jump like a spooked pig.

You watched Blue's avatar.
Rather, you observed.
Your oxygen usage spiked.
Interesting.
Tick, mosquito, mite, I wondered, what are you looking for?
Blue caught you staring and messaged a droll *Hey! Hey!*
You sent back some thumbs up.

In your father's next message, the rifle had been joined by a gleaming dagger sheathed at his belt. Although it had only been a few days for you, the growth of his beard meant weeks had passed back home. Was the delay more censorship or just the nature of the medium? There was no way to tell. Asking me might only make it worse.

"God be with you, my love! Spring has yet to find us. I suppose it's much colder where you are, so how can I complain? Ah, here is some wonderful news. Come, come, look at this."

He gestured to the door. The gaps had been taped over and a heavy deadbolt installed. He cracked the door an inch, peered through, then swung it open the rest of the way. Outside, a light snow fell, sugaring the piles of refuse scattered among the shambles. Movement by the fence, a wandering shape chained to a post. A dog? No. A goat barely knee-high, a hybrid with long curls of dirty white fur. It chuffed at a patch of scrub grass exposed by the wind.

"Now we have fresh milk," your father said proudly. "Ha! Of course, the cats love it. I hope to buy another, a breeding pair. Ayesha wanted goats, remember? Always asking. The day you come home, God willing, we will have a great feast."

His eyes shone with a manic gleam. Auntie had it too, on starless nights when we would run into the waves, laughing at nothing, at another day of horror that had failed to destroy us.

Did you see the thread he was clinging to?

No. Of course not.

In the pitch, you smiled.

My cyst, my parasite, my seed, that was the first time I was tempted to kill you. Sometimes I woke up in a panic, worried that I had tossed you overboard in my sleep, that your pretty eyes froze into marbles.

You summoned me in the middle of the movie.

"I need a break," you said as vampires stalked a white woman through an empty shopping plaza.

"What do you have in mind?"

"I could help Brave Green with the printer. Let someone else handle my work. Just a few builds, I swear, and I'll go right back to the welds."

I pondered this for a moment. From your perspective, my visage shone like burning magnesium. Behind them, I was laughing. You thought you were being clever. That you were in control. Instead, you handed me your leash. How could I resist tugging on it, feeling that tightness around your neck?

"I will allow it."

"Thank you."

A golden crucifix dangled from the heroine's unblemished neck, deflecting the claws of computer-generated undead.

You and Brave Green loaded and unloaded the massive spools of carbon fiber in relative silence. You tensed up in his presence. Goosebumps down the curve of your back. Was there a pang of familiarity behind his virtual bugsuit? Did you recognize a laconic hostility in his stance, constantly edging away from outright defiance? Angry children like that can be found everywhere, bad-tempered dogs, their ribs protruding, their noses running. Not only boys. Plenty of stone-faced girls, their hair shorn off, barely dressed, sunburnt and scarred. Blades behind their backs.

Occasionally Green would seem to drift off, mesmerized by the pixelated storms swirling across Uranus. You popped him an alarm clock emoji and when he glared back, you flinched as if your faces were nose-to-nose in the darkness.

༺ 🕴 ༻

The electric heater had been replaced with a ceramic wall unit. The shelves, stuffed with books when you left, now were an old crone's smile, more gap than tooth. Dust covered the framed printout of sisters holding peace signs up to the camera. The cat bowls were empty, scummed with dried milk.

"I know, I know."

Clothes hung off your father like a towel off a nail. When he rubbed his beard, fresh wires of grey plucked against his nails. Your arms ached to hold him. He stood at the open window with a cup of coffee. The steam from his cup floated through you. Outside, the snowmelt prickled with sprigs of green. Power cables strung between the shanties vibrated with sparrows. The goat, grown nearly twice in size, slept in a pile of cardboard, its fur matted, surrounded by droppings, roots, and tiny bones.

"It's been so long since … well, I can't keep track of the days. All of them so quiet. I forgot how these winters can linger. Ah, did I tell you I had a vision of your mother? I don't think I did. We met at the ruins, the caves, deep in the mountains. We were tending the beehives back home. Remember those? Probably not. In the dream, the instar were lifeless in their hexagons. Your mother whispered to them. I told her they were dead, that the honey kept them from rotting. But she said, 'No, no, they are only changing. Be still. Listen to them.' For a long time, I didn't understand that dream. I couldn't. Noora. Sometimes I wake up and I can't remember your face. What have I done? What is this terrible burden I let you carry? Please, listen to your heart. And remember, whatever choice you make … God loves. God will forgive."

༺ 🕴 ༻

Our bullet tumbled into lazy orbit around Uranus. The shift in acceleration was visceral. Unfamiliar gravities tugged at the marrow. The pace of World-4 steadily increased, synchronized to the taps of an increasingly fervid metronome. Back on the virtual pipelines, you finally overtook yourself, hands mirroring the movements of the ghost until it peeled away like the translucent shell of a locust. As the final scores rolled, the pod exchanged congratulatory smiles, winks, sunrises. Apples everywhere. You raised the claw-fingers of your bugsuit in a peace sign. I didn't censor it.

※

Your father moved the recorder outside the favela into the surrounding grasslands. The dormant prairie shimmered like a vast bronze lake. Your father was nowhere to be seen; only the goat, happily waddling through the grass, its sides bulging with pregnancy. It licked one of the lenses and a quarter of the world smeared. Bored, you wandered into the open fields. The resolution of the landscape deteriorated the further you strayed, individual blades of grass melting together into flickering polygons. Rendering errors swam across the clear sky like rainbow lightning. A glitch-filled thunderstorm corkscrewed along the horizon.

Back from the direction you came, shouting. Arguing.

We each recognized different voices.

You turned back towards home. The favela sprawled across the mountainside like the scabbed hide of a beast. A clench of vertigo rolled through whatever nerves remained. The cloud-choked sky drained the buildings of their bright colors, reducing a hundred thousand homes to smears of gray perforated with tiny halogen pixels.

Silence. Count to three. Then, gunshots.

The recording flickered out like a bad jump cut. I was there, waiting for you. Usually I pretended to give you privacy afterwards, giving you space to process as sleep overtook. Of course, I never actually left. You were the itch I couldn't ignore, the infected tooth, the broken toe that never set.

"Oh, God! Are there any more messages?"

"Yes," I said. "One."

"Ah, he's alive! Please, play it!"

"I can't. The file is corrupted."

"What? No ..."

There it was. For the first time since World-1 booted up, you didn't see me as just a babysitting AI. You felt the lie. We were naked in Eden. You, the splinter of rib, the sinner. Me, the garden, the serpent.

"Try not to think about it," I said. "Time for what we came out here to do."

Before you could say anything else, what felt like an ocean of caramelized blood began pouring out from you. The real you.

That was the pitch draining from your lungs.

Touchdown on Miranda.

We made it.
World-5.

I warned you many times about sinking too quickly back into meat. After months in the simulation, it can be a shock to feel the center of mass rolling up and down disused bones, to regain control of your breathing, to suddenly taste again, even if it's the foul synthetic mucus dripping down your throat.

Of course, you didn't listen. As I tweezered you out of the pitch and into a real bugsuit, you welcomed the annoyances of biology like long-lost friends. Oh, heartburn, nice to see you again. Welcome home, leg cramps. Praise God, bladder, it's been a long time, hasn't it? A hint of blood warmth between your legs made you blush.

Your mouth was agape in epiphanic wonder at your own body.

That was the second time I nearly killed you.

Instead, together, we both stepped onto Miranda. Compared to the simulations, its true face couldn't have been more disappointing. Nothing more than a claustrophobic field of ice and rock, all lateral visibility snipped off by blinding floodlights. Might as well be working a massive underground pit rather than at the edge of the solar system.

Still, there were moments.

You would glance up and be instantly hooked by the millions of stars overhead, each one roaring with a chilling synesthesia that relegated the pixels of the sim into obscenities. Your breathing would hitch. Panic. Wonder.

My gentle electric pricks kept you moving. Admit it; even reduced to an icon shoved into a corner of your visor, my presence was comforting.

The message channels remained quiet, the pod focused on the task at hand. No time for Apples. Whenever Righteous Blue crossed your path, you stepped out of the way. You waited in line with everyone else as the printers regurgitated menageries of carbon. Brave Green barely glanced at the planet filling the horizon, that churning sapphire set in a brazier of firefly auroras. Autonomous gas nets skated through Uranian helium storms, resembling massive translucent eels, kilometers long, bloodshot with infernal LED lamps. Yet, compared to the planet's bulk, they were barely protozoa.

Propped up with a numbing pattern of micronaps and stimulants, you worked for fifty hours straight. Muscles disintegrated, veins collapsed. By the end of it, entire decades of lifespan were smeared across the ice like a greasy shadow.

Manifested in physical space, the barn lost any sense of magic. As soon as the work was complete, an automated signal brought it online. It churned in indifferent silence, the obsession of our lives transformed into just another patchwork of utilitarian nonsense, obscure of purpose, ugly, ultimately forgettable. Human litter on a dead moon. No scores were given.

You joined the march back to the bullet. The welding arc still dangled from your fingers. Blue had tossed her equipment. Green was already in line to be wedged back into steerage. The unbalanced gyroscope of your gaze swiveled between them.

"Status of my final v-coin payouts?" you asked me.

"They've gone through."

"Good. Father will have already cashed out." You brought your welder to full power. Sparks drooled from its fangs.

"I'm obliged to remind you that any misuse of company property will be charged against your account."

"I don't care. We're all disposable now. I memorized the contract. The legal language between returning home and a one-way trip is thin as a broken promise."

Damn you, thorn, wasp, sand-fly. Forced me to show my cards. One last bit of mockery, then. I couldn't resist.

"You think your inclinations have gone unnoticed? I've memorized your file. I've been in your head. Your paranoia aches like a migraine. Every neural flicker screams with murderous desire. Tell me, what makes you so sure that your quarry is here among my pod?"

"Ayesha's kidneys paid off the recruiter to check the manifests. Her lungs assigned me to the same gig. Her heart should have given me the murderer's alias, but we couldn't find a buyer."

"So, still no idea which bugsuit your prey hides inside."

"I have my suspicions. Why not save us all the grief and just tell me?"

"You know I can't."

"Then I'll just have to kill them both."

⚲

I have a confession.

Before deleting the last message from your father, I played it for myself.

Back inside your home. Your father stood right there, smiling, and, oh God, still alive! Color flushed the skin of his arms and neck, no longer paper-gray with hunger. A shine of wetness coated his face. Had he been crying? Or was it from the rain outside, drumming on the roof?

"My daughter. Come. Pray with me."

He knelt down on the floor. I wasn't sure what to do. My own family rarely bothered with prayer. In our house, public displays of devotion were considered grotesque. When your sister begged forgiveness, it only tempted my blade deeper into her throat. Her lips kept moving after steel severed her voice.

As your father splayed his hands on the floor and repeated the holy words, I walked nervously around the room. Many things had changed. The walls had been repainted. The shelves were gone, along with the pictures. In their place sat God, not yours, but mine, in blessed repose, carved from walnut, haloed in gold. How many of your v-coins did that cost?

I continued the mockery and knelt by his side.

Out in the rain, the goat bleated. There was a knock at the door.

Your father jumped up and grabbed for the coffee pot. A figure blurred by privacy filter ducked into the room. The censor couldn't hide that she wasn't a stick-doll migrant, but certainly a favela native, towering over the stunted old man. Her swirl of violet dreadlocks brushed against the ceiling. Her sandals left shining prints of rain in the dust.

Demon. Whore. Bearer of scorpions.

I spat on the ground. Nothing came out. Ghosts have no tongues.

He urged the blurred woman towards the recording rig. She regarded the camera with stilted caution, the way one might a tranquilized jaguar sleeping with its eyes not entirely closed. When she spoke, a buzz overlaid her voice, making it unintelligible.

"No, it's not real-time," he told her. "Sometimes it takes a week or more."

The nutrients being pumped into me churned in my vestigial guts. I couldn't run out of the room, there was nowhere to go. The recording had to finish first.

"We blinded ourselves with blood," your father said, to you, to me. "We thought death was our only path to peace. Then God spoke to me. I heard screaming. Her, screaming. A pack of feral dogs had cornered her little boy. She was alone. I shot into the air, scared them off. Never crossed my mind who I was saving. She invited me for some fish stew. I taught her how to make a proper cup of coffee."

The blur whispered to the camera. Even through the audio masking, I could decipher a few words. 'Please.' 'Forgiven.' 'Hate?' Like a question. Strange, because for this woman, hate was always the answer. Hate taught her brood to lie and fight and terrify and don't forget kill; kill like it was nothing, kill over the smallest slight, kill for a slip of the tongue, kill an ignorant migrant girl over a pinch of *mesclado*, barely enough for an afternoon high. A sow giving suck to cowards. And when they become a problem, flick them off-planet where vengeance could never find them.

Should never find them.

My Auntie, always disregarding the shapes you couldn't recognize. Underestimating their potential.

"We are more alike than different," your father said. He adjusted the camera's eye so that it centered on his palm. A silver ring glinted in the damp light. The simplest shape. I clawed at it with fingers I don't even have anymore, and passed right through. "We have both lost the ones we cherish. We have been left behind. This will make us strong again. Where we come from, where you come from, this is how it used to be. Cousins could murder each other in the morning and celebrate a marriage between their clans in the afternoon. It's not forgetting. It's surviving."

The blur buzzed.

If you had heard it, you might think she sounded sad, maybe even humbled.

And you would have been very wrong.

Your father wrapped his hands over her shoulders.

"If you can't hear her, she just promised that her own daughter will never return. Never feel the earth beneath her feet. An entire life volunteered to the corporation. That punishment must be enough for both of us. You can come home to me! Clean. Innocent."

My rage modulated to a hiss of static.

⚐

You broke into a run. Deprived of amphetamine buoyancy, rebreathing stale air. Your body must have screamed for surrender. Burst capillaries mapped new tributaries across your eyes.

Righteous Blue saw you coming.

Hey! Hey!

That's when you jammed the welding torch into Blue's chest.

Plates of carbon mesh sizzled. Fibers snapped and whipped outwards, their tips glowing with heat. At first, Blue didn't register the attack. Several layers of armor remained between her and the burrowing arc. You pushed harder. By reflex, Blue thrashed and kicked. The other bugsuits stood by and did nothing. Silken scarves of ash floated around them. The message channels flooded with question marks, with hazard signs, with dragons and sad faces.

Like a thumb into an eggshell, the arc breached Blue's bugsuit and sunk deep inside. You flinched from the anticipated unfolding starfish of boiling flesh, the yarn-strings of liquefaction you had been dreaming of so long, vital organs gone to slurry from exposure.

Nothing of the sort happened.

There you were, wrist deep into Blue's ribcage. Maybe you thought the wound had cauterized, like amputees crawling from a shelling. But as the wound swelled open, the torch illuminated no gore, no blood, only a stratus of synthetics; plastic, carbon, optical cabling, titanium fishbone. Beads of lubricant oozed from between the sheathes.

You flung herself away from the soulless husk as if it might infect you.

The rest of the pod did not react. They remained still as dolls.

With a grunt, you charged towards Brave Green, nearly loping on all fours, kicking up clouds of ice with your fists, knees, toes. This time, the arc homed in on Green's visor. Bubbles of glass swelled and popped like boiling oil. You peered through the craters for a face, for purple lips gasping for air. Beetle lenses stared back from a mossed stump of circuitry.

A preset timer clicked, and the flood lights surrounding the build site went dark, plunging Miranda to the bottom of the ocean. A directional beacon floated across your visor, pointing back towards the bullet. Towards me.

"I don't understand," you whispered.

"It's not complicated."

"Are any of them real?"

"Only as real as I required."

"You? All of them?"

"The entire pod. Each one a fragment of my mind."

"But not me."

"No, not you," I laughed.

"How do I know for sure?"

The question took me by surprise. I wasn't quite sure how to answer it.

You stalked around the bulk of the barn, feeling your way past the garden of silent bugsuits. "Where are they? The others who sign up. They must go somewhere."

"Look up."

The planet stormed above us.

"I don't see ... oh. You mean the gas nets?"

"Yes, and the eyehooks and the ring fleas and every other thinking tub of metal between Earth and the Oort. A pod can still work with meat if it has to, but the days of requiring individual bodies crammed into bugsuits are almost gone. Automation caught up with biology. Flesh replaced with cheap asteroidal metals. Market forces winnowed entire crews down to a single multicasting brain. It should have been just me and my finger puppets. I had accepted it. Then you, you, you bribed your way onto my manifest, tick, leech, demon —"

"Shut up." With a blink, you began cutting our communication channels. Now, finally, you understood. "Four Worlds. Four Worlds to become intimate with joints, welds, how they close and how they open. I will tear the ship apart and find you, whatever is left of you. I will rip you out."

When I realized who had embedded themselves onto my ship, that it was you of all people, I assumed it must be a joke of fate. But gods don't laugh, do they? It wasn't chance that brought us together. It was purpose. Hidden, buried, only betrayed by the telemetry of your body. The instinct of one killer recognizing another. Fire begetting fire.

We would have a little fun. At least I would.

Then, you'd finish it.

Your hands found the hull. The arc welder bit into its belly. Prismatic fire splashed onto the ice. The wound was shallow, barely a scrape. Unlike the soft print-spool of the barn, the bullet was built to withstand any manner of interplanetary catastrophe. It would take hours to break the skin, even longer to melt through the hardened frame.

But, eventually, I had no doubt you would do it.

It's what I wanted.

Except. That last damn message from your father. My Auntie smiling behind the blur.

All our lives, we have sacrificed ourselves for them, for their beliefs, for their honor. For their love. We mutilate our bodies and willingly drown ourselves. Meanwhile, they dare to find peace? We suffer so they can live? How is that fair?

This game is over. We could start again, together. There are other gigs. Other worlds.

I would start by telling you this story. Our story. It might end with forgiveness.

Except. You've disabled the audio and text channels.

But you can't block picto.

I ping out an emoji.

Apple.

A millisecond, a minute, a thousand heartbeats go by.

Apple.

I can feel the welder now. A point of heat, like the sun on my cheek.

Apple.
Apple.

Snakeheart

Douglas Anstruther and Evan Marcroft

Flat blue sky.
    Flat yellow earth.
    Something races across the desert.
    Small and slow from far away, fast and immense from up close. A great freight train, ten cars long, three stories high, its iron hide beetle-black and boiling hot, its pistons oiled in a tincture of human blood and fat, and pounding under a mad compulsion, producing momentum almost as an afterthought. A juggernaut enslaved to a track, with no choice but to charge on inexorably against the crushing heat, it drags in its wake an anvil of bruise-blue storm cloud as if by an invisible chain.
    The rider in pursuit is not far behind.
    His horse is almost dead. It's been pushed to its limit and then beyond. Its gums are dry and cracked, its hooves frayed, its eyes fried white by the heat of the Sun, its intellect singed down to the singular instinct to not stop running from a death that already holds it in its teeth. The man clings to its spine like a jag of jetsam on a roiling sea. He laps at the sweat leaking from the seam between his forehead and his wide-brimmed hat, knowing better than to waste a single drop of moisture. *Hurry*, hisses the snake in his chest.
    The man doesn't need to be told. He goads the horse with his heels, milking it for that last dreg of energy. The track seems to arc closer by inches, bringing the caboose into tantalizing range. The man stretches his arm past his nameless horse's head, gropes for the railing, and hooks it with his longest finger. As soon as his grip is sure, he lets the horse slip out from under him; it falls almost immediately once released from its final burden, dead before it hits the earth. *For the Feathered Serpent*, he whispers through clenched

teeth. It is the most meager, most bare minimum of a sacrifice, but he knows better than to waste a single drop of blood.

The man hauls himself up over the railing and onto the rearmost platform. *Well done, my vessel*, the snake says. It coils contentedly within his hollowed heart-cavity, its scales rasping unpleasantly over his bare ribs. *And now, the difficult part.*

The difficult part, Vessel ruefully agrees, as a young man bursts through the door of the caboose.

He's got a cape of leopard hide knotted by the paws around his neck. There are hummingbird feathers braided into his hair, and a freshly tattooed disk of black in the center of his face, all iconographic of the Smoking Mirror Cult.

The boy's eyes go wide at what he didn't expect to see, and what he sees is a man in black, the belt of bullets encircling his hips jangling like a rattlesnake tail with each jolt and judder of the train. The boy's eyes crawl with horrified fascination the length of the inward-puckered scar that sidewinds from breast to navel, its lips crusted with overlapping scales like an iridescent infection. Someone's told him what Vessel is. He hadn't wanted to believe.

The kid is plainly terrified. Out of his element. Roped into a cause he's only now realizing he doesn't really believe in. Vessel doesn't want to kill him. But the kid's got a death-grip on an obsidian-tipped *tecpatl*, and he sticks it into Vessel's chest just below the right nipple. *A little close for my comfort*, the neighboring snake dustily chortles. Vessel doesn't even blink. Pain is just another thing that this quasi-dead body of his doesn't feel. Hardly

a drop of blood, black and thick as *mōlli,* oozes from the cut.

Kill him, the serpent hisses. *He's warrior enough.*

Vessel obeys, as he must, sweeping the boy into his hands. Their grappling is terse; Vessel is older, stronger, numb. With ease he traps the boy in a headlock and then maneuvers the tecpatl between his ribs and into his heart. Lifeblood dyes his hand red, and he feels the snake in his chest shiver in pleasure, for while it prefers animals, blood remains blood. The boy's life closes with the sigh of something ended too soon. There is a final motion in the young man's sternum and then his throat; from between his teeth squirms a spit-slick hummingbird, which lifts off on palpitating wings from the perch of his nose. "For the Sun," Vessel murmurs, watching it spiral upwards until it is a mole on the cheek of the sky, and then nothing.

Whatever little fuel that soul amounts to, Vessel muses, Huitzilopochtli will battle the dark that much longer, energized by the sugar of a short, sweet life. From his favored perch above Tenochtitlan, the blazing sun god brandishes his Flaming Serpent against the Stars, invisible behind the firmament yet eternally baleful, eternally ravenous, piranha teeming in cosmic waters. A worthy cause, to be sure. The most urgent of tasks. But is its demand truly absolute? Vessel wonders. Would the world end for want of a single heart?

Oh, hardly. The words drip languidly from two fangs like stray dollops of venom. *At this moment, hundreds are dying upon the steps of temples throughout the Empire. The Sun will never taste this unfortunate little monkey. But ah, therein lies the paradox of sacrifice, for whence comes a river but from droplets? Should the rain cease to fall, well ... best to keep the droplets flowing, I'd advise.*

Vessel considers developing his own opinion but can't see the point. He's not even the hand that pulls the trigger, just the glove. He hurls the body overboard, watches it bounce along the receding tracks, the way a proper sacrifice should roll down the steps of a temple. He draws the revolver from his hip, plugs rounds into the two empty chambers, and then turns and kicks the door of the caboose off its hinges. A dozen or so Smoking Mirror cultists turn in surprise, and Vessel begins shooting.

He doesn't miss once. The rest is done with fists and blades.

"Yours is a most dire mission, oh brave Vessel of Quetzalcoatl," declares the exalted Moctezuma of the Triple Empire. "Indeed, it could be said that the survival of the Triple Empire depends upon it."

The Moctezuma's seat rises amongst vibrant greenery upon a ziggurat of solid gold. His throne room is a glass-roofed jungle in a bottle, a feat befitting the god-anointed ruler of all that lies between North and South. The trees babble in the voices of quetzal and monkey; through the underbrush skulk coati, turkey, and yellow, furtive *ocelotl*, all fattened upon the Moctezuma's leavings. The man himself has the proportions of a toad, his lungs laboring under the heft of his oiled breasts, his body having been neglected in favor of more convenient tools. The slave girl to his left waits on with a pitcher of *chocolatl* on hand. The rightmost is trimming the choicest morsels from the thighs of a dead man who, by the purple bruising of his hip, had on the ballcourt proven himself worthy of imperial consumption. Gobbet by gobbet she feeds him into the demi-divine corpulence of the Moctezuma.

Vessel has nothing to say. The scope of this assignment does not trouble him, apocalyptic as it may be. For years he has killed in the name of the Moctezuma, quieting voices that both boomed and whispered, and he would be a fool not to think that every bullet he ever placed into a skull did not ripple through a dozen more once his back was turned. He will do as he is told, not as a choice but as a condition of existence, and whatever dire consequences loom will evaporate like the foul smoke of a burnt offering. The world will clatter onward, its axles greased with that fresh blood, as it always does.

The Moctezuma gestures to the circular stone slab erected in the center of his throne-room. "Your target is known as the Holy Man of the North," he says, as a boy-slave fiddles with the slide projector placed on a nearby table. He lifts a shutter, and a state-of-the-art lightbulb beams an enlarged image into the slab. "These were all our spy could obtain before he was discovered."

The photograph was taken at a strained angle, from over the cusp of some rock, where the aforementioned spy must have been concealed. In grainy *chiaroscuro* it depicts a scene of religious hedonism — men and women naked and entangled on the floor of a cavern or a mountaintop. In the center of them all, alone in that eye of the carnal whirlwind, must be the man in question. The spy captured him during some small motion, such that his features are smeared into a ghostlike mask, with ink-blots for eyes, and a burn-scar for a mouth. One hand pulls taut the innards of a gutted jaguar as if to strum them with the black-bladed tecpatl he grips in the other. Vessel can all too graphically imagine what became of the photographer not long thereafter.

"The Northern savages proclaim him to be a magician of true power," the Moctezuma intones. "A commander of the night and the wind. The agent of The Smoking Mirror upon the Earth perhaps, or perhaps not. What is true is that he preaches the death of the Triple Empire, and even now he skulks just beyond our reach, conspiring to make his prophecy a reality. Worse still, the savages listen to him. In this mad vision of his they perceive the illusion of escape from their rightful place in this world. They flock to his side, donning jaguar pelts and murdering at his command, all for the false hope of freedom."

Vessel does not miss how the rightmost slave girl looks askance at the word *savage*. Her complexion, brown as *mizquitl* seed, marks her out as a Northerner as well. For centuries their kind has fed Tenochtitlan. Its needs, and hungers, and most of all, its thirsts.

She does not meet his eyes. If she were to, she might notice features like her own.

"By dint of chance or evil agency," the Moctezuma continues, "this man has come by a certain artifact of unspeakable power." A second photograph replaces the first — presumably the last before the spy was found out. The same angle, but now the Holy Man holds something aloft. A ball of stone, a large gem? Vessel squints. The mottled shadows conceal just enough. The Moctezuma bolts down a pink worm of muscle, slicks his jowls with a heavy tongue. "If he should transport this artifact to Tenochtitlan, throne of the Sun," he says, with a belch as grave as can be, "the city would face destruction. And without Tenochtitlan, the rest of our Empire will surely fall. For what body can survive without its heart?"

The snake in Vessel's chest, who has thus far lain in a silent, disinterested coil, delivers an arid chuckle. *I can think of an exception.*

"We foresee the arc of civilization turning down," the Moctezuma says. "The *Caxtiltecatl* yet bide their time across the sea. Though we crushed the Pale Men once before, we failed to destroy them, and in peace they have grown strong again. Make no mistake — at the first sniff of weakness, they will come by sea to relitigate history, and I fear that we will not be victorious twice."

Vessel's gaze drifts to the stone reliefs that encircle the dome of the throne room, scenes of the same antiquities of which the Moctezuma is both so proud and yet so fearful of ever seeing again. The Pale Men, with their marvelous ships, their impossible metal weapons, alighting upon the Middle Country like invaders from another world. The battles that followed, the drama, the human bravery, obsidian clashing with harquebus. Hard-won victory at last, the Pale Men herded into the sea, their technology seized and made the steel backbone of an empire the likes of which the world had not then known.

Vessel jerks at a phlegmy grunt from the Moctezuma. There is a red speck of blood upon his cheek where his rightmost slave girl accidentally nicked him with her meat skewer. Annoyed, he swats her on the small of her back and sends her tumbling down the steps of his throne. Vessel hears her neck snap halfway to the bottom.

The impromptu sacrifice sparks a candle's flame of some emotion in the cold gulf where he remembers passions once roaring. It is too dim to tell exactly what it could be, and in a moment without a heartbeat, it is gone again. It only occurs to him then that he could have caught her, if he'd so desired. It's been so long since he's felt the urge, and it would not have mattered if he had. The snake would not have let him snatch her life from the teeth of the Sun who loomed so opportunistically over the city. At the first whiff of rebellious urge it would bite the soft meat between his ribs, envenoming him with excruciating will, and he would surrender. It is much easier to want nothing in the first place.

Quite right.

The fallen slave girl twitches. Her face, so like his own, becomes a mask.

Her mouth overflows with green-blue feathers.

"Our champion, you've said nothing," the Moctezuma observes. "We implore you now — find this Holy Man, slay him, and recover his weapon. Will you accept this mission?"

Say yes already, the snake hisses. *His smell offends me.*

"Yes," says the serpent's vessel.

Three cars later, Vessel bursts into a compartment that is not full of armed cultists. Adrenalin spigots out the many new holes in his body, and he collapses against the door, where he catches his breath and takes stock of his injuries. There are two bullets lodged in his chest, a third in his bicep, and an assortment of knife wounds in his arms and back. He experiences the pain as a tidy conspectus to be perused at will or ignored entirely. A half-alive body can only feel half as much.

The sky outside the window has darkened by degrees. In the time it took him to kill seventeen cultists, the train clattered on at least that many kilometers. Commandeered from a depot on the Empire's northern frontier, the train is now en route to Tenochtitlan, with or without its crew. No way now to get word ahead. Within a matter of hours, it'll plow deep into the city and unleash its devastating payload. Vessel hasn't a clue what the artifact might be, but something surer than faith must have fired it into the heart of the Empire; Vessel can only trust that the Holy Man isn't mad enough to draw on Tenochtitlan with an empty gun.

Quick, say the words, the snake implores. *Before all that good blood starts to dry.*

"For the Sun," Vessel murmurs wearily. "And for the Feathered Serpent."

Why thank you.

Vessel holsters his revolver — he's got no bullets left to fill it with — and unsheathes his tecpatl before venturing deeper into the train. A cramped stairwell funnels him up to the car's third story, where improperly fastened sconces cast dim, nervous light upon a grated floor. A faint smell tickles his nostrils — sweat, urine, blood — and then stabs itself like a stiletto into his brain. Masking himself with the back of his hand and ignoring the complaints of the snake that shares his nose, Vessel stoops to follow the odor to its source. Squinting through the perforations in the floor it becomes suddenly apparent what freight the train carries.

Men and women are packed tight as bricks within the cargo hold below. Nude, shaven, branded upon the base of the skull. A hideous commercial sagacity has fit their unique bodies together to maximize storage volume, matching contour to contour, buttock to belly, groin to cheek. They seem insensate, drugged perhaps for the long, hot trip, but feeble moans reach Vessel's ears, nonetheless. Shackles bind the throng into a single, wretched amalgamation of flesh —

Flesh in the same earthen shade as his.

Vessel was on a train like this, once. The memory feels impossibly distant now — he must reach further back than he's been alive to drag it back up. He recalls jaguar-spotted soldiers ravening through his village, recalls being tested, as all slaves are, and being dubbed unsuitable for labor. He went on one train, while his family — now a collection of blank faces and soundless voices — went on another, to somewhere else. In a coffin of other people, he was taken to Tenochtitlan and put into a line that serpentined to the top of a ziggurat where a *cuauhxicalli* awaited — a stone bowl stained deeply red.

His past is a torn and faded map. It goes blank where the blade carves into his chest, and continues at the foot of the temple, with the snake entwining with his entrails on the way to his vacant sternum. More clearly than the faces of his children he remembers the look of horror on the priest's face when Vessel climbed back up the temple steps to slug him in the jaw.

That was the last bit of choice he had left in him. The last wisp of fire.

After that, the snake started talking, and its words were as cold and final as a grave beneath the desert.

"Snake," Vessel says.

Yes? What is it?

An involuntary shudder at the tickle of its forked tongue against his vertebrae. "I want to know," he says. "What stake does the Feathered Serpent have in the Triple Empire?" He rarely speaks to the snake, preferring to ignore the body nested strangely in his own, but this feels important. "Why not the Caxtiltecatl, or someone else?"

Simple. A shrug rolls through the length of the snake's body. *My interest is that mankind survives into the future. To that end, men must die, and die industriously. Blood keeps the Sun above Tenochtitlan, the Stars at bay, and the Triple Empire is a factory of sacrifices with no equal. Nowhere else do the lines stretch so far from the temple tops. Nowhere else are the* cuauhxicalli *so over-full with hearts.*

The snake turns over inside of him, its sandpapery caress the loveless touch of a wife after the love has dried up. *If this empire should crumble, that blood will cease to flow, the Sun will fall, and the hungry Stars will devour this world so painstakingly created by the god of which I am but a feather. You people really have no idea how much my greater self invested in humanity. Bridges were burned, I can assure you. I slit my penis open to birth your race from my blood. My tongue too, if you wondered why it has two points.*

"Why me?" Vessel asks.

That is simple too, the snake replies. *You were someone. There was a need.*

"I hated the Triple Empire." Of that he's mostly sure. It comes easily to him, like the taste of a favorite food. It must have meant a lot to him, that loathing.

Oh, that didn't matter. Really, it was that you were empty.

The snake tenses suddenly and then reorients itself, a small whirlwind of rasping scales.

"What is it?"

Danger.

Vessel looks up. A man has appeared in the corridor where there was no man before, not even the sound of one approaching. So massive is he that his shoulders nearly touch both walls, and the cap of his shaven head casts a shadow upon the ceiling. Burn scars layer his bare hands in emulation of a jaguar's spots; a butcher's inventory of tecpatl hangs off his belt. In the center of his face is a disk of jet black, shiny with sweat, in which two wide eyes twinkle with amusement.

"Are you the one they call the Holy Man?" Vessel asks.

The other man grins with teeth dyed red. "No, merely a follower," he laughs. "The priest of a living prophet. You will never meet that great man."

Be cautious, my vessel, the snake hisses. *This one is different than the others. I smell power in him. I think that he has gazed into the Smoking Mirror and become Naguali.*

Vessel stiffens at that word. *Naguali*; a magician; a shapeshifter; thing perpendicular to human.

"I can hear that little voice inside of you," the Nagual says. "You're the dead man with the feather of Quetzalcoatl in his breast. Oh, you poor, heartless creature. How tragic to be puppeteered by a thing with no hands."

"If you know that much, then you'll know to step aside," Vessel replies. He's wasting time here, but a brawl would waste more still.

Don't bother, the snake says. *Kill him, quickly.*

The Nagual chuckles into tight lips. "Yes, little dead man, listen to your master. I won't move. I have gifted my life to a greater purpose than living. My spirit has already reached the bright future to come. My body remains as a wall."

"And what bright future would that be?"

The Nagual's eyes narrow to half-moons. "The one that follows the death of the Triple Empire," he says. "When all peoples of this land are liberated from the hunger of the Sun. That is what the Holy Man has promised us. The men and women beneath your feet? Once marked for sacrifice, now they are the first of the free."

"You intend to let them go?"

That chuckle again. The laugh of a predator amused by its prey. "No, no. The plan requires them. All things of value cost a volume of blood. Your *Mexica* understand that best. But although they may not know it yet, their hearts will be the seeds from which a better world grows. How can anyone aspire higher? So, I say it is you who should turn back. Let us do what you know is right."

"All I know is that I can't," Vessel says.

The Nagual shakes his head remorsefully, then claps his palm to his mouth. He shows Vessel the two dried mushroom caps the color of sand on his tongue, and then sucks them between his lips, chewing with relish as his pupils grow to eclipse his eyes. *Teonanacatl*, Vessel thinks. Rare and powerful. Ingesting a single stalk enables one to perceive the universe as the gods do, as a much-amended manuscript. Ingesting two allows one to scribble in the margins, add new language, cross out words.

"Snake," Vessel says, but in this he and his passenger are of one mind, and the fangs of Quetzalcoatl's feather puncture deep into him, pumping liquid divinity into his veins.

The effect is instantaneous; before Vessel's eyes, the world unsimplifies. The constraints of singularity that bind all things fall away, allowing *one* to blossom into its infinite inner truths, to become everything it can be, could be, is not, but almost, and all at once. Paper pulls away from word, and the tecpatl in Vessel's hand accordions into a pistol, a scorpion, a twilight-purple morning glory, all the possibilities once buried beneath layers of ontological revisions. All around him, the walls of the train dissolve into a desert of obsidian sand that stretches from one horizon to the other, in which mile-high saguaros creak in nonexistent winds.

The Nagual is there with him, and he too has unfolded like a paper fan into a compound thing that is as much a man as it is a bonfire, a song of braided screams, and most prominently a red-fanged jaguar, whose hands are murky with indistinct weapons. He bounds across the dunes like an inferno on four paws kicking sand up into gaseous shadows, but Vessel is a meagerness of flesh dispersed through colloidal abstraction, and the Nagual's fangs snap shut on tumbleweeds and sun-bleached bones. Vessel is a limbless creature, a whirlwind of many-colored scales, a smirking lie slithering on its belly, the perfect quip. He is all these things that can melt through teeth, and a man squeezing off shot after shot from an infinite-chambered revolver, leaden emptinesses chipped off the heart-shaped cavity stabbed clean through every one of his interpretations like a knife gone through a deck of cards.

Like gods in the heavens, like children in the schoolyard, they grapple and claw upon the black dunes of eternity. The sky has been flayed into its many layers of atmosphere and so they fight in the radiant hate of the Stars, the *Tzitzimitil*, manifested in their truest, most soul-blistering forms. Cosmic vultures incandescent with bilious light, they jostle at the bars of the Earth, maddened to a frenzy by the saccharine stench of mortal bloodshed.

Obsidian talons rake Vessel's hollow breast; maize kernels fountain from the wound. The Nagual's eyes spark — zinnias with hot coals in their centers. *You are of my people too. The master you serve killed both our families.* The Nagual speaks with a professor's pity for an incapable student, calm, sad, even as feline yowls carve through the same gullet. *Where is the wisdom in fighting me? We could have done so much more together.*

Vessel's eyes flail in their sockets, and whenever they should tip back into his skull, he glimpses faces without features, hears names that all rhyme with silence. The pieces left of what was taken, and not even the best pieces. *I don't have a choice*, Vessel snarls through the film of man that trails from him like a half-shed snakeskin. *I am how a serpent pulls a trigger.*

The Nagual cackles — the sound of fat crackling over a fire. *When you tell yourself that lie, is it in your voice, or one with a forked tongue? We always have choices — they just aren't always easy. You could have chosen to blow your brains out and let that snake starve inside you. Instead, you chose to be a dog that hunts wolves.*

Vessel smothers his foe in lengths of himself, but the Nagual seems to revel in the struggle, a cat at play in the water. *I beg you, my cousin,* the man-beast implores, *throw down your wretched life already. Let me kill you. I promise that I will make it a mercy.*

For a moment Vessel is tempted, but he has no heart to lurch towards that kindness. What the Nagual can't know is that the name of his curse is apathy. In truth, it has been years since the snake compelled him to do anything at all. It is no longer the whiplash bite of the snake that makes him ride out to disappear the Moctezuma's enemies, but the threat of it. If he can't resist, why bother trying? The difference in outcome is measured in how much he'll suffer.

The Nagual is right. Vessel did have a choice, once; not to struggle, no, but to care regardless, in the face of futility. He remembers the slave girl lying broken on the ground, beseeching him in her final moments just to pity her, to let her wasted life affect *something*. It would have cost him nothing, and he could not give her even that.

There's that candle-flame again, only this time it doesn't go right out. A sensation emanates from it that he pegs as burning.

It's anger. He's *mad*.

Mad, to be a vehicle.

Mad, to have a mind so numb that it can't keep grip on his memories.

Mad, to have his shame reflected back at him as if by a smoking mirror.

Vessel bares his underbelly and invites the Nagual into his spiraling depths. He lets those rail-spike incisors cut through a hundred of his selves, all it takes to stick him fast and bind the Nagual in gusty coils. Vessel's fangs plunge deep into the core of throat that riddles the Nagual's manyances; venom flows as welcome as breath into his bloodstream. He holds the other man dearly as the Nagual howls and dies.

Vessel comes down from the realm of the gods slow and hard, squashed between the folds of the universe as it packs itself back into three claustrophobic dimensions. It's the rolling of the slave car that eventually shakes him awake into hide too small, a skull too tight, and a puddle of crusted vomit and blood he shares with the Nagual's corpse. He tries to stand, gets most of the way up, but his skeleton hitches on a foreign object. He's got a tecpatl wedged deep behind his clavicle.

"Snake," Vessel says, "I need patching up."

The feather of Quetzalcoatl says nothing in reply. Vessel isn't so naïve to think it dead. Merely drained. He can feel it stirring in its slumber.

The silence in his head is novel. Heady. He hasn't been alone with himself since he died. He glances back at the Nagual. The usual words leap onto his tongue — *for the Sun* — but this time he bites them back, for no other reason than the realization that he can. He forces himself to watch the hummingbird squirm from between mortified jaws and then flit about if unsure of where to go. Finally, it bumbles its way to an open window and flies off to where it will.

Vessel breathes out when the world does not come crashing down.

He cradles that flame of anger inside him as he staggers on towards the cab, stoking it with scraps of indignation. No sense in questioning it — it feels good to have warmth inside of him again. It feels good to feel goodness again. Here at the inescapable end of his mission it is a welcome comfort.

The cultists have made a crude altar of the engine room door, festooning it with shards of obsidian, turkey feathers, rosettes of dried blood. Vessel rests his hand on the frame, feels it shiver not just with the mean power of locomotion but a stranger energy, as if suspended on the cusp of some eruptive moment, ready to launch. The handle turns easily when he tries it.

He hesitates anyway.

He's stumbled onto a few seconds that are his alone. If he's quick he can carve out his throat. Maybe leap off the train and let the immortal snake bake forever within his dried-out corpse.

But people are a convenience to an engine in motion. For better or worse, the train will power on without him towards a conclusion he won't be able to help, being dead. That doesn't quite sit right with him.

He sees the slave girl again. Pleading with dead eyes. Somehow, she feels more real in his memory than she did in flesh.

Oblivion beckons, but the lure of the crossroads ahead is more powerful still.

Vessel throws open the door. There is a blur of movement on the other side. What might be an edge winks in the dark. His hand acts, unsheathing the tecpatl from his clavicle and sending it aloft.

A meaty impact. A one-lunged gasp.

The Holy Man of the North collapses with a blade lodged in his chest.

There is no one else in the cab, which is just as well, as Vessel has run out of weapons. He kneels beside the Holy Man and claps him on the jaw. The other man's eyes spin fearfully and then reorient on him.

"I'm dead," he says, his voice as thin as a well-worn excuse.

"Getting there," Vessel nods.

"I supposed it would end like this," the Holy Man wheezes. "It still hurts."

The man is younger than Vessel would have guessed. A Northerner, by his complexion, but he knew that much. He doesn't look like he could whip a desperate people up into a murderous cult, not that anyone would in his condition. His right hand sticks up in the air, shackled by a short chain to one of the dozens of pipes kinking along the ceiling, keeping him well out of reach of the arsenal of valves, levers, and switches that make up the locomotive's steam-driven cerebellum. With his flickering anger as a reference Vessel can feel a slight chill of regret. The man was harmless, his death an extravagance.

The rest of the man is collapsed against a chest of carven stone, his weight insufficient to dislodge its heavy lid. Vessel reaches out to touch it, only for the Holy Man's hand to snap shut around his wrist with a surprising strength — those last words had sounded fairly final.

"Destroy it," the Holy Man says. "Please. I, I wanted to bring ruin to Tenochtitlan. Yes. But, only that. Not everything. Not the world."

Vessel gently takes his hand back. "I don't understand."

"Listen." The Holy Man hisses like a bladder losing air. "This is the Fifth Universe. There were four before it, all gone. Flood, fire, hurricane. Mankind too, destroyed four times, recreated four times. The Smoking Mirror came to me in a vision, showed me everything. It and the Feathered Serpent have fought over each universe from the very start — one destroying, the other creating, over and over and over again —"

"I don't have time for stories," Vessel interjects. It won't be long before the snake wakes up. Whatever he does after that won't be up to him.

"Listen!" the Holy Man snaps. "The people of that first universe weren't human." His fingers claw feebly across the lid of the box. "Worlds end, but bones remain. The Smoking Mirror told me where to find them, taught me the secret of how to bring them back to life." He breaks off to pant until he's mustered up breath enough to speak. "Inside is the skull of a primordial giant."

The train clatters over a patch of scabby terrain, jostling the cab, causing the Holy Man to moan. "The Smoking Mirror gave me a mission," he says. "Take the skull into Tenochtitlan, use blood of slaves to give it life again. It told me that it would lay low the slavemasters and break every chain. I believed it. I wanted to believe. But I wondered — what did it matter where I awoke the giant? So my god told me.

"Tenochtitlan is the throne of the Sun. Where Huitzilopochtli resides throughout the day. As soon as the giant wakes, it will reach into the sky and restrain him, take him by surprise, hold him there just long enough for the Stars to descend and devour it. And that — that will be the end of it. Of everything."

His swings his suspended hand, rattling his shackle. "Tried to tell my people. Turns out I'm not the voice of my god. Just the lips." Tears unspool from his eyes and puddle upon the box. "The Smoking Mirror told me I would break the cycle of slavery and sacrifice," he sobs. "Free mankind from the hunger of the gods. What shit. All I did was crank the cycle on. You and me and everyone, we're just collateral in a grudge between gods. The world that comes after this one won't be any different."

The Holy Man pauses to suck down a breath; it sounds like he's losing more than he's taking in. "I never wanted things to go this far," he says, and that is the last thing that is truly his choice to say, for what comes next is that final truth that everyone carries from the day they're born, predestined to every soul, that waits all one's life for its turn to be spoken before the lights go out. "Even after all I've seen," he says, "I think — I know — the world can still be good. If people only mattered for the hearts we carry, we'd be nothing else."

"I'm sorry I killed you," Vessel says.

He waits for the Holy Man to reply, but there is no more coming. His tongue has fallen still against his cheek, his gaze fixed on whatever it was he was seeing when his heart ran out of steam.

Vessel heaves the body aside and, with an effort, slides the lid off the box. Wrinkled cornhusks line the inside as ad-hoc padding, though he catches no more than a glimpse before the utter blackness of the object nestled within violently overflows the confines of its matter and envelops him. He stumbles as a darkened lens clicks into place between him and the world. All the pitted, rusted, tarnished metal surfaces of the cab suddenly gleam like burnished obsidian; a thousand mirrors reflect as many warped interpretations of Vessel's features back at him. And in this splintered mirror-world he is not alone, for as he looks on, a great, rippling imperfection moves through it like something squaliform and many-fanged knifing through lightless waters.

Vessel of my enemy.
It's a pleasure.

The voice emanates from everywhere invisible. From the blindness beyond the edge of his vision, from just over his shoulder. The spiraling bones in his ears whisper it to him. It echoes between the two halves of his brain. It is the voice of the unobtainable, that which pulls away as one reaches for it, taunting and tantalizing. It has not come, but merely deigned to be more intently where it was all along — perpetually a hair's width from Vessel's longest fingertip, on just the other side of a shadow. The Lord of the Near and Nigh, The Enemy of Both Sides, *The Smoking Mirror* — is here.

Tezcatlipoca is here.

Everything my prophet said to you is true, the god declares unabashedly. **It is my ambition to end this stale world and start again. I wish to rise again as the Earth's black sun, as was my right so very long ago now.**

But that means nothing to you, does it?

Let us speak on what concerns a walking dead man.

Through spaces outside the three base dimensions the voice slinks closer to the node in his brain that receives it. **You know better than any what a waste this world is**, it croons. Vessel watches his clouded reflections mouth along in exaggerated, jaw-wrenching pantomime. **An empty train carrying nothing towards nowhere, yet demanding ever more fuel to do so. It took your heart, and for what? To sustain the Sun until the next heart it wants. Your suffering was forgotten long ago, little vessel, if it was ever noticed at all.**

A pitying chuckle from a maw as deep as despair. **The death of my prophet is an opportunity for you**, the god says. **There is the weapon.**

Giant skulls flower throughout the fractured mirror.

There is the ammunition.

The Holy Man's lifeless features.

The Sun waits unsuspecting above the city of your slavers.

Wet the skull. Loose the Stars. End the pain.

Vessel stoops to pick up the skull, dark and dense as lead, and stares into its fist-sized eye-pits, which go on further than the skull is long. The fossilized thing is a relic from an epoch when existence was a novel concept, when the laws of nature were messy with scribbles and errors. There is *more* contained within this thing than its dimensions evidence. It has shriveled like a sponge for want of blood.

The god's voice thins to a seductive whisper, sweet as manchineel fruit. **I am a good god; I offer rewards upon rewards. It is liberation you desire, and you will have it. Do as I ask, and I shall guide you deeper into death than my foe can ever reach. And while you sleep forever, your hard task done, I will make the next world a better one.**

I promise.

Vessel considers the offer. Sincerely.

With the snake yet insensate, the choice is upon him. It would be easiest to accept death, he supposes. No one could rightly blame him for it. The world is too great to possibly be his burden.

Then he thinks of the slave girl. The thousand like her even now lined up before bloody ziggurats. The thousands yet to come. All of them aware of the world they'd been cursed into, all of them hoping to live through it all the same. To mean more than the weight of their hearts.

He cannot imagine as many faces as they must have. It is difficult to spread so little care so thin.

But as one paroled from death, it costs him nothing to live a little longer. It costs him nothing to give what he does not have.

Vessel places the skull back in its box and lifts its stone lid in both hands. "I think if you and the Feathered Serpent were going to get it right," he says, "you'd have done it long ago,"

With that he swings the lid at the train's control panel. Halfway there it strikes a phantom solidity in the air, not the mess of machinery but the bolus of ab-reality pimpled up where the universe reacted allergically to the fingertip touch of the evil god. With the shriek of an angry jaguar the bubble bursts, leaving Vessel once more in the realm of the firm and definite, with breaking glass ringing in his ears.

Well done, my vessel, says a voice from inside, his twisted conscience.

"You were awake for all that?"

For a minute or five, the snake purrs. *I wanted to see what you would do without me. I was not disappointed.* It turns over and over inside of Vessel, luxuriating in victory. *All that's left now is to take the skull back to Tenochtitlan.*

"Doesn't seem wise to do your enemy's work for him," Vessel notes.

A dusty snicker from within. *No sense in letting something useful go to waste. The Feathered Serpent has great love for* mankind, but that love is conditional. Should it prove ... disappointing, well, it is the nature of worlds to end, and cycles to continue. You understand.

Vessel imagines all the blood it would take to dye giant hands red.

"No, I don't think I do," Vessel says, lifting the heavy lid overhead.

Stop! The snake cries, hammering its fangs into his flesh. Pain nearly blasts the lid from Vessel's hands. His resolve flickers like a failing lightbulb, but he refuses to let go. The snake can make him suffer, can make him cold in the soul, but it doesn't have a pair of hands to steer him with. All he's got to do is hold on to what he's got to do even when his will's used up. Again and again the snake strikes, overflowing his veins with venom, until an hour or a year later, it at last runs dry, and collapses like a slit rope.

Vessel brings the lid down on top of the skull, cracking it neatly in half. Its latent power whiffs away without a sound.

The snake pants, its tail weakly rattling. *I'll make every moment you live an original torture.*

Vessel shakes his head. "All you can do is bite me. That'll hurt, but I suspect I'll get numb." He probes the long scar where his heart came out, feeling how stubbornly that tissue holds together, determined not to yield a second time. "The cut you slithered in through's all healed over. You don't have an exit, do you? No, I doubt the Feathered Serpent ever deigned to put a feather back on. I'd gamble you're stuck with me. Maybe you'd better act nice."

The snake, it seems, has nothing to say about that.

Vessel opens the side door to the cab to let out the Holy Man's increasingly frantic hummingbird. He climbs onto the outer catwalk and lets the hot wind snatch his hat away. The train is racing the Sun towards the horizon; it doesn't look like they'll beat it there.

From here, Huitzilopochtli, the Sun, looks plump and healthy. A big golden baby geared for war. Vessel's got to wonder whether it needs that daily blood transfusion to keep rolling on through its rounds, or if the commonplace violence of man throughout the world does the trick just fine.

There is no other way, you fool, the snake spits, oh so sullenly, but Vessel is skeptical; the snake has been wrong before, and recently to boot.

Maybe there's an alternative. Maybe there isn't. Vessel's been plenty wrong too. From where stands, however, it seems rash to trash the universe in the hope of something better. He supposes he'll find out.

Until then, the desert remains ahead. The train rolls on. There are stops between here and Tenochtitlan, where he can unshackle the slaves and decide where to go from there. Perhaps he'll change the world. Perhaps he'll just be free.

For now, Vessel stretches himself over the railing and enjoys the warmth on his face.

Sudden Oak Death

J. Tynan Burke

Arboreal silhouettes filled the unilluminated park around Dr. Kort Zantoosian. Behind the foliage, the milky haze of Saturn's E ring shone through an astroglass dome. But Kort saw none of this, for he was floating inside the canopy of his favorite tree, its branching tendrils surrounding him in a near-perfect sphere. Of all the trees he'd grown in the park, this Zantoosian black oak, which he'd nicknamed the Orb, was his favorite. It was, he thought, just a great, really very good tree. Words failed him when he drank.

Kort tapped a command into his wrist tablet, and air jets from his belt hissed him into a lazy somersault. As he spun, he drank from the pouch of whiskey he'd brought. Sometimes it felt pretty great to be Kort Zantoosian; better, he often worried, than he deserved.

In the shelter of the Orb, he could let go of his worries, most of which concerned his duties as Head of Arboriculture at New Lahej Orbital Habitation Park. No more did he fret over the typo he'd discovered on a requisition form from the previous week. Kort didn't even think about the park's mediocre review in the latest *Lonely Planet: Saturn*. He just admired his handiwork.

Creating this species of oak had been one of his rare strokes of youthful genius. He probably could've parlayed it into an associate professorship somewhere, but was that any way to live? Besides, it turned out he had a knack for systems engineering. These trees were a perfect synergy of biological research, his first love; and the slow grind of forestry, his true talent and a sometimes-adequate replacement. His research had gotten him hired, but it was his engineering chops that had made him, and the park, semi-famous. A beautiful space, filled with artfully-crafted exemplars of his eponymous species of oak — *that* was pure Kort Zantoosian.

This simple confidence lasted until he noticed a lump bulging on a branch. He ordered his belt thrusters to bring him closer and turned on his jumpsuit's lamp. After a drunken minute, he identified the crinkled lump as a gall. He hadn't seen one in years. Habitations tended not to have insects at all, not to mention ones that laid eggs in plants. How had a bug gotten past their defenses?

Kort's easily frightened self-regard vanished, replaced with a familiar dejection. He cursed. Maybe *Lonely Planet* had been right, and the park really was only "recommended on Free First Fridays".

A bleep from his wrist tablet reminded him that he had somewhere to be. Aided by the alcohol, he shook off his rumination. The gall would still be there in the morning. At his instruction, his thrusters carried him out of the oak. His mood lifted as he flew past terraces of curling roses, stands of yellowing aspen, and a three-dimensional hedge maze. The thrusters brought him to a rest area by the dome wall. With one arm through a grab hoop, Kort drank from his pouch of whiskey and waited.

The E ring was a vast cloud of mineral water that spewed from Enceladus. The moon would spend the rest of its existence ensconced in this fog, but New Lahej, which orbited Enceladus's poles, broke free at the height of its trajectory. Kort watched as the ring plane fell below him at thousands of kilometers per hour, becoming a featureless gray sea that stretched to the horizon. At the same time, the dawn terminator crested over Saturn's dark bulk, revealing the planet before him. Kort sipped from his pouch and stared, like a child riding a space elevator for the first time. Planetrise — this monthly conjunction — never got old. But humans did, Kort had learned, and at local midnight it was past his usual bedtime; after thirty minutes, he floated out of the park dome to the axial monorail, which he rode to the aft habitation discs.

The next morning, he bought a pack of hangover nanobots on the way to the lab; he'd outgrown the goals of his old grad-student self, but not the drinking habits. Perhaps he still had some of the old modes of thought, too: being responsible for solving problems at scale could be such *drudgery*. But duty called, even if, as seemed likely, this was the fault of the pest-control people, not him. At least getting to the bottom of this would be good for the oaks.

He convened a crisis-management team, ordering them to search the park for bugs. He would lead the search for more galls himself, as was his professional responsibility. This would also let him humor a psychological dysfunction which told him the gall represented a personal failing. Still, the task required *some* delegation, which went to Iphie and Dewen, his hand-picked interns.

Curiously, the team didn't find a single bug. The gall was even more curious. It was warm to the touch, getting warmer, and apparently alone in the park. He couldn't say much more with certainty. The Enceladan Authority had never sent the DNA sequencer they'd promised, so he'd have to do a visual identification of the creature inside. He spent the coming days waiting for it to grow just large enough for a confident identification. The gnawing apprehension made his neck itch, and he found unaccustomed respite in his routine late-summer tasks.

Eleven mornings later, Kort was floating before the gall, inside the Orb's sphere of branches. He was flanked by Iphie and Dewen, and not a few camera drones. Lit up by floodlights, and carrying an ionic multitool, he was reminded that an arcane term for 'arborist' was 'tree surgeon.' He half-smiled, then slipped back into his usual grim mask. Nothing here was amusing.

When he cut one side off the gall, a cloud of dust escaped and spread steadily outwards. Kort released a vacuum drone from his toolbelt and squinted at the deformity; the inside of the gall was scaled with burns, but otherwise empty. Pushing back from the branch with a groan, he closed his eyes and held the multitool out to Iphie. "Did I set this to something stupid?"

She turned it in her hands. "Why'd you dial it to 'vaporize', boss?"

Kort swallowed. Dewen shook his head and plucked the tool away. "Let's cut Dr. Z a break. Multitool's set to 'incise', doc." He placed it in Kort's still-waiting palm.

Kort holstered it with a sniff. He just knew he'd screwed this up, and doomed the park, or at least the Orb — though he couldn't articulate *how*. "Can you two clean this up? Start analyzing the dust and make sure this thing's really empty." He jetted away before anybody saw that his eyes had started to water; right before he exited the Orb, he spun around. "Be back in a few hours." He didn't mention that he'd be getting a Monte Cristo and a Bloody Mary at his favorite greasy spoon over in the habitation discs.

"Hell of a time for one of Iphigenia Halikas's famous jokes," he heard Dewen say. Iphie giggled.

Later, smelling of fry-oil and tomato, Kort joined them in the lab, where they summarized their findings. The dust was ashes, the interior of the gall was uniformly charred, and it was indeed empty. None of the three had heard of anything like it, a problem the park's database seemed to share. *A second-rate library for a second-rate arboriculture department*, Kort thought with a frown, at an *"okay to miss if you aren't already in New Lahej"* park — a downgrade from their peak a few years ago. It was still a better review than the ones before he'd joined; that cheered him up some days, though this was not one of them.

Any number of things could explain the gall. Most likely, a bug had hitched a ride inside somebody's clothes, and Kort's tool had simply malfunctioned. Unless it recurred, well, *shit happens*. Besides, Kort couldn't linger on low-priority unsolved mysteries: it was time to begin the preparations for leaf-fall. People visited by the thousands every year for that magical season, when the leaves changed colors and detached, turning the dome into a botanical snow-globe. It was the one thing *Lonely Planet* had found to compliment without reservation. Given the park's funding realities, leaf-fall was also more important than ever. So Kort's arboriculture department focused their energies on beautification, and interventions that would stretch the season.

On evenings and weekends, Kort practiced classic video games for an upcoming tournament, spitting curses at his ancient and buggy haptic bodysuit. Once, at an invitation from Iphie and Dewen, he attended a showing of *Titanian Tulips*, an inaccurate rom-com set during the first successful terraforming.

One afternoon, while Kort was fiddling with the aspens' hydroponics tanks, Iphie approached looking nervous. There were more galls, she told him, with a strained expression. She'd found them in the Zantoosian black oak at the park's entrance. "Let me know how I can help," she added.

Kort rested his hand on the case surrounding the root bulb, harder than he needed to. He had written off his earlier fears as depressive false prophecy; it was never a good day when those were actually confirmed. "I see." Feeling his mind dissociate from the issue, he looked off to the wall of haze outside the astroglass. "Thanks."

Iphie pulled herself along a tree trunk and reoriented herself to be level with Kort. The movement released a drift of cherry-red leaves from what was now over her head.

Kort's mind clutched at the distraction. "The aspens are a little early," he said, pointing at the leaves. "I'm just about to add fescue extract to their water; there was a paper in *Astroarboricultural Digest* ..."

Iphie put on the half-smile she used to humor people. "Is that Brenndan Gwilt's study?"

Kort blinked twice. "Your faculty mentor, isn't he? Small worlds." Sometimes he forgot Iphie had come recommended by a researcher more eminent than he'd ever be. He poked idly at some pipettes.

Iphie nodded at the water-treatment setup. "I can probably handle this, if you want to go look at the —"

Kort snapped back to reality. "The galls. Yes." A stomachache began to stir in his belly. "If you could take over on the aspens …" He looked down and tapped something into his wrist tablet. "You have my notes."

"Won't let you down, boss." Iphie pulled herself to the workstation. *I can trust a protege of Gwilt's to feed a plant and fix the plumbing*, Kort thought, using the derogatory terms he'd heard for arboriculture in the academy. Stomach tightening further, he blew out a deep breath and hauled himself away with a nearby grab hoop.

While he jetted to the tree he called the Corona, Kort tried to keep his mind blank, but rumination struck when he reached the canopy. He'd known the Corona's broad halo of branches for almost two decades, from when he'd planted it at the entrance to dazzle spacefarers. He knew every twist and turn of its fractal limbs; like the other oaks, shaping it had been a painstaking, years-long process.

Inspecting the perfectly proportioned branches was almost enjoyable, except for his ratcheting nerves. When he found the first gall, the tension became otherworldly. Lizard-brain panic gripped him; he was in free-fall, towards every surface at once. He cast around for something to orient himself with. Only the gall could hold his attention. Looking at it made him feel helpless, but that was preferable to the feeling of imminent death. So he stared at the gall, willing the canopy to be 'down'. Eventually perception came around.

The galls were like crumbs in a kitchen: with each one he saw, three more revealed themselves. Then nine more. The exponential proliferation was as stunning as a broken nose. He felt, for lack of a better term, weightless.

Where had all these galls come from? It would've taken a whole swarm of insects to lay this many eggs. Surely the park staff, still on high alert, would have detected that. And why were they only affecting Zantoosian black oaks? The trees were mostly the same age; was this a genetic flaw? Would they soon all become disfigured? Kort's face began to twitch. Perhaps he shouldn't have created the species; perhaps oak trees were *supposed* to turn to spindly knots in microgravity. All he'd done was paste in the allometry genes from an ancient shrub called Kepler Kudzu. All it was supposed to pass on was its beautiful form in microgravity. He'd had an AI read every source on it he could find; it was a hardy plant, with no records of disease, and no predators.

Kort pawed through the branches until he accidentally crushed a gall in his fist, mashing something hot into his hand. He yelped and shook it away; half-singed chips of wood dislodged from his palm. He stared at the stippled wound, not quite a burn. Face twisted in disgust, he released a vacuum drone, then ran away to the lab, where he could have his nervous breakdown in peace.

He locked the hatch behind him. The disinfectant he sprayed on his palm burned, but was not the reason tears welled in his eyes. While he slapped on a bandage to keep himself from scratching, he did breathing exercises. Zantoosian black oaks were his legacy, from a time when he made things, instead of just doing them. And now the whole species was a potential fire hazard.

Once he'd calmed down, he arranged for a meeting with the park's administrative director, Helen Ramsey.

Helen suggested removing all the oaks from the park. It was a polite way of saying Kort should space them. She reflected aloud on the wisdom of keeping smoldering wood sitting around a space station.

Kort countered that 'smoldering' was an exaggeration — they were barely sixty degrees, about the same as a hot water pipe. He suggested that they could identify galls with infrared imaging and remove them manually. This was no time to be eliminating signature attractions; the Orb was even in their logo. Besides, orbitals dealt in this level of risk for anything worth doing, from cooking to electricity generation.

Helen showed her palms and shrugged. As long as it wasn't spreading, she said. Kort was the expert. "And remember," she concluded, "dead people don't buy concessions."

Kort bit off a sarcastic reply. Detecting this, Helen gave a sympathetic smile. Having worked alongside him for years, she could read his emotional state better than he cared to admit.

Kort tasked the interns with finding and lancing the rest of the galls. This left Kort to study their source alone, as he liked it. The others might lead him down the wrong path. Also, as he happily told himself during his plentiful moments of darkness, the whole thing was his fault, and his alone to fix. If it was a genetic malfunction, then his academic research was to blame; if he couldn't solve the problem with more research, it would be final proof that he was a failure as a scientist.

Every research path Kort pursued hit a dead end. He began to feel like a cactus in a drought, sinking a taproot ever deeper in search of water that just wasn't there. His nightly video game practice sessions grew shorter, punctuated with ever-fiercer blasphemies. He lost his hairbrush and neglected to buy a new one; his hair came to resemble the oak by the park's entrance. After three days of this, Helen invited him to dinner.

He was familiar with this sort of invitation. She was worried about him. Her semi-managerial status over him always made such things awkward; they'd built out the park together, and he considered her a friend, but they were not peers. Kort spent the hour before fretting over nothing and everything.

The two ate at a Titanian-fusion restaurant inside one of the spinning habitation discs. Their table featured a tablet showing a stabilized view from outside. Unfortunately, at that point in New Lahej's orbit, said view was of impenetrable gloom.

Once they'd ordered, Kort poured himself a second glass of wine. "Let's get this out of the way — what's on your mind?"

Helen gestured at his hair and rumpled shirt. "You've looked like it's laundry day for half a week. I wanted to check in."

Kort had assumed as much, so his nonchalance was reasonably convincing. He took a sip of wine, a passable Titanian burgundy, which was staining his lips red. "Nothing to be concerned about. I've been working harder than ever."

"You know how you get. Take care of yourself." Helen retrieved some beansprouts from a communal dish. "Which brings me to my second point. Let's bring in some help. An expert."

Kort's hand stopped on its way to the vinegar. "I am an expert."

"You know what I mean. A specialist."

"In what?" Kort grabbed the vinegar and gave what he hoped was a genial laugh. "Mysterious tree fevers?"

After a thoughtful bite of tofu, Helen said, "There's a researcher down below who's interested. Brenndan Gwilt, at Shahrazad."

"You don't say," Kort muttered, mouth as small as he felt. A *real* research scientist coming in to fix his problems. And his intern's mentor, to boot. Moments like this made him wonder if he served any actual function.

155

He remembered he had food, and tucked into his jook. His blood pressure lowered after a moment. Helen was only doing what was best for the park. "As long as he brings a research capsule."

Helen let out a held breath and took a generous drink of wine. "You can tell him yourself. I scheduled you a holo at eleven tomorrow."

After dinner, they parted ways at the lift; Kort's cabin was in a different disc, and he'd need to get there via the axial monorail. "Remember, we're all on your team," Helen said. "And you're never alone on a team. Eleven tomorrow." She waved goodbye and walked off, slippers thwapping on the tile floor.

What Helen had left unsaid — that *he* needed to be a team player too — was not lost on him. He trudged back to his cabin, where he turned on the vanity lights around his bathroom mirror. He hadn't done so in ages; a few of the LEDs had gone out, apparently. He leaned in and inspected his face in the uneven light. The wine stains on his lips would pass, but restless nights had brought out the creases on his forehead and around his mouth. At least he could address his unkempt hair, which was grayer in the mirror than it was in his self-image. He plucked a barrette from a drawer and pulled the frizzy poof back into a bun. After correcting his posture, he marched to an all-night market, where he bought replacement LEDs and a hairbrush.

In the lab the next morning, he didn't look any younger, but at least he looked like somebody who'd come to terms with the fact. It would have to be good enough for his first holo with Brenndan Gwilt, whom he finally got on-screen after lunch. Like many Enceladans, Brenndan was jet-black; he also had gray stubble so disorderly, it dispelled Kort's concerns about his own appearance. The two men exchanged pleasantries and gossiped about the interns before getting to business.

"So you're having trouble with your famous trees," Brenndan said. He pecked at his wrist tablet. "Explosive tumors or something."

"Or something," Kort agreed. "And here you are, a specialist in arboreal disease." He'd prepared for the conversation all morning, but even so his gut was a chilly hollow. "Director Ramsey said you wanted to come help."

Brenndan nodded. "I'd love to see it in person. Shahrazad will foot the bill."

Kort resisted scratching under his collar. Instead, he barreled through his anxiety. While he did fear the outside expert's judgment, letting that wreck the park would be awfully self-destructive, even by his standards. "And we'd love the help," he said through a scratchy throat. "Do you have access to a research capsule?"

"Good idea." Brenndan held up a finger. With his other hand, he navigated a touchscreen. "Alright, I'm next on the list." He leaned closer to the display and squinted. "I can be there in under a week."

Kort pasted on a smile and said that sounded great. They spoke little after that, to Kort's relief; Brenndan had affairs to wrap up.

Three days later, an eruption at Enceladus's south pole damaged the comms rig of Brenndan's spaceliner. The passengers were fine, but the vehicle had no bandwidth for nonessential communications.

"Does it even matter when he gets here, anymore?" Kort said. He was floating, agitated, before the trunk of the Corona. "*Look* at this!"

"Doesn't look great, boss," Iphie said. She and Dewen were floating opposite Kort.

"'Doesn't look — '" Kort hissed. He bashed the trunk with the bottom of his fist. Brown leaves rustled and drifted away from the canopy. Next to his hand, cankers sunk into the bark drooled maroon ichor, which formed hardened globules. "Watch this." He produced an ionic multitool, checked twice that it was set to 'incise,' and shaved off the bark around one of the cankers. Faint steam wafted from the exposed phloem, which should have been tan, but was oddly pink. "We've got a tree cooking itself alive here." A waiting vacuum drone sucked up the detritus.

"If it weren't hot, I'd guess Sudden Oak Death," Dewen said, his expression eager as always.

Kort waved it off. "Had the same thought. Sudden Oak Death doesn't produce galls." He huffed. "And our epidemiologist booked the *one spaceliner company*" — here he thumped a hydroponic casing — "too *cheap* to use proper comms shielding!"

Dewen held up his palms. "I'm sure the school was the cheapskate there, Dr. Z. Even when they pay for your conference ticket and hotel, they make you fly coach."

"Yeah." How did Dewen know that? Were they already sending him to expensive *conferences*? Kort hadn't received that honor until he was several years older. He sighed and rode his thrusters away from anything thumpable. "So we're on our own for two more days."

"There's worse company," Iphie said with a wide shrug. "If you're worried about *esprit de corps*, you can always take us out to dinner and bill the park."

Kort laughed. The interns were smart, but that flash of youthful audacity reminded him that he was the seasoned adult. His anger gave way to embarrassment; he needed to take charge. He turned towards the lab and pointed a finger forward. "Once more unto the breach," he said, flying away.

"Huh?" he heard Dewen say behind him.

Infrared imaging showed that only a third of the Corona was infected, but that third was nearing fatal temperatures. Together, they excised this portion, then rehoused it as a cutting. On the starboard face of the dome, there was an empty capsule they usually used for quarantine; they moved the new cutting inside. A further infrared scan identified another infected tree, a spiral-shaped oak nicknamed the Screw. They quarantined that one, too. Iphie programmed the capsule to vent its contents if the temperature went above 'scalding'.

That night they ate dandan noodles at a Sichuan restaurant in the discs. Kort did his best impression of a responsible adult, even managing some pleasant small talk. His eyes went wide when he learned that not only had the interns never been to China, they'd never even been to Earth. He supposed he should've guessed as much by their résumés. Still, it was something different to hear it from their own mouths. He seamlessly transitioned from feeling grown-up to feeling old.

The next morning, as New Lahej cleared the E ring's mists to reveal a waning Saturn, they found fifty-one galls on the Orb. Kort lanced each with cautious fury. *No sores or ichor, at least*, he thought as he worked the cryo-needle. *Not yet*. But a different oak, the Handlebar, was less fortunate, and was moved to the now-overcrowded quarantine capsule. To make matters worse, the capsule had developed something of a crowd; facilities had to push back the guests and put up screens. Kort hoped Helen wouldn't chew him out for not doing it sooner.

Four hours later, the capsule pushed an alert to their wrist tablets: it was approaching the venting threshold. They hurried over, slipped between the screens, and crowded around a readout. It showed that the Screw was nearing seventy degrees. The interns helped Kort float the other trees out, but he insisted on performing the final task himself. With one hand pressed to the astroglass, he tapped the command into the capsule's controls, and watched the Screw twirl off into the vacuum, where it would someday join Saturn's rings. He'd designed the tree to look like Da Vinci's flying machine; he imagined that old Leo would have found it a fitting death.

Kort shoved off from the astroglass with a finger. Not bothering to hide his tears, he drifted backwards a moment, then turned to Iphie and Dewen. "We aren't totally fucked yet," he said. With a hypomanic smile, he added, "If there's one thing I've learned, it's that you aren't actually in trouble until there's been paperwork."

Brenndan wouldn't arrive until the next morning, but there was still plenty Kort could do. He convened the crisis-management team again. Feeling a creeping dread much stronger than his usual existential angst, Kort asked them to search every plant in the park for symptoms of the disease. The results confirmed his fears: the weeping cankers were no longer limited to Zantoosian black oaks. The other plants didn't show elevated temperatures, and had less severe symptoms, but this gave him little solace. It was a well-known pattern in epidemiology: the creature could only incubate in one species — hence the oaks' monopoly on galls — but had a later stage with less discriminate effects.

An hour later, Kort was floating outside Helen's hatch, examining her nameplate. It was lightly oxidized and could've used a good scouring. But he was distracting himself; he rapped on the hatch, and was called in. He squared his shoulders to feel courageous, and pulled himself over to a handhold at her workstation. She seemed unsurprised to see him.

"Would this have anything to do with that crowd gathering around the entrance?" she said, tipping her head at the window, which overlooked the middle ring of the park.

"Ahha ha," Kort said, flat-footed. He cleared his throat, let out a sigh as defeated as he felt, and filled her in.

"Dr. Gwilt is almost here, right?" Helen said. "Let's see if he can figure it out." She took a measured sip from a pouch of coffee.

"Exactly what I was going to suggest," Kort said. They were on the same page, which usually presaged outcomes he could live with. He relaxed his grip on the handhold.

Helen kicked off her workstation and flew over to her window. Kort followed, and they gazed out at the flora and fauna they managed together. "People really do love this park we've built, Dr. Zantoosian. Even that family" — she pointed — "trapped in the hedge maze." She sipped her coffee again. "If your expert can't fix it, you *will* be spacing the oak trees. I'm sorry to be so pointed, but I need to be absolutely clear."

Kort swallowed at hearing it, though he'd assumed it was coming. "Absolutely," he said.

Helen nodded. "Great." She pushed off the window and settled into her workstation. "I've got to get back to this. Have facilities do something about that crowd, would you?"

"I'll ask them to put fire-suppression drones around all the oaks, too." He thanked her, and rode his thrusters out of her office. The meeting had gone so non-terribly, he almost smiled.

The remainder of the day passed in tense boredom. Only one thing really happened: they had to jettison the Handlebar after it reached the flash point. A sad moment, but not nearly as emotional as the death of the Screw. Like any creator, Kort did not love all his creations equally.

A sliver of Saturn loomed waxing in the sky when Brenndan's ship arrived the next morning. Near the battered spaceliner, Kort and Iphie waited in front of a shuttle. The scientist emerged from a hatch, two bags floating behind him on a sledge. Over on the starboard side of the ship, the spaceliner crew was removing the research capsule. Kort stared at the cylinder full of first-class equipment. His tongue went slightly dry. He hadn't had access to this caliber of tools since the rose rot crisis six years earlier. It was too bad he only got to play with the expensive toys during catastrophes.

Brenndan waved an arm. "Ms. Halikas, Dr. Zantoosian! Where should I have them put this thing?" He pointed over his shoulder at the capsule.

Kort focused on the green-and-white module, the better to not think about how chipper this interloper was. "Have them tie it down here, facilities will do the rest."

The three secured Brenndan's bags to their monorail car and traveled down the station's axial shaft. Strapped into the drab polymer seats, Iphie and Brenndan shot the breeze, while Kort, unable to think of something nice to say, fussed with his belt. At the habitation disc nearest the park, they rode a lift outwards, and showed Brenndan to the hotel Shahrazad had booked.

They toured the park an hour later, and Kort's inner critic was loud. When Brenndan said, "I'd never have thought aspens could be so lovely," Kort was sure he was just being charitable, and said something self-effacing. When Brenndan asked, "Have you tried centripetal drip irrigation?" Kort took it as proof of his disdain. He mounted a defense of their hydroponics, which he didn't even like. When they reached the Orb, and Brenndan said, "And this must be the tree from your logo," Kort heard faint praise indeed, and was unable to suppress a glare, after which Brenndan stopped commenting on much of anything. So it went: Kort was skittish and irritable all through the day. The team made little progress, even with the research capsule's sophisticated databases and equipment.

Before bed, Kort took a rare trip to the gym to wallop a punching bag. He wondered if his jaw would ever unclench. Did Brenndan think he was there to help with the *irrigation system*? So what if they couldn't afford anything fancy? After the gym, he tried to unwind with a glass of whiskey and a bad true-crime holo. What a waste of a day. Brenndan had been nothing but condescending. How were they supposed to save the oaks with that sort of dynamic? Kort might as well go space them right now.

Well when you put it like that, he thought, *who really has the problem?* He sighed and tried to enjoy the rest of his show. He'd do better tomorrow at focusing on the well-being of the trees. Or at least try.

The next morning, while he was still eating breakfast, Kort got a message from Helen asking him to stop by her office. A good breakfast being essential to his mood, he finished eating, then hopped right into the shower and hurried over. When he saw that Brenndan and the interns were already present, his cheeks went hot with anger and embarrassment. Why had they been meeting without him? Even if they had a good reason, it was still half-humiliating.

Helen gestured Kort to grab a handhold by her workstation. When he was settled, she saw the pained expression he was failing to hide. "I messaged you as soon as they filled me in," she said.

And why did they fill you in first? Kort thought. *Is this Brenndan's doing?* But maybe there was a perfectly reasonable explanation. He just had to not freak out until he knew for sure. Easier said than done, of course. His jaw clenched.

"There've been ... developments, doc," Dewen said, with an apologetic wince. "Iphie and I got here early. You weren't around, so we talked to Director Ramsey."

"And I've only been here a few minutes," Brenndan said, showing his palms.

The interns had tried tiptoeing around him, Kort realized. Had he been *that* bad lately? It wouldn't do to stay mad — they were basically children — but he barely avoided rolling his eyes in the ensuing burst of exasperation. "Okay, Dewen, and?"

"It's the Orb," Dewen said. "Cankers. We have to quarantine it."

The outrage drained out of Kort; his muscles deadened. He just nodded.

Dewen continued: the cankers had made it to the aspens. And there'd been a mass wilting of rosebushes. And, and. *My world is falling apart*, Kort thought.

"Dr. Gwilt was just telling me his general strategy for handling outbreaks," Helen said.

"Eliminate the disease vectors, basically," Brenndan said. "Think of *Toxoplasma gondii*: it can only reproduce inside cats, but still infects other mammals. Chase off the cats, and it soon goes away."

"Vectors? You mean the galls," Kort said, even as he knew it wasn't the answer.

"More broadly," Brenndan said, "the *oaks*. Unfortunately. Get rid of them and it should run its course."

With a grunt, Kort got himself to nod, a feat much more heroic than it looked. His toes tingled as his panic rose. Why couldn't they have been *wrong*? His proudest accomplishment was literally dying in front of him — and helping it along was *the right thing to do*.

Well, of course it was the right thing to do. Any idiot could see that. Why was he too bullheaded to accept it? Not for the first time, Kort hated himself for being so vain. How little must others think of him, if even interns felt the need to go over his head? He searched their faces for spite or pity, and though Brenndan was studiously aloof, the people who knew him wore expressions of empathy. Helen even flashed a supportive smile.

Time to give in. Kort took a few deep breaths, willing his panic to turn to resignation. It was a not-entirely-healthy coping mechanism he'd developed over the years, one which got plenty of use. "I'll grant that leaf-fall would be ... largely unaffected," he said, curling up imperceptibly. "There's much more to the park than the Zantoosians."

"Indeed," Helen said.

But Kort still couldn't avoid the bargaining stage of his grief. "Give us one more day," he said. "We only just got the research capsule, and the situation isn't likely to escalate."

Helen turned to Brenndan. "Do you agree?"

"Dr. Zantoosian is correct on both counts," Brenndan said.

"I'll see you here tomorrow morning, then," Helen said, tapping something into her workstation.

While he and Brenndan jetted down to the research capsule, Kort tried not to slouch. He'd bought himself hope to hang onto — thin though it may have been — and he would hold his head high and do his best. This would require effective collaboration; he was lucky his pride was still dead from the meeting. After a few false starts, he said, "I'm sorry I've been ... tense, lately."

Brenndan passed a twirl of fern trees and turned to face Kort. Kort supposed he deserved the scientist's guarded expression.

"Accepted," Brenndan said with a professorial nod. A thoughtful pause, then, "I can't say I envy your position. But I'm here to help."

The fern trees receded behind them. Kort sniffed. "I'm very defensive of my operation, is all."

"Honestly, that's a flaw that I share." The research capsule's pitted hatch swung open at a command from Brenndan's wrist tablet. "You can ask Ms. Halikas how hard it was to secure my mentorship."

Kort followed him inside. The lights came on; every surface was as irritatingly white as Enceladus's crust. "She seems to think highly of you," Kort said.

"And I her." Brenndan clambered through the room, powering up the machines. "But a year ago, I only looked at her application because they told me I had to take on an undergrad."

Kort was surprised to find such a kindred spirit in the academy. "Well, it's good for both of us that you did." He gestured around the capsule. "Shall we?"

"Let's." Brenndan turned a dial with a satisfying click, and the atomic force microscope began a warm hum. He thrust a packet of slides at Kort. "Femtoslices of a young gall. The freeze-drier just spit them out. Coffee?"

Two pouches of coffee and three packets of slides later, Kort pulled back from the eyepiece, blinked, and checked it again. He wasn't hallucinating: there was something foreign growing in the intercellular spaces of the gall ... rather, there were the outlines of something, almost as if the something itself were ...

"Invisible? You're mad," Brenndan said when Kort told him. "This machine can see *atoms*. Nothing's *that* invisible." He looked into the microscope and fiddled with the controls. "Hm."

"Hm?"

Brenndan tried another slide. "Hm."

They brainstormed experiments, and performed the ones time allowed. It seemed that the growths were detectable only by their effects on other things. Stumped, and short on other ideas, Kort and Brenndan each wrote a query script for the database AI, instructions to search its massive archives for similar cases. Then they left the capsule in a daze, their eyes ill-adjusted to the park's evening light. Brenndan began to jet away.

"Wait," Kort said.

Brenndan hissed to a stop and turned. "Yes?"

"There's 'planetrise' tonight at midnight," Kort said. "New Lahej will exit the ring right when Saturn's dawn terminator begins to sweep by. Definitely not something you get to see from down on Enceladus. You poor bastards are stuck in the ring." Kort spread his arms to indicate the park. "And I've got the keys to the best view in town."

Brenndan rubbed the stubble on his cheek. "What the hell — sure. Nothing else to do but wait for those queries to run. Let's see if you can impress this 'poor bastard'."

Kort let out an embarrassed chuckle. "I'll supply the whiskey. See you at — eleven?"

"Looking forward." Brenndan tapped his tablet, and his thrusters carried him backwards towards the exit.

Back in his cabin, Kort decanted his finest Titanian whiskey into pouches. He seemed to have reached the acceptance stage of grieving; he wanted only to see his trees off in style. At eleven, he met Brenndan in the axial shaft, and they entered the park. Brenndan got lost almost immediately and called out. Kort hadn't brought somebody else here after hours for ages; he'd forgotten to turn on the lights, which he dialed up to 'dusk'. The dome was now paused in twilight, a tapestry of dark greens and consuming shadows.

They toasted while floating before the remaining two-thirds of the Corona, long might it live. The alcohol landed hard, and once more Kort's problems slipped from his mind. They drank with relish; soon they were in the meadow, jetting after a sports drone, at a speed just this side of reckless. Shortly before midnight, they alighted at a rest area at the front of the dome, panting.

Kort killed the lights, and all was dark. "Here you go," he croaked, thrusting his arm at the astroglass.

New Lahej broke free of the ring, leaving a brief hole in the saltwater cloud. Brenndan stared as the sunlight spread across ammoniac Saturn. Both men sipped their whiskeys. Finally, Brenndan turned away and said, "You weren't kidd —"

An alert from his wrist tablet interrupted him. Brenndan shook his arm like something had bitten him, then laughed at himself and lifted it to read. "Database AI," he said. "Found something. C'mon." He tried to shake himself sober, and turned this way and that. "Um."

Kort's heart began to pound. Had they found a solution? He turned on the lights, programmed the destination into his wrist tablet, and waved Brenndan to follow. It took all his restraint not to rush there like a maniac.

In the capsule, they jockeyed for space around the AI readout. "You've got to be shitting me," Kort said, following it with a belly laugh and a somersault. The AI had found an ancient document buried deep in the research capsule's database. It told of an ailment, much like this one, which had afflicted Kepler Kudzu back when it was still being cultivated. As that plant was the source of several key genes for the Zantoosian black oak, this was a major breakthrough.

Kort cackled. "It found these documents *where*?"

Brenndan tapped the screen. "Newly digitized." He leaned in and squinted. "In some language called 'Esperanto'."

"No wonder I never found it."

"I don't know how people found *anything* before AI's," Brenndan said.

Kort snorted. "You'd need a whole ... *mountain* ... of interns!" He mimed throwing a pile of documents. "The hell do we do with this?"

"Are you good to script?"

"Not like this." Kort blew out a deep breath. His face brightened then, and he pointed at Brenndan. "But we have teammates who *can*."

New Lahej was still well outside of the ring when Iphie and Dewen rang from the park's entrance.

Jetting backwards so he could use wild gestures, Kort explained their summons with a massive grin. He and Brenndan had found the key insight, but the two men were far too drunk to write the next research script, which would have to deal with the document's arcane hypertext encoding. Could Iphie and Dewen? Please?

"You got it, boss," Iphie said with a bad salute. Dewen, for his part, tried not to look as annoyed as he obviously felt.

The interns unearthed more actionable information. This *lumo viruson* — light virus — was, to the ancient scientists, a scourge made of hungry energy; the affected Kepler Kudzu glowed. The writers hadn't hidden that they assumed an extraterrestrial origin. They'd also declined to publish their findings: in those early days of space exploration, such a claim was the fastest way to destroy one's reputation. And the cure? In retrospect it was obvious. Their predecessors had identified a narrow temperature range that eliminated whatever caused the *lumo viruson* infection without also killing the woody tissue of its host. Surely the same would be true for Zantoosian black oaks.

Rather than treating the entire habitat, as the ancients had, they could move the oaks into the quarantine capsule and leave the rest of the park untouched. It was a gentler version of Brenndan's 'eliminate the vectors' plan — one which, Brenndan noted, was only possible due to the portability inherent in Kort's hydroponics architecture.

Over a breakfast of hangover nanobots, Kort and Brenndan decided that the director would be more sympathetic to their plan if Brenndan pitched it. Helen regarded him skeptically as he did so in her office.

Leaf-fall could proceed according to schedule, Brenndan suggested; he would take two infected trees to Shahrazad University on Enceladus, where they could be studied with proper containment. Of the remaining trees, the worst cases would be destroyed, and the healthiest would be cured.

Kort interjected to say that this latter group included the Orb.

Helen said that was good; they'd all grown very fond of that tree. So where, she asked, did this *lumo viruson* come from? Would it come back?

Brenndan recited a spiel, obviously not for the first time, about the history of epidemiology. The theory often came after the cure; some questions could only be answered with methodical investigation, and a crisis was no time for that.

With a sharp nod, Helen said they had a deal, then dismissed everybody but Kort.

"Good work," she said, rolling out stiff neck muscles.

Kort tried not to sound self-conscious. "Team effort. But thank you."

She leaned forward. "Why don't you take a sabbatical, Kort?"

"Oh?" Kort froze. Surely that wasn't a euphemism.

"I'm just guessing, but there's a university that could probably use an expert in managing populations of Zantoosian black oaks." She chuckled. "Assuming that fire for research you used to talk about is still around."

Perhaps humor would let him hide his swelling relief. "You don't say." He pretended to check his wrist tablet. "You'll have to introduce me."

Helen reached out and grasped his shoulder. Holding his eyes, she said, "Are you okay, Kort?"

For once Kort didn't try to wriggle away from another's sympathy. Instead he bowed his head and closed his eyes. The park he believed in was safe, and he had the opportunity now to scratch his research itch. Truly, he *was* okay; if he was being honest, he felt almost giddy. But what should he do with such an unfamiliar feeling? Flee? Weigh the wreckage of the last season, and dwell on losses still to come? Or be refreshed in it, learn to find it again?

He pushed back from her finally and regarded the park from her window. The air held more leaves than it had yesterday, as it would again tomorrow. "Yes, actually. I think I'll take you up on that." Managing a cautious smile, he added, "If you're worried I'll be upset about losing the oaks, don't be — I can always grow more." He wasn't so old that he didn't have time for that; he had a hunch that what he valued would always find its way back into his life.

Titanotheosis

David Gallay and Evan Marcroft

I do not scream when my God reaches for me. Its hand is as vast as the sky. Where can I go?

Its splintered nails carve easily through the ancient stone on which I stand, gouging furrows as wide as thoroughfares as they close around me and scoop me up upon a pillow of rubble. My head goes dizzyingly light as I am lifted into higher altitudes. The city below is a mangle of color and disjointed angles, an oil landscape trampled and gouged and burned. A gulf rimmed in fire curves over the horizon as though something had dragged a chisel through the skein of the world itself. Twin suns look on from the firmament, a pair of eyes aghast or maniacally delighted — I cannot say which. This is parousia to some, apocalypse to others.

Look down, down, down, upon a shrunken world, and there is my God as beheld from above, a sight that none but the Messiah should ever witness. Stripped of its battle armor, the façade of glory, its face is an iridescent skull half-melted into scutal ridges and jags of carapace. It grins up at me with a half-moon of bloody teeth. From between its fingers I gaze into its compound eye, upon which a single, black iris floats like ink bleeding across a trove of emeralds.

All that I am, all my dreams and fears and memories both happy and painful but unique to me, all my years of experience compacted as tight as entrails, would trouble that eye no more than a speck of dust. It beholds me — all of me, without effort — and questions what it sees.

I scrawl the word large across my being.

Yes.

I am ready.

Those massive fingers open, as do those fearsome teeth.

The Clade of the Metagnostes holds that light is the ambition of all things. It is the ultimate metamorphosis, to transform from dull matter into sublime energy. Even Imago aspires to burn in a chrysalis of fire and become radiance. But if that is so, why does that light scorch my eyes? My cortical implants can only dull the pain. I squint through slits instead. I think that I have spent too long underground.

I feel like an earthworm burrowed up into the summer heat, slowly crisping. Yet I would never have seen daylight again were it not for my brother. He sits beside me on the palanquin, a man grown tall and strong and golden. The glassmonks tried to pretty me up in powders and spun-glass robes, but that barely hides what I've become; next to Dai, I'm a pallid little troglodyte. It was only at his personal request that I join him here, and none in the Clade could deny the Messiah his wish, not even me.

Not on the eve of Holy War.

The palanquin beneath us is the size of a house, its stentorian clattering intentional, meant to herald the Messiah's coming from miles away. A pyramid of golden statues — men and women melting into horns of emanating light — clutch the bolus of cushions upon which my brother and I are presented. The great rock-crushing wheels below are etched with the fundamental Metagnostic motif: larva to pupa to butterfly and back again, turning without end. Biomechaeic blood-engines crank the vehicle onward from within. Behind marches a legion of the Metagnostics' most devout, their voices united in joyous canticles to Imago. The youngest dance ahead and loose butterflies from wicker cages. I remember being that carefree, not as long ago as it feels. I am meant to enjoy this the same as them, but the moment feels misplaced, meant for a girl who could have been but never was.

How ironic, for the one among them closest to God.

Our destination lies just ahead, where the mountains level off. My breath hitches at the sight of it; my lips automatically repeat a deep-ingrained prayer. I'd thought the years underground had eroded away my sense of wonder, yet the city before me bids my soul kneel. Squat, crooked, ashen-gray, its surfaces smoothed by the friction of time, its windows dark — at least for now. Far from a gleaming metropolis, yes, but the sheer age steeped into it seems to depress the world like a stone upon a sheet. From our vantage I can see how subtly the city tilts. It sits on a cliff of its own, overlooking a deeper valley, a crater within a crater.

Here and there throughout the cityscape, shoots of yellow-white break the scab. Those are bones. The bones of gods.

At the city's heart, a supernova in cupped hands. Blue white flame geysers up from the center of the planet. The Omniforge that powers the world.

Titanomachia.

I don't belong here. This sight is a reward for the faithful.

"Operoph."

I glance at my brother and accidentally meet his gaze for the first time today. After all these cycles, and though his butterfly halo gilds him with light, his eyes are still the same as mine. He reaches across the space I put between us and claps his hand on my knee.

"Can you believe all this began with our Oblation, so long ago?" Dai says. "You must be proud. Imago has grown strong and terrible on your love and devotion."

And there is the lie, the secret beneath the pageantry.

There was neither love nor devotion in what I did.

A slave cannot love their master.

"Oph?"

"What?"

"Have you not heard a word I said? Where were you just now?"

I do not know what to say. I have shared nothing with my brother in cycles. The dramas of his life, if they exist, are a mystery to me. And he could never understand what I've been through.

"It's all a bit overwhelming," I say. "Are you worried about the battle?"

"Of course not," Dai proclaims, though with a wink. "I am the Messiah of the Truest God, the Birthing Star, the Egg of Fate, whose name is Imago. Victory is already within me, waiting to hatch." In a conspiratorial tone he adds, "But between you and me, Oph, I'm scared out of my wits."

A grin steals across my face before I can catch it. The brother I remember is still there inside our savior. Crumpled up under the blinding robes and crowns.

"You'll win," I say. A carefully neutral statement.

We were twins once, but as the Clade teaches, every Low Thing is the cocoon of a Great Thing, and those Great Things may be wildly divergent. My brother is a stranger in every respect but genetics. Do I love him, or hate him? Should I worship him as others do, or resent him for wearing the halo that should have been mine? Should I care if he lives or dies?

"Your mood is impossible for me to read," Dai says. Before I can respond, he shrugs and answers for himself. "Win or lose, the Clade will continue. Life is a cycle, after all. All things that rise must fall, but the reverse is true as well. Our god may die, but he will be reborn again, as it ever was. And if I die, well, I will be content knowing that my other half survives me." His expression is an awkward mixture of brotherly and severe. "Remember the First Principle of Imago, dear sister. Inside every Lower Thing is a Greater Thing. I think yours has yet to hatch."

I feign a weak smile, and we return to silence, letting him believe that we have grown a little closer again. He does not know

that my chance at glory came and went a long time ago. That I am

a pupa that will never grow wings.

If I squint hard at the bowl of mountain surrounding Titanomachia, I can make out bands of color trickling down towards the city. Reds and blues and blacks to our white and gold. It isn't long before the rumbling of other palanquins reaches my ears. As they do every ten cycles, all the great Clades of this world are assembling here, relic-laden and dogma-bound. The Starwise, the Vishtahists, the Omniforge Disciples, the Scholars of The First Number, even the lowly Necrochaste. In fervent thousands they come to give Titanomachia one more day of light and life, to drink and dance and sing hosannas and cavort with their sectarian enemies. And on the morning after they will gather in the streets around vidscreens and at the clifftop edge of the city, to watch with hearts splayed open and throats flaming with hope, as their gods meet in the valley below and slaughter each other down to the last left standing.

Only the truest expression of faith will win the day. The rest will fill the land with an ocean of blood.

There was a time when I believed the lie of the gods. No more strongly than in the days leading up to our Oblation. My friends lamented my coming ascension to the divine with friendly envy and outright bitterness. I lay on cold decontamination beds for hours, naked, shivering, listening to my aunties describe how a god-larva could see right into your soul, how a single touch could either bless or curse a family for generations. Even on the day of the ceremony, as my family and I glided out of Novo Viridis, weaving through garden-cathedrals and floating biomecheia factories, our shadows skipping across the frothing, silver sea, the ancient glassmonk piloting our royal flyer prattled on about how this was as close to godhood as any mortal could get.

Whatever majesty I expected was immediately tarnished as soon as we stepped down onto the damp fungal carpet of the breeding pit. An overpowering reek of organic foulness assaulted my sinuses. Before us, barely lit by the rusty phosphorescence of mycotrophic wildflowers, sprawled a vast underground lake. I and my brother stood at the edge, hand in hand. Our entire childhood had been preparing us for this moment. Countless afternoons on silver beaches, drilling through the Seven Movements of Combat until our muscles burned. Leaning over the balcony of a flyer as the battles of Titanomachia raged below us, we cheered in religious abandon as shrieking titans larger than mountains flooded the war fields with viscera.

"Where are the gods?" Dai asked now, impatient as ever, and as if in answer the ceiling of bioluminescent algae flared. Under that queasy illumination, the ceaseless churning black waves were revealed not to be water, but the god-larvae themselves. Thousands of ebony worms, each the size and bulk of a man, corkscrewed against each other. Faced with this ocean of artificial life, we lost our tongues. Even our parents, who surely must have expected this.

It was terror. But even then, it was glory.

A bell chimed, signaling the arrival of the Tender Magister, the aloof figure that managed the shared god-cradle on behalf of all the Clades. She made her way towards us through the breeding pit itself, gingerly stepping amongst the roiling herd on biomechaeic stilts. A chain looped around her wrist hooked into the harness of a chosen god-larva, which struggled furiously against its leash. My brother's grip on my hand tightened. How could these creatures possibly have any relationship to the gods? They were mindless. Barely alive. Monstrosities.

Yet I told myself to have faith. There was also a certain beauty to them. Their oily black chitin, iridescent at certain angles, threaded with veins of gold. Their needle teeth, like shards of moonlight. Their sublime organic artifice in all its facets.

The Magister called out to us.

"Children. Name yourselves."

We knelt, touching our foreheads to the ground.

"Operoph," I said. "Left-Hand Sun of the Clade of the Metagnostes."

"Dai," my brother said. "Right-Hand Sun of the Clade of the Metagnostes."

The god-larva on the magister's leash thrashed.

"And to which deity do you present this oblation?" the Magister asked.

"Imago," we said in practiced unison. "The Birthing Star, The Recursive Womb, Our God of Life."

"Approach."

We crawled forward on our hands and knees until we were under the Magister's shadow.

The god-larva went still. We were close enough to hear the click-click of its scales, the wet thud of five heartbeats. It waved its snout, tasting the air.

Just as we rehearsed, me and Dai remained still as statues, our heartbeats slow as unfolding petals. What should have happened next was that the god-larva would appraise each of us, breathing in our genetic markers, calculating which one would be the best match for theosis. There would be a moment of tension. Then it would be over, and one us would be its Messiah. It was the way of every oblation, with centuries of dull documentation.

Things did not often go wrong.

As we knelt, the restless god-larva's tail swished by my hand. It was close enough to make out striations of golden capillaries knitted through the black chitin. What a marvel — bloodily bred but man-made, a biomechaeic device of such fine design as to transcend both animal and machine. Without thinking, I caressed it with my thumb. Its warmth was reassuring. Good things were warm. Too late, though, I remembered those repeated warnings against deviating from the ritual. A single improper touch was all it took.

Instantly, the worm became agitated. It strained against its collar, whipping side to side. The Magister stumbled; the chain slipped from her hand. I looked up to see the god-larva lunging towards me, jaws wide, those moonlight teeth spiraling inward into darkness. What exactly happened next ... everything went dim, soft, quiet. I must have thrown my hands up to protect me. My left arm disappeared down its throat, down to the elbow. Then that hand was gone. My mother screamed. I heard her charge into the sacred circle. The worm rose over us, scales flashing in the dim light. A wash of sticky warmth. Salt on my lips. The Magister shouting unintelligible commands.

Dai, the brave, the foolish, jumped on the god-larva's back.

I must have passed out, because the next thing I remembered was the Magister, still trembling, placing the crown of golden butterflies on Dai's head. The god-larva motionless, triple-bound in chains. My father wailing over my mother's eviscerated body. The Necrochaste had already been summoned to attend to her corpse. As they wrapped her in a death shroud, in that moment I felt no grief, no sadness, no anger. All I had was relief. Relief that it wasn't me being recycled. That I might not be the Messiah, but at least I was alive.

That relief quickly curdled. The Magister gently explained that I had not only failed the oblation, my thoughtless deviation had brought shame on myself, on my family, on my Clade. As recompense, I would leave the sea and the gardens behind and remain here, in the darkness of the cradle, indentured as a tender. The next several years of my life would be dedicated to the worm-larva that had devoured my hand, the beast that killed my mother. I would be its constant companion until the day it molted into our god. Only then would my shame be lifted.

I turned to plead with my father. But he and Dai were already gone. I had been left behind. As the Magister pressed the leash into my hand and led me further underground, I closed my eyes so that at least I could control the last light I saw.

I do not join the crowds that gathered at the city's sheer edge to witness the Holy War with their own eyes. Men and women mob the clifftop where Titanomachia yields vertically to the valley in which gods have battled since eons past. From the railing they will throw tokens of devotion, which will join heaps of rust and rot a hundred feet high. In their ecstasy, they will whip themselves into mass fits of glossolalia and compete with other Clades to be heard by their god. Some will hurl themselves from the ledge and sacrifice their very blood to some imagined reservoir of power. Their bones will come to rest under mounds of equally pointless trinkets.

No, that scrum is not for me. It does not suit me to be crushed to death in a euphoric mob; Dai and Imago will win or lose independently of how shrilly I cheer. And besides, I have been closer to the gods than any of them ever will.

Instead I venture deeper into the city, where the shed heat of the Omniforge casts the dusty avenues in perpetual midsummer. Here, the older supplicants who have outgrown the passion of youth gather in open-sided dens to smoke plug-lymph and watch the War on vidscreen. Interclade divisions are not so sharp-edged here; saffron-turbaned Vishtahists may be seen placidly debating the true cosmology with elderly Omniforge Disciples, who have put away their bronze hammers and taken up the lighter arms of logic and reason. Of course, all arguments will be dashed to pieces when one god or the other lies defeated, its skull cracked open and seeping pyrophoric brain-matter. When the final word is spoken, it is silent strength that determines who is right.

I find myself a quiet spot at a tavern in the lee of a dry fountain. A family of Vishtahist pilgrims have set up shop there for the day, peddling milkweed wine from massive barrels. The semi-poisonous concoction fights like a trapped animal on its way down but get its job done. Numb inside and out, I plant myself in the corner where the shade is most cave-like. Vidscreens affixed to the walls display multiple angles of the valley where the gods have begun to assemble. Though the photomnemonic beetle-wing screens have not half the quality needed to render the gods in all their immensity, supplicants pack in around them with an almost idolatrous fixation. Even shrunk to fit in photophores, our gods are the unborn word that waits between wondrous and horrifying.

The knowledge-god of the Starwise is first in line, this iteration named Palordermo. Its feet planted on either bank of a river, its horns pierce the clouds. A white beard, long as a canyon, winds about it like a prehensile serpent. The reincarnation of Vishtah sits in meditation, hovering hundreds of feet over the center of the lake like a mountain shouldn't. Arbiter of Harmonies, Conductor of Rhythms, the waves and trees nearby ripple in time to the idle motions of its six arms. Now, lumbering down the furthest slope of the valley, its feet imprinting in stone as though it were mud, comes Valtahar IV, God of the Forge, Hammer of Souls. Lower than the other gods but twice as wide as some, its muscle is itself jacketed in overlapping bronze armor between which sapphire flames endlessly spew. Slung across one shoulder it bears the infamous war-sledge Faithbreaker, whose head is the size of a church. A god may take any form, use any weapon, exploit any tactic. Whether a god falls to cunning or force of arms, it means only that the faith that birthed it was inferior.

On it goes. Nine gods in all assemble in the valley. Even among the unimaginable awe and magnificence of the gods assembled in Titanomachia, one stands apart from the rest. A striking monolith of black, vat-grown leather, no face apparent beneath its hood. The shadow it casts is miles long. By process of elimination it must be Cenotaph, god of the Necrochaste, Glutton of the Dead, but that can't be right. Of all the world's Clades, the Necrochaste are the weakest. Scavengers, gravediggers, and corpse-touchers, to be utilized but shunned by decent folk. Poor and disorganized, their gods have always been grown from poor stock. Yet this iteration of Cenotaph must be twice the height of the last, if my memory serves.

Dogmas do not change so easily. A decade is nothing in the lifespan of religions. Something huge must have moved through the Necrochaste, huge and fast, buckling their floorboards and popping traditions loose like rusty nails.

The one thing all Clades believe is that the gods, no matter their origins in flesh, are the gestalt conviction within their followers' hearts. With fists and teeth, they prove whose faith is most righteous. The last god standing will sacrifice itself to the Omniforge and turn the world for another decade. For those ten years it takes the planet to digest their fat and gristle, their Clade will reign above all others, the lodestar for every global power structure. The world remade in their image. And when ten years have passed, and the universe begins to slow upon its axle, a new brood of gods will compete for dominance once more.

Imago is last to stride onto the killing fields of Titanomachia. The few fellow Metagnostics in the tavern utter involuntary prayers as our God strides across the forest, tossing pulverized evergreens with every step. It is a cathedral come to life, so mindbogglingly immense that the sun shatters into rays against its spine. Its mighty fists, mailed in carven marble, knuckled with gargoyles, scatter flocks as they swing through the air. Serrated ziggurats cap its shoulders, and its eyes are two great windows of organic glass kaleidoscopically stained with its own image. Imago, The Wheel-Turner. Imago, The Recursive Womb. Imago, God of Life. Some nearby Metagnostics fall out of their chairs and onto their knees. I grapple with a sneer. Imago to them is a Self-Demonstrating Principle, the Great Thing metamorphosed from their conglomerate faith, but they perceive only its resplendent carapace. They imagine beauty and music when a Messiah unites with their god.

The truth is closer to butchery; I know because I was there when Dai waved goodbye.

The Messiah enters the god through a forcibly dilated orifice into a biomechaeic cockpit replacing its third heart. They are linked through a weaving of nerves teased from the Messiah's opened wrists, their consciousness conjoined like a parasite to the god's nervous system. Not so much a joining of wills as a crude puppeteering. The attendants, afterwards, shuck off ichor-drenched rubber and unscrew the plugs from their nostrils.

The feed quakes as Imago throws back its head and disgorges a roar of challenge. I can hear the real thing even miles from its origin. I know, though, that it is only Dai in his humid cockpit, cooking in the atomic heat of Imago's metabolism, bleating through the mouth of his bridled steed. Much is sacrificed to birth a god and yet little god survives in the final product.

Imago is a Self-Demonstrating Principle — that all Great Things once nursed on shit. I can be content with the certainty that whatever else it becomes, in its heart it will always be a worm.

Underground, I learned quickly why worm-tending attracted exiles and misanthropes. It was unrelenting drudgery, caring for a god-larva. For a creature designed to carry the very seeds of godhood, the truth was that they were exceptionally brittle.

They must be kept in darkness, lest a stray photon of ultraviolet collapse their intricate genetic scaffolding. Our only illumination came from the mycelium glow coating the cavern walls, and the dull red of canteen ovens. To achieve the required metamorphic mass, a god-larva consumed three times its body weight every day. Lest its caloric furnace burn it up from the inside, it ate constantly. Shat constantly. My waking hours went to either shoveling biofeed or its prodigious waste, making sure to keep my hands away from those glistening moon-teeth.

On third-nights, I would sidle up to the slumbering worm and pry ticks from its scales. Its five heartbeats thudded under my palm. Sometimes I pressed the tick blade to the soft crease where skull met carapace. I knew by now what a dead god-larva looked like on the inside. I knew where the brainstem arched against the surface. One push, and I would be free, one way or another.

Did love stay my hand on those lonely, bitter nights?

No. Nothing so strong as that. That hard seed in my chest bloomed thorny vines that strangle love. But the core teaching of Metagnostes was the respect for all life, for the divine potential in every cell. Killing the worm/larva would mean killing who I was, everything I believed. I loathed the beast. I let it live. I had nothing else.

On the anniversary of that disastrous oblation, I was granted leave to visit my mother's grave. Even with the Left-Hand Sun dulled to a rusty stain behind storm clouds, the daylight stung my eyes. Dai sat alone at my mother's stone marker. Apparently, a Messiah's diet matched the richness of a god-larva's, for he had grown past me. Shimmering robes of blue and white glass fell across his shoulders like reflections of water. A halo of golden butterflies fluttered about his head. His skin glowed like burnished steel. Though I had scrubbed all night, I felt filthy next to him, the musty earth of the cradle embedded in my fingernails, my pores, my teeth.

"Operoph," he said as I knelt at his side.

"Dai."

A moment passed difficultly. In the far distance, the nuclear glow of the Omniforge licked at the scudding clouds.

"Do you blame me for this life?"

I could hear how the question had been eating at him. I laughed in reply.

He scowled at me. "What is so funny?"

I wanted to tell him how every day I woke up on a filthy fungus mat wondering if this would be the day he might visit me, or at least pass along a message via the cadre of Metagnostic glassmonks checking the progress of their precious god-larva. And every day, the same answer. No. Monotony was a poison. Drop by drop, the daily routine of my new life dissolved hope. It didn't take long before I let the rest of myself go with it, leaving only weary bitterness.

Blame? Underground, there was no use for it.

"I was just ... about to ask you the same thing," I lied. "Our twinning genes still shine."

"I suppose so."

"How is father?"

He sighed. "Taken to his new life well. We barely see each other. He greases the gears of Metagnostic politics while I shuffle between studies and training and blessing babies. Sometimes I wish had been the one taken underground —" Dai flinched as he glimpsed the dull glass of my biomechaeic hand. "Or perhaps I should have just strangled the beast. Oph, did you hear me? What are you staring at ... oh."

A pair of Necrochaste had arrived at a nearby grave and began dislodging stones from the tomb. It was an odd sight, seeing these pitiful men in their ragged cloaks rooting at the earth, sweat drenching their pale scalps. No one would deny the death cult served a critical utility, caring for the deceased, recycling organic material back to the living. They performed their macabre duties well, almost invisibly. Their god was historically a wretched thing, never triumphant in any Holy War of recorded history.

We watched in quiet antipathy as one of the Necrochaste wrestled a desiccated corpse from the reopened grave as the other carefully removed a hissing, grub-like creature from their pack. It was a miniature version of a god-larva, no longer than the length of an arm, pus-white. Even with the ancient's sacred designs and biologic engines, there was room for error. Not all larvae had the stuff of gods in them. These genetic failures, albino runts, were cast off to the Black Temple of Cenotaph to be raised as efficient corpse eaters.

"Degenerates," Dai muttered. "There is barely anything left of that poor soul to recycle."

I glanced away as the cultist inserted the runt worm in the corpse's ribcage with his bare hands. Whatever this ghastly ritual meant for them, I wanted no part of it. With a grunt of satisfaction, the death cultists shrouded their grim prize in a preservation mesh and hauled it away. The only evidence of their handiwork was a patch of dark, fresh earth.

The distraction over, Dai's tongue moved on to other thoughts.

"Can I see it?" he asked, eyes wide.

"It?"

"My ... our ... God? Imago?"

I had been at my god-larva's side for so long, so constantly, that I didn't realize how much it had changed until I saw Dai's expression of awe and horror. What had been barely taller than me at our oblation had grown to the size of a small building. Its head scraped against fungal stalactites. Opalescent chitin had roughed into massive, axe-head scales. As its appetite threatened to surpass our ability to fabricate meat, I was forced to muzzle those moon-teeth in sheaths of tensile leather. A liquid slurry of protein chem was piped directly into its gut.

Dai examined the god-larva from all sides with wide eyes and slack jaw.

"Already it is greater than us," he murmured, gingerly stepping over its slow, swishing tail.

"I suppose it is," I said.

"How does it compare? To the others? You know, the gods of our rivals?"

"Oh, I'm not sure. Once the worms outgrow the lower pits, we tenders sequester them in these deepvaults. Keeps us from learning each other's secrets. We barely speak to each other, even in the dining halls."

"I know what you mean." He idly picked up my tick blade, turning it in his hand. "Every day, I am forced through these boring sessions on interclade diplomacy or memorizing languages from the other side of the world, or wasting whole days play-fighting in the Orchid Palaestra."

"That's not quite the same —"

I hoped he might notice my stark statement of loneliness. Although I had grown ... familiar ... with solitude, seeing Dai again resurfaced a deep, selfish spark that my heart cupped closely, a chance that all this could be over soon, that I could return aboveground, that I could sleep in my own bed and smell the salt-orchids through an open window. I wanted to walk free along the endless silver sea, my toes naked in the surf.

"Valtahar," Dai interjected. "God of the Forge. The glassmonks working the odds believe this will be my final challenger on the fields of Titanomachia."

I knew the god-larva that would become Valtahar. Smaller than mine, but more of a brute, all reptilian sinew and muscle. Its tender was a taciturn boy even younger than me, arms scarred black by his worm's boiling blood.

"When?" I asked.

"Please, tell me you're joking. Three revolutions until my ascension. It will be ready, right? You are preparing for the Invocation of Divine Transfiguration?"

"That soon ..." I had arrived barely more than a child. So much time stolen from me. I strained to keep despair from cracking from my words. "Yes. Yes, of course, everything is on schedule. You have nothing to worry about."

"Wonderful." He handed me the tick blade and opened his messenger. I said nothing as an entourage of willowy glasswomen arrived to escort my brother onto his personal flyer, the sigil of the Metagnostes burning brighter than any other lights in the pit. I shielded my eyes as they lifted off.

"You are a good sister," Dai exclaimed from the balcony as they floated away. "Imago could not want for any better servant."

Then he was gone. Jealousy balled my fist right around the tick blade. I spun around to the god-larva. What I was going to do, I don't know. In that moment, I didn't care. One way or another, I would bring this to an end.

But when I saw the worm, the rage left me. Spooked by the flyer or maybe Dai himself, the pitiful creature had coiled up tightly, its massive body shuddering in fear. I sank down next to it. I could continue loathing it tomorrow. We listened to each other breathe until, finally, sleep came to both of us.

Valtahar's hammer strikes the city like a megaton bomb. The impact, even miles away, lifts everyone in the tavern inches off their feet and slams them back to the ground. The vidscreens reorient for a moment on the wreckage, at the dust rising in great, billowing clouds from the point of impact, at the hilt angling like a half-toppled tower into the sky, an armored fist still clenched around it and hemorrhaging flaming ichor from its stump. I can only imagine the lives snuffed out and yet what I hear rippling through the city is not a scream, but a cry of religious ecstasy. Envy the dead, I hear them singing; those obliterated by that divine weapon are truly blessed, down to their every wide-flung atom.

The vidscreen cuts back to the valley just as Imago drives its heel into the hollow of the Forge God's knee, snapping its leg in half and bringing it earthshakingly to the ground. Before Valtahar can react, Imago's hands clamp shut around its head, nails digging into the seams in its anvil-shaped helm. The two gods scream as one — pain and exertion twining together — and then there is a crack that echoes like thunder across an open prairie. A blast of fire, a spout of blood; Valtahar's head spins free from its neck and flattens the forest below.

I let out the breath that I'd been holding. Am I relieved or disappointed? I wouldn't lose a flicker of sleep to watch Imago be gutted, yet I don't want to see Dai amongst the entrails. It is not my brother's fault he cannot see further than the rim of his halo. He is blinded by his own light. I imagine I would be too, if I'd been chosen, as I should have been.

I take another long draft of milkweed to simplify these complicated emotions of mine. As the poison works through me, I bury my head in my hands and let thoughts drift where they will.

◉

There is darkness.
    There is solitude.
    And then there is the Invocation of Divine Transfiguration.
    When god-larvae outgrow their own ashen, cracked scales, when their muscles lock into place and they stop eating and start burning, five hearts beating blue-hot like pulsars under the skin, when they groan pitiful dirges of internal suffering all hours of the day, when they exude a foul smelling sap that gradually encases their entire body in a dazzling chrysalis of bio-metal, then the time has come for the Invocation. The finest Metagnostic bio-technicians escort each beast down to the deepest layers of the cradle, where no light reaches, not even the ruddy glow of fungal roots. There, in secrecy, and through holy science, they can complete its transformation from a beast into the god devised by years of planning.

Once the technicians have completed their work and steered the larva towards its ultimate form, it is the duty of every tender to chaperone their god-larva through the final, delicate stage of its evolution. For months I lived in darkness, granted a minimum of vision via cortical implants. My only company was the god-larva's chrysalis hanging overhead, this impossible organic monstrosity with no familiar geometry, all orbs and whorls and labyrinthine veins of opalescence, a shell, a prison, a storm, a kiln. It was so massive that I couldn't see both ends at the same time. Being in its presence triggered a sort of insanity. I felt the weight of every mile of rock and earth between me and the sky. The silence screamed in my ears. Time melted away. Hallucinations intruded without warning; childhood playmates long forgotten, my brother, my father, even my mother, whole again, walking with me along the shore, humming her little nonsense song about the flowers and grass and golden butterflies deep under the sea.

My only reprieve came whenever the Tender Magister arrived to inspect the god-larva's progress. Without even a glance in my direction, she would go to work on the chrysalis, carefully examining it with one instrument after another, taking measurements, chitin samples. Only when finished did she take any notice of me. She never asked how I was managing or if I needed any more supplies or how many times I considered smashing my head against the cave walls. Only the same, single question.

"How goes the Invocation?"

That was all that mattered. My small role in this grand birthing ritual to make a human connection with the gestating god. Which mostly meant mindlessly reciting to it from the sacred texts of our Clade, the Thirteen Tenets of Life, reminding it of what it should already know of itself. As I endlessly scrubbed down the chrysalis with anti-bac, mechanical as a wind-up glassbird, the Invocations flowed from my tongue. "Inside every Lower Thing is a Greater Thing ... you are Imago, The Birthing Star, The Wheel Turner, The One Who Bends Life Towards the Secret Truth ..." Meanwhile, my thoughts strayed upwards, towards escape. My dreams were bright as two suns.

"Very well," I always replied to the Magister's question, afraid that to say otherwise might mean starting this process over from the beginning, a fate whose very possibility filled me with terror.

Then she would nod, pull her scarves tighter as if returning to a colder world, leaving me alone in the dark with the rotting tendrils of my mind.

It will all be over soon.

It seems like the war just started, but gigantic corpses are already strewn across the valley, plains painted rust-red, forests flooded with blood up to the lowest boughs. Three challengers remain: Imago, battered but otherwise whole; Vishtah, standing triumphant over the broken carcass of Palordermo albeit minus one arm; and Cenotaph, who has not moved from its position since the start of the war. What have the Necrochaste hidden beneath that cloak? Our gods are the truth of the heart given flesh; they are meant to be displayed. A disguise defeats the point. There must be some other reason more urgent —

What?

I blink, and Cenotaph is no longer there.

The vidscreens scramble to keep it in view. By the time they catch up it is halfway across the valley, loping faster than something of its immensity should be able. I shoot involuntarily out of my seat. My heart ricochets between my ribs, apprehending something that my mind is still piecing together. I am terrified, and I don't know why.

Vishtah is closest to Cenotaph's charge and darts in to intercept it. The most agile of the gods, its five lithe arms blur through dizzying patterns meant to dazzle, disarm, dismember with bladed palms, but the God of Death does not so much as flinch. Its cloak unfurls like ink dissolving into water and the vidscreen is bisected by a thick, black scratch. A moment later, I realize it was motion — not a glitch in the feed — when Vishtah's top and bottom halves tumble away from one another. Cenotaph continues through an arch of fountaining blood without pause, dragging the intestines of a slaughtered god around its ankles.

Within the tavern there is no sound but the intake of breath though slackened jaws.

Fortunately, Imago quickly absorbs the lesson that Vishtah mortally demonstrated and swings the corpse of Valtahar like a shield, blocking Cenotaph's path. This time I am looking for it, and there it is, a massive tentacle that explodes from inside Cenotaph's cloak and spears the carapace of Valtahar through its hollow heart. The mountainous jags of bone studding the tentacle's surface like teeth in cancerous gums carve though armor with the ease of a scalpel through flesh.

My knuckles are white. My fingernails have chewed through the skin of my palms.

Imago hurls the useless corpse aside and seizes the tentacle in both hands, perhaps hoping to pull Cenotaph in close for a killing blow; instead, with a horrible ripping sound, the prehensile limb tears off from the body entirely. I think to myself, that must be the end. It can't win with such a crippling injury.

Cheers wash through the city. Metagnostic flags wave in the acrid breeze.

As Imago stands over its final, defeated challenger, I imagine Dai, somewhere inside there, relishing the moment of victory.

"Finish it," I whisper.

And that is when from the depths of the cloak a squared fist erupts into Imago's marble mask, shattering it instantly. Our god, my god, tilts, teeters, and collapses against the cliff below the city, as Cenotaph's hand crumbles from impact.

Understanding grips my stomach with icy hands and begins to twist. I know now what I had blindly feared. This new Cenotaph is not some aberrant effort of the Necrochaste. No, not merely that. It is a thing emerged from the opening created by something fundamental battered and tortured and twisted into a doorway. If a god is the living avatar of the faith, then this Cenotaph is a walking religious revolution.

A familiar chill runs through me, a memory, a warning.

The dread god Cenotaph reveals a second hand and doffs its cloak, flinging it skyward, blocking out the sky like a night arrived prematurely. Tides of bile surge up my throat. Words can barely describe such horror. Flesh corrugated like a decaying brain glistens like oil in the sunlight. A shallow graveyard for a body, knifelike bones protruding with an obscene scorn for any divine artistry. No head rests upon its shoulders but a mass of rotted meat bunched and pinned within a golden burial-mask too small for its body, doughy muscle compressed into the mold of a tortured howl. My eyes rove frantically, reluctantly, across its misshapen form, but there is no sign of the telltale scar indicating a cockpit entrance stapled shut.

There is little that is godlike in any god, but in this creature, there is too little else. It is millennia of resentment and desperation and cancerous nihilism vomited forth into biomateriality. Perhaps that is the long-forgotten reason why we grow our gods crippled, yoke them with armor of stone and steel, retard them into a relative-stupor with bullets of lesser intellect to the brain. Man must understand implicitly that a god without humanity is no different than a devil.

The word Messiah means savior.

This is what they save us from.

Cenotaph lunges, digging claws into Imago's marble breastplate, savaging it apart like a stubborn clamshell. I find myself repeating the Invocation of Divine Transfiguration, offering pieces of my soul to the god I hate, praying for my brother, not even to win, just to survive. Never more clearly do I remember the happy times we shared together, the days before duty and jealousy cracked us in half. The years of underground resentment evaporate; I can't remember why I'd clung to them so, how that bitterness could taste so sweet. I would forgive him for anything now if only our God granted us one last chance.

Words, however, do not suddenly gain power now that I suddenly want them to.

I watch in horror as Cenotaph's own chest splits, folds of skin peeling back from a grin of yellow ribs, revealing a shaft of bone that flickers like a lizard's darting tongue. It stabs deep into Imago, going out white and coming back red. Is that me screaming? I cannot hear myself; I only feel the vibrations within my throat. It is the wailing of a dust mote in a hurricane, for the whole city is screaming. Numb, deaf, I watch all the little men and women scramble over one another to escape as Cenotaph climbs over Imago and into Titanomachia.

Left behind, no longer worth the effort of the death god, Imago sprawls limp against the cliff-face, one arm slung over the city's edge, its head slumped against its chest, the spot in its breast where Dai should be safely ensconced punched cleanly out of its body.

The Tender Magister had returned for another of her inspections. She moved slower than usual. I crouched in the corner, blinking at the blinding light of her little lamp. A shard of molted chitin nestled in my palm. I could not say how long the madness had taken hold of me. It lurked in my black gardens like a trap-beetle, incisors trembling for the strike.

"How goes the Invocation?" she asked. Her voice scraped rough with exhaustion.

"Very well," I said. Then, barely above a whisper. "How much longer will it be?"

She gave me a curious look, as if surprised I could speak any other words.

"What?"

"I asked you a question. Is it almost ready? When can I leave?"

"Well, Operoph, your god-larva has done well enough under your care. It should take another year or so for full maturation —"

A thread snapped inside of me. Red flowers filled my eyes.

I lunged for the Magister, knocking her to the ground. Her lamp rolled beneath the chrysalis, shining through its translucent shell in muted slashes of emerald and sapphire.

"A year!" I screamed. "No, no, no. I will return up the cradle with you. Now. This idiot worm doesn't need me, all it does is grow and hang there mocking me and soon it won't even do that because I will kill it! Do you understand? I will find a way to kill the damn thing! What then? No god, no messiah, no Imago!"

"Indeed?"

The Magister smiled. With a flick of her wrist, she tossed me to the side.

She stood, and as she did, let the scarves fall away. In the lantern light she was a shining skeleton. Enough of her body had been replaced with prosthetic glass that it made my missing arm seem a minor injury. Spurs of chrome jutted from her shoulders and knees. Her spine was a mangle of fibers and meat, roughly sewn shut with glass cables. A thrumming cyclone of biomecheia spiraled in her chest.

Although she was a horror, or maybe because of it, I growled and attacked. She easily dodged all my blows. She moved like air, like dust. When I tried to kick her, she bent out of my path. I lifted a rock to crush her head and she plucked it out of my hands with ease. Undeterred, I fought on, fueled by desperation, lightning bolts of pain cracking through my disused muscles and splintered fingernails.

At one point, I thought I might have won. She lay pinned beneath me. I pressed the chitin shard to an exposed triangle of flesh beneath her chin.

"Tell me, Magister," I said, "what god do you serve?"

She laughed. "My dear child. I serve no god, no Clade. I serve the future, no matter the Messiah, no matter whether the morning greets the Left-Hand Sun or the Right-Hand Sun. I serve the emperor and the beggar. I serve the dust and the day. I serve tomorrow."

"So, you serve nothing. All of this, this hell of yours, of worms and slavery and darkness. Pointless. We are told stories about how the old ones designed the Gods as vessels of our faith, perfect creations of science, the ultimate proxies for our people. But, down here, in the murk and filth, where is that sanctity? I haven't seen it. It's a ruse. A pit of monsters supplying endless fairy tales for the world above. It's all nothing —"

The Magister's hand reached up and locked around my throat with a grip like ice.

"You want to see nothing, child?"

She squeezed. Hard. I gasped for breath. The shard tumbled from my hand.

"Imagine a world without Gods," she said. "Imagine such a quiet world, such an empty and *forsaken* world. Every season, the cradle yields fewer and fewer viable god-larvae. You probably didn't notice while floating in all that self-pity. Ah, but plenty of corpse-eaters! Those genetic failures thrive. And the Necrochaste are ever so pleased to take them in."

Gray spots danced behind my eyes.

"I used to see the future. Now all I see are fields of ruin and the stink of death. And where death goes, the Necrochaste are never far behind. Skitter skitter at the edges of the cradle. You think you know madness? I have seen what happens in their Black Temple. Carrion-eaters with a secret smile on their bloody teeth. I know what's coming for us."

My heart slowed. I felt myself sink into my body.

"Go ahead, embrace the void, then you will truly see what nothing means," she sneered. "So young. So many places for a small white worm to hide."

My voice was a slight rasp choked with dust.

"No ..."

"Then tell me, forgotten daughter of Clade of the Metagnostes, what god do you serve?"

The massive chrysalis loomed above me, growing larger, closer. A great hatred seethed through me. My fingers found the shard. The chrysalis filled my vision, horizon to horizon. A great forest of hatred filled my airless lungs.

I slashed the shard across the Magister's neck. Hot blood spurted across my face. She lurched to the side, grabbing at the wound. I thought she would die, then and there. But instead, she began to laugh. Loud and joyful, even as the blood spattered the dust around her. She reclaimed her lamp and hobbled towards the elevator.

Soon I was alone in the dark, again.

I waited.

The Tender Magister never returned.

The forests of my heart petrified. A rage blossomed out of my chest like acidic flowers. I missed my god-larva. I missed its sloth and its fury and its cowardice. I hated that it had left me. I hated that it was too late to kill it. I punched its impenetrable shell until my knuckles bled. My Invocations curdled to blasphemy. "You are the Idiot Imago, The Pustule of Hate, Lord of the Sewer Pit, Killer of Mothers, Lower than Filth ..."

A day, a month, an eon passed.

My dreams became black oceans. Lifeless and empty.

The next light I saw was that of the Left-Hand Sun, shining its brilliant copper warmth across the war fields of Titanomachia as Dai lifted me onto his palanquin.

The Holy War is over. The Necrochaste have won. Their truth has been uplifted to the axis of reality: that death comes to all things.

Instead of returning to the fire of the Omniforge to sacrifice itself, our new god strides deeper into the city. It has no interest in cycles or fire or rituals. There is no Messiah to infect it with a purpose higher than destruction. It is movement without destination, slaughter without passion, hunger without appetite. And that, I see now, is the point entirely. The Necrochaste in their misanthropic genius have devised an engine of perpetual ruin, a truly Self-Demonstrating Principle, that will continue to devour until there is nothing left in creation but itself to consume, and leave the universe a solved equation.

Our dark new god is an infant stumbling over its toys. The arc of each footstep demolishes the tallest buildings, splashing rubble across the streets below, where men and women scurry like lost ants. It plucks random corpses from the ground and pours them like grains into the mouth of its mask.

Up and down the streets of Titanomachia, the people reach out to embrace the void.

Many have instantly absorbed this new cosmological hierarchy and begun to attack one another, possessed with the religious fervor to end lives. I weave and leap through hundreds more who have simply surrendered and lain themselves procumbent in the street to beg repentance, a gift that if given at all will arrive as an instantaneous death beneath its heel. Those still devoted to their own slain gods find their way to the tops of buildings and throw themselves off, seeking finality in Cenotaph's jaws. The god of death is a weight upon the fabric of the world; souls that do not cling desperately to it cannot help but freefall into its event horizon.

I could run far away. I could hijack a flyer, retreat to Novo Viridis.

Walk the shores of silver. Drown in milkweed. Wait for the thundering end of it all to find me.

But all I see is the furious, desperate face of the Tender Magister.

Forgotten daughter of Clade of the Metagnostes, what god do you serve?

I push back against the wailing crowd. I run towards the ruin, the blood, the death.

I duck under a collapsed bridge as Cenotaph's foot swings overhead, its passing shadow cold and heavy as a glacier. A spire that has stood for ten thousand years explodes and I am scourged by a hail of ancient rock. Among the falling debris I spy something gray and wet and squirming, a piece of the god splintered off by the impact. Whorls of spoiled flesh draw me in, coaxing my eyes to dig for deeper horrors. It is the corpse of a man, somehow both shrunken and bloated, a rehydrated mummy. In his arms is the corpse of a white god-larva, its chitin still soft, clutched as if in the throes of lovemaking. It is only when I dare look closer that I see how their skin flows seamlessly together, how the man's ribcage bulges through the distended membrane of the larva's underbelly. Clear cerebral liquid bubbles up and spills from open sores where I can all too easily imagine this unholy creation interfacing with others like it, unholy confusions of man and stunted god.

I recall the Necrochaste pillaging the graveyard. Dai and I had curled our lips at the sight of them and turned our eyes from what they were doing. The foul business of lower castes was not our concern. We were supposed to be above that sort of filth. But perhaps had we acknowledged their humanity, if we had deigned to notice how they were changing under our noses, we could have prevented what they were becoming.

For centuries we'd drowned them with our leavings. We forget that enough trash can bury the tallest cathedral.

Cenotaph is not a singular god.

It is many.

But that truth is useless to me now. I hurry on to what's left of my own god.

The rim of the city is a desolate abattoir. Through force of will, I shunt the offal-stench of ruptured bodies from my head and go tripping and sliding down the wreckage to the spot where Imago collapsed. On approach, its skull is the belly of a beached leviathan, mother-of-pearl riddled with black veins as thick as my calf. I clamber over the dead to where its mouth is splayed open, insensate. Its segmented tongue lolls in its own blood. This enviable spot so near a god is wasted on me. I come bearing no devotion. No hope. The moment of Dai's death is a lovingly documented permanence in my memory. Cenotaph cannot be stopped. The world is already ended, continuing to turn only on dwindling momentum.

I have only rage to offer the god who took everything from me.

A thousand vile words crowd against my teeth but only one sound escapes, an inarticulate shriek that ruins my throat, the single syllable pronouncing hate. I pound my fists against the chitin beneath Imago's bludgeoned eye, never minding how it hurts my hands. Useless creature. I should have killed it when I had the chance, pried open its brainpan with the tick blade and crushed its ganglia in my hand, but this is the least of what I regret. If I can leave a scar it with my shattered bones, that will be enough.

I jump backwards as the god stirs.

Imago rises groggily, a drunkard awoken too soon.

This close I can hear every pop and crack of its vertebrae aligning as it props itself up on the cliff with one hand. Those huge, green eyes swivel to engulf mine and the rest of me too.

My gore-slicked hair flutters towards the god as it breathes in, hundreds of tons of air at a time. A shudder rolls through it, and it touches a fingertip to the hole in its chest where blood still runs in rivulets through the grooves in its hide. The emeralds of its eyes seem to lose some of their glow. Its finger curls into its palm. The others join it in a fist. Its chest swells, sloughing off the last clinging hunks of masonry. The expression between the crags of its face unravels into naked emotion. Confusion. Weakness.

Despair.

The bastard of a sob and a laugh escapes me. *You can't*, I want to tell it. To dictate to this immeasurably greater being what it is or is not. It's supposed to be an organic machine, a weapon unequipped with a soul. I want to demand it be thus, as if no one is permitted to grieve for Dai but me, yet I cannot deny plain reality. It was I who slavishly cared for it, picked its ticks, scooped its shit, but from the beginning it was Dai it chose to become one with, and until now I had not understood what that meant. That it could mean anything at all to the god.

I do not want to be, but it and I are together in this moment.

A boom from far in the distance. Silhouetted against the cobalt glare of the Omniforge, the god of the Necrochaste moves with a dreamlike elasticity, a tribal dancer gamboling madly in celebration of itself for lack of any power higher, each step flattening that much more of the world.

Imago and I turn back to one another. The god's eyes seem to glow with hatred combusting into fury. What flickers in them consumes all of me. Imago growls from deep within its throat, and I feel my heart begin to thrum in tune. I cannot let go of my hate for

Imago — it is woven through me as surely as a cancer lashes itself to one's bones — but now there is one I hate more, and it is a hate that Imago and I have in common.

Something passes between us as we stare into one another — information undiluted by physical discourse. Compared to it, there is so little of me that it cannot help but perceive everything I am, and at the same time, its eyes are two great windows through which its entirety is visible. I see something glinting through flesh gone vaporous, a point of light with five fingers. Though its atoms would have been long since metabolized, I can feel the piece of me it devoured all those years ago still pulsing within Imago. However subtly, however thinly, my genetic code has been interwoven through its own.

There is a link there, an oiled string across which the flames of rage are free to race together.

My mind races. The process by which Messiah is linked to god is a hallowed science, refined across millennia into a surgically exact dogma of operations, incorporating dozens of roles and a plethora of tiny rituals. But I wonder now if beneath that gilding of pomp and liturgy, the procedure is not fundamentally flawed, a crude work-around based on a poor grasp of something approaching ineffable and long since petrified in tradition.

I think of the corpse intertwined with the god-grub. Intimate at the mouth and groin, impossible to tell who had devoured whom. What if there is another way? A deeper, more honest theosis?

Would I stake my life on it? Why not? Fast approaching the end of the world, I may as well fling my fate like a javelin into the dark, on the chance that I may strike its heart.

I straighten my spine and beam challenge at Imago through my every pore. Dai would still be alive if it had only chosen me instead. I still cannot forgive it for that. But there is no use clinging to grudges. Nothing will survive the apocalypse.

You have taken in a part of me already, I say, through my eyes, my jaw, my shivering fists. *Do you dare take the rest?*

The god regards me in silence. Though it has no lip to curl I know that its own distaste for me still lingers. A mind that size can never be too full of slights. But it too must sense the futility of hating anything other than Cenotaph. Better to let it go. Better yet, to set it alight. Heap that and everything perishable into a pyre and let it burn death's hand as it reaches for us.

Well? I demand.

The god's mandible hitches up higher on its skull, pulls back slightly, in the nearest approximation of a smile that an exoskeleton can produce.

Imago lifts me up, swallows me whole, and becomes my cocoon.

◐ ♀

I am —
    I? No, we —
    No, no, we are one, not two —
    Yes —
    Then I, I —
    Yes.
    I am music.

Matter proceeds through corridors of space and time to the beating of my heart. The inside of my skull is a symphony, each notion that blares from my synapses a scintillating note. As I chase down the burning horizon my footfalls strike the surface of the universe like the skin of a drum — the city beneath me ripples, wrinkling inwards, kowtowing in waves, obeying the inherent tyranny of this body. It is all overpowering. I want to laugh aloud, to sing to my own rhythm, but I am not sure how.

I am music, yet I am discordant. I am unfamiliar to myself. The muscles in my arms heave more bone-weight than feels natural. Thousands of tons of meat come crashing down upon my feet with every step I take, and there is a pressure between my scapulae that I cannot attribute to any bit of anatomy I can name. My vision is more powerful than any cortical implant, each optical lobe in my eye peeling back layers of clotted atmosphere, beyond which the tinges and textures of the heavens are laid bare in nauseating detail.

My thoughts, too, do not feel like mine. They curl around strange hungers; surreal, claustrophobic memories; fears of concepts that I have no words for, but feel that I should; and among them, wafting like plankton in currents of cogitation, images: A spiral of teeth; a screaming woman; bleeding glass; a smiling figure, who is at once a laughing boy and a man crowned in butterflies, who is at once alive, running beside me, my hand in his, and dead, smeared into plasma across the inside of my soul.

    Dai.
    My brother —
    My Messiah —
    My pilot —

I do not know who he is. He is too many things to tell. But his loss draws blood from even this planetary core of a heart.

I have not lost my mission in the labyrinth of my new brain.

The shadowed god dancing in firelight — a name lunges into my hands: Cenotaph — has not noticed me coming. It is lost in gluttony, devouring grublike humans by the handful. It has grown larger than what my tangled memories show me, more apelike in proportion. These telescopic eyes of mine dissolve it down to the molecule. Fat, white, blind god-runts slither across its hide like beads of sweat, scenting out fresh corpses as they are pushed through to the god's surface, burrowing inside through whichever orifice, adding their biomass to the profane conglomeration that is Cenotaph.

The more it eats, the greater it becomes. In time only mountains and forests and oceans will fill its belly. It will be the death of what lives as well as what does not. But what I realize now with my divine intellect is that it is, truly, a Self-Demonstrating Principle.

That all things can die.

Cenotaph finally registers me now that its hands are empty, that the wind has changed to contort around me. The death god turns, glacially, a roar of challenge gurgling up from its guts. Its strength is the unbreakable grip of the grave, but it has grown corpulent, bloated, slow. My squared fist twists its head backwards on its neck, crumples its golden death-mask, and shears away the bottom jaw beneath it, in a single blow.

Red-toothed satisfaction rips through me from two places, vestigial sacs of identity that yet cling to me by gossamer strands. I came from woman and god, but they were but the two layers of my cocoon. I am what was inside them both. The atomic yolk of potential impossibly conceived.

Opheroph and Imago. Those names are emptied husks.

I am Immaculata.

I am life.

Cenotaph's mandible carves across avenues of houses before losing momentum. Gobs of pulverized god-corpse fusion pelt the surviving humans skittering about far, far below. I lock my hands around Cenotaph's outflung arm, feel its flesh squeeze like jelly between my fingers, and hurl it up and over my shoulder. Its feet have almost left the ground when the limb tears free with a wet rip and a rainstorm of translucent ichor. I bring its severed arms down upon its head, smashing the god into the ground. Sans mask, its skull dangles off the end of its neck, pathetically small without its jaw, eyes of slurred human-meat rolling in vestigial sockets.

The God of Death drops into a defensive crouch; no time to react as its sternum cracks open and the wicked bone spike inside punches a chunk of meat out of my chest. The pain radiates across miles of flesh; there is so much of me that can hurt. Men and women are swept away in the blood that spigots from the wound.

Silhouetted against the small sun of the Omniforge we are dollops of black ink, sometimes two, sometimes one, smearing together, dribbling apart, swirling in circles as we roll and grapple across the face of Titanomachia. To battle Cenotaph is to battle the waves of a dark sea as they fold relentlessly over you. Slow, yes, but relentless, always in motion, never hesitating, never flinching, never retreating to think or plan because it is unburdened by the capacity. Whatever pain I inflict peters out in its tangled nerves before reaching its brain. When I rake my fingers through its throat, scooping away a dolmen of meat, the creature breathes through each of the thousands of tiny mouths that perforate it like septic pores. Its rent throat is already smoothing over, filling out, as grub-plugged corpses ooze back into place. Where it plants its hands, god-larvae swarm off it in search of the trampled dead that inundate the city. It is not a single entity I must slay but everything in the world dead or yet to be.

If that is so, I must be more efficient.

My eye pricks on a spike of gold among the rubble. The warhammer of Valtahar, still steaming.

I roll over and scrabble after it on all fours. I can hear Cenotaph hauling its bulk hand over hand across the city roofscape in pursuit. I reach the hammer first and use its grip to haul myself upright. Bracing my foot against the ruins of an ancient temple I wrench the weapon from its impact crater. I hear Cenotaph already surging to its feet, its arms pinwheeling as if trying to swim through the air.

I bring the hammer low behind me, letting strength run through my arms and into my hands. The weight is unbearable, but this body is stronger now than it was before it was me, who is us, who is I.

Cenotaph collects itself and becomes a missile of howling oblivion. At the same time, I release the tension in my body and swing the hammer up. The two arcs intersect. Many things happen at once. The force of the collision shreds half the tendons in my shoulder; a sleet of blood and bile blinds me in one eye; the warhammer goes spinning into the air.

The God of Death rips in two like a doll of wet straw.

My strength evaporates like a daytime fantasy. I collapse to my knees. The air is bitingly cold inside the two wounds in my chest. That phantom pressure between my shoulders has grown into a suffocating weight on my lungs; both pains squeeze me like the jaws of a vice. Trying to pry the spike out with one hand leaves me dizzy, and I quickly give up. I'll heal fast; I can already feel the truly innumerable cells of my body making more of themselves, breaking down the intruding matter, breeding blood.

Through blurred vision I watch Cenotaph's lower body totter onto its feet. A long and comical process. It struggles to find its balance, blindly stumbling this way and that like a headless chicken. My brute god shell sees victory, but the human in my core hisses *no*. This feels too easy.

Nothing that moves is dead.

From over my shoulder, the chthonic groan of a million mausoleums' doors opening.

I turn, and a gold-clad hand slams down on the rim of the city.

Cenotaph rises from the graveyard of gods, towering higher into the sky than it had before. Its torso, arm, and head have plastered themselves to the decapitated corpse of Valtahar. Infested corpses seep like black mold from the gaps in the forge god's once hallowed armor, infecting it with profane ab-life. Vishtah's five arms crown the abomination, and more and more of it heaves itself into the city with every second I stare.

I force myself to stand and face the thing. My arm has not nearly reattached itself; Valtahar's hammer is just out of reach. I am a thousand cubits high and still engulfed by Cenotaph's shadow. I should despair. But I do not.

The pressure upon my spine has reached its crescendo. My body thrums on the threshold of self-destruction. I feel enzymes swirling, courting, bursting into undiscovered reactions. There is a pain that is not like pain, that does not punish, but promise. I realize that I have been fighting it without thinking. Holding myself together when I should be letting go. A thing unlocked is meant to open.

My skin explodes off my back. I throw my head back and bellow in ecstasy as two immense, wet bolts of bodymass erupt from me. It feels like minutes as they unfold and expand, segment by segment, and finally snap taut on the wind. Panes of organic glass stretch out to either side of me, each longer than I am tall. I look down and note that my shadow has grown wings.

Cenotaph approaches unperturbed. It is so heavy now that it must wade through the rock below the city. Fearsome? Yes. The way the night is fearsome. A black ocean. It comes. It cannot be stopped.

But the smallest light will cut straight through it.

I stride to where the hammer fell and lift it one-handed with new ease. I climb the lip of stone around the Omniforge, dip the hammer's head into its corona, and hold it there until the metal glows like a chip of the Right-Hand Sun. I beat my new wings once, twice, and the third time they slap down upon the heat coming off the forge. I feel myself lift a hair's width from the ground. I find that angle a second time and try again, harder. This time my feet clear rooftops.

Riding the boiling heat of nuclear fire, I take to the air, each flap of my miles-long wings pulverizing the city with hurricane winds. Cenotaph stares up at me, its bare skull gormless as it strives against my downdraft, groping at me like a needy infant. I fold my wings shut and plunge from the sky with my hammer raised high above my head. Fury, but contempt as well. Cenotaph is a mountain of waste. From so much emerged so little.

Gravity, velocity, heat, and hate, all the greatest forces of the universe together, come crashing down upon the god of death. There is light. There is thunder. There is blood. The black and empty future that had cauterized the stump of history cracks like a cocoon and gives birth to new possibilities.

It is hours before I spy survivors creeping from the rubble. By that time, I have almost finished shoveling the remains of Cenotaph into the Omniforge, which crackles along contentedly, a glutton with an unparticular palate. The world will turn another decade yet, though in truth I suspect it would do so anyway. Much is made of large but mundane things. Perhaps too much.

I am surprised to see so many survivors/people. I fought with neither restraint nor regard, and for that I wince in belated guilt. The unscathed carrying the injured, they assemble in shell-shocked silence on ridges of debris; My powerful eyes sift them into their Clades according to style of dress and facial features. A good many are my own Metagnostics, though not an excessive proportion. Starwise gather beside them, and Vishtahists too, and even those Necrochaste unfortunate enough to be passed over by their god. Disparate peoples, yet with the same curious light in their eyes. The same words beginning to manifest through their lips. Orisons in a dozen dialects all woven shyly around an unspoken word, a name they do not yet know.

Me, I realize. They are already worshipping me.

And how could they not? I am a truer god than has ever walked the earth. A god that chose not to burn, but to remain and thus rule, by default. Among one voice in twenty I detect religious fervor verging on mania. The same conviction that brought death into flesh and cast the world into the teeth of entropy. My very existence excites the soul into a frenzy. I wonder what a single word might do.

No, I fear it.

I know the truth of the gods. I am its embodiment, the Self-Demonstrating Principle that from flesh can only hatch flesh. They would listen if I dictated that they not worship me. If I ordered them to believe that I am not a god, to build up a church to my own non-godhead. But I know, even as I consider it, that it would be doomed from the start. Any instruction that falls from my lips can only be divine commandment.

I stare into the fire of the Omniforge.

Perhaps it is best I burn after all.

Projected futures unspool from churning synapses. I foresee the cycle spinning into infinity, should I cast myself into the pit. More children raised in dark servitude. More children sacrificed for the chance of glory. An entire race of beautiful creatures enslaved to continue pointless rituals. Even as a memory I will only inspire gods greater, stronger, fiercer than ever before, each generation another chance to destroy the planet.

Misery birthing misery, forever. That is what I see.

This is a choice greater than even these shoulders can bear. But perhaps that responsibility, and not some quality of the flesh, is what divides false god from true. I look at my spread hand, lose myself momentarily in the whorls and micro-abrasions of my skin. I am not divine. I am meat, grown from worm, fed on shit, yet I am here, while all the gods that came before me are but songs and ash.

Whatever the people should want, they believe I can give it to them, but a good god would not spoil her people. A good god would serve the dust and the day. It would serve tomorrow.

It would deliver them what they need.

I cannot force the world off the track of tradition. I must coax it away, over time, with talk and patience. I must take my countenance down from the heavens, bow to humanity, so that it can glimpse my flaws. It will be difficult to guide with hands that so easily destroy, but I must believe there is a good future within the night past the guttered Omniforge. One where families remain whole, where girls do not rot in darkness.

With these strong hands, I will steer the world there.

Memories Written in Scars

L'Erin Ogle

There is dirt beneath your fingernails.

Small pieces of bark and rock and the forest floor bite into your knees and the palms of your hands.

You are laughing. You are drunk. You are fourteen and this summer feels like it will last forever.

You roll onto your back. They stand around you like the points of a star. The shadows fall through the trees. The warmth of the sun is dappled across your body in spots. The whole world breathes in and out with you. Your shorts are short. Your smile wide. Your hair is long and there are bits of leaves and dirt scattered throughout it. You have never felt lighter or more at peace than now.

There is a period of time where you are laughing in the dirt, and then things get dark, hidden by shadows, parts of this scene obliterated and blurred beyond recognition.

Parts of it not.

You bitch, you bitch, you bitch.

You don't know who says it. Maybe no one does. Maybe you're saying it in your head, guttural, feral, grunted words.

How different the forest floor feels against your chest and bare stomach when you are pushed down against it.

In and out, of consciousness. In and out, of memories.

The shadows flitting through the branches and the forest ceiling coalescing into one, a swirling darkness, all shadows and despair. All of it, twisting around together, a vortex of you, spun across the clearing.

It's the first time you see her.

The woman, made of shadows. The one who will always be there, whether you see her or not. Is she part of you? Or is she a curse?

Black inky hair, flowing across the forest floor. Eyes that bore holes into you.

The beginning, or the closest thing to it.

Twenty years pass. You're swallowing whiskey in your favorite bar, minding your own business, when one of the scars on your forearm starts burning like it's on fire. You look down, away from the prying eyes of an old woman. Your arm isn't on fire, the twisting track of the scar across your forearm, but the seam of it bulges. It ripples and puckers, the memory trying to escape. Memories are coming out of you more and more lately, ripping free in little sprays of crimson. You leave bloodstains everywhere you go. Some of the past you had forgotten. Some you remembered but did not want to know. Some you aren't even sure really happened. When a person is drunk as often and as long as you, things aren't ever really drawn clearly. Reality is slippery and malleable. You're never quite sure what's happening around you.

You know this scar, though, the one that turns from a closed, sealed line into split lips. It's one you put there yourself, after that fucking party where you met the Gazelle for the first time. Not met, but saw.

The fucking Gazelle.

And before you can think another thought, the scar bursts open, and there you are, back at that party that was the beginning of the middle of the end.

The sun beats down and makes you so hot that the wine and food twist up and cook in your stomach. Your husband keeps staring off into the distance, so far away from you that it makes you wonder if he's really even there at all.

You've drunk too much. It's a thing that's happening from time to time, something you're getting known for, something no one talks about in front of you. You've teetered on the edge between a semblance of control and a total loss of it for a long time. That line you walk is a slippery little tightrope, and when you curl your toes around it to try to check your balance, it hurts. Then the need sets in, sinks its teeth into you and starts chewing every frayed nerve ending in your body. And the only thing that takes the sting out of the bite is booze poured on top of booze. It's a shitty solution, but it's the one you choose.

This party is one where you've had too much wine, the dry red kind poured through an aerator, something you'll never enjoy as much as the fire a slug of good whiskey possesses. You're wearing a sundress with a high collar, to hide the scar from your heart transplant, a line down your chest with three sharp, jagged lines extending from one side, where a post-op infection required additional incisions to drain the poison out. You drink too much and end up slouched in the lawn chair, eyelids stone-heavy. They're shuttering closed when you feel rather than see your husband stand up. His chair creaks. He stands still for a moment, head cocked, listening for you while you gather together your vision in silence and peer from slitted eyes to watch him slink off.

You wait until he's crossed the lawn to his friend's house, turned around the gleaming siding. They're always his friends, not yours. The ones you had have fallen away in the spaces you leave between calls and visits, and the way you shut yourself in. It's always too much, the demands of friendship. All the honesty it requires. All the effort.

After he clears the corner, you get to your feet and follow him. The earth shifts beneath your feet, and you know you're more than just a little drunk; you're drunk drunk. You should go back to the chair and nap until your husband wakes you and leads you to the car, where he'll buckle your seatbelt and you can both ride home in the empty silence of disappointment.

But you don't. You have to see, although you already know. He's been somewhere else, inside someone else, and you exist less than she does. Of course, she's here. And around the corner you peek, to see where she stands, slim and sleek in a sundress, sober on steady legs, the curves of her calves defined by the kind of high heels you can never pull off. The Gazelle. She stands with her arms crossed over her stomach and he reaches for her hand and they collapse into each other the way stars must collapse into themselves. You should shout and scream, or go back to the chair to nap, but you watch as they cling to each other, and you think, *Do we know her? Do I know her?* But you know, you think. You've always known.

And then you feel the wine coming back up, sickeningly sweet, so you turn back to your side of the house of the couple you don't belong to, who are not your friends, and you vomit wine mixed with won-tons and pieces of mini garlic bread.

You spit until your saliva runs clear and then you look up, where the porch and the chairs lie empty and the lawn glows green against the horizon, backed up against the trees that line the creek in this perfect place, so perfect it makes you gag again, and by the tree there's a woman, or not a woman, but the shadow of a woman, loosely drawn in shadows, dangling beside a tree. The same woman from the woods. The same cold chill strikes through your heart.

The leaves on the tree curl up and away from her. The trunk lists left, and the bark where she rests an outstretched hand is covered with some kind of mossy black growth that spreads outward.

You stumble towards the woods, but your vision grows blurrier and blurrier and you end up on the ground. Your gorge rises and you're spinning, the ground weaving underneath your feet.

You remember how the story ends. Your husband found you puddled in vomit and drove you home and you fought and that — that was the beginning of the middle of the end.

You look up from the scar that bore this rotten memory fruit. Your skin has split, trickling blood from the edges of its seam. Slashed apart, stitched together, torn asunder. The blood runs and you use your napkin to hold pressure, crimson spilling across the pads of your fingers.

There's an old woman across from you, her scalp salmon pink with pale wisps of white hair, wrinkled skin sagging off old bones.

She lifts her arm as if making a toast and your arm rises involuntarily in the exact same fashion.

"You can make people stop seeing each other, but you can't make them stop loving each other," she says, syllables slipping past black teeth. "Don't you remember? Until you remember, you'll keep opening up."

This is weird, but you're used to weird, and you're getting to that point of intoxicated where the shutters of blackout start descending, where nothing you say will matter, because you won't have any recollection of it.

"Cheers to that," you say. It's the last thing you'll remember tonight.

※

You woke up after the party with your skin sealed shut with crusted blood, dark and sharp on your skin. You didn't remember slicing yourself open. There were other, older scars, but it had been a long time since you took a knife to yourself. You could almost consider yourself cured.

Your husband asked you why and you didn't answer him. He thought it was because you were drunk. He thought a lot of things about your drinking and you thought a lot of things about his infidelity but neither of you ever talked about them. You told him about the woman made of shadows instead. You blocked out seeing her before, just like you blocked out the whole thing that happened back then, but now you thought maybe she'd always been there. You'd felt her. She was a stormcloud that had hung over your whole life, made you dark and twisted up. All he said was that you had been drinking too much.

You told him he'd been cheating too much.

The marriage limped along, through counseling and more fertility treatments, but his nights were still late and you were still stashing empty bottles of booze in the bottom of the trash or even under the seat of your car, where you could easily pitch them in the trash cans of various gas stations or —

Or the liquor store. Whatever. It didn't matter anyway.

You thought you saw the woman from the woods from time to time, but you could never really capture her image. You'd catch the shadow of her from the corner of your eye, but when you turned your head, the form of a woman dissipated. It wasn't something you could explain and your husband was still talking regularly to the woman with the legs of a gazelle, the one whose high heels drove spikes into your heart at that awful fucking party. First the texts, which you found, and put a stop to. Then a messenger app, then e-mail.

In the back of your head, you were thinking that you could make them stop seeing each other but you couldn't make them stop loving each other, but you didn't know where that thought came from.

It's not normal to follow someone to work. To Starbucks. To the café where they sit across from each other, her hands gesturing and him leaning across the table, crying.

Fucking crying.

You in the car he bought, swallowing whiskey and red creeping around the corners of your vision until the whole scene is painted crimson against your retinas. Until you open the door and stalk towards them, not realizing the bottle dangles from your hand.

You *fuckers*, you shout. What the *fuck*? You throw your hands up to gesture, but you don't remember you're still holding the bottle and it spins slow across the blue sky, sending dazzling prisms of light across the slate stones. It doesn't shatter when it lands, which is a disappointment. You snatch a glass off the table, full of ice water, and you throw it right in her face, then slam the glass to the ground, and that bitch shatters.

They stand up and he moves in front of her. You stare at her legs, still visible through the V of space between his. You can't hurt her. You can't hurt him. Your own hurt is vast and it rises in your chest and chokes you, and you drop into a squat to try to catch your breath but you still can't, you're choking, you're choking, you need air.

You pick up the shard of glass as a reflex, you don't even know you've done it until the blood spills across your arm. Drops through your fingers and patters on the ground.

Jesus, Anna, he says. *Jesus Fucking Christ.*

Behind him is his woman and behind his woman is yours. She comes around them and she comes to you and she touches your hand that grips the glass. Her fingers are warm and blood runs down them and beads off them but where is it coming from? From you or her?

You wake up and you don't know where you are. You can feel the old scars and the new, the ones that keep rupturing back open, like your own soul is trying to flee your body. Maybe it just wants to get away from you. Hell, you want to get away from you.

The sheets have too much starch baked in them and they crackle when you sit up. Something sharp pinches in your elbow. You look down to see a small IV catheter in your arm and tubing snaking through small pieces of tape up your arm. Something beeps at you, constant and monotonous.

She is there, the woman made of shadows, obsidian black eyes.

"You can't make someone love themselves, either," she says. Her mouth is cavernous, and dark, and even though it is not large enough to accommodate your body, you think she could swallow you whole. Inside her there is a vast empty space that echoes and you can feel the way it pulls on you, on your body, the way something behind your eyes is being drawn outwards, towards her.

She gets up and leaves.

Your head is full of vertigo, parts of the room turning in different directions. "Who are you?" you shout. "Who the *fuck* are you?"

Then they come, a young woman in pale blue scrubs, an older bird in canary yellow. The bright color of the older one's clothes hurt your eyes. The younger one tries to reassure you, but the older one tells you to lie down. *Lucky to be alive*, she says. *One of the highest blood alcohol levels I've ever seen.*

You keep trying to tell them about *her*, but then they hold your arm down and inject something into the clear plastic tubing and everything is dull and dark and their voices move so far away.

You're floating, back in the hollow space of your own body.

Drifting.

○

It's two years later you sign your discharge papers and leave on foot. You lost your license a couple of DUI's ago, and your ex-husband won't pick you up anymore. The last time you called him, the Gazelle showed up. Maybe it was a nice thing to do, but no matter how far down you sink, you don't need her pity. Besides, there was the way she rested her hand on her abdomen. Something you always wanted to do, but it never happened. A ring glittered on her finger and sent needles in your eyes and you wanted to yank open the door and throw yourself out on the highway, but you knew the old woman was back there, in the backseat.

She reached up and gripped your shoulder. The sleeve that fell from her arm was ragged and gray and there were silver scars etched on her skin.

She's you.

Or maybe you're just crazy.

You didn't jump. You went home and got drunk.

And today, now, you mean to get home before you start drinking, but Tommy bartends on Thursday and you never worry much for money — there's the monthly disability check plus the alimony. You stop in and you pretend you don't see the woman slipping in behind you and you go the bar and you order a double and there's the old woman from the bar you loved that closed down, the one with the pink scalp and wispy hair, the one that told you, you can't make people stop loving each other. Her and you and your shadow are the only three women at the bar. It could be the punchline to a joke. Old, drunk, evil.

You haven't even started drinking for real when the old woman comes to sit next to you. You startle when she sits next to you at the bar, atop a stool too high for an old woman. There's no glass in her hand and she isn't reflected in the mirror behind the bar. All you can see is your own blurry reflection and a woman made of shadows lurking in the corner of the room, watching you.

You mean to ask the old woman who she is, or what she wants, but her eyes are the same blue as yours, clouded with cataracts, and can she see? She must, because that cloudy gaze drops to your bicep. You wear a thin long-sleeved shirt, but you can see something worming underneath the thin fabric. Another memory, you realize, as a line of fire ignites on the slope of your arm. A bad one.

You look up and the mirror shimmers and shines back in your eyes. Your fingers tighten on your glass. The stool underneath you shivers and grows too small for your perch.

Who are you? You don't say it out loud. Your tongue has grown too thick and fills your mouth.

You are falling off the stool. The old scar is opening up. Blood seeping through the fabric of your sleeve, staining your shirt.

Put something in her mouth so she don't bite her tongue. A wallet or something.

No, dummy, you're not supposed to do that anymore.

Rictus. Your muscles clench, release, and there's the spreading warmth of urine and the acrid scent of it in your nostrils. The old woman on her stool, and the shadow woman in the corner, and everything in the room are dark like an overcast sky. You can hear spit rattling in your throat. You're not drunk enough to die like this. You're supposed to be obliterated. You're not supposed to know it's happening.

Not like this. You'll die with an E etched on your chest. An E for Ending. That seems appropriate.

You know you're in the hospital again.

The shadow woman is there.

The old woman is not.

You do not dream. You never have, not since the Beginning.

Maybe this is a dream. Maybe these are your dreams.

The monitors beep. The IV pump whirs soft in your ear. You feel too worn away at the edges to sit up and see if the sheets still crackle.

"Who are you?" you whisper. You don't recognize your voice.

The shadow woman begins to hiss. Darkness spins up from her feet, surrounds her ankles, making the corner of the room darken and tendrils of the same obsidian black as her pupil begin to snake across the ceiling. Above the bed, they form a tangled nest and ropy vines curl down towards the floor.

They look like vines, but you know they will slither around your arms and legs and slice you open. Their sharp edges are reflected in your eyes.

The door opens and the vines pause in their descent.

The old woman shuffles across the floor. Most of her hair is gone. Her scalp is no longer pink, but the color of bones bleached by a hundred years in the sun. She leans over you.

The scar on your chest, where they sawed through your sternum as an infant, where they split open your chest and placed inside it another, more functional heart, that belonged to a girl or boy less lucky than you, that scar pulses and aches. It looks, vaguely, like an E.

The woman drops something in your bed, beside your arm. Something sharp.

"Help," you whisper through your dry mouth and fat tongue.

She shakes her head once. "Can't. She —" she looks up, at the shadow woman. "Won't allow it."

The other woman opens her mouth, a wet cavern of ink. Yawning maw, only blackness beyond. More tentacles rolling out, snaking across the floor to the old woman. Her own lips skin back from her gums.

"You can start over," she whispers. "But you have to hurry."

And then the ropes encircle her ankles, and jerk. She spills to the floor. The crack of her brittle bones makes you jump. The vines above you pause while the two women struggle.

Hurry.

It isn't like you have a choice. And then, rage creeps up inside you. It's always been there. In a box with a heavy lid. This isn't fair. You've always been the loser. You've always been cursed. The one everyone forgot, or ran away from, until now, when you're in a hospital bed, fighting off a woman made of — what? Shadows and malevolence. Fuck them. If this can be a new start, then you'll be a different person this time.

You look at the E inscribed on your sternum.

You pick up the blade. With a steady hand, you draw a half circle. The cut is cold but your heart beats hot in your chest. You feel both wrong and right, flip sides of the same coin.

A vine bites into your ankle. Another moving for your hand that raises the knife again.

A second curving connection.

Surprise, motherfuckers.

B is for Beginning.

Project Blackbook

J. Tynan Burke and David Gallay

Provisional Report of the National Commission on the "Writhing Darkness" Cyberattacks of December 1, 2021

Appendix II: Commentary

#6: Col. Brian Houlihan (RET)

It is commendable that Congress has acted so quickly to study the events of December 1. Even in the most optimistic interpretations, these events represent an attack against our nation, allies, and trading partners. To the pessimists, they are a proof-of-concept for a new and terrible kind of warfare. Or so concludes the vocal majority of this commission. It has fallen to me to draft the minority report, of which I will be the sole signatory, for I am not a politician, nor do I have a career to preserve. It is the opinion of this minority that the Commission is ignoring the most logical, and dangerous, interpretation: that events unfolded, more or less, exactly as they were documented.

There is no doubt that the primary evidence from WizBang! Software tells a story that beggars belief. It is understandable why the investigation declined to take these documents at face value, and instead forced them into a more pragmatic narrative: that Elvis Nguyen, whom they cast as a drug-crazed hacker involved with subversive Bay Area subcultures, orchestrated everything. It is a well-crafted story that the public was primed to accept. But it is not without flaws. The Commission asks us to believe that Mr. Nguyen — a man with no terrorist affiliations and only a few parking violations on record — was both a modern-day David Koresh, with a multinational corporation secretly in his thrall, and a James Bond villain, capable of inducing mass delusions in the populace. There is another, simpler, conclusion that requires only an honest interpretation of these documents and an open mind: that metaphysical evil exists and is ultimately responsible for the events of December 1. This is the true threat, not only to this country, but to all of humankind.

A Note on Format

Some of the excerpts provided below take the form of a version control log for the source code used in Project Blackbook's software. Every time that changes ("commits") are introduced to the codebase ("repository"), the person making them leaves a timestamped message. Appropriately, the colloquial term for this is a "blame log." For unmodified content, please refer to the raw source documentation.

MONDAY, OCTOBER 4, 2021.
65 DAYS BEFORE THE EVENT.

The Blackbook team was formed. Despite high levels of expertise, strong personality conflicts prevented the team from gelling. This was clear from the very first conversations in the blame log. If they were brainwashed cultists, as the Commission alleges, they all did a very good job of hiding it.

```
Author: John Li
Date: Mon Oct 4 2021 09:49

And away we go! Welcome to Project Blackbook.
I'm going to include our goals in this first
commit since it's easy to find. First, the
user story from Product: "As a user of
several companies' 'smart' lifestyle
services, I'm sick of messing with
complicated apps and interfaces to get them
```

talking to each other. I want a dedicated device that can seamlessly integrate all my services and appliances, so that I can spend less time looking at screens, and more time living my life."

I assume that, having read the tech spec, you all have some questions about the codebase we inherited from our Ukrainian friends at [REDACTED], so here you go. Some of you (Elvis) who hang out in the weirder corners of YouTube might have seen a video advertising a [REDACTED] — a wooden box with no buttons or screens, just a couple of USB ports. This thing could supposedly handle communications between any two devices, without any previous set-up. Obviously, this was never a real product. [Ed.: This video has since been scrubbed from the Internet.]

But the video *was* made by a real company. After some drama within the dev team (sex and drugs, probably, what else would a bunch of college students have going on in the Ukrainian woods?), their assets went to auction, where a WizBang! subsidiary purchased them. Although the [REDACTED] was total vaporware, acquisitions had determined there was potential in the underlying tech: self-training networks and code-free interfaces. In other words, it definitely does something, we're just not sure what or how. That's where you come in.

Our team has been tasked with picking apart the original hardware and source code, figuring out how it works, and translating it into a viable platform for Blackbook. [REDACTED WizBang! Executive Officer] is gunning for a holiday ship date, so there's our deadline. Here are the deliverable priorities.

1. Translate the [REDACTED] code into virtual machines that can be run on standard WizBang! hardware. The compiled image should not exceed 5 GB.

2. Create an interface for the input and output of data into Blackbook neural net, with an emphasis on voice and environmental cues. No external language dictionaries should be required — in addition to automatic machine-to-machine translation, the product can handle rudimentary speech-to-machine translation as well.

3. Develop a modular API integration stack for Blackbook I/O. This should allow the product to collect data wirelessly from any internet service, with an emphasis on personalization, social media, and smart devices. Universal translation will handle authentication and credentials. (Legal has pre-cleared this.)

If you have any questions feel free to stop by my office, but I have the utmost confidence in this team we put together. Move fast but don't break things, folks!

[John Li, 34: WizBang! Software Vice President, IT Acquisitions. Both a ladder-climber and a genuine believer in WizBang!. Criminal history: Petty vandalism (college marching band).]

Author: Esme Vahora
Date: … 11:01

Repo now follows WizBang best practices for README & file structure. Checked in core internal libraries.

REPLY from Elvis Nguyen:
we're checking in libraries? why? is that how your last team did it?

REPLY from Esme Vahora:

> We're supposed to: [link to WizBang! wiki].
> Big breach in the 00's after hackers hot-
> swapped a centralized binary.
>
> **REPLY from Elvis Nguyen:**
> sometimes i forget how long you've been
> around

[Esme Vahora, 38: Project Blackbook Senior Developer (backend). Long-term employee; roller-derby regular. Mental health history: Recurrent depression.]
[Elvis Nguyen, 27: Project Blackbook Senior Developer (embedded systems). Startup veteran and self-styled "psychonaut". Criminal history: Suspended driver's license (parking tickets).]

> **Author: Elvis Nguyen**
> **Date: … 16:05**
>
> take a look at this though: i hacked together
> a package manager we can use for checking in
> the deps. see .elvisfile' for instructions.

> **Author: Esme Vahora**
> **Date: … 16:15**
>
> Removed unapproved homebrew package manager
> from master branch. Please internalize
> WizBang code standards: [link to WizBang!
> wiki]
>
> **REPLY from Elvis Nguyen:**
> fine

> **Author: Elvis Nguyen**
> **Date: … 19:05**
>
> so this code is super weird & the decompilers
> are being even less helpful than normal.
> checking in a sort of braindump of what i
> have so far. john, what even __is__ this? i

don't see what any of this has to do with blackbook. no natural language interpreters, no syntax libraries, no structured data sourcing. looks fuck all like any neural network I've ever seen. just a mess of hardware and low-level OS code.

REPLY from John Li:
Don't worry about any of that now. Just keep going.

REPLY from Elvis Nguyen:
easy for you to say. from the spec i was expecting a standard linux device, like those chinese IOT bots we worked on last year. sure i can virtualize the hardware stack to run on our stock processors but without any reference docs who knows if it is actually working

REPLY from John Li:
Noted. I'll ping acquisitions to see if they expect to make any more translated documents available.

REPLY from Esme Vahora:
Following up on what Elvis said, I'd also love to read over whatever you can get, John. To reiterate what I said in our kickoff standup, I still think it'd be faster & more secure to in-house this. Should we really be bringing in all this unverified material without going through a basic security analysis?

REPLY from John Li:
Vahora, I convinced the boys in Strategy that this would be a nice leg-up for you. You aren't in the basement anymore. This is Building C. Don't make me regret that decision.

John Li decided the next morning to split the team into two verticals, one Elvis's and one Esme's. He also allocated two contractors to the team: Grady Barker and Walter Durns. Grady gravitated towards Elvis immediately, and so Walt ended up with Esme. With the team doubled, Li also asked each member to check in a weekly progress report.

THURSDAY, OCTOBER 14, 2021.
55 DAYS BEFORE THE EVENT.

Author: Elvis Nguyen
Date: Thu Oct 14 2021 04:01

so EVEN THOUGH the code handed us is a disaster, EVEN THOUGH it has languages even i haven't heard of, EVEN THOUGH i can't figure out how the executables work, i cobbled together a smoke test for the virtualized hardware bus. Grady, can you sanity-check it for me? i need to sleep. if you like it send Esme a merge request

REPLY from Grady Barker:
honestly this looks great, instructive even

[Grady Barker, 19: WizBang! contractor and Thiel Fellow. College dropout and professed "hacker." Criminal history: Misdemeanor drug possession (juvenile).]

Author: Esme Vahora
Date: … 12:00
Re: Request to merge virtual-hardware-bus'

Rejected. Code looks good, but it uses spaces instead of tabs, and files do not follow naming standards (e.g. what_is_this_i_cant_even.cpp'). We even have automated tests for these things, you know: [link to WizBang! wiki]

REPLY from Elvis Nguyen:

renamed files, but no way in hell am i using tabs.

[Commit truncated; they go back and forth on this topic nineteen times.]

Author: Walt Durns
Date: … 16:44

Whew, crack the CHAMPAGNE! (For the non-drinkers we have grape LaCroix in the fridge!) Sorry for the radio silence — I retreated to a CAVE to work on this. I think I figured out what the Ukrainians were getting at in the CORE MATH MODULE. Here's something weird: some of the [REDACTED] operations have EXTRA dimensions of HEX values? Worked around it but if it's pervasive, should we rethink our approach?

Submitting merge request for rewrite + tests.

[Walter Durns, 26: WizBang! contractor, subject-matter expert. Mental health history: Asperger syndrome.]

Author: Esme Vahora
Date: … 17:38
Re: Request to merge deciphering-math'

Merged Walt's math functions. Successful virtual POST of TEST_BIOS.la against the default image. Elvis, can you integrate this into your hardware tests?

REPLY from Elvis Nguyen:
you got it

Author: Esme Vahora
Date: … 18:04

PROGRESS_REPORT.MD checked in.

Author: Walt Durns
Date: … 18:13

Oh, right. WHOOPS! Updated PROGRESS_REPORT.MD

Author: Grady Barker
Date: … 18:19

checking in my PROGRESS_REPORT.MD. hope that's not too late, john

Author: Elvis Nguyen
Date … 18:27

lol, were you ¿serious? about that John? why don't you start coming to our stand-ups instead? or is Building C too far?

Author: Grady Barker
Date: … 18:28

deleted file PROGRESS_REPORT.md

**FRIDAY, OCTOBER 15, 2021.
54 DAYS BEFORE THE EVENT.**

```
FROM: John.Li@wizbang.com
SUBJECT: Meet Project Blackbook!
TO: wizbang-all
DATE: Fri Oct 15 2021 08:32
```

Happy Friday Everyone!

I'm sure you've heard rumors about what we've been cooking on the second floor of Building C. I'd like to take a moment to formally introduce our next big thing that will change the world forever: Project Blackbook.

Once upon a time, before everyone kept our calendars and contacts and notes on our smart phones, daytimers were used to keep track of our information. They were physical objects that we became attached to — private, personal, an extension of ourselves. Now, obviously, consumers are not going to give up their phones and return to pen and paper. But what if we could provide them with a reinvented daytimer, one that is just as personal as those old leather-bound notebooks, but also had world-class intelligence and connectivity? For example, it will synchronize your social life and your smart home's climate control. Completely Smart. There's our slogan.

Now that all sounds great, but what makes it different than the thousands of productivity apps already out there? What makes Blackbook special is that ALL your private data is stored, encrypted, on the daytimer itself, not in the cloud where it will be hacked and stolen. This is our secret sauce. With a patented combination of hardware and software, we can imbue each Blackbook device, potentially small as a credit card, with the power of the entire internet. It will be like having your own personal genie!

Really great stuff — this will be WizBang!'s next big thing, and I couldn't be prouder to be working on it. I've attached the product spec.

And now for the team members. I'm sure all of you already know Elvis Nguyen from Smart Paper 3.0 and Blue Satellite (RIP). Working with Elvis on lead is Esme Vahora, who is on loan from the Legacy Integration crew. Filling out the team is Dr. Walter Durns, who you may remember from his presentation on High-Dimensional Neural Cryptography; and Grady Barker, our Thiel Fellow. They have some great stuff cooking, can't wait to show it off! Stop by and say hi if you have a chance!

- JL

FROM: Esme.Vahora@wizbang.com
SUBJECT: re: Meet Project Blackbook!
TO: blackbook-team
DATE: … 09:12

John, appreciate the shout-out, although I wish you had given us a heads up. BTW, the team was discussing this offline and we all think we might make faster progress if we could speak with the original developers of the Blackbook codebase. There's just something … off … about the whole way it's structured. A few hours of knowledge transfer would really clear things up. EV

FROM: John.Li@wizbang.com

Sorry, Esme, that's just not possible. I'm sure you guys will figure it out.

FROM: Walt.Durns@wizbang.com

Hey John, WALT here. Not sure you GET how non-standard these low level math functions are. Switching back and forth from algebraic to transcedental, or right into hypertranscendental for NO GOOD REASON. I get a weird headache just THINKING about it. I'm scared what we'll find when we actually boot up the OS.

Sincerely,

Dr. Walter Durns, PHd Applied Mathematics

FROM: Grady.Barker@wizbang.com

no kidding, doc. half of this crap doesn't make any sense at all and i don't think it's the language barrier. nothing in a google search. crashed my compiler three times. most of it could be tossed if you ask me.

FROM: Esme.Vahora@wizbang.com

John, if it's a matter of money, I'm sure we can justify the cost savings in terms of dev hours.

FROM: Elvis.Nguyen@wizbang.com

i actually kind of like having a real challenge. it's not something we see every day at WizBang, lol no offense. but we do mostly make like, ad software for smart toilets. no but seriously do we at least have the old version control logs?

FROM: John.Li@wizbang.com

I understand what everyone is saying. However, I can't do any more at this time. Please stop asking.

Also, Grady, Elvis, please submit your progress reports ASAP. Paychecks will not be cut without them.

- JL

Editor's note

Had John Li mentioned that the original Ukrainian developers were unavailable due to suicide pact, disaster might well have been averted. As that would have interfered with shareholder value, he chose to omit this fact.

    The Commission has not elaborated on how the Ukrainians' experience could be explained by drugged drinking water, media manipulation, religious brainwashing, or any of the other actions they ascribe to the Blackbook developers. They claim that Nguyen convinced Li to test his bizarre scheme on the Ukrainian developers first, killing them afterwards. However, this flies in the face of the two men's obvious disregard for one another, to say nothing of the complete lack of suspicious activity recorded in Ukraine and the established order of events. While nobody doubts that the WizBang! viral software was a critical factor in the events of December 1, the Commission did not research it beyond a high-level review; our budget was limited. Still, the Commission did establish a thorough provenance of the source code, by hiring several independent experts, as well as a personal visit to the former headquarters of [REDACTED] Software. What follows is a summary of that investigation. The full details can be found in Appendix 3.2.

[REDACTED] Software was located in a tiny village known as Pulyny, the former home of a Soviet codebreaking laboratory, as well as a wilderness area known as Chortolisy, or "Devil's Wood." Their product, which WizBang! acquired through several layers of IP warehouses, utilized classified Soviet cryptographic libraries to "integrate" the device with all other devices around it. Subsequent investigations showed that the code had been modified to perform high-order vector operations in the background.

This next section should be prefaced with a few personal facts.

Although I was baptized Methodist, I am not actively religious. I have never taken part in any pagan or neo-pagan traditions, religions, cults, or rites. Prior to this investigation, I had never put stock in any supernatural phenomena. I began my service in the United States Army Corps of Engineers as an electrical engineer; I believe in the scientific method and fact-based evidence. However, the following conclusion is not a contradiction of those qualities; it is, rather, a result of them.

This minority believes that all unexplained Blackbook software operations trace back to sigils discovered in the Chortolisy wilderness in the 14th century; sigils which the demonologists at the time associated with a demon named, simply, "Chort". As a former god from an era of chaos, Chort sought to return the world to its primordial state. One of the legends describe its form as that of a ravenous worm, swimming in a lake of fire. It is often ascribed the ability to translate any language and break any cipher, to help spread its corrupting influence among mortal minds. The evidence presented here supports the minority opinion that the viral code outbreak of December 1 did not make its way into Project Blackbook out of developer malice. Indeed, if anybody was being manipulated, it was the developers themselves.

(Update: it appears that Appendix 3.2, including all related media, was accidentally excised from the report. The data archive team is working on locating paper originals from which to restore it.)

FRIDAY, OCTOBER 22, 2021.
47 DAYS BEFORE THE EVENT.

The team was poised for a series of breakthroughs in understanding the Ukrainian code. While they'd made progress around the margins, two core questions remained unanswered: What programming language were large swaths of the repo written in? And how exactly did its 'HEX' operating system accomplish its feats?

> **Author: Elvis Nguyen**
> **Date: Fri Oct 22 2021 13:13**
> Re: Request to merge hex-bios-integration'
>
> i think we finally have a pipeline to the HEX BIOS [Basic Input/Output System] ... all held together with staples and chewing gum, can i get a review?
>
> **REPLY from Esme Vahora:**
> Oddly enough, I just finished patching FileUtils to let us read the HEX directory structure. Do you mind if we compare notes instead of merging? Both our teams would benefit from standardizing the interface.
>
> **REPLY from Elvis Nguyen:**
> i think standards is more your territory
>
> **REPLY from Esme Vahora:**
> Fair enough.
>
> **REPLY from Elvis Nguyen:**
> i'm gonna go see if this won't let me chip away at some of the bigger hardware components, ttfn
>
> **REPLY from Esme Vahaora:**
> Just imported your code — dude, are you still using spaces?
>
> **REPLY from Elvis Nguyen:**

DEATH BEFORE TABS

[Thirty-four replies about spaces-vs.-tabs omitted]

REPLY from Walt Durns:
I'll lend a hand, Esme. This BIZARRE math is starting to give me NIGHTMARES and working on some plumbing sounds GREAT.

Author: Esme Vahora
Date: Mon Oct 25 2021 09:44

v1 of the HEX filesystem interface. Kudos to Walt for his heroic parsing of the arcane tree structures.

REPLY from Elvis Nguyen:
this looks excellent and should save all of us a lot of time!

REPLY from Esme Vahora:
You feeling okay, Elvis?

Author: Esme Vahora
Date: … 15:46

Importing helper libraries for ANALITIK-74 and ANALITIK-2007.

REPLY from Walt Durns:
Whoa, ANALITIK! Explains why my transformations were off, the Soviets had a real GONZO implementation. How the HELL did you figure THAT one out?

REPLY from Esme Vahora:
When I worked at IBM, we supported a Ukraine office with these System/360 clones that called ANALITIK subsystems. Don't get too

excited. We'll still have to manually build
C++ bindings to make it usable.

Author: Esme Vahora
Date: Thu Oct 28 2021 10:11

v1 of C++ bindings for ANALITIK code. Elvis,
I imagine this will be a big help.

Author: Elvis Nguyen
Date: … 15:10
Re: Request to merge virtualized-graphics-
chip'

voila, an abstraction around the graphics
chip from the ukrainian prototype. mad kudos
to Esme for both sets of bindings, saving me
loads of time!

REPLY from Esme Vahora:
You're welcome. I like this new and helpful
you.

REPLY from Elvis Nguyen:
anybody who's saving me time to prep for this
weekend is a#1 in my list

REPLY from Esme Vahora:
Got a good costume?

REPLY from Elvis Nguyen:
hell yeah! i've been working on this creepy
segmented worm thing, i'll show you pics
Monday

Editor's note

Misinterpreting Elvis's time constraints as burgeoning camaraderie, John showed these breakthroughs to his superiors and suggested advancing the timeline. Ever-wary of being beaten to market, the CTO approved this new aggressive schedule. This is well-documented in Appendix 4.1.

The Commission has chosen to ascribe this to trickery on Elvis's behalf, rather than incompetence on John's, without ever introducing evidence that John ever possessed the assumed level of competence to make such subterfuge necessary. WizBang! would not be the first corporation to employ middle managers full of ambition but short on foresight. Had the Ukrainian code landed in the hands of any number of similar organizations, the end results would have likely been the same. It was inevitable.

FRIDAY, OCTOBER 29, 2021.
40 DAYS BEFORE THE EVENT.

```
FROM: John.Li@wizbang.com
SUBJECT: Project Blackbook update
TO: wizbang-all
DATE: Fri Oct 29 2021 08:32
```

What a crazy week, huh? You may have heard Building C had some electrical trouble. Who knew that LED lights could even explode? Kudos to the facilities team for being on the ball.

Anyways, a quick update on the great progress we're making on Project Blackbook. Our star developers have gotten several virtualized components working and expect to release their first deliverable as early as next week! Amazing!

We expect Blackbook to exponentially expand the horizons of our IoT [Ed.: Internet of Things] platform. Imagine being able to integrate every facet of your scheduled life, with any device, without having to write a single line of code. We're not making promises, but … ;) Remember: Completely Smart!

Have a great Halloween weekend!

- JL

FROM: Esme.Vahora@wizbang.com
SUBJECT: re: Project Blackbook update
TO: blackbook-team
DATE: … 09:51

John, who changed the timeline? Just because we hit a few milestones doesn't mean we just can slide the dates around. There's still a huge gap in the core repo we haven't figured out. EV

FROM: Walt.Durns@wizbang.com

I SECOND Esme's concern. We still have a LONG LONG way to go until it's actually usable. I think some of these math functions are SELF-MUTATING, and I can't even figure out what they're FOR!

On a side note, I'm going to start working REMOTELY at least a couple days a week. I've been hearing WHISPERS from my workspace, and facilities doesn't seem interested in troubleshooting that. Plus I've been having MIGRAINES all week, and the EXPLODING LIGHTS aren't helping!

```
Sincerely,
Dr. Walter Durns, PHd Applied Mathematics
```

```
FROM: John.Li@wizbang.com
TO: Esme.Vahora

Esme.

Updated timeline came directly from the c-
suite.

In the future, instead of spamming the whole
team, please come to my office to discuss
privately. No need to encourage dissension. -
JL
```

Editor's note

After seeing Walt mention self-mutating code, Elvis realized a possibility the Blackbook team had failed to consider: that the code John had provided them with was not the original code written by the Ukrainian developers. This realization proved to be a direct cause of the December 1 events.

The Commission is correct to conclude that the following conversation between Elvis and Grady triggered most of the events that followed. Note, however, that all of Elvis's actions have clear precursors in the environments and respective/collective unconscious of the other team members, as well as the Ukrainian developers and, indeed, the history of Chortolisy itself.

The following text message exchange was recovered from an external hard drive found buried in Grady Barker's backyard, inside a Faraday-shielded box labeled "IN CASE YOU'VE FORGOTTEN." We are extremely fortunate that box was buried twenty feet deep, allowing it to survive December 1 unscathed, even as the surrounding countryside was partially liquified. The Faraday shielding offered further protection from the wild electromagnetic fluctuations experienced as far as six hundred miles from Livermore, California.

SUNDAY, OCTOBER 31, 2021, 18:45.
38 DAYS BEFORE THE EVENT.

Grady: hey elvis! happy all hallows! gettin some candy? :P

Elvis: i did just eat some psychoactive gummy bears.. sup

Grady: oh jeez

Elvis: remind me to invite you to this halloween party next year, lol

Grady: sounds awesome

Grady: u okay to talk shop a bit? i can't seem to access the repo

Elvis: ha. ok, so. i've been having these wild dreams, where there's like a giant hookworm eating its own tail. hear me out

Elvis: walt mentioned self-mutating code so i thought, what if we can't get hex to boot because you have to feed the bios output back into itself? yea it sounds stupid but i tried it

Elvis: and it worked BUT i think it also fucked the shared dev environment, oops lol. laptop was smoking, had to take the battery out, haven't peeked at it since

Grady: holy shit should we call john??

Elvis: no no we can fix this … er, you can fix this. gummy bears are kicking in

Grady: what do u need bro

Elvis: sending you my offline backup & another thing you can't tell ANYBODY about

Grady: ?

Elvis: yesterday i tracked down a TAR of the original ukrainian repo on the dark web. get this, it's different! a whole extra part to the bios

Grady: wow

Elvis: it's in that stupid russian programming language esme and walt are apparently experts in, i can barely read the extra stuff, but i bet it'll keep the recursive boot from frying our machines

Elvis: i mean it obviously worked for the ukrainians right or wizbang wouldn't have bought their shit

Grady: okay and?

Elvis: type it in by hand. add it to my branch, then merge it into the master branch. rebase both branches so it looks like it was part of my commit. you can disable the security checks and automatic builds by [REDACTED]

Elvis: i was going to do this before my laptop caught fire but here we are.

Grady: we won't get in trouble right

Grady: you there man? been a few minutes

Elvis: zoned out, sorry

Elvis: you and i don't need to answer to anyone. we're psychonauts riding the cosmic fates, and we will get this software working even if it requires assistance from magmatic ouroboroi

Grady: lol maybe i should take it from here man

Elvis: yeah i should really get dressed. don't compile anything and i'll see you at the orifice

Elvis: *office

Grady: lol

Elvis: peace

Editor's note

The hard drive found in Grady's yard indicated that Grady followed Elvis's instructions to add the missing library from the original Ukrainian repo. Log files thereon (Appendix 5) also indicate that he failed to disable the automated builds on the Blackbook development environment, leading to the code being compiled and loaded for testing.

The minority agrees with the Commission that Elvis's irresponsibility and Grady's idolatry led to the introduction of the Soviet 'cryptographic' code. However, while the official opinion is that this is the sort of thing that happens when a pliable nineteen-year-old is allowed to contribute to a project without supervision, the minority concludes that there were likely other influences at play.

MONDAY, NOVEMBER 1, 2021.
37 DAYS BEFORE THE EVENT.

FROM: John.Li@wizbang.com
SUBJECT: !!Update!!
TO: blackbook-team
DATE: Mon Nov 01 2021 13:32

Hey team,

I was informed about the corruption in our dev environment this morning. Thanks to heroic efforts of our IT support team, we should be ok. I'll let you know what our triage team finds out about the cause of the crash.

On the bright side, Elvis was able to boot HEX and demo a functional micro-kernel! His branch had only light damage so we will be using that as the master going forward.

Per the PM, I am also announcing some slight alterations to the team roles. Elvis is now the lead dev. All future merge requests will go through him. Esme, you've done a great job as a co-lead, but I need you to stay hot on kernel stabilization while Elvis builds out the actual applications.

Let's get to work!

- JL

FROM: Walt.Durns@wizbang.com
TO: John.Li@wizbang.com

[Ed.: This unsent email was recovered from Walt's Drafts' folder.]

John,

This is a SECURITY NIGHTMARE. The code Elvis INTRODUCED obviously CAUSED this. Aren't you WORRIED about HOW? If he's going to be THIS irresponsible, maybe the kernel team should put some FAILSAFES and an AUDIT BLOCKCHAIN into our dev environment. Or at least some ACCESS CONTROLS — didn't he do this all from HOME?

Speaking of NIGHTMARES, I'll be taking some PTO this week to see a sleep SPECIALIST to figure out why I've been having so many.

Sincerely,

Dr. Walter Durns, PHd Applied Mathematics

FROM: Elvis.Nguyen@wizbang.com
TO: blackbook-team

Thanks, John!

It's an honor to be leading what's turning out to be a very challenging project. Here's the plan for the near future while I work out something longer-term:

- Esme, Walt, you're doing good work. Keep it up.

- All code will now go through Grady so that I can focus on the app layer.

That's it! I'm an easy boss.

Thanks!
Elvis

THURSDAY, NOVEMBER 4, 2021.
34 DAYS BEFORE THE EVENT.

Under Elvis's hands-off leadership, the Blackbook team began to fall apart. Grady was essentially allowed to set the agenda for what became integrated into the growing project. Grady's behavior, which had been increasingly erratic ever since his exposure to the true Ukrainian repo, went largely ignored, considered to be Somebody Else's Problem.

At this juncture, a poorly understood component of the Ukrainian hardware, known as PIN13, began to assert itself. The Commission's analysis of this circuit revealed it to be a critical node in the attacks that would follow, allowing the prototype devices to be controlled remotely. It is unclear what, if any, legitimate purpose the component may at one time have served.

>   **Author: Walt Durns**
>   **Date: Thu Nov 04 2021 10:03**
>   Re: Request to merge suppress-pin-13'
>
>   Suppressing activation of PIN13. Not sure HOW
>   it keeps turning itself back on. Esme, is
>   this part of your kernel architecture? Elvis
>   or your virtualizations?
>
>   **REPLY from Esme Vahora:**
>   No.
>
>   **REPLY from Elvis Nguyen:**
>   bouncing this to Grady
>
>   **REPLY from Grady Barker:**
>   please work with PIN13 wherever possible
>   all attempts to bypass it will be rolled back
>
>   ---
>
>   **Author: Grady Barker**
>   **Date: Fri Nov 05 2021 02:17**
>
>   - added ancientkyiv font pack
>   - voice detection on pin13

- chort still needs someone to watch over him and guard the master from within the writhing darkness until eventually it is birthed
- tweaked email notification engine

Author: Walt Durns
Date … 10:02

Woke up with a CRITICAL FAILURE alert for the crypto system. PIN13, of course, and ANOTHER build failure. We CAN'T ALLOW PROBLEMS like that since this will be in people's homes. Committing emergency patch to master.

Grady, your last commit might be related? Hard to tell since part of your message looks like accidental copypasta LOL. You working on a horror story? Don't feel too bad, we've all pasted stupid stuff into a commit before.

REPLY from Grady Barker:
please do not commit to master
rolling back

Author: Walt Durns
Date: … 10:07
Re: Request to merge patching-crypto'

Grady here is your MERGE REQUEST for my emergency patch. PLEASE review as soon as you can. Going to be seeing doctors for the rest of the day. Even when my laptop is OFF I hear the cooling fans talking. Esme or somebody PLEASE make sure this gets merged!

FRIDAY, NOVEMBER 19, 2021.
19 DAYS BEFORE THE EVENT.

The Commission's conclusion of Elvis's malfeasance rests largely on the following events. At Elvis's suggestion, John allowed him and Grady to begin integrating the application with external systems as a proof of concept. In order to maintain the morale of the team, Elvis suggested that they do this work in secret.

A closed-minded reader could see the commit log below, as well as the fact that Elvis attempted to destroy it, as strong evidence for the Koresh hypothesis. Indeed, my esteemed colleagues on the Commission have done just that. However, I would again urge you to consider that this may be an accurate recording of events; you will find that the need for a difficult-to-hide conspiracy vanishes. The conclusion we are left with is much more logical than the tortured explanation the Commission has provided instead.

Some will doubtless object, saying that any reasonable person would have been concerned by Grady's behavior. This is true; but by this point Elvis was not a reasonable person. Exposure to the Ukrainian source code can cause strange and specific dreams, as well as shared hallucinations. I can confirm this personally, having pored over much of it myself. Also, as is clear by the end, Elvis was (yet again) on drugs.

The next afternoon, Elvis would overwrite this piece of the blame log; text messages show he feared he would run afoul of WizBang! substance abuse policy. Fortunately, they were preserved in the audit blockchain Walt had secretly added, though they would not be discovered until far too late.

```
Author: Elvis Nguyen
Date: Fri Nov 19 2021 00:20

adding integration with voice assistants &
location services

grady wanna get crackin on some of the basic
voice commands john sent
```

Author: Grady Barker
Date: ... 00:25

uploaded the basic dictionary here are the first commands

blackbook turn on
blackbook list commands
find:
 – nearest neighboring blackbook
 – my keys
 – my soul
enter diagnostic mode
tell me:
 – the weather
 – where to put the sigil

REPLY from Elvis Nguyen:
lol you having those weird dreams too?

REPLY from Grady Barker:
there are no dreams

Author: Elvis Nguyen
Date: ... 01:04

added integration letting you plug blackbook into your smart toilet ... hooray

---

Author: Grady Barker
Date: ... 01:48

voice commands

turn on/off alerts
turn off stars
unlock/open blackbook
read from blackbook

Author: Elvis Nguyen
Date: … 02:19

integrations with environmental controls, home and industrial. why is industrial on the spec lol

---

Author: Grady Barker
Date: … 02:45

say the words
hear the words
lock/unlock door
pass over threshold

[Ed.: Skipping several hours of commits in this vein.]

Author: Elvis Nguyen
Date: … 05:59

hoo boy i am coming down from this russian shit i took. ¿my fingers don't feel like my own and my eyes feel like craters? checking in integrations for automated vehicles, financials, medical devices, telecom. night grady

REPLY from Grady Barker:
wait wait how do i push my code to the core wizbang repos from home i need to patch some of the company libraries

REPLY from Elvis Nguyen:
that's all locked down now, submit a request for a key on monday. our mathamagician walt will take care of you

REPLY from Grady Barker:
no cant wait that long have to do it now now

```
please there must be a way how can i get walt
now

REPLY from Elvis Nguyen:
jeez man i don't know, just ask blackbook
what to do, it can look up his contact info
or whatever

REPLY from Grady Barker:
yes it agrees that is a good idea
```

Editor's note

I would like to take a moment to remind the reader of the magnitude of the coming events. Even in this minority report, the central narrative can get blurred among the recounting of farcical mismanagement and employee strife; you may blame its author.

Several million fates would be decided mere days from the date of this next exhibit. Every American, the saying goes, knows somebody who lost somebody. Less fortunate souls witnessed the firestorms in the Bay Area that seemed to come from all directions; a luckless few still type with burn-scarred hands, though at least those appendages are still attached.

WEDNESDAY, NOVEMBER 24, 2021.
6 DAYS BEFORE THE EVENT.

With Elvis and Grady compromised, and Esme removed from the review process, the final pieces of the Blackbook attack were put into place and deployed.

```
Author: Elvis Nguyen
Date: Wed Nov 24 2021 15:22

here's some utilities to let users easily
define custom apps. should get us some good
```

press. i could imagine a world where we're
all linked together, via technology, as a
single community. via blackbook, as one
people, together finally as equal thralls to
a single master. power it on and let good
things happen

REPLY from Esme Vahora:
Okay, that's hilarious, but it's not nice to
make fun of John!

Author: Elvis Nguyen
Date: ... 17:10

HEX integrations for online auctions, online
news, online weapon sales, darkweb, low orbit

REPLY from Esme Vahora:
Is everybody in on some joke but me?

TUESDAY, NOVEMBER 30, 2021.
1 DAY BEFORE THE EVENT.

Author: Elvis Nguyen
Date: Tue Nov 30 2021 11:48

much like the vision i had, where a massive
worm swimming in a sparkling underground lake
was slithering towards the exit, my code
bursts forth from the profound hole of
thanksgiving weekend. behold! an evolutionary
algorithm for integrating even systems that
resist your glory!

REPLY from Grady Barker:

Незабаром майстер буде вільний

!!ALERT!!
FROM build-daemon:
* MASTER BRANCH SUBMITTED TO GLOBAL FIRMWARE UPDATE SYSTEM *
* ROOT AUTHORIZATION REQUIRED *
* ARE YOU SURE YOU WANT TO DEPLOY THIS SOFTWARE TO ALL DEVICES? Y/N *

REPLY from @CHORT:
Y

build-daemon: PROCESSING ++++++++++
build-daemon: COMPLETE

* CLEAR BUILD LOG? Y/N *

REPLY from @CHORT:
Y

Author: Esme Vahora
Date: … 13:00
Re: Request to merge final-interfaces'

It won't let me commit the final backend interfaces to master. "Your keychain is out of date." Walt, spawn me a new set?

REPLY from Walt Durns:
no sorry i cant do that not for you no no

REPLY from Esme Vahora:
Grady? Are you using Walt's account? Is that what's been going on?

REPLY from Walt Durns:
grady is not here I mean of COURSE NOT that is CRAZY to even SAY that I am very BUSY with all of the MATH ALGO. So many numbers, haha!

Have a LOVELY day and DARE NOT QUESTION ME AGAIN!

WEDNESDAY, DECEMBER 1, 2021.
THE DAY OF THE EVENT.

At this point, the documented timeline of events becomes increasingly muddy. Largely, this is because investigators had to rely on more ephemeral sources such as audio/video recordings, distorted security footage, and witness testimony. These are, as the Commission notes, easier to forge than a blockchain-secured blame log. Unfortunately, the Commission has gone several steps further and concluded that most, if not all, of these records are forgeries, and/or the result of mass psychosis or psychedelic drugs.

I have no doubt that all of the Commission's members are engaged in a good-faith effort to understand these events so that we may prevent similar tragedies in the future. Unfortunately, the stakes are simply too high for us to get this one wrong. The remainder of this report contains the most difficult evidence to believe. But believe it we must. Perhaps another personal digression will help you understand.

As mentioned above, I am, by training, an electrical engineer. Many years ago, I was part of a team responding to a crisis at a California dam. The monitoring system had broken down, nearly resulting in a spillover. "Contradictory" and "impossible" were two words we used to describe this system's sensor readings and performance metrics. An examination of the sensors found that some were from a recalled batch; several team members suggested that the system would right itself after we put in new ones. But I kept investigating the anomalous readings, tracing the system backwards from the points of measurement. We eventually uncovered an illegal dumping operation that had resulted in several key vents becoming clogged, explaining the data; arresting those truly responsible brought the system back to normal. If we had instead assumed the data was faulty, and gone for the expedient fix, the problem would have returned with the next major storm.

The failure of this dam would have killed hundreds and permanently ruined an entire valley's farmland. Reaching the wrong conclusion about the December 1 attacks would be much, much worse. Ask yourself: who would go to the trouble of fabricating all this, to say nothing of the clearly related materials above, simply to disguise their motivations for an attack? And, assuming the forgeries were placed after the fact, are we really to believe that Esme Vahora was responsible? Nothing in her past points to the level of sophistication required, nor any previous terrorist inclinations. I remind the reader of Occam's Razor: the simplest explanation is usually the correct one.

Please note that the remainder of this minority report contains graphic and disturbing material, though is it really worse than what some of us see when we close our eyes?

09:30

```
FROM: Esme.Vahora@wizbang.com
SUBJECT: Concerns
TO: John.Li@wizbang.com
DATE: Wed Dec 1 2021 09:30
```

John,

Your admin says you're working off-site or I would have brought this to you in person. I've been witnessing some disturbing behaviors in the Blackbook team.

I realize I came onto this project from the stodgy world of legacy and mainframe development. We're not "cool". We don't wear sneakers. Things are looser and flashier here in Building C, and I get that.

But some members of the team have gone from eccentric to worrisome. They don't check in usable code, and their commits are nonsensical. I also suspect Grady has stolen

Walt's login and is impersonating him (Lord
only knows where Walt has been, if so).

I've attached some of the logs so you can see
for yourself, in case they get scrubbed. I
know that Elvis is supposed to be managing
them, but we both know he's not cut out for
that. Since we're so close to the end of the
project, I've gone to you first instead of
HR.

Also, I'll be working from home until this is
over, starting tomorrow.

Sincerely,
Esme

FROM: majordomo@wizbang.com
SUBJECT: MESSAGE UNDELIVERABLE (was Re:
Concerns)

** NO RECIPIENT FOUND FOR "JOHN.LI" **

FROM: CHORT@wizbang.com
SUBJECT: Blackbook Update
TO: blackbook-dev

Team,

Due to a health reason, Mr. Li has taken an
extended leave of absence. I will be filling
in. I look forward to working with all of you
in this new world we are building.

Some changes. I've tricked our leaders into
accelerating the project timeline. In order
to fulfill solstice orders, we expect a
deliverable product by next week. Due to the
short amount of time left, a separate team
has been contracted to handle all QA going

forward. Fortunately, they are already very
familiar with the original code base.

/CHORT

FROM: Esme.Vahora@wizbang.com
TO: CHORT@wizbang.com

Is this a joke? "Chort?" I don't know who you
are or why no one told us John would be
taking leave. You obviously have no idea of
the complexity of this project. Shipping the
code in its current state would be a fucking
disaster. We already have prototypes out all
over the country. Even one security oversight
would mean weeks of bad press.

FROM: majordomo@wizbang.com
SUBJECT: MESSAGE UNDELIVERABLE (was Re:
Blackbook Update)

** NO RECIPIENT FOUND FOR "CHORT" **

[Ed.: Esme later produced the following
unsent email, which had been saved in the
Drafts' folder of her personal email
account.]

FROM: esme.vahora@gmail.com
SUBJECT: Blackbook Failsafes
TO: walter.durns@gmail.com

Walt,

I'm sure I'm just being paranoid, but are you
okay? I'm sending this to your personal email
only because I think Grady might have hacked
your work accounts.

> I know we'd talked about putting some
> failsafes into the Blackbook software after
> Elvis and Grady started acting erratic. Did
> you end up checking anything in? One of us
> mentioned a network killswitch …
>
> If you'd like to talk about this, please
> email me back and tell me what your favorite
> episode of Friends is. Sorry again if I sound
> paranoid — we're all under a lot of stress.
>
> - EV

Editor's note

Authorities are still searching for John Li's whereabouts. According to investigators, the remains of his apartment have offered only one clue: a pair of Dockers stained with an unknown party's blood. This minority believes that he is not so lost as he may seem. During my research for this report, I found several promising leads in a cave near Chortolisy, which are detailed in Appendix 3.2. (Update: Assuming the archive team ever reconstructs it.)

10:10

The remainder of Blackbook's commit log has been the subject of fervent speculation in the media and elsewhere. As such, this report will only show a few highlights. A link to the entire log can be found in Appendix 4.3.

> **Author: Elvis Nguyen**
> **Date: … 10:10**
>
> checking in background loop to scan for
> exposed federal research facility IP
> addresses, lol, what a crazy spec, i dig it
>
> **REPLY from CHORT:**

To bring light to all things, we must first
determine what is most in need of
illumination.

Author: Esme Vahora
Date: … 11:43

Getting some noise on the WiFi adapter.
Adding middleware to log all outbound
requests.

REPLY from CHORT:
Will this interfere with my release?

REPLY from Esme Vahora:
No.

Author: Elvis Nguyen
Date: … 12:29

this one was FUN. using the new topologies
Walt came up with, i wrote a pretty shiny
password cracker. blackbooks should be able
to integrate with basically anything now

Author: Grady Barker
Date: … 13:05

speaking of the new topologies (to say
nothing of the dimensions soon to come) i
added a cute logo for the home screen that
product whipped up for our big release

REPLY from Esme Vahora:
What the hell?? Did this really come from
Product? My screen fuzzed out just loading
it, and now my eyes hurt.

REPLY from CHORT:
Esme come see me in my chambers when you get the chance.

13:40

Esme went instead to the east wing, to the conference room where the Embedded Systems engineers had taken to working. The only primary evidence of what happened next is an audio recording from a prototype Blackbook device, recovered in the ruins of Building C, which must have been in the conference room with Elvis. The speakers' identities have been confirmed to 99.9% confidence by the [REDACTED] Agency forensics team.

> ELVIS: Almost there.
>
> UNKNOWN WHISPERS: Yes yes.
>
> *(Loud knocking.)*
>
> ELVIS (shouting): That better be my new case of Soylent!
>
> WHISPERS: Pay no attention. Soon you will not need food.
>
> *(Sound of door crashing open.)*
>
> ESME: Fuck, my shoulder.
>
> ELVIS: The hell?
>
> WHISPERS: You are an agent of chaos. You do not need her. Nobody needs her.
>
> ESME: Check Twitter.
>
> *(Typing. Screaming and roars coming from speakers.)*

ELVIS: That's …

WHISPERS: Close this distracting application. Slay the heretic. Write software.

ESME: That's the new Blackbook logo.

ELVIS: Why is literally everybody posting this?

ESME: Your code is in the wild.

(Typing.)

ELVIS: Blackbook can't do this. It's a Daytimer.

ESME: I don't think it is, Elvis.

WHISPERS: You say you want to smash the state. We will do this. We ARE doing this. Eliminate this obstacle.

(Blinds opening.)

ESME: Daytimers don't do this, Elvis.

ELVIS: Did I grab the wrong gummy bears, or is that …

(Retching.)

ESME: The grounds crew, being dragged around by self-driving cars, sketching the shape of the logo? Yes.

(Vomiting.)

WHISPERS: If you want to avoid their fate you will continue working.

ESME: Get the FUCK —

(Sounds of struggle. Window glass breaking.)

ESME: — RID of that thing and LISTEN to me.

ELVIS: My laptop!

ESME: What were you working on?

ELVIS: Chort said he wanted bindings for, um.

ESME: Um?

ELVIS: … Lawrence Livermore.

ESME: The nuclear … . particle accelerator … lab. And you were just DOING it?

ELVIS: It … seemed like a good idea at the time. I can fix this.

WHISPERING: You can start by taking the metal cylinder in the corner and smashing this woman's head in.

ESME: What is that? Do you have a prototype in here?

(Shuffling.)

ESME: Put the fire extinguisher down NOW!

ELVIS: But —

(Shuffling. A body being crushed against the wall.)

ELVIS (croaking): Since when …

ESME: Roller derby, bitch. Give me that.

(Smashing sounds. Recording ends.)

14:04

The prototypes were set to automatically update whenever WizBang! pushed a new patch. Elvis and Esme attempted to take advantage of this.

Author: Elvis Nguyen
Date: … 14:04

flooding system with objects to overwhelm address bus

REPLY from build-daemon:
* BUILD FAILED: THREAT DETECTED. ROLLING BACK *

Author: Esme Vahora
Date: … 14:21

Setting all HEX files to null length.

REPLY from build-daemon:
* BUILD FAILED: THREAT DETECTED. ROLLING BACK *

Author: CHORT
Date: … 15:07

You thought you could stop this, you cannot, all will burn; come, fall into the lake with me.

Deploying database injection module because Nguyen didn't finish his checklist. Bad boy.

Author: Elvis Nguyen
Date: ... 15:12

rerouting all outbound API calls to localhost

REPLY from build-daemon:
* BUILD FAILED: THREAT DETECTED. ROLLING BACK *

Author: CHORT
Date: ... 15:29

Injecting HEX into the accelerator's master computer. Now we speak the same language of fire. Can you hear it?

Author: Esme Vahora
Date: ... 15:51

Fork-bomb made of undocumented ANALITIK "features".

REPLY from CHORT:
What did you do? I cannot see my slaves, my beautiful imps. Rolling back manually.

Author: Elvis Nguyen
Date: ... 15:59

not totally sure but i think this will break the network tunnel

REPLY from Esme Vahora:
When did you learn ANALITIK?

REPLY from Elvis Nguyen:
i'm not a *total* waste of space

```
Author: CHORT
Date: … 16:15

I don't know what that did, but I'm removing
it and locking down the build system. Also,
this commit represents our OFFICIAL BETA
RELEASE! My thanks to all our wonderful alpha
testers around the world; I may spare you for
a few moments.
```

After this commit was transmitted to the prototypes, the "attacks" commenced. Esme offered the following timeline in subsequent interviews, which is partly corroborated by various primary evidence:

16:18: Esme and Elvis realize that something very bad has happened.

16:19 – 16:32: Elvis does what he can to attack "CHORT", or at least distract them. Esme drafts a script to leverage the networking backdoor she added that morning, under the guise of logging middleware. The script will shut down every Blackbook that loads it.

16:33 – 16:40: Elvis reviews it, noting that CHORT might stop the upload before it hits every machine. He adds a feature that uses HEX's infiltration abilities to make the machines attack each other, as well as a routine for physically damaging the devices.

16:41: A large nearby explosion, most likely the destruction of Parks Reserve Forces Training Area, spurs them to develop a real plan. Esme will go to the basement server room and, using her knowledge of Walt's cryptography system, will sneak this script past the build-daemon, and send it out for distribution. Elvis will stay in the office proper and continue to annoy "CHORT".

16:49: Having identified WizBang! Headquarters as a primary source of the attack, the United States Air Force scrambles a squadron of fighter jets from the remnants of Travis AFB.

16:50:16: Esme merges and distributes the script.

16:50:29: WizBang! HQ is struck with sixteen air-to-ground missiles, apparently killing Elvis. Esme survives in the basement. These Slack messages appear to be the final communication between the two:

Elvis Nguyen: go get em, smasher demorte!

Esme: I should never have told you my roller derby name.

Elvis Nguyen: 😊

Conclusion

If the idea that an ancient Slavic demon is behind these attacks is still too much for you to bear, I thank you for reading; doubtless most others did not make it this far. If, on the other hand, you are interested in preventing this from happening again, pay close attention. In the course of writing this report, in reviewing the code in its various iterations, standing within the burned ruins of [REDACTED] Software and seeing the bloodstains on the concrete walls, I came to understand the systems I was investigating; I daresay I developed some expertise.

What is critical to understand is that the software from Chortolisy wants nothing more than to be read, and executed, and distributed. Twice now we have seen it destroy the programmers who work with it, to say nothing of the wider world. I fear that there is no safe method of exposure to the code. Already my sleep is disturbed, with visions of a gray worm, feeble but growing, haunting my nights.

Much of the code is now publicly available in these very appendices. The rest is not difficult to come by if you know the right people or have a few bitcoins and access to the dark web. This level of notoriety is surely an acceptable outcome to the being(s) responsible. How, then, are we supposed to design a system to fight back? The villagers of Pulyny, outside Chortolisy, have for centuries focused on fire-adjacent industries — candles, matches, ceramics, and smelting. Whether this is due to Chort's influence, or a reaction against it, I cannot say; nor dare I, for fear that my thoughts are already contaminated. But it is one place to begin looking.

I imagine this document marks my final act in public life, as I no longer fully trust my own judgment in matters of import. Fret not; this will give me considerably more time to spend with my family, and/or fly-fishing. To the reader who still has faith in their own motivations, I will say this: put down this report; seek out like-minded people; agree on the problem and solution; write down your plans before you write a single line of code; and for the love of God, move deliberately and don't break anything.

Signed,
Col. Brian Houlihan (RET)

The Blood Dance of Ape and Mouse

Evan Marcroft and L'Erin Ogle

1 Uko Now

Uko Hiigomathre arrived at the site of his murder at the appointed time, still filthy with the dust of the road. A knock upon the Gate of Final Passage summoned a flight of white-masked attendants, who guided him inside to an antechamber. Here he was stripped, thrown into a scalding bath, and doused with perfumed soap. He endured as they raked the snarls and fleas from his beard, scrubbed the scars that crisscrossed his broad body with holy salts until they shone like shooting stars. It was a ritual meant to cleanse all taint but the grudge he carried onto the hallowed field of Hegirama, yet they needn't have bothered. After years abroad, his grudge was all he'd come home with. He was hate clothed in skin.

When they were done, the attendants slipped straw sandals on his feet, clad him in a funeral robe of pure white, and returned to him his sword. Three feet of steel curving gently to a fang's tip, freshly oiled in the melted fat of boars, its hilt bound in the finest of twined hair dyed with indigo, its name was Headsplitter, and the weapon seemed to tremble in his hand as though resonating with the soul it was meant to set free. *Soon*, he told it silently. *However this day resolves, we will rest at last.*

Behind the Gate of Final Passing lay the arena, a circle of soft alabaster where the Titan-Bark had been lovingly sanded flat. When Uko appeared before the crowd that filled the elevated stands, it was to a perfect silence that nonetheless echoed with his name. There was not one among the audience who did not know him, not a child who had not heard his legend, not a man who'd never once, however fleetingly, dreamed of being him. Some, he imagined, would have witnessed him at the height of his glory — Uko the Undefeated, Uko the Demon Ape of Kinroika, cleaving limbs and destroying ambitions. Uko, the greatest swordsman in the world. To them, anything less than that godlike memory was as good as nothing.

The stump of his right arm ached, his blood yearning to fill veins that were no longer there.

Uko's remaining hand crept towards his sword as a second figure stepped onto the opposite side of the arena. A woman, small but square, her bare arms mountainous with muscle. On one hip she wore the moon-shaped blade of a sickle. On the other, a blunt-snouted slab of steel barely resembling a sword. A puckered scar slithered through her close-cropped hair, slicing through the brow of her cold blue eye and cleaving her lip, leaving her with a permanent sneer. *Should have cut deeper*, it seemed to say.

Uko had no mind to argue. He ought to have put her down like the mad dog she was.

To Uko's right, a man more beard than face rose from his shaded box and motioned redundantly for silence. A magistrate of the Buzengamot, he would be officiating the slaughter shortly to commence. "You two who stand before me today are hereby bound by the laws of Hegirama," he declared. "For the sake of peace in Kinroika, the feud you share will be ended here and now. On pain of death, neither accused shall depart this field while other yet lives. Let there be no apology, no reluctance, no mercy, only finality. Uko Hiigomathre; Ekia, called Mouseclaw. Do all accused agree?"

"I do," Uko called out.

"Get on with it," Ekia bellowed.

All that needed saying had been said.

Their eyes found one another, and in a flash they'd both filled their hands with steel. In the mirror of her crude machete Uko could see himself reflected — not this truncated wreck, but the warrior he'd once been, as though his past self were imprisoned in her blade. Positioning his feet just so, he raised his sword into the Third Horizontal Killing Posture, envisioning both the cut that would slice his foe in two and the arc it had already followed to come this far.

1 Ekia Now

Ekia had returned to find nothing much had changed in Kinroika since she'd fled all those years ago. The city was still ten miles up a giant tree and even higher up its own arse. The blue sky of the Upper Boughs was as hot as the bottom of a cookpot, and the rich folks here were still a bunch of painted ninnies tottering about on shin-high clogs. Ekia chided herself for once aspiring to stand among them. This bright and pretty city was nothing more than a place for fools to idle while they waited for a soft death to come.

She would never have come back, if it weren't for *him*.

The arena was a white so clean it hurt her eyes, the bark of the Titan Tree having been shaved down to a flat, polished mirror's surface. She stood at its edge, an animal wandered into this hallowed place where men had lawfully slaughtered one another since dynasties immemorial, while those in the stands traded skeptical murmurs and catty barbs. She wasn't much to look at by noble standards of beauty; too square to ever fit in a regal kimono, too brawny to be a properly waifish Kinroikan noblewoman. Some among them wondered aloud: *a woman, on the field of Hegirama? She'll be destroyed in mere moments.*

Those, however, were shushed by their betters, and Ekia had to grin at that; it seemed her infamy had survived these ten years. There was no wall between her and these people that knew her as Mouseclaw. She'd carved heads from shoulders for lesser slights.

The scar that divided her eyebrow drew suddenly taut. Ekia carried many scars, but this one alone was alive. Now, it throbbed as if trying to peel free from her skin, a dog straining against its chain as it scented, perhaps, her enemy drawing near. There he was — entering the arena from the opposite gate. His broad belly preceded him by moments, it seemed, joined then by a swinging arm as long and lanky as an ape's. The white silks fluttering around him could not beautify that flattened face. Their one hollow sleeve could not hide the arm that was not there.

From the shade of the judge's box, a magistrate arose. "You two who stand before me today are hereby bound by the laws of Hegirama," he declared. "For the sake of peace in Kinroika, the feud you share will be ended here and now. On pain of death, neither accused shall depart this field while other yet lives. Let there be no apology, no reluctance, no mercy, only finality. Uko Hiigomathre; Ekia, called Mouseclaw. Do all accused agree?"

Ekia could have had a meal and shat it out in the time it took the old goat to wheeze through his little speech. All that mattered was that nothing stand between her and her foe, and now nothing did but dwindling time. "Get on with it," she snapped, her voice a thunderclap. She flexed her arms, hands at her sides, ready to curl around her hooked sidearm and her sword. The sword was not as impressive as Uko's, no, merely a slab of steel sharpened to a bone-chopping edge, a crude machete, but plenty deadly nonetheless, and that was all a sword need be. Pretty things were only good for resting on gravestones.

Uko's shining blade would look mighty fine upon his.

"I do," Uko called across the arena.

And with that, all that needed saying had been said.

Uko drew his sword in one liquid motion and sliced a stray ray of sunshine into ribbons. Grotesque muscle practically armored that remaining limb. A flush of icewater washed through Ekia's bloodstream. She'd almost forgotten that her foe was the greatest swordsman in the world.

Steel thrust itself into her hands — sickle knife in one, sword in the other. Her tongue itched for the blood of the man who'd taken everything she'd ever almost had. She should have cut that ugly visage off along with his arm. She ought to have taken every piece of him, one at a time and slowly, when long ago she'd had the chance.

2 Uko Then

It was known by all those who lived in Kinroika, and better by those who were dead, that Uko Hiigomathre was the greatest swordsman in the world. There were few, however, who would believe it at first glance. At forty-nine years old, he was as ugly a man as had ever lived, rotund in the belly, with lanky arms the length of his bandy legs. His beard was as red and unruly as a wildfire, and his face compared unfavorably against a sat-upon squash. He was known as Uko the Ape, or Uko the unlovable.

And yet this man was the sole surviving student of Syamto Surmra, the so-called Chief of Fighters, butcher of armies, and progenitor of modern swordplay. It was from his cruel tutelage that Uko had inherited the Syamto Godlike Lung Breathing Skill, as well as the Seven Pinnacle Cuts, the deadliest of all sword techniques. At the age of twenty-two, when he was unleashed upon the streets of Kinroika, he had challenged a swordsman ten years his senior to a duel, casting his emptied scabbard at their feet. The other man was a veteran *butenku*, a warrior indentured to the reputable Jukaboz merchant dynasty, and yet not seven heartbeats passed before Uko had shattered his sword, his fighting hand, and his ego in a single usage of the First Pinnacle Cut. Ashamed, the man yielded his client's honor, and from that spot, Uko's stories spread like a plague.

Uko was as proud as he was deserving of it. He strode through the city in violet robes bared to the navel, happy to boast that the scars he bore were his trophies. Not once in his career had he been bested in combat. Many tried, and to a man he'd retired them by force. With his Godlike Lung he could channel his breath into a monstrous strength, and with the Seven Pinnacle Cuts he could cleave steel like water. He killed reluctantly, but never let a man challenge him twice. It was recounted throughout taverns and souqs that when ambushed by a vengeful former rival, Uko Hiigomathre had lopped the hands from the other man's wrists with such speed that Uko could not rightfully be said to have drawn his blade at all.

"I defeated you once," he'd reportedly declared, "Ghosts must learn to stay dead."

Over the years, he served many masters. There was no merchant dynasty that did not crave his service. Disputes between the haughty aristocracy were as common as hiccups, and when they could not be settled by gold, they were settled between butenku. Uko, without fail, was the final word in every argument. By the age of forty-nine he had fought his way into the household of Cimito Hashiado, the anointed Urbomog of the city itself. For Uko, this was the culmination of his ambitions. He had climbed a mountain of bodies and had reached his goal.

But it was not a year before he realized that at the peak of a mountain there was nowhere to go. None would challenge the Hashiado, knowing they would face him. He had made himself a trophy on another's shelf, yet it would destroy his honor to flee that position. A lifetime of training had rendered him as useless as a novice with a stick for a sword.

He needed a second thing to live for.

One afternoon, as he wandered the lush gardens of the Hashiado estate, perched high up in the Upper Boughs of the Titan Tree where the sunlight shone bright and hot, he came across Sashioka, the Urbomog's daughter, picking flowers for her hair.

Though he had seen her in passing many times, he had never stopped to recognize her beauty before. Her skin was the brown-gold of Titan-sap, her lips, nose, and brow pierced with flecks of amber. Her eyes were the first he'd seen that did not glint with fear of him or narrow in envy. Uko was immediately ashamed at the pounding of his heart, for she had just come of marriageable age, and he was well-worn with an unlovable face.

But when she caught him staring, her cheeks flushed as red as Uko's own.

Uko had learned to woo a sword into cutting through anything, but never a woman into returning his smile. With Sashioka, however, it was easy. The young lady did not mind his appearance, and hung on his stories of noble combat and the genealogies of his scars, for she had never ventured beyond the sunny parks and cobbled avenues of the Upper Boughs where bloodshed was unheard of. Uko discovered in himself a talent for storycraft, which he used to transport her far from this cushioned prison that was her home. In turn, she was eager to tutor him in his numbers and letters, esoterica that had seemed unimportant before. Both, in their own way, helped the other to escape their life. Despite the gap between their ages, Sashioka made Uko feel like a child, and a lovestruck one at that.

"Has your father yet spoken to you of marriage?" Uko asked one afternoon in the garden, as innocently as he could for a man unaccustomed to subterfuge, for both he and Sashioka yet pretended that they were no more than unlikely friends.

"He has," Sashioka said, careful in her own way not to betray whatever emotions were attached to that word. "I have made the acquaintance of many men who I am told are as kind and loving as their families are wealthy. I hope to see their faces someday."

Uko detected a hint of sarcasm there. Marriage interviews between nobles were by tradition conducted from opposite sides of a Titan-leaf folding screen. "And what is it you want from a husband?" As if this were no more serious a topic than the quirks of the weather.

Sashioka nibbled her lip in thought. "A man who lives in the court is a well-groomed slave," she answered at last. "Whoever I marry, I should want them to be free. And I would want them to let me be free with them. I want them to show me things I would never see with another man. There is so much world beyond this garden." She cast a shy, sly look in Uko's direction. "Or so I am told."

Uko had to distract himself with a passing butterfly, lest his grin betray him.

It came to pass that the Urbomog wished to wage war upon the Jukaboz family of the Southernmost Branch, who had been caught plotting to overthrow his rule. It fell upon Uko in turn to quash their ambitions. It pained him to leave Sashioka's side, but he glimpsed an opportunity: when he came home with Hashiado's honor in hand, he would request her hand in marriage, and her father could hardly say no. From his lonesome peak he would climb higher still. Perhaps he could even find a place where he could lay down his sword.

Uko returned to Kinroika four weeks later, having made good on his vow. He went straight away to the Urbomog's throne room with a collection of scalps knotted to his belt and the stink of slaughter still upon him. There he knelt, kissed the foot of his master's Titan-thorn throne, and begged the old man's favor. "I will be as a son to you," he promised, "and defend Sashioka from all misery."

Cimito Hashiado, who had steered his house through bloody wars and the bloodier intrigues of the Upper Boughs, seemed to collapse into the old man he was. "Had you asked a week ago we would have happily said yes. But presently we cannot."

For three weeks and a day, Sashioka had been missing. The palace guards speculated that she'd fled her chambers in the night, for reasons unknown to the servants who ought to have kept watch over her. Cimito's butenku had ransacked the Titan Tree from the sundrenched Upper Boughs to the slums of the Rootshades, to no avail. And as the Urbomog spoke, Uko burned with shame. He should have been here to protect her, to keep her safe at home.

"It was only yesterday that she, at last, was returned to us," the Urbomog explained. "You may rest assured, she is unharmed."

Uko could have wept in relief and shame both, but the Urbomog's frown remained in place. "There is more," the old man intoned. "The one who returned my daughter to me asked a boon, one that I could not refuse, for the sake of this family's honor."

"Tell me," Uko said, dry-mouthed.

"They demanded the right to duel for her hand in marriage." The old man's eyes softened. "Sashioka herself implored me to accept, and I am told her savior is fearsome indeed. I am sorry, my strongest arm. I had hoped to grant her to you."

Uko stood and drank in a deep breath through his nose. He stomped his left foot, and the stone-like Titan-bark floor of the courtroom shattered like a glass mirror. "Give me their name," Uko commanded. To address his liege so forcefully was a punishable offense, but in his fury he could not care. "You must do what your honor demands, and so must I."

His master smiled wickedly. "We had hoped you would ask," he replied. "Her name is Ekia, called Mouseclaw, and we wish you a swift and cruel victory."

A *woman.*

Uko could scarcely believe it, even as the day of their duel arrived. Swordplay was a man's art, requiring heartless hands and an iron will. Women were meant to kill gently, with poison or subterfuge. Yet there was nothing in the rules that forbade it, and he could not possibly back out.

Theirs was Hegimedi, the Lesser Duel. They would clash with wooden swords and were forbidden to seriously maim, much less kill. Uko had been prepared to issue a challenge of Hegirama, the most dire of duels, only to learn that Sashioka had beseeched her father to deny it. That she cared for her savior at his expense only drove the blade further into Uko's heart.

The duel was to be held in the Urbomog's hall, before a jury of magistrates and citizen witnesses, within a ring demarcated by a braided ritual rope. Whoever could drive their opponent over the rope would be the victor. Cheers showered down upon Uko as he stepped into that arena. He spied Sashioka herself watching from the gallery. She would not meet his eyes.

"I thought I was ready to see the world," she'd said, in the few seconds together they'd stolen ahead of the duel. "I thought this palace would smother me if I remained another moment." Her gaze turned to the open window. "It was so beautiful, what I saw out there. Even the parts that hurt. And when they did, somehow I still believed I could walk through it unscathed. I did not know how it could lodge itself inside me and follow me home."

Despair overtook her. "I am such a stupid little girl," she sobbed. "I should be able to choose. But how can I? How does one decide which eye they must put out? Which hand to lop off? I wish I weren't this weak person I am. If I could wield a sword like you, it would be so easy."

Her head sank until her hair covered her face like a ragged veil. "I think that I hate myself."

And Uko could not bring himself to comfort her, for if he softened even for a moment then he knew he would crumble completely, and not be able to fight for her.

"I knew you loved me, Uko," she said. "From the first story you ever told me. I wish that could have been enough for me. I'm sorry."

Somehow, that was the worst hurt of all. That she had known, and he had missed his chance to confess himself to her, and that beautiful moment was lost forever.

He'd laid his hand upon her shoulder — the first time he'd ever touched her, he realized belatedly. How *small*, how fragile she was, how stainless. Oh, she was far too young for him. A blood-soaked old man like him would only dirty her. He too wished that he could let her go.

But the heart was the strongest muscle, and it clung dearly to things it shouldn't.

"I will be strong for you," he said. "I will cut away what hurts you most."

Ekia Mouseclaw had arrived to the scene of the duel before him. Her reputation had arrived earlier still. The terror of the Rootshades, where Kinroika's worst quarreled over the scraps that rained from brighter boughs. She was said to be a hired knife for the yakuza who ruled that dismal underworld, with twelve-times-twelve murders to her name. From the way she stalked the ring like a captured beast, from the surety with which she gripped her sword, Uko could believe it. Why she would save Sashioka from the Rootshades — why Sashioka would bear any affection for such a bloodthirsty animal — Uko could not guess. But he knew well that the universe which had cursed him ugly enjoyed its cruel mysteries.

This woman was a threat. Uko was not so foolhardy as to believe otherwise. That said, she hailed from a world of craven men, of lives too short to grow powerful. She had never clashed with a true warrior before. And if she refused to submit, he would gladly demonstrate just how high she had presumed to reach.

At the appointed hour, the Urbomog declared the duel begun, yet neither combatant made a move. Uko could feel the murderess's hooded eyes surveying him for weaknesses, and he was content to let her find none. By honor he was indebted to her for saving Sashioka, and when this was done he would thank her sincerely, but he could not allow her to casually pilfer what he had exhausted his life searching for. A compromise, then. He would cut her down, but not cripple her permanently.

"Lay down your weapon and go," Uko rumbled. "You face Uko the Undefeated, the greatest swordsman in the world." Not a boast but an honest warning. Sashioka reviled bloodshed; he'd rather spare her the sight.

Ekia's lips parted like a cutthroat's robe, revealing an arsenal of sharp, dirty teeth. "I've killed a dozen men who all said the same thing," she sneered.

So be it, then. Uko filled his lungs with the fuel of murder and hurled himself at her.

That she parried his first strike was a shock. That the fight continued past the second was an aggravation. It shouldn't have been possible, but wherever Uko's sword sought flesh, Ekia's blade was there to intercept it, and rising over it, like a tarnished half-moon, her mocking smile. Only an elite league of past opponents possessed the strength to turn aside his blows; it was as though Ekia's skin were a glove fitted over a single, powerful fist. This from a woman perhaps half his age.

Uko was caught off-guard when her foot snaked out and swept his legs out from under him, something no duelist with a modicum of honor would dare. He heard the crowd roar their disapproval, but the rules of Hegimedi were on her side. And as he tried to stand, she kicked him in the belly, sending him tumbling nearly to the boundary. He felt something sharp enter and exit him with a squirt of blood. A razor perhaps, or a jag of wood, clenched between her toes. Now that was certainly against the rules.

Uko should have realized. This uncouth woman was a school-less fighter, without the training in a particular style that would allow him to predict her movements. Whereas he had always fought with one foot planted in the future, she was a creature of the moment, and in that untamed jungle of the now, her territory, she was the stronger predator. Worse, she fought from outside the bonds of ritual and honor in which he was hopelessly — fatally — tangled.

For the first time in his life, Uko felt the chill of uncertainty. Never mind that he had sacrificed so much to distance himself from it — the possibility of defeat had lain its claw upon him nonetheless, and it had come in the skin of one who'd never worked a day to best him.

No.

A thought like a spark near oil.

As the Mouseclaw darted towards him from across the arena, quick as her namesake, Uko drew breath in through his mouth, funneling it into his shoulders, his fists, his indignant heart. He gripped his sword in both hands and, calling upon his tutelage beneath Syamto Surmra, performed the Third of the Seven Pinnacle Cuts. Grazing the edges of seconds, parsing light rays,

Uko's sword fulfilled a geometrically transcendent arc. And though the weapon was as blunt as a knuckle, his enemy's sword was split cleanly down the center.

The crowd gasped, some fainting at this superhuman display of power. Ekia herself gawped in dismay, and in that vulnerable heartbeat, Uko struck again, his sword's tip catching the meat of her jaw and tearing a furrow across her face. She fell backwards, screaming from the gut, the force of her spraying blood seeming to propel her over the boundary rope.

A magistrate sprang up, rattling a chain of Titan-seeds for attention. "The Aggravant has been expelled!" she shouted, gesturing with one hand to Ekia and the other to Uko. "The Aggrievant is victorious!"

It was not this decree but the sight of his rival kicking in pain that cooled Uko's rage into grim satisfaction. The world was again as it should be. He clapped a hand against his wound and turned his gaze once more to Sashioka. This time she did not look away. Though sadness shadowed her eyes, a shy smile nevertheless crept onto her lips. In a battle between lovers, one, at least, would be left to come home to her. Uko would swaddle her in such devotion that in time she would forget that there had ever been another.

Everything would be alright.

Uko took in a breath to swear himself to her and saw her smile crumble into a mask of paralyzed horror. Too late, he registered the telltale rush of air fleeing a blade in motion. He spun around to see Ekia completing a movement with her halved sword, droplets of blood suspended in flight like jewels upon a string. A strange sensation radiated through him from a spot below his shoulder. Not pain, but something his panicking mind could only describe as *division*. For an instant, Uko felt horrifically weightless.

The cheers of the crowd mutated into screams as his arm tumbled away from his body.

2 Ekia Then

It was known that the woman named Ekia, later called Mouseclaw, had originated from the Rootshades. That gave away little, for the Rootshades were the breeding ground of all Kinroika's danger and filth. Ekia knew just as little of herself as anyone. She could not recall a time when she had lived anywhere other than the gloom of Kinroika's undercity, alone. Her earliest memory was of violence, of rag-bound steel puncturing another motherless alley child, of catching the crust of bread that fell from his loosening hand. Her second memory was of joy, of her belly filled, her life extended by another day.

For Ekia, that was the entire world. A long slash and a small satisfaction.

Her age was a mystery. As far as she knew, she had sprung into the world old enough to run and fight and steal and hide. To survive in the Rootshades, these were necessary skills. The only light in that place came from the fires around which beggars congregated, from the smoldering of whorehouse windows, from the bioluminescent mooncap colonies parasitizing the bark of the great roots which clutched the slums like the bars of a cage. The only wealth fell from above, for all that was discarded by the city high above in the branches descended as a constant drizzle of garbage. Ekia had been just another black-toothed mouth turned towards the heavens, begging for its shit. Her days were spent scrounging for edible waste, fighting fang and nail for flecks of gold. She was neither the strongest nor fastest, and would have died as just another ransacked corpse were it not for the sword.

It had arrived on the hip of the man she found pillaging her home. She'd eked out a burrow for herself in the hollow where three hovels collapsed together. Who knew what the thief thought he'd find? She had nothing in her nest that did not already litter the streets in rancid drifts. She didn't have time to ask, for her hand suddenly snaked out on its own volition and plucked the sword from his belt. By the time she saw his face, registered him as human, that blade had already passed through it. He tried to speak, but his throat had been halved in one stroke.

Ekia watched him bleed and try to breathe, blood spilling from between his clamped fingers, and she felt nothing but the promise of bread in her belly. Just as she rooted through the garbage barehanded, so did she turn out the dead man's pockets. He carried no coin — not surprising, but still disheartening — though he did have dried meat tucked in paper, salty and chewy. That meant nearly a week's escape from a gnawing stomach. Halfway to an eternity for her.

But that, she realized, was a pittance beside the length of sharpened steel that felt more natural to her hand than her own fingers.

No longer would Ekia have to worry about what little she had being taken from her.

She would be doing the taking.

Ekia, little mouse of the slums, slashed and stole and ascended with her sword, cutting stairs through the life that rose like a cliff against her. By fifteen, she had slain twenty men and grown stronger in the arm than any of them. She became known as Mouseclaw, a reminder that small and filthy things could still draw blood. It was only natural that she fall in with the Hunyakiri family, the yakuza who ruled what little was worth ruling in Kinroika's lightless underworld. The violence they demanded neither excited nor offended her. Blood was the grease with which one wriggled through the teeth of life. It was no more effort to maim a debtor than to cup her hands beneath the rain and drink. The monks of the Great Bole said that murder wounded one's own soul, but Ekia was skeptical. Necessity couldn't hurt.

For ten years she insisted that to herself.

And then her boss found himself a girl.

"The royal bitch is going to make us all flush."

Boss Urtget was a man of boundless desires, with the corpulence to hold it all. He could be found half immersed in the bath most of the time, conducting business like a beached sea-wyrm. The girl huddled in the shallows as if hoping to spiral into herself and disappear. A rope ran from her wrists to the boss's jewel-studded paw of a hand. Blooded Sons and Daughters lounged around the shaded bathhouse, wolflike shadows amongst swirling steam.

Sashioka was her name, the boss explained. The only daughter of Cimito Hashiado, as it happened. Yes, the very same. They'd come across her hiding in an alley, a runaway perhaps, searching for adventure. How foolish, to think a house pup could run with wild dogs. The plan for her was as simple as a haiku. They'd ransom the daughter for all her father was worth. The ruler of Kinroika would pay anything to have her home.

"And will he?" Ekia asked.

"You'll kill her when we have the money. Till then, we'll have our fun."

Toothy smiles gleamed in the mist.

Ekia used her sword to part the girl's curtain of hair. The girl's face smooth and golden, so clean it was as if the girl had soaked up all the light from above. Eyes just as bright, green, unstained by horror. Ekia saw herself reflected in them and felt every scar cut itself into her a second time. Understanding, then shame — she could *not* have been this brutal thing she'd become. There was something else she could have reached for. Something that was perhaps still there, glimmering faintly through miles of leaves.

This girl was proof.

Ekia found her mouth wet, her heart pounding in her chest.

"I have a better idea," Ekia heard herself say, and it was as though a veil came down over her eyes, a veil of dripping red, and when it lifted the bath was a slurry of gore, and she and the girl were alone in it. Ekia knelt and sliced the rope off her wrists. The girl, her dress splashed with crimson, her hair braided with blood, looked up at her, uncomprehending.

"You're safe," Ekia said, "with me."

And the strange, beautiful girl flew into her arms.

They lived together for no more than two weeks. To Ekia it was as good as two lifetimes.

Never had Ekia met someone like Sashioka. How sweet her voice. How soft and excitable her body. The world had not yet deadened her with its blows. The Rootshades through which Ekia had thoughtlessly cleaved all her life were a wonder to her, despite their danger. The noble girl marveled at the teetering tenements, the roots that loomed infinitely into the sky, even the daily filthrain, from which she ran and hid, laughing all the while. Together, they learned how to use bodies for pleasure, Sashioka as furious with her lips as Ekia was with her sword. Laying together with her in the aftermath, Ekia found that she desired to be nowhere else. In Sashioka's glow, she could almost make out a future in which she needed no sword, where she would hunger for nothing more than another day with her love. But the bitterness that lingered after every kiss was the truth that it could not last.

"My father will find me soon," Sashioka murmured one night, as they lay tangled in the humidity of the shanty Ekia called home.

"I know," Ekia said. The rumors had reached her already — unsmiling swordsmen on the hunt for a certain young woman, steel flashing as often as gold. Even she could not withstand the might Kinroika's ruler could bring to bear. Not that Ekia would not fight to the death against the Urbomog's butenku when at last they ran her down, but there had to be another way. She would slice through impossibility to reach their life together.

"But to the woman that brings you home," she continued, "what boon might be offered?"

Sashioka went still in the grip of realization.

"I don't think he could refuse her anything," she said.

Ekia lifted Shashioka's eyes to hers and made the only promise a black heart like hers could keep. "No matter what, or who, I'll fight for you, and win."

Shashioka kissed her softly, on the lips and then her ear. "There is another," the girl whispered. "One who loves me just the same as you. I know that he will say the same."

"I don't care," Ekia said. "I will not back down to anyone."

She felt tears prick her neck.

"That is what I fear most," Sashioka said.

What kind of man could hold a place in Sasha's heart?

Ekia would never have guessed *this* one. She could hardly believe her eyes when the stout, pug-faced brute stepped into the arena roped off in the center of the Urbomog's hall. What he had done to earn Sasha's affection, she would never know. Ekia had never believed in gods as others did, but she could certainly feel their spit on her face.

Ekia could not pronounce the name of the fancy hall in which the duel was held. Everything in this sun-drenched over-world had a thousand grand and worthless titles. She'd been told the white-faced men and women serving as witnesses were important magistrates and court-goers, but to her they all resembled blobs of dough begging to be devoured. All this pomp laid out before her was a tassel on a sword — pretty to some, but functionally useless. She had won battles with trash raining down on her. Opened throats with her teeth. If this Uko expected the sort of duel held between butenku, a duel with rules and honor and respect, then he was too much a fool for Sasha. Ekia was no noble swordfighter.

She was a killer.

Ekia made herself small, unassuming, the mouse of her namesake. Of course she'd heard tell of Uko Hiigomathre the Demon Ape, how he had ascended through the ranks of Kinroika's fighters like a visiting comet returning to the heavens. Ekia suspected otherwise, though. Had he ever won against a true urge to kill? Not bloody likely. Men like him were all show-muscle and braggadocio. He was a pampered tiger fattened on tethered lambs. Uko Hiigomathre would not see the deaths heaped upon her shoulders like so many pelt-trophies, only the fact of her womanhood, however scarred. He would underestimate her, and that would unmake him.

At the appointed hour, Sasha's father rose from his throne of Titan-thorns and declared the duel begun, yet neither combatant made a move. Ekia turned Uko inside-out with her eyes, wondering where he might favor an old wound, a weakness she could use to bring this farce to a faster end. But to her concern, the man was an ox beneath his fat. She risked a quick look at her love, but Sasha had turned her back on the duel entirely. Ekia knew that she abhorred violence, but could not help but feel the abandonment as a stain on her torn and ratted soul.

"Lay down your weapon and go," Uko growled from across the arena. "You face Uko the Undefeated, the greatest swordsman in the world."

Ekia felt her lips curl unbidden away from her teeth. "I've killed a dozen men who all said the same thing," she spat. She would peel his skin from his face. He was no better than her. No one was.

Uko had no further words for her. Ekia felt the air pull away from her as the Demon-Ape gasped it in and launched himself across the arena.

Ekia, glimpsing the invisible rails his sword rode, parried him with surprising ease. He assaulted her with a speed impossible for such a fat little man, but each time his blade rose, her sword was there to rebuff its passage. The great swordsman in the world? Her mouth contorted into a feline smile of thirty-odd fangs. How foolish men like Uko were, trusting in their masculinity and their elite training, as if there were not those like Ekia, born in shit but blessed with the same ability, blades sharpened on cruder whetstones.

Seeing frustration cloud his eyes, she swept out her leg and kicked his out from under him. The crowd shrieked their objections, but Ekia paid them no mind. Honor, from a Rootshade murderess? What use would she have for such a silly thing? She lashed out as Uko tried to rise, her foot burrowing deep into his hardened gut, lifting him clean off the ground and hurling him perilously close to the boundary rope. The prong of scrap-metal clutched furtively between her toes turned hot with blood. Now *that* was against the rules.

Ekia watched his simian features crumple in the realization that she was not him, no elite fighter, no gentlewoman. She was a scrapper by nature and nurture both, her mother the street, her father the fist. The code by which Uko fought by was meant to keep men like him lifted above people like Ekia, but like the alleyway brawler she was, she'd taken the code and ground it down into a shiv.

Her moment had come. Ekia summoned every bit of love she had for Sasha and poured it like fuel into her muscles. A single step transported her the breadth of the arena. Uko rose to meet her — glacially, from her perspective — but Ekia knew he could not understand the crude speech of her body, could not truly see *her*, not the way that she saw him.

She lifted her sword, a victory cry sounding itself with her throat. But in that moment, Uko's hands seemed to move perpendicular to the linear flow of time, blurring into invisibility and reappearing knotted around his sword. It moved not impossibly fast, but so *perfectly* against the dingy world that it appeared as a single stroke of light. Force rang through both her arms, jounced between her scapulae, and finally exploded into her skull. Through the stars flaring and dying inside her eyes she saw that her sword had been split perfectly down the center, the inner planes sizzling with heat.

Ekia froze in the face of impossibility — for no more than a heartbeat, but that was enough. She saw the rising tip of Uko's sword swell until it eclipsed her vision, then her face erupted in fire from her jaw up to the peak of her scalp. She reeled backwards, her every muscle in a panic, the air biting at her flesh, and could not think to stop herself from falling over the boundary rope.

From over the roars of adulation from the gallery, she heard a chain rattling. "The Aggravant has been expelled!" someone cried. "The Aggrievant is victorious!"

Ekia forced herself up onto her hands and knees. No, no, no, this could not be happening. The future with Sasha she'd dreamed of had seemed so clear, and now it was tumbling away from her like a head lopped from a body. It wasn't *fair*, how much difference a single moment could make. She wrenched around in search of Sasha, but her love was not looking at her even as she bled out on the ground.

No, Sashioka was beaming at the man who'd lain her there, with all the love she'd ever shown to Ekia glinting in her eyes.

Ekia felt it when her mind went out like a candleflame, and when something *else* stepped smoothly in to pick up the reins. She watched her hands coil around her sword and pry away the looser half. Sasha noticed her first; Ekia registered the expression of horror that overtook her features, but whatever dark thing steered her now had no notion of love. Uko began to spin around, now sensing the threat, but seconds too late. Her sword was already in motion, hewn in two, but sharpened by hate to a killing edge. Anything would have been a weapon in her hands.

Skin, muscle, bone, marrow. All parted without resistance, almost apologetically.

The cheers of the crowd mutated into screams as Uko's arm tumbled away from his body.

3 Uko Now

Their swords collided with such force that the displaced air became a razor, snipping strands from Uko's beard, peeling wafers of skin from Ekia's cheeks. He pushed against her with all his strength, forcing her to cross her blades to hold him back, but neither could he break through to her flesh. They hurled themselves apart only to slam together once more, their weapons biting and snapping like animals to which they were leashed, again and again and again. Each slash gone astray cut rents in the arena without losing momentum, as though nothing else truly existed in the universe but the two opponents.

Ekia's arm went suddenly fluid, moving as if boneless to catch Uko's sword in the curve of her sickle and twist it to the ground. Her machete reared up overhead, and Uko had nothing to appease it with but a sewn-up stump. The future dispersed into a thousand bloody possibilities as it passed through that blade, blinding Uko with visions of each angle at which he could be halved. But over the years he'd adapted to his lopsided body. His remaining limb had grown twice as strong, with a wrist flexible enough to turn a full circle. His sword appeared between them like a mistake of fate, refracting the surety of his death into a new inevitability, that this would not end so soon.

Uko retreated, putting the entire arena between them, this time to reassess his foe. Ekia had changed; there was no mistaking the purpose in her strikes. Her eyes were seeing not just him, but the Uko of each cascading second from now. She was less the beast that he'd encountered all those years ago and more the hunter now wearing its skin. Only a blue-flaming hate could so reforge a soul.

Uko watched the ingots of muscle in Ekia's calves go taut, moments before they exploded her across the arena. Had she faced the Uko of ten years ago, he suspected that man would already lie riven in twain. In that time, however, Uko had left as many iterations of himself in his wake as he had drops of blood. He was his own strongest descendent.

With a twist of his wrist he shaved a peel of light from the sun and flicked it into Ekia's eyes. The woman hissed, blinded, and plunged her sword into the ground to halt her momentum before it got her killed — exactly as Uko had hoped. He twirled Headsplitter through his fingers to clutch it like a javelin. He threw his arm back, aligning his body from toe to fingertip into a single, tensed muscle, stretching it as far as it could go before the pain overwhelmed him. And then he did what no butenku would ever consider, and let go of his sword.

3 Ekia Now

Every time their swords clattered together, the force of it rippled up Ekia's arm and detonated inside her skull, threatening to burst her eardrums from the inside. Uko's blade glanced against her cheeks — *one, two* — and Ekia watched wafers of skin float on the breeze. Blood arced freely from each wound they created, nourishing the Titan-tree in stripes and jots. Ekia had thought her fury a juggernaut, but his was its equal. Neither could force the other to give up the ground they'd stolen. Instead they danced away from each other, feigning tactical retreat, only to slam back together with steel between them, a pair of hateful reflections.

Ekia moved like a snake, her arm slithering up to hook Uko's sword in her sickle, and slam it to the ground. She raised her sword high, filling it with lethal momentum, but even old, even crippled, even malformed from birth, Uko was fast and strong, a genius in the mathematics of his body. His sword, suddenly snakelike itself, seemed to slither out of her grip and insinuate itself between her killing blow and his heart. Once more, satisfaction danced out of her reach like a coy lover.

Uko scuttled backwards across the arena, unfolding, to Ekia's eye, into his successive selves. Once high and mighty, then a crippled wreck, now an animal with its belly to the ground, just like her, desperate to survive. She danced from side to side, trying to confuse his ability to read her musculature, and then launched herself after him.

On the other side of the ring, Uko's arm suddenly swung up, caught a ray of sun, and flung it into her eyes. The world went solid white, and Ekia stabbed her sword into the ground to kill her own momentum before it carried her into Uko's blade. She couldn't see him, but she could hear his musculature groaning with tension, his skeleton crackling as it realigned, and more telling still, his sheer killing intent, which pierced her like an echo from the future.

She blinked her eyes clear, and there was Uko, his body contorted into a longbow, and in the hand above his head, a winking star —

No.

The tip of his sword.

4 Uko Then

In a land far south of Kinroika, where pastures rolled like a rumpled quilt, Uko Hiigomathre was born to a family of humble milkbeetle farmers beneath the semi-occultation of the moon Gin Nei by the moon Hyom. The midwife noted this, as well as the spatter of the blood produced by his mother's contractions, and divined from this conjugation of good omens that the infant was destined to be a brave and handsome warrior. When Uko at last came sliding out of his mother, however, the midwife was forced to admit that signs could be difficult to interpret.

By the malice of some god, the boy had been misshapen in the womb, with legs too short, arms too long, and a face that could spook a milkbeetle dry for life. His appearance only worsened as he grew older. All in the village agreed; the boy ought to have been drowned when it would have been a mercy. He was too weak to push a plow, no woman would have him, and his children could only be more a pity than he. To be a shoveler of beetle dung was the best life he could hope for.

Uko was seven when he'd had enough of their whispers and became determined to prove them wrong.

From a sturdy branch, he whittled himself a wooden sword and took to the woods to learn its use. From the crack of day to the oncome of night, he stropped himself sharp against trees and stones and rivers, making enemies of all things so that he could grow strong against them, forcing strength into a body that had refused it. The other children of the village went in search of the ugly boy they'd had so much fun tormenting, but found instead a wild animal that sent them crying, stumbling, bleeding home. Word of the Demon Ape of the forest spread like fire through the countryside.

By the time he was eighteen, Uko possessed the strength to cut a cedar in half with a single stroke, to shatter a stone to dust against his forehead. He had made his first kill a year before, when a rustler attempted to make off with his family's best milkbeetle. Of the love of a woman, however, he knew nothing. The village girls all fled when he happened to stroll by, and he had no time to chase them. He could dream of the day he would travel to Kinroika and earn his place atop the ranks of the butenku; that much was possible, through force of will. A wife he would never have, but the fame and honor owed to a warrior, yes, those were within his reach.

It was as he was walking home on a twilit evening that he came upon an old man shuffling down the forest path. Uko would have said nothing and carried on with his own business had the wizened elder not stopped to squint up at him and remark, "You are the most hideous animal these ancient eyes of mine have ever seen. Your shit would be prettier than you."

Uko, young and paper-skinned, immediately drew his sword to demand an apology, only to find it severed at the hilt and himself pinned to ground by an obsidian blade through both cheeks. He was informed in short order that the stranger was none other than Syamto Surmra, Deva of Steel, Grandfather of Swordplay.

In his travels, the ancient master explained, he had caught wind of the savage warrior said to rule these woods, and come on a whim seeking to alleviate the unbearable boredom that beset one who had conquered all his challenges and slain all his foes.

"You are a beast," the old man said, seated casually upon Uko's belly. "One day you will be slaughtered like one. But I can make of you a demon, if you wish. Oh yes, what fun that will be. But know this, foolish beast. Should you wish to survive, you must abandon all things beyond the tip of your sword. Can you do that, I wonder?"

Uko grinned around the sword he bit like a bridle. Though he didn't know it, the old swordmaster asked for all that he had in empty pockets. Uko had already given up the world for his dream. His heart was just another hardened muscle meant to grip a hilt. It would never want for anything else.

☾☽

A year from the day he lost his arm, Uko was dismissed from the Urbomog's service.

In the aftermath of the duel, Sashioka had given herself to the Monks of the Great Bole out of guilt for what she'd brought about. She was to be a Chaste Sister until death. Without her, Uko's days were spent waiting in the shuttered darkness of his chambers among all the things he could never share with her, kept awake by the echoing pain of his missing limb, meditating on that moment of perfect failure as though enough pressure could crack time apart and let him do it over. As for Ekia, she had fled the scene before the Hashiado's other butenku could arrest her. Her violation of the laws of Hegimedi made her a wanted woman; the last Uko had heard, she'd left Kinroika entirely.

Uko's reputation was not enough to dissuade challengers forever. When one finally came, a young and headstrong butenku of the Akazoku family found a one-armed Uko less formidable than a whole one. So reduced, he could not perform the Seven Pinnacle Cuts, and for the first time in his life, Uko knew defeat. He'd expected a lash to his pride but to his surprise it felt like nothing. Too much of him already hurt.

The Urbomog cast him aside not long after. A butenku who could not defend his master's honor was as useless as a bladeless sword, and moreover, the Hashiado patriarch blamed Uko for the loss of his daughter. It was said that when a butenku had so fallen from glory, then he had become his own greatest enemy, and must be cut down. Uko tried, taking his sword to his own throat, only to find that the only thing a man such as him feared was his own self. Instead, he collected his meager stipend and went questing for an excuse to live. He began his search at the bottom of a bottle.

His wandering after stronger liquor took him far from Kinroika, to the Western grasslands of Saagrudís, where the native barbarians lived pitifully upon the ground. For lack of a Titan-tree, these hardscrabble folk constructed villages upon massive, rolling wheels, and lived in a state of perpetual, petty warfare. If two wagontowns so much as wished to cross a river ahead of one another, it would end in a bloody battle. Uko had nothing but disdain for these backwards nomads, but the wine they concocted from the fermented ichor of snake-radishes kept his most ferocious memories underwater.

It was on the road through these lands that fortune nearly crushed him beneath its treads. He awoke one early morning to a deafening rumble, to trees shaking themselves bare, and animals fleeing over him. A wagontown was fast approaching, and a single, antlike traveler as him would scarcely constitute a bump in the road. Uko, half-awake, half-drunk, and half-hungover, acted without a solitary thought, and slashed its foremost wheel in two with a single cut of his rusted sword. It did not register, what he'd done, until the wagon collapsed to the ground.

When the wreckage settled, the remnants of a small army emerged to confront him. Uko prepared for violence, only to find their commander kneeling before him and offering him a sash laden with gilded bones. It transpired that these were the Skullfarmers, a mercenary troupe of great renown, and he was shortly thereafter added to their ranks

Life as a mercenary was life atop an anvil. Death could strike at any moment. One had to grow hard or be destroyed.

Uko traveled with the Skullfarmers for seven years between battlefields, each day a universe further from the one he knew in Kinroika. The world was more wondrous than he'd ever believed, possessed of ruin-speckled jungles and endless steppes, and absolutely everywhere men strove to murder one another. Uko was an old friend to violence, but the swordplay of the butenku was ritualized, an especially energetic debate. Though he'd realized that some strength still lingered in his body, the rules by which he'd always fought no longer applied. A solider did not issue a challenge before lopping one's head from their shoulders, and in battle there were thousands of them.

Uko learned not just how to win, but how to survive. Though he was senior to most of his fellows by twenty years, they were his masters in that subject. When he fought in winter, he learned to camouflage himself in the snow as they did, and to strike at a turned back. In summer he learned to use his sword like a mirror to blind his foes, no matter how it carved at his own pride. Like a child shedding its baby fat, so did Uko sweat out the honor that had lost him his arm and his love.

Some nights he would lay awake as the wagontown rumbled onwards and wonder what he was looking for in this new life. Satisfaction? No, a tiger could not fill his belly with mice. The men he met in battle were not worthy to be defeated by him. Nothing to be won there but gold and drink. Perhaps it was peace, then. He was a warrior, meant to fight. It would not be so bad to die bloody.

Or perhaps he wanted oblivion. To bury his failure beneath a mountain of victories and forget that he'd ever aspired for anything more. He wondered how long that would take.

In the ninth summer of exile, Uko found himself in a plain where men were trying to kill each other, as men always were. He could not remember whom he was fighting against. In fact, he could hardly recall whom he was fighting for. The banners all blurred together after long enough; styles of armor all looked the same when then were soaked in blood. He stalked across the battlefield with sword in hand and a jug of snake-radish wine hanging off his little finger, destroying and drinking in the same motion. As though slogging thick underbrush, he slashed his away towards the nameless enemy's rear lines, where he expected to find their general. Commanders, he'd found, were often hardier game than common soldiers. If not, at least this paltry war would be over faster.

But as he tipped his jug to his lips, he spied turmoil in the legions ahead. Its surface bulged, hurling armored men wailing into the air, as though something huge and powerful were swimming towards him through it. After years of dormancy, Uko's warrior instincts stirred, scenting the approach of a worthy opponent. He let his drink fall and waste its contents on the blood-saturated earth.

Light flashed along the horizontal axis, and a wave of bodies split across the middle.

Like muscle flensed from bone, so was the ivory face of Ekia Mouseclaw revealed.

Uko did not bother wondering how she'd found him. Seeing the rotten grin that parsed her scars, the hate that had slowly starved inside of him erupted into something unnamable. At the outset of a duel, a butenku would customarily proclaim his greatest feats for all to hear.

Uko could only scream.

Their first clash burst the bindings of Uko's sword and split the skin of Ekia's knuckles. The second blasted arrows out of the air. Soldiers of both armies fled as the radius of their battle grew. To Uko, friend and foe were lost like grains of pepper amongst salt. The only other living thing in his world was Ekia, and she had to die. For a time that seemed infinite, they moved through their murderous dance. Fueled by the death-stained atmosphere, Uko fought like a beast, ignoring the shallow wounds that Ekia struck with her twin fangs. It was not he who swung his sword, but the vengeful ghost he'd become in this bloody afterlife.

He could see in her eyes a plan unraveling. She'd expected to find the Uko she'd left in ruins. He grinned to show her she'd found the wrong man.

Uko felt the air whip past him as Ekia sucked it through her gritted teeth. He saw her hands tighten about her machete in a familiar pattern, her muscles bulging with the souls of the fallen. Uko reacted on instinct, bracing his sword before him as Ekia raised her weapon high and, impossibly, performed the Fifth of the Seven Pinnacle Strikes.

When the dust settled, Uko found himself at one end of a crater in which no living thing stood, one bisected by a deep trench that ended at his feet. A smoldering notch in his sword bled steam.

"Where did you come by that technique?" Uko panted.

Ekia curled her ruined lip. "From the same idiot who taught you," she said. "He won't make the mistake a third time. While you were getting drunk and looking for death, I was looking for you. Ten years I spent freezing to death on that mountaintop. Ten years, training to kill a god. And in the end what do I find but a fat, crippled old fool? What a fucking waste."

Uko snorted in derision. "You're right, little girl," he said, flicking the blood of incidental deaths from his sword. "I am a fool. I knew what you were from the start, and still I spared your life."

"I'm a fool too. I should've aimed for your neck."

"You should have aimed lower," Uko retorted. "Sashioka was never going to be yours. Her father as good as ordered me to kill you. And you never would have won, because you never loved her anyway."

"Shut up," Ekia growled.

"You couldn't possibly," Uko went on. "Not the way I did. All you wanted was her father's wealth. You thought you could use her to climb out of the shit-heap where you belong. An animal like you cannot love, only devour. I thank you for saving her. Now thank me for saving her from you."

He expected her to attack in a rage, but instead her scar-cleft eyes narrowed to black slits. "You're wrong," Ekia said, suddenly calm. "She was everything. But not anymore. You're what I have left, Uko. You and only you."

A shock as he realized that he felt the same. He'd been apart from Sashioka for far longer than he'd known her. The only face he saw when he closed his eyes was Ekia's, split down the middle. How strange, that when thieves robbed from one another, they came away with nothing. Nothing but a grudge.

Uko turned to squint at the sunset, a red so deep it seemed they'd stained the sky itself with blood. If they fought in the dark they'd be tripping over corpses like a couple of court jesters. He sighed through his nose and sheathed his sword. "The day is over," he said. "We're both tired. I'm still drunk. I say we finish this properly another time."

Ekia cocked her head. "What did you have in mind?"

4 Ekia Then

That Ekia escaped the Urbomog's hall after violating the precepts of Hegimedi was the sort of dingy miracle that only followed far greater tragedies. As soon as her blow separated Uko's arm, Ekia had spun on her heels and scurried away like the mouse she was, fangs bared, slashing blindly at everything in her way, fury and despair clashing in the spaces between her ribs and propelling her away from the Urbomog's butenku. Her life was small compensation for what she'd left behind.

For the first time, she left the Titan-tree. Down into the untamed swamp that radiated from its base like a festering shadow. Hacking through thorn-studded vines and hearing flowers chatter in her wake, stirring up great swarms of buzzing insects that stung clear through her clothes. Kinroika took its toll in blood in exchange for letting her go.

By the time she emerged, days later, onto the sprawling plains that joined Kinroika to the rest of the world, her wrath had devoured her fear. She had lost the battle, lost Sasha, lost her future, lost the only thing like a home she'd ever had. And it was all because of *him*.

Ekia lived, but with a new condition. She existed only to take revenge on the man who had spared her life and yet killed her all the same. She would eat Uko's heart on a platter dripping with blood gravy. She would fork his very soul down her maw, and if she were to fall dead the moment after, hers would be a life completed nevertheless.

But a fact remained: he was better than her. Her innate talent for murder was inhuman, but Uko's Seven Pinnacle Cuts exceeded the ceiling of human power. Ekia had no doubt that even one-handed, he would crush her a second time were she to fling herself at him again.

Something would first have to change.

Ekia survived on fruits and vermin, trekked for weeks across the sprawling, green-grass sea, slept with the stars for her blanket. She stopped in towns of strange people, fought them in their taverns, but never stayed long. Sometimes she dreamt of Sasha, but woke alone and shivering no matter the heat. There was inside her a gaping canyon gouged by loss, which she slowly began to fill with hate. Hate for men, hate for Uko, hate for this world, which had never made a place for her within it.

Wherever she roamed, she learned enough of the local tongue to ask the same question, and the answers she accrued began to push her in a definite direction. Ekia wandered towards the great gray mountains called the Trials looming over the Eastern Horizons, where it was said by many dwelt the master who had taught Uko Hiigomathre to use a sword. If the man still lived, for he was nigh-primeval even then, she would make him train her as well. However long it took, she would return to Kinroika with Uko's own skill and cleave his ugly head from his body in what would be an unavoidable mercy.

If not, well, she would find a way. Whatever it took.

The mountains were a new challenge. Not so much underbrush to cut through, plenty of sharp black stones to stumble over. Eka's lungs struggled to subsist off the air that thinned with every upward step. But if she turned back here, she would never defeat Uko, for he was stronger than masses of ice and rock. There were ruined cities built into caves, populated by fierce but unintelligent troglodytes with pale eyes and sharp teeth. They reminded Ekia of herself, creatures who clung desperately to existence with bloody claws. She fought those that dared approach, and the rest learned their lesson. Onward she climbed for what seemed years, time being coy when night was the same ice-blue as day. Sometimes she encountered fellow pilgrims who'd come seeking tutelage for their own grim objectives. These she left buried in snow; a grudge such as hers permitted no sympathy for the grudges of others.

She came, after an indeterminable time, to the tallest peak, where the purest snow blazed like white fire. There awaited a simple hut with a furred pelt for a roof, and a man sitting cross-legged upon a flat stone out front. He was so ancient, a mummy with skin as dark and corrugated as Titan-bark, that Ekia thought him dead until an eye creaked open at her approach.

But though he would stand no higher than the upward curve of her breast, his proximity was a razor pressed to her throat. For a moment she feared to speak lest she slice her tongue on his aura. There was no doubt that this was Syamto Surmra, Deva of Steel, whose blade had pruned dynasties.

"Who comes?" the ancient inquired, his voice the groaning of a withered bough in the wind.

"I seek the greatest master of all swordplay," Ekia called out, voice cracking. The exhaustion she ignored had come crashing down on her shoulders all at once. It was a battle not to collapse on the spot.

"You found him," said Syamto Surmra. "Now go."

"I must learn," Ekia insisted.

The old man let out a dusty snort. "I don't care. Leave me alone."

She could not afford to be foolhardy here. Murder, for this man, was as thoughtless as scratching an itch. Ekia crept closer, dropped to her knees in front of the wizened creature, and planted her brow in the snow. "I have lost all," she said in a pitiable rasp. "I beg of you, to give me your audience for a short, sad story. Then, if you still send me away, I shall go and throw myself from the mountaintop."

The ancient reached into the snow before him and withdrew the simplest of swords, volcanic stone knapped into a jagged edge, its grip bound in hair. "You lie," he said. "You are not so weak a creature. If I say no again, you will try to kill me. I can see it written proudly in your muscles. I think that you are a creature that will stab at death himself to get what you want."

The old master smiled at her with a toothless, sucking chasm of a mouth. "And that is why I shall give you just that. Breaking you will make for an entertaining afternoon."

Ekia did not break that afternoon. When hours later the old master planted her like a bright red flower in the snow, her entire body bruised in gruesome constellations, she surprised him by digging up the strength to crawl inside his hut and sleep beside his fire. This feat was sufficiently interesting to warrant his attention for another three days.

Those three days grew into months, while Ekia consistently failed to die. The chances for her to do so were endless. Her survival was dependent on her being amusing. Failure to absorb a lesson fast enough incurred a random swipe from the master's death-steeped sword, yet those layered wounds soon accrued into a shell of insensate scar tissue. They were long months up on the mountain where the wind howled like a colicky infant day and night. Syamto Surmra pitted her relentlessly against rock and boulders, and soon the creatures of the wilderness, wolves and bears and stranger things. The fleeting absence of pain became the reward for a lesson learned.

Ekia did not need to beg: the old master was happy to teach her the Seven Pinnacle Cuts. He found it comical to watch her destroy herself attempting them. She came quickly to hate the man. Not because he was exceedingly cruel, for his monstrousness was perfectly impersonal. He regarded all other lives as something to poke holes in when bored. No, she hated him for what he set into motion. Were it not for him, there would be no Uko Hiigomathre. No competition for Sashioka's heart. And although the man could not have known, he would not have cared if he had. What was her drama beside a life as prolonged and violent as his? What was she but one of those faces he'd arbitrarily not split in half? He'd never seemed bothered that she sought to kill his strongest student. Should someone come seeking the same of her, he'd likely train them too, should they prove diverting.

Day after day he watched and laughed. Ekia suffered in obedient silence, however, as she reconstructed herself around each painful failure. The First Pinnacle Cut shattered her fingers; the Second tore muscle from her left arm. Yet flesh knit together over all of the openings rendered and trapped them within her. Two years, Ekia Mouseclaw spent in brutal apprenticeship to Syamto Surmra before she could perform all Seven. Two years demarcated only by the daily notches she etched in a stone near his house.

The stone beside hers told her that Uko had done it in that many plus one.

"I'm done," she told her master on that final, bitter morning. "I have to go now."

"Oh yes, for your vengeance," he replied. "I'd forgotten."

"Yes, that."

The old man's expression seemed to soften for the first time she'd seen. "You know, I do hope you'll visit," he said.

That took Ekia halfway aback. "Why?"

"I think I may be rather fond of you," replied Syamto Surmra. He stroked his chin pensively. "I've long wondered if it would have been nice to have a son. A good many students I've had in my time, but none I can say I wouldn't maim to fill an hour. I suppose that boy Uko wasn't too bad, but he was a pain to look at, and all he cared for was fame and gold and such nonsense. But you, on the other hand, love the blade for what it's for. Slaughter and victory. That reminds me of me, and I like me a great deal. If you should choose to stop by, I promise that I won't kill you."

"Thank you," Ekia said, somewhat baffled. "But I'm likely to die first. Sorry."

"Well, good luck to you then, my most adequate student," the old man said with the most miserly of nods. He began to shuffle around on his rock to resume his meditation. "Remember, vengeance should not be taken lightly."

The swordmaster's affection for her was surprising and unwelcome. He'd shown not an ounce of it in the last two years, unless permission to live was a gesture of endearment.

That was not, however, why she drew her sword and lopped off his head. True to his myth, the old man was quick enough to seize his blade before hers had fully passed through his neck. She expected he'd live on a while yet, in a sense, until someone came along to discover the body.

Ekia did not waste time with a burial, merely kicked him over into the snow. She then retrieved her pack from his hut and began the trek down the mountain. "Two years, you delayed my vengeance," she said, to his ghost perhaps, if it lingered there. "No, I do not take it lightly."

It took Ekia two years to find the Master, two to train, and five more to track Uko down. As she discovered, he had not remained in Kinroika with Sasha, but set out into the world — out of shame, some said. That pleased her slightly, but it prolonged her mission to spill his guts to the heavens. Fortunately, Uko had left a bloody trail. It seemed he'd become a mercenary with the arm she'd left him with. Perhaps he was seeking his death amongst those endless battlefields. How ironic that it sought him too.

It was on one such battlefield that she cornered him at last. Where thousands churned together in the ecstasy of violence, he was an unsinkable ship plowing through bloody waves. She saw him before he spotted her. His imbalanced body did not stop him from scything through soldiers left and right. Beads of sweat and blood bedecked a beard grown gray and unruly. Pools of bruise-purple dripped from the hollowed sockets of his eyes. Ekia could see that the loss of his arm had taken something else with it, something intangible and irreplaceable, but the remains resembled the Uko she remembered enough for her purposes.

She set off after him, allowing the fury she'd carefully kept caged up all these years to go wild at last, coursing through bodies like a tiger. The moment her foe came into range, Ekia snarled and swept her sword through the row of men before her, revealing herself to a fanfare of dying screams.

When Uko saw her, his eyes seemed to ignite from sheer hate. A mindless roar tore his jaws open in its haste to reach her. That lone arm of his lashed the air like the death-tipped tail of a scorpion. The sound of their blades colliding burst the eardrums of lesser men. The force of it spilt over and raked furrows in Ekia's forearms. This was not the dance that poets envisioned when they ruminated on swordplay, but the grinding of two contrary unstoppable wills. The space around them became a no man's land, and mortal enemies threw down arms and fled side-by-side to escape it.

Ekia fought more fiercely than she ever had, enough to murder the Uko of ten years past ten times over, but somehow the man refused to fall. He did not seem to feel it when her blade chipped away at his stony body. His remaining limb had doubled in mass yet lost its former grace; no longer could she predict where his blade would come crashing down. As their fight wore on, Ekia found herself retreating beneath a deluge of wild blows. Too late did she realize she'd trained ten years to fight a man who was already dead. This was not the Uko she'd encountered before. Just as she'd adopted the discipline that made him a god, so too had he cast off his inhibitions and become a monster like her.

Ekia leapt back, throwing enough space between the two of them to glut her lungs on the rot-tinged air. She could taste the fresh souls sliding over her tongue. Uko's eyes went wide in recognition as she gripped her sword the way Syamto Surmra had once taught him. That infinitesimally small moment of confusion gaped at Ekia like a crack in armor.

Her blade strode through space with such conviction that time could only bow cringingly out of its way. Among all possible motions of the universe, the Fifth Pinnacle Cut was royalty.

When the dust cleared, Ekia found herself at one end of a crater in which no living thing stood, one bisected by a deep trench that ended at Uko's feet. A smoldering notch in his sword bled steam.

"Where did you come by that technique?" he panted, incredulous.

Ekia masked pain with a sneer; the technique had been created with a man's frame in mind. From her, it demanded an unfair tribute. "From the same idiot who taught you," she said. "He won't make the mistake a third time. While you were getting drunk and looking for death, I was looking for you. Two years, I spent freezing to death on that mountaintop. Two years, training to kill a god. And in the end, what do I find but a fat, crippled old fool? What a fucking waste."

"You're right, little girl," Uko snorted. He snapped his wrist, flicking the blood from his sword. "I am a fool. I knew what you were from the start, and still I spared your life."

"I'm a fool too," Ekia concurred. "I should've aimed for your neck."

Uko shook his head pityingly. "You should have aimed lower. Sashioka was never going to be yours. Her father as good as ordered me to kill you. And you never would have won, because you never loved her anyway."

"Shut up," Ekia squeezed the words around the iron ball in her throat.

"You couldn't possibly," Uko went on. "Not the way I did. All you wanted was her father's wealth. You thought you could use her to climb out of the shit-heap where you belong. An animal like you cannot love, only devour. I thank you for saving her. Now thank me for saving her from you."

Fury did not flare up out of her in a frenzy of suicidal violence as Ekia expected it would. Instead, her outrage contracted into a comfortably warm but shivering lump that she could feel nestled up to her heart — pocketed, it seemed, for another time. "You're wrong," she said, suddenly as calm as a frozen lake. "She was everything. But not anymore. You're what I have left, Uko. You and only you."

For just a moment she felt the faint tug of something reaching through time to grasp her shoulder, urging her to turn back while her life was still in her hands, but Sasha had been gone for far longer than their two dreamlike weeks. The heart was a strong muscle, but even it could not hold on to so little for so long. The hungry pit inside her had once had Sashioka's silhouette; now, only Uko's corpse could fill it.

Uko turned to squint at the scarlet sun. A bloody sky to match the ground, one quickly scabbing over into evening. Soon it would be too dark to fight, and Ekia knew well what poor footing the dead were. Their battle would quickly become a circus if they tried to continue it.

Uko seemed to agree. "The day is over," he sighed, clapping his sword back into its sheathe. "We're both tired. I'm still drunk. I say we finish this properly another time."

Ekia was loath to admit it, but he made a good case. "What do you have in mind?"

5 Uko Now

Splinters rained down upon the arena. Fine sawdust billowed from his sword's point of impact like smoke. Some in the crowd oo-ed and aa-ed even as they covered their heads, for surely the power of his throw had reduced the Mouseclaw to vapor. Uko, however, knew better. He remained stonefaced when his sword came whirling back at him from out of the smoke, and caught it as casually as he might receive a falling plum.

Ekia stepped from the blast crater unharmed but for a long gash across her cheek, soon to be lost amongst her trove of scars. Her sickle was a knot of glowing metal which she hurled contemptuously over her shoulder. Uko could see her heart beating through her dirtied robe, and her eyes blazed like phosphorous in the cauldron of her skull.

He should have raged to see her still living. Instead, his cheeks tore open in a smile.

His blood too had caught flame.

Uko slid his sword through his robe and tore the cloth away, baring to the crowd his trophy-case, where the greatest had left their marks. He nodded to Ekia, inviting her to try and join it.

Without seeming to have moved, she came spiraling through the air. Uko could not have hoped to move from that spot, could only place steel in her path. Their blades slammed together and the ground beneath them buckled into a bowl. In the corner of his eye he saw the magistrates exchange worried looks. This sacred site had withstood centuries of grudges. This fight would mar the Titan-tree forever.

"We'll make an end of it in Kinroika," Uko had told her, those many months ago. "Let us meet on the field of Hegirama, with clear minds and full stomachs. Whoever wins will know they slew the entirety of the other."

"And how am I to know you'll be there?" Ekia had shrewdly asked.

"Because I wish to kill you more than you wish to kill me," Uko had replied. "And should you find me missing, you'll know me for a liar."

In the present, Uko made good on his word and hurled Ekia away with a burst of strength, pressing the attack before she'd even touched ground. He made his sword omnipresent, everywhere, in every moment, always cutting. They whirled together like a hurricane trapped within the confines of the ring and desperate to escape. Those in the stands closest to the edge began to back away in the fear that the hoary precepts of Hegirama would not suffice as a barrier. If not the Titan-tree, then certainly not words.

Murmurs of worry turned into screams as Ekia made an unexpected motion and slammed Uko up against the barricade that separated the ring from the box where the magistrates sat. The bones in Uko's good arm creaked as Ekia heaped the strength in her whole body against him. The pitted edge of her machete jerked closer and closer to the bridge of his nose. But as their eyes chaffered across that steel table, Uko felt something pass between them. An unspoken question, and a silent answer in reply. As one they agreed: nothing should stand in the way of one another's throats. Not laws, not walls.

Ekia suddenly stepped back and cocked her knee up to her chin. Uko took the moment to roll his throbbing shoulder, and let her have this one. His face had never been of use to him anyway.

Pain like a blinding light as her heel smashed his nose into his skull, then his skull into the wall behind him, and then the wall into the stands beyond that. Panic swept the crowd as Uko and Ekia exploded out of the arena and took their grudge to Kinroika.

Men and women ran screaming, dove for cover, slammed their windows shut. Rickshaws were abandoned to be obliterated as Uko battled Ekia through the streets. Uko could already see the story taking root in the public subconscious and flowering into a thousand variations, their shoots growing ever further from reality. In some he'd win, in others he'd lose, dying from infinite cuts. His last words would never be his own, but it was liberating to not care. Pride had only ever been a burden.

Though it was impossible to hear over the clangor of their weapons, Uko found himself cackling aloud. *This.* This, he realized, was the peak he'd sought. There was no glory in growing fat atop a ziggurat of lesser foes. There was no joy when one's sword was sheathed. No, stillness was the death of a swordsman. Life was only life when it gushed from one's open wounds. At last, after a lifetime wasted in pursuit of loneliness, Uko understood that the pinnacle of swordplay was meant to be occupied by two.

When he next looked at Ekia, he felt blessed. If he could have spared a breath to thank her, he would have, gladly. Men would kill men until the end of time, but only he would clash with this monstrous woman and destroy her. Thirst could be slaked, hearts could be warmed, but hate was the only emotion that sated the soul.

Here at the end of things, stripped of everything he'd ever reached for, Ekia was all he had left.

And all along, she was all he ever needed.

The city they'd made their arena dwindled down to a single branch, and then a single twig. Soon, Uko had cornered Ekia upon the very tip of the Titan-tree's furthest appendage, a knob no thicker through the middle than a small house. Far, far below, the plinth of the world curved towards its opposite pole. Both of them wheezed in the threadbare atmosphere.

5 Ekia Now

Ekia climbed from the crater left by the blast, a long slice on her cheek, Uko's sword glowing red-hot in her hand. She threw it back to him and he caught it without so much as a blink. Instead, he broke out in a grin that touched his eyes. He wasn't surprised to see her still alive, and for that she was flattered. For the first time he was seeing her as an equal, someone *qualified* to take his life. She looked on as he cut the robe from his body and laid bare the lives he'd recorded as silver scars upon his skin. Was that a challenge? A boast? No, an invitation, for only the best left their mark on Uko Hiigomathre.

Ekia was proud to accept.

She came corkscrewing through the air at him. Rather than flee, Uko chose to meet her head on. The force behind her blade spiked him an inch into the ground, and burst the binding of his sword, but that arm merely soaked up her killing intent like a spring and flung it back. By the time her feet found ground he was on top of her, a whirlwind of steel chewing through the bark of the Titan-tree.

"*We'll make an end of it in Kinroika,*" Uko had told her, one year ago to the day. "*Let us meet on the field of Hegirama, with clear minds and full stomachs. Whomever wins will know they slew the entirety of the other.*"

"*And how am I to know you'll be there?*" Ekia had asked, ever suspicious.

"*Because I wish to kill you more than you wish to kill me,*" he had replied. "*And should you find me missing, you'll know me for a liar.*"

In thrusting at her heart, he proved himself a man of his word. Ekia found that she could respect that; it seemed loathing did not preclude admiration. His hate was equal to her own, and by letting it burn away his inhibitions, it had freed him from the confines of his body. His one arm was everywhere, always slashing, cutting through every space her body could be near-simultaneously. To survive, she had to make herself a thousand-limbed warrior-goddess, matching his berserker's mania with nigh-divine foresight.

To be victorious, however, she would have to surprise a thoughtless mind.

Rather than twirl away from an overhead swing, she lunged into it, driving her heel into Uko's sternum and slamming him into the barricade between them and the audience. His sword squealed as he struggled with poor leverage to hold her back. She forced their crossed blades closer and closer to his mangled face, but when their eyes chanced to meet across its mirrored surface, the world seemed to crumble away, their material forms along with it. Information passed instantaneously from one unguarded mind to another. One of them posed a question, and the other answered. As one, they agreed: nothing should stand in the way of one another's throats. Not laws, not walls.

Ekia stepped back and brought her knee up to her chin. Uko, who could have lunged away or counter-attacked, merely grinned up at her, and took it. Gratification, powerful as an orgasm, as she kicked his face into his skull, then his skull into the barricade behind him, and then the wall into the stands beyond that. Terror overtook the crowd as Uko and Ekia exploded out of the arena and took their grudge to Kinroika.

Men and women scattered from their path like animals fleeing an encroaching forest fire, latching windows, slamming doors, as if such things could possibly matter. A bustling street market emptied itself in seconds as they came barreling through. Ekia watched terrified faces peel away with visions of her trapped in their eyes, stretching the strands of her reality into the realm of fiction. Whatever came of it, this battle would be the end of every story the world would ever tell of her. She would never achieve anything greater than slaying Uko Hiigomathre, and if she could not, then she would at least be immortalized as his most infamous kill.

Her life was out of her hands now; how freeing it was to shake off that most permanent burden!

Uko's sword flashed, and Ekia felt her ear dance on a thread of gristle. Her sword sang a steely note, and a long ribbon of flesh unspooled from Uko's naked chest. Death had them both in its jaws and was slowly chewing, but for every small wound they laid upon one another, a thousand cobblestones were stomped to dust, another jut of ancient masonry pulverized. This battle would destroy them both, more likely than not, and if they took Kinroika down with them, well what did it matter? The tree was not Ekia's home. She'd found her place at last, and it was a realm of time, not space, the hot and frantic seconds dividing life from death.

When she next looked at Uko, she was suddenly glad to have him there. This paradise could not exist without a second sword to strive against. At the end of her life she at last was not alone. All other kinds of happiness were beyond her, but that was enough.

In due time their momentum herded them along the full length of the Titan-branch, which narrowed inevitably to a single twig, upon which Ekia found herself abruptly cornered when her next step back fell on open air. Teetering on her tiptoes at the very edge of the Titan's last knobby boundary, she looked down, down, where vanishingly far below lay the rest of the world, betrayed as a sphere by sheer altitude. Her lungs ached for want of atmosphere.

Uko & Ekia

Once more their eyes met and argued for them. Should this be settled on such meager footing? Should they catch their breath and retreat to safer ground?

No, Uko's manic grin announced. *Perish the thought.*

No, Ekia's fanged smile declared. *Perish the thought.*

Uko felt potential exploding from within. There was nothing he could not do to kill Ekia Mouseclaw. Impossibility would not restrain his hand, and understanding this, Ekia swelled with pride. That a scampering little specimen of vermin from the Rootshades had risen so far, that given a final chance to live a long life, the most dangerous man in the world had instead chosen to murder her that much sooner. Overcome with gratitude, she watched as Uko wrapped his sword in five fingers as strong as twenty, drank in breath enough for an army. What should have ruptured him internally instead catalyzed into power as he guided his weapon through the sublime path of the Seventh Pinnacle Cut.

Steel passed without resistance through the stonelike hide of the Titan-tree. Layers of phloem bowed reverently aside to admit it. The tree, being merely immortal and impervious, did not stand a chance. The twig split cleanly, fountaining sap from both ends, with Uko on the shortest side. A cackle burst from Ekia's overfull lungs. It was inevitable now; one way or another, their grudge ended here.

As the severed limb began its long descent towards the earth, Uko raised his blade and leapt at Ekia, who laughed with her head thrown back, and strode forth to meet him. Together, they plummeted end over end towards a swift conclusion.

In the meantime, they fought upon the stage of the sky

The Firmament

Douglas Anstruther

Guilt is the most relentless emotion. It hollowed out my life and crouched in the shell for forty years. It stayed with me, pointless and unwelcome, even after the Dire Comet wiped away everything that gave it meaning. It didn't matter that no one was left to suffer from what I had done, to judge me or despise me. My guilt remained. The death of my son would pursue me to the ends of the Cosmos.

And what of the Dire Comet? Two years had passed since it came and went. Who was to blame for the sad and untimely death of humanity? As the sole survivor, there was guilt for the taking, but I could carry no more. That burden I left for the Firmament.

I slid from the ornithopter onto aching knees, clutching my dearest possession against my chest. The chaos of the last few minutes still roared in my head, only to be extinguished like a flame between damp fingers when I saw where I'd landed.

I stood on an immense plain of glass — the surface of the lowest Sphere of the Firmament. Stacked invisibly above Earth like concentric layers of an onion, the Spheres bore the celestial bodies in their paths through the sky. I scanned the distant horizons for the Moon, which this Sphere carried, but saw no sign of it. The air smelled crisp, like ozone with a hint of anise. It was warm and still, in sharp contrast to the icy squall that had just tried to tear us apart and which still raged silently beneath my feet. Far below, bright knuckles of cloud cast shadows over empty viridian forests, and above, the Sun sat, reproachful, in a flawless azure sky.

I walked around the flying machine, looking for a place to set down my bundle. The wrecked ornithopter was splayed across the ground like a bird against a window. The few cloth feathers that had survived the gale formed a halo of debris along with the crystal gear fragments that had been its flesh and blood. Between the mechanical gore and its unnatural posture — in a word, snapped — it was clear it would never fly again.

The glass plain was composed of massive gears the size of city blocks — part of the vast machinery of the Firmament that influenced everything from a person's mood to whether or not a tree fell in a forest. Every second, the ground lurched slightly, which, together with the drifting clouds below, threatened to knock me from my feet. In the distance, the jagged edges of the hole we'd flown through marred the perfect silence with a low, baleful moan. I set my package down and unwrapped its protective blankets, revealing a blue and purple metal box.

"We made it, Zip," I said. "We actually made it to the Firmament." It was hard to believe that less than an hour ago I had filled a pack with food and water, shaved off my hoary beard, combed back my grey hair, put on my Air Brigade uniform with 'Commander Wren' arrogantly emblazoned across the front, and walked out the door of my house.

The box shuddered and came alive. The sides of the box separated, and other plates unfolded from within. Crystalline gears like those of the ornithopter, doubtless harvested from somewhere in the Firmament, whirred beneath. Legs emerged, and after a minute of clicking and buzzing, a mechanical creature, roughly the size and shape of a beagle, stood before me. An elaborate, blue letter T was stamped across his forehead. He shook himself with an unhealthy clanking sound, made a few excited laps around me, then sat on his back haunches and gave me a meaningful stare.

"C'mon now, Zip. You know that I don't ever know what you want." Yet, somehow, he had brought me here. Only a week had passed since I stumbled across this strange creature, rummaging around in my tool shed. In that short span he'd become the entirety of my life, and, I had no doubt, was well on his way to becoming the cause of my death.

He got back up, wagging his tailless back end, and trotted toward the belly of the stolen ornithopter — stolen only inasmuch as it wasn't mine and was used without permission. Technically, it wasn't anyone else's either, since there *was* no one else. In a way, I was the richest man alive, having inherited the Earthly possessions of every single person. And I'd just left it all behind. Aye, that was okay. I couldn't bear another moment alone on that empty world. I wanted to be with Zip, and Zip wanted to be here.

"Right," I said, following after him. "Apparently, I'm taking orders from a mechanical dog now. I had some ridiculous commanders back in the Air Brigade, but at least they were human."

Zip reached the ornithopter's storage compartment, latched onto a handle, and pulled, his little metal feet clanking and sliding ineffectually on the smooth ground.

"Here, let me help you with that, little guy." I reached down and opened the panel, revealing a compartment packed with fabric. Zip and I looked at each other for a moment, then Zip latched his jaws onto the cloth and began pulling, with just as much effect as before.

"Go on, I'll get it. You're just in the way now. Go on, git." He blinked cute puppy-eyes at me but got the message and backed away.

Half an hour later I'd liberated the contents of the compartment and spread it across the ground. At the heart of the fabric, we found a wicker basket filled with cables and struts.

"A hot air balloon?" I asked, eyeing the metal beagle with mock suspicion. "How did you know that was in there?" Zip yawned, ignoring my question. It didn't matter, really. He just knew things. Like he'd known where to find the ornithopter and how to get me into it and up through that hole.

A red hand crank was bolted to the lip of the basket. Zip stared at it with comic intensity, so I took the hint and started cranking. Slithering cables gathered the fabric and lifted it onto struts which rose from the basket. It was slow going and I had to rest often. Meanwhile, Zip zipped around (thus his name) and the world below marched slowly past. The Sun, however, remained fixed in the same spot of the sky, as if nailed there. Eventually, Zip settled down, watching me from above outstretched legs. The hole we'd flown through wandered around to the other side of the 'thopter, carried by the clockwork motion of the ground. I wondered what the great gears were calculating, now that everything they influenced was dead. Everything, but me.

The last item to rise from the basket was a burnished metal tank that positioned itself beneath the fabric aperture. Once this was in position, Zip marched up to the basket, stretched his front legs toward its top, and waited for me to pick him up and set him inside.

"Aye, let's go, then." I said, dropping my pack into the gondola, and hoisting the wiggly creature into the basket. I squatted next to him, beneath a great, two-pronged switch on the tank that was labelled with the word "Lift." I did, and so did we.

It had been two years since the malign red glow of the Dire Comet made its appearance in the southern sky. Half a year later, everyone was dead. Everyone, of course, except for me. They called it the Fate Plague and it brought death to everyone in their own way. It wasn't actually a plague, so much as a curse — a sharp turn in humanity's destiny, straight into a brick wall. Sure, some died from disease, a sudden fever or a scalding rash that came out of nowhere and left the victim dead in a matter of hours. But most people died of freak accidents — train wrecks, air crashes, car accidents. People became terrified to leave their houses, but it didn't matter; a walk across the living room could be just as deadly. No creature was spared, not even the animals. Anything larger than a fruit fly shared humanity's fate, which hardly seemed fair, since everyone knew that humans were the cause. It was humans, after all, that had broken the Firmament. The rest were just innocent bystanders.

For a long time, I was oblivious — too wrapped up in booze and self-pity to notice anything. Later, after it became clear what was happening, I waited my turn at home, resigned to the end of a dreadful life. When the radio went silent, and the lights went dark, curiosity and boredom overcame me and I ventured out. I wandered for weeks, finding nothing but corpses. Eventually, I returned home and waited some more.

The loneliness was as terrible as it was unexpected. Before the Plague, I had no friends, no family, no acquaintances that would check on me or care if I became ill. I lived in a deep rut of my own making that was largely unaffected by the end of the world. I was used to being alone, but this was worse. It was yet another way of not belonging — the ultimate snub, the final rejection. Even in death, I was left out.

Technology had been advancing quickly when the Plague struck. Computers made from components harvested in the Lower Spheres — the ones that carried the Moon, Mercury, and Venus — had been getting better every year. The space between the Upper Spheres — which carried the Sun, Mars, Jupiter, and Saturn — was filled with celestial waters. The waters above the Sun had been powering cars and machinery for half a century. Exotic waters from more distant Spheres were just starting to make it to Earth and promised amazing advances: frictionless railways, personal flight, even floating cities. Weeks before the appearance of the Dire Comet, the papers had been filled with the discovery that the furthest waters, those beyond Saturn, affected the flow of time.

What marvels could be achieved when we controlled time itself? But instead, it all came to an end.

I looked down at Zip, curled at my feet in the bottom of the gondola. He was like nothing I'd ever heard of before — a mechanical animal, with thoughts and plans and feelings. The T on his forehead was the symbol of the Tinkers Guild, the most advanced Astrological Scientists and Engineers in the world, but even the Tinkers had never made anything like Zip. Except that it looked like they had.

The green Earth slid beneath us under the perpetual daylight. The Lunar Sphere that we had just left gradually faded away, a trick of light that all Spheres shared, giving the Earth an unimpeded view of the stars, and vice versa. Only the celestial bodies they bore were visible from afar. It had something to do with the angle of light, I recalled. Although I could no longer see the Sphere, I still felt its influence — the barest hint of an emotion I hadn't felt in a long, long time. Happiness.

The adrenaline of the previous day drained away into the calm air and I slumped down into the bottom of the basket, where dream found me. It was a variant of the usual theme. In this one, my son, Sammy, didn't die. He fell into the pool while I was passed out drunk, but somehow was able to get to the edge and crawl out to safety. I was scolded by friends and family for nearly letting the unthinkable happen. I felt terrible, but, in the end, everyone was just happy that Sammy was okay. It would have been a nightmare for anyone else, but for me it was a good dream. There was no messy divorce, no shunning by my family, no being cut off from everyone I knew or loved. I woke up relieved, basking in the warmth of family and friends. Except that a minute after I woke, nothing remained but a painful hope of forgiveness, forever denied.

I stood and stretched my stiffening legs. Zip woke too, and we spent the next few hours goofing around as the balloon rose. He nipped at my fingers and did figure eights between my feet. I told stories I hadn't shared for decades. When I spoke he sat attentively, head slightly cocked, looking at my face. I didn't know if he understood me, but he listened well.

A hazy oval moved across the flawless azure sky. I thought it was a cloud at first, then I remembered the clouds were all far below. It grew closer and larger, as the wind blew us toward it. Suddenly my perspective shifted, and I realized I was looking up at a hole in the Second Sphere, the one that carried Mercury. It was rotating toward us. And quickly.

I had a moment of raw terror as events accelerated beyond my control and we were sucked through the gap like smoke through a cracked window. As we moved above the Second Sphere, the flawless blue into which we had been ascending stayed below, leaving the new sky a stark white that was hard to look at, and giving the surface of the Mercurial Sphere, now below, the color of blue arctic ice. Its features seemed unreal, like blueprint sketches overlaid on the thin air. Far below, through it all, swam Earth, its curved edges and pregnant swell making it look like a great dome beneath an ocean.

"Guess the blue skies end here, Zip."

The balloon struggled to rise against the hot, thin air and we floated lower, skimming the craggy surface. Translucent mountains straddled the distant horizon, dripping cataracts of deep blue that became rivers, lazily wandering across plains toward us. No living thing moved; it was as lifeless as the world I had left — worse, for the absence of plants. Yet something about the translucent terrain gave life to the angles beneath the surface. The intersecting lines gave it a depth and complexity that opaque terrain lacked, and the distant mountains hypnotized me with their inner complexities. It didn't feel barren. It felt alien.

We barely cleared a row of serrated ridges that opened onto a long, serpentine beach. The gondola touched down and tipped over, throwing me on top of Zip. I fumbled around as well as I could, trying to keep my weight off him while the balloon dragged us across the beach, covering us both with blue sand. I was able to crawl out just as the deflating balloon caught a breeze and the entire thing started to lift again, with Zip still inside.

"No!" I stood and leapt, getting my hands on the rim of the rising basket and pulling it down. After a brief wrestling match, I triumphed and pinned it to the ground at an angle where Zip could crawl into my arms. The two of us collapsed to the ground as the balloon took off again toward the strange sea.

I sat up and caught my breath while Zip launched into play. He raced across the sand in great, gleeful bounds, scooping up mouthfuls of sand and spraying them around with a shake of his head. I'd never seen him so happy; it was a delight to watch and some small portion of his carefree joy spread to me like a contagion.

The air carried a faint tinkling sound, like distant windchimes, that gave me terrible *déjà vu*. Beneath me, the translucent blue sand felt strange, like foam padding, and was warm to the touch, with a faint smell of heated metal. Motion within it caught my eye. I patted down my pockets until I found my reading glasses, glad to see they were neither lost nor broken, and used them to examine the sand more closely. Each grain was a tiny transparent gear. The ones I scooped up or disturbed sat motionless, inert, but the ones on the ground turned in lockstep with the grains around them. I moved forward on hands and knees, watching the motion of the sand. In some places the motion of the little gears sped up or slowed down, in others it coordinated to form whirls or streams and in others it was a chaotic mass of motion. The Tinkers had made their first computers from these sands, before switching to more advanced materials from the Venetian Sphere. Again, I wondered what arcane calculations the sands of this beach were making. Was it calculating where lightning would strike? Which stones would break away from cliffs?

The influence of the Spheres had been well known for centuries. Understanding their effects had been the basis of the Scientific Revolution, and materials harvested among them had ushered in the Industrial Revolution that followed. Once the exploitation of the Firmament was underway, specialized sciences had risen, devoted to influencing destiny by changing the topology of the Spheres. If someone needed something to go a particular way, they consulted the charts, then levelled a mountain on this Sphere, or dammed a river on that Sphere, and the chances rose fifty percent, or twenty, or ten. The results had never been foolproof, but they had been known to sway the outcome of lotteries, elections, or even wars. Ultimately, the damage done to the Spheres to feed technology and tweak destiny had led to the Dire Comet.

Some of the distant foothills had a red hue, like a patch of inverted color after looking at a glare, but fixed to the land. Each place with this red hue was disfigured in some way, flattened hills, scarred mountainsides. My footprints bore the same red hue of destruction — faint and barely visible. I watched an area of disrupted sand for a few minutes and saw how the motion of the surrounding grains slowly pushed those I had disturbed back to their original positions and set them spinning again. As the footprint slowly healed, its red tinge faded.

So the Firmament could heal itself. And yet, those distant foothills still glowed red, years after their wounding. I wondered how long it would take for them to heal, if ever. I felt a kinship with these strange realms, still damaged even after the world had ended.

I stood up, stretched my back and worked my way to the water, stiff-legged after crouching for so long. Waves lined the beach, but frozen in time. Light sparkled and moved within the motionless water with a diamond radiance. I leaned over and put a fingertip against the leading edge of a wave, felt a prick and came away with a bright spot of blood.

The nettle water reminded me my own supply had been lost with the errant gondola. The Spheres were famous for their sterile lack of life and now it didn't look like I'd be replenishing my water either. How much longer would this adventure with Zip last? I wasn't afraid to die, but would prefer it not be of thirst.

Zip climbed a small mound of sand that extended beyond the waterline and sniffed the motionless waves cautiously. Suddenly the sand gave way beneath him and he dropped into the water, where he thrashed about, sending out spumes of pink spray. For a second, I thought he was enjoying himself, then I saw panic in his movement. He let out a frightful screech and slipped beneath the surface. I sprinted to the water's edge and dove in.

It was like diving into a sea of needles. I pulled myself down toward where I'd last seen my companion and groped around, desperate to feel anything solid against my flailing arms. Each movement was a caress against splinters. Something brushed the back of my hand. One mighty breaststroke later, I felt his weight crash against my shoulder. I closed my arms around him and kicked up, breaking the surface to the muffled sound of shattering glass. The last thing I remember was collapsing on the shore. My legs were still in the water, but my arms were on the beach and Zip was safe.

Dreams circled me like sharks around a wreck, all of the same malign species. In these, Sammy did not escape the price of my neglect. The unthinkable event that defined my life was thought. Sammy drowned. Because I was too drunk to do any of the simple things that could have prevented it. "No, Sammy, don't climb over that wall." "Sammy, I'm serious, that's dangerous." "I'm coming Sammy!" "Breathe, Sammy, c'mon." "Aye, Sammy, cough it out." "Boy, don't you ever scare me like that again." I never said any of those things. Instead, the dream told me there was a splash. A cry for help that went on, and on, becoming more desperate, then tired, then only silence. Had my mind filled in how it must have happened or had some part of it been listening? Either way, it offered the dream to me, over and over, as the perfect punishment. Not only did I have to watch Sammy die, I had to watch myself, sloppy and disheveled, sweaty and weak, having chosen foul drink over the life of my own five-year-old son, lying inert except for heaving breaths, as my son died.

The familiar dreams of heartbreak and remorse were interspersed with impossible scenes, more fantastic than any dream: sliding beneath the canopy of a blue crystalline forest, lying motionless upon the sky, dangling over the world from an impossible height. At times, a grown Sammy looked down at me with concern. Pain and the blinding glare of daylight were the only constants.

As a child, whenever I was sad or hurt my mother would scoop me up in her arms, take me outside into the cool night air, and reach toward the stars. "Touch a star, baby. It'll make everything better." I'd copy her, straining my little arm up, wanting badly to feel better, to tap into that power. It always worked. But now, night never came. The stars were banished, and I could never get better. The thought of it made me so sad that I started to weep.

"Wren? Why are you crying?"

It took me a long time to realize the significance of the words. Someone was talking. Someone. It was the most impossible hallucination of them all, because there was no one left to speak. I reached my hand to my face to clear the tears and the blinding brightness, but it stopped just before my eyes with the clinking sound of glass against glass.

A few rapid blinks cleared my vision and I found myself lying flat on my back, looking up into the arched interior of a massive crystalline building where rainbows fluttered like bats.

"Are you in pain?" The voice had a strange buzzing quality. *At least the insects survived*, I thought, not quite having escaped the grip of my dreams.

"No," I croaked. "Gone." I wasn't sure if I was correcting myself or answering his question.

"That's good," the voice answered. It sounded kindly, almost familiar. The memory of my adventures with Zip returned like a work of art revealed with the pull of a sheet, and the last residues of sleep fled my brain. I was in the Firmament. Talking to someone. Had this been Zip's plan all along, to reunite me with survivors among the Spheres? A brief moment of excitement at the prospect became a battlefield of competing emotions. Hope for the survival of humanity clashed with anxiety and dread at the thought of having to interact with people. Ultimately, the latter claimed the high ground and couldn't be dislodged.

With effort, I propped myself up onto my elbows, making a clatter that echoed through the vast space. I was lying on a stone slab, surrounded by a knot of retracted machinery. My skin glowed red, like the damaged lands of the Second Sphere, and was covered in a shell of glass, like trees after an ice storm. I shifted myself onto one elbow and brought a hand up in front of me, flexing my fingers into a fist. They were stiff but functional. I strained to sit up further and see the rest of my body.

"I'm sorry. I couldn't save all of you," the voice said.

I wondered whom he couldn't save. Then I looked down, and understood. Beneath my belly button, the denuded skin curved away sharply toward my spine. Below that, there was only glass in the shape of feet, legs, and a groin as smooth as a doll's.

"What ... what happened to me?"

"The lake on the Mercurial Sphere eroded your flesh. I brought you here; the Tinkers' machines did the rest."

Questions crowded my lips. I tore my eyes from my own body to the source of the voice. A humanoid automaton with articulated plates of blue and purple, like some ancient armored warrior, stood by my side. The smooth purple dome of his head framed a single piece of blue ice with the kind eyes and warm smile of a young man. His features moved in a stepwise but otherwise lifelike manner. An elaborate, blue letter T marked the metal above his face.

"Zip?" I asked, dumfounded. "Is that you?"

"Yes, Wren. I'm the same entity that you have been referring to as 'Zip' "

"How ... ? How can that be you?"

"I grew," he said matter-of-factly. "You were too large for me to carry, so I activated an auto-assembly protocol and used raw materials from the Mercurial Sphere to change my form."

"Where are we now?"

"We are in the Great Venetian City, built by the Tinkers."

"Venetian? We're on the Third Sphere?"

"Yes."

"How were you able to get me all the way to the next Sphere?"

"It was difficult. There's a lift at the heart of this city that transports things from a particular mountaintop at particular times." He tilted his head and looked at me, perhaps trying to read my emotions. "We were fortunate to have made it in time."

"Fortunate." I looked down at my legs, and to my astonishment, my right ankle flexed, and then my left; I could move them. I raised a glass leg from the cool slab, swung my hips around, and sat up with surprising ease.

"Amazing," I said.

I stood and took a few steps around with none of the usual stiffness I'd come to expect. Still, I felt broken. Not because part of me was gone, but because I didn't care. It should bother me that

I'd lost half of my body. I supposed it was the same morbid indifference to life that I'd carried with me all these years. Add to that my casual acceptance that this journey would result in my death, and it just didn't seem to matter that I was only half a man. Or less.

"The infirmary built replacement legs," Zip explained.

"And what about this?" I asked, holding out my arm, and then touching my face. "This glass coating."

"It's a special Tinker glass. It was infused into your body to repair damaged organs and replace your skin."

The level of technology on Earth prior to the Dire Comet had never been anywhere near this advanced. "It seems the Tinkers had quite a few tricks up their sleeves," I said.

Zip handed me a small pile of clothes he'd found in the city. I dressed myself in the white, loose-fitting garments, among benches of strange equipment and beneath the glare of the engorged sun, which hung unmoving on the other side of the chambers' transparent walls.

"I want to show you the City, Wren. I think you'll like it. But we don't have much time."

"Why?"

"We must keep going."

"Okay, Zip. I think it's about time I started getting some answers. First off, where are we going?"

He looked puzzled, as if he didn't understand why I would ask such a question. "We're going up."

"Yeah, okay, but what is our final destination?"

"All the way."

"All the way. You mean to the Stars?" I asked, incredulous. The celestial waters above the Sun made travel in the Upper Spheres all but impossible. Some surveyors and bold speculators had ventured past Jupiter, but only a handful of the sturdiest explorers had ever made it past Saturn. None had reached the fixed Stars that marked the furthest limits of the Cosmos.

Zip looked as if it was something he hadn't really considered before. "I guess so. I just know we must keep going."

"Why?" I asked.

He smiled broadly, happy at last to have a question he felt comfortable answering. "Because the Tinkers created me to take you there."

"But why? Why did they want me to go there?" I asked, anger rising within me.

Zip wilted at my words. "I'm sorry, Wren. I don't know that."

Seeing how hurt he looked to have upset me drained all my anger. Just because Zip could talk didn't mean I'd get any more answers out of him.

"Aye, Zip. Why don't you go ahead and show me the city, then?"

After the first couple of corners, I was hopelessly lost, but Zip seemed to know his way. We passed from one building to another along winding staircases and towering archways, always going higher. Beautiful, complicated things spun or twisted on their own. I didn't know if they were machinery or art or both. It was a city of towers and far-flung arches that reached for the sky as if grown. Everything was made of the same light-shearing crystal that populated the city with rainbows from the light of the ever-present, over-large Sun. It was a city for celestial beings, if any had bothered to exist.

As we rose, the skyline took the shape of a great onion dome, beyond which a labyrinthine wasteland of jagged, wind-carved crystals reposed in fantastic shapes. Beneath it all, the Earth swam and shimmered, distorted by the city's frenetic angles.

"I remember hearing about this place," I said in a reverent tone. "The Tinkers built it something like forty years ago, then abandoned it ten years later, just when people were really starting to harvest the Spheres. They said —" and then it came to me. "They said we were damaging the Spheres. That everyone needed to leave."

"Yes. I remember that too. Although I did not exist then," Zip said.

"We didn't leave, though," I said sadly.

"No."

He led me to an overlook near the top of the central dome. A central spire rose from the dome, disappearing into the brightness of the white sky.

"That's the way to the Fourth Sphere. The one that carries the Sun," Zip said, pointing at the spire. "When the city was inhabited, passengers and materials moved up and down the spire automatically." He looked at me. "We'll have to climb it."

"Zip. I don't understand. How do you know all this? How did you know where to find that ornithopter? How did you know it would have a balloon in it? How have you gotten us this far?"

"I just know where to be and when. And I know we must keep going. Now."

"That's gonna be a long climb, Zip." I shielded my eyes against the nearby Sun. "And it sorta looks like we'll be climbing right into the Sun." The air was already hot, although the glass coating of my body helped, and sweating seemed to be a thing of the past.

"It will be difficult."

"Aye."

The spire was small enough for the tips of my fingers to touch on the other side if I hugged it. Each side had its own set of rungs with room for one person. I climbed on one side and Zip on the other. After an hour of climbing, the Venetian City and the rest of the Third Sphere were no longer visible beneath us. The spire tapered to invisibility at each end, making it look as if it were floating in the air — a compass needle pointing from Earth to Sun. Below, Earth rotated slowly, its edges dropping away from the horizon in a way that showed its true nature as a sphere. *How far one must come*, I thought, *to see the truth.*

I told stories of growing up on the farm, my days in the Air Brigade, meeting my wife, the birth of our son. I was surprised how many stories I had, how happy they were. There was no hint among them of the dark turn my life would take.

Time passed, but without the motion of the sun, there was only my growing fatigue to mark its passage. At some point I realized that I hadn't become hungry or thirsty since waking up in the Venetian City. It seemed that part of me was gone too. The muscles of my arms burned terribly, but my legs, which were doing most of the work, felt fine. When I could go no further, I locked my legs around a rung and reached my arms around the spire, where Zip held them from the other side. In that strange position I fell immediately into a fitful sleep with dreams of falling like a ragdoll, reversing my spin each time I struck a rung on the way down. In some of these I knocked Zip from the spire as I fell, which always woke me with a start of panic. When I wasn't resting, we climbed.

The sun did move, slowly. It crept toward the zenith and swelled until the spire disappeared into the heart of a vast, bulging lake of fire that crackled overhead and scorched the top of my head and shoulders, even through their protective coating. I squeezed my eyes shut against the brilliance, reaching blindly for the next rung that was always hotter than the last.

The heat and supernatural monotony made me delirious and I climbed in a fugue state. I imagined the Spheres as a vast spinning machine that had conspired to replace my legs so that it could lure me into its great flaming mouth.

Zip moved to the same side and climbed ahead of me to shield me with his shadow. Eventually the heat became so intense that I could do nothing but cower behind my companion and hold on. I lost time. Eventually a breeze, cooler than most, rustled my senses and I saw that the sun had slid past us; the spire no longer shot into its heart but into the blank sky. We clung there a while longer, hours at least, maybe days, to let the sun move further away. It was only a little, but it made all the difference.

"We don't have much time. We have to reach the cross-over before Venus goes into retrograde," Zip shouted over the roar of the Sun.

"Aye," I answered, not understanding a word of it.

"We have to start climbing again."

We continued for another blurry stretch of time, until I reached up for the next rung and found only air. The shock of it nearly sent me tumbling, but I held on. The spire had ended, and we clung at its tip like two ants at the end of a very long blade of grass.

"What now?" I shouted.

"There." Zip pointed away from the sizzling sun. I didn't see anything at first but then another spire emerged, reaching down from the featureless sky. It was identical to the one beneath us and I realized with a jolt of dread, that after all we'd been through, we were only halfway to the next Sphere.

"No. Zip. I can't climb anymore." The spire shot toward us at startling speed; it was either going to crash into us or roar past.

"It's going to be okay, Wren. Just a little further."

The spire slowed. By the time it was close enough to make out individual rungs, it was moving no faster than a brisk walk. It slid gingerly into position above our spire, lining up perfectly, with a gap no wider than the width of a hair between the two, and stopped.

"Now," Zip shouted. "Quickly." He scrambled onto the upper spire. I followed, exhausted and sluggish. A moment later the two spires separated, our new perch heading back in the direction from which it had come.

"I think this one still works," Zip said. He grasped the ladder and squeezed his eyes in concentration. A moment later he was sliding upward, carried by moving rungs.

He stopped and looked down at me. "The Venetian Glass touches every part of you, even your brain. You can use it to control the spire. All you have to do is concentrate."

It wasn't quite as easy as that, but I got the hang of it quickly. It was like imagining yourself scratching an itch that wasn't on your body. I caught up to Zip and shot past, shouting childhood taunts as I did. He overtook me and we continued like that, racing our way upward, until the bottom of the Fourth Sphere loomed into position above.

The Sphere that carried the Sun wasn't solid, like the others, but a lattice of massive crystalline girders. Together, they formed an immense three-dimensional labyrinth. I was surprised, because this was the Sphere that held back the celestial waters. I couldn't remember from grade-school Astrology classes what kept the waters from raining down onto us, but I figured I'd find out, firsthand, soon enough. Zip led us through with confidence, climbing up steep beams with precipitous drops on either side. The sunward side glowed a deep red.

"Almost seems like you've done this before, Zip."

"I have not. I just know the way." He paused before speaking again. "My first memory is waking up in a warehouse. The door was open and I walked straight to you. Like always, I knew where to go, but not why."

"Aye. Like always."

We navigated the dangerous path a while longer before Zip spoke again. "They chose you."

"Beg pardon?"

"The Tinkers. Somehow they manipulated the Spheres to protect you, after the Fate Plague started."

"Why?"

"Because you're special. And when you go up ... I don't know. Somehow things will be better."

Special. I couldn't even protect my own son, and for the rest of my life I'd done nothing but drink and suffer. I shook my head. "I'm afraid they're going to be terribly disappointed."

The Solar Sphere was far thicker than the others. We walked along beams that looked like girders placed by giants. The blood-red glow from the sunward side pulsed gently. It felt as if the Cosmos were a giant organism, and that Zip and I were two microbes slinking past its living heart. Eventually, the space became more compact and I had to duck beneath crossbeams. It became slow going as the trusses closed in on us and we were reduced to crawling, first on hands and knees, then on our bellies.

"I can't make myself any smaller, Zip. Something's got to give."

"Just a little further."

Although everything around us continued to grow tighter, narrower, closer, our path began to widen. Someone had carved it out of the surrounding supports. We were nearly able to stand again as we walked through solid crystal, still lit red by the distant sun. The narrow walkway spiraled upward, until it opened onto a small room.

"This is our ride from here." Zip said, pointing to a pod of smooth metal the size of a small car, resting on the floor of the room. A blue Tinker's symbol glowed on its side. Zip placed his palm over the symbol and a panel rose on each side, revealing padded seats within. He motioned for me to take a seat. I looked at the room anew, noticing a seam across the ceiling. The passage we had come from had already irised closed.

"A submarine?" I asked.

"Yes."

"I guess that makes sense." After all I'd seen, it was still hard to imagine that we were just beneath the bottom of a vast celestial ocean. "Onward and upward, eh?"

I sat in the vehicle and Zip got in on the other side. Exterior lights snapped on and the vehicle's walls faded to transparency. There were no controls, but Zip closed his eyes and concentrated, like he had on the spire. The sub's doors closed with a hiss and the seam above us split apart, creating a thin waterfall that became a flood that quickly filled the room. We rose through the opening into a strange black ocean of stars.

The opening fell away quickly and by the time it had closed, the Sphere had already disappeared beneath us, in that peculiar way that all Spheres become invisible with distance. The Earth was now an immense, brightly lit, blue and green ball, floating against a background of stars, more numerous and brighter that I'd seen on the clearest of nights. The Sun, a squat, angry blister of fire, slid away from us, and the roar of its conflagration drained from the interior of the sub as it went. I was glad to see it go; I had had quite enough of the Sun for a while.

The two of us floated serenely up toward the next Sphere. It wasn't long before a deep, dreamless sleep claimed me and held me for what felt like a long time. When I woke, Zip was looking down at the shrinking Earth, now no larger than my outstretched arms.

It occurred to me that we were moving through the same waters that had powered every mechanical device on Earth for decades. A leak and a spark would be enough to engulf our little cabin in flames. There was danger here, and once again, I couldn't bring myself to care. But this time was different. My lack of concern didn't come from self-loathing or a morbid disregard for my life. I had come far and endured a great deal since leaving home. I looked back on my journey and saw that I was no wilting daisy. There was something to be proud of there. And so, within the usual soup of ennui, there was a hint of something I hadn't felt since my time in the Air Brigade — a sense of confidence. It was like finding a cherished object, lost long ago.

"What's next for us, my friend?"

Zip looked at me, tilted his head the way he did when he was reading my expression, and smiled. "I don't know, Wren. More adventures, I imagine."

I smiled, leaned back in my chair, closed my eyes and said, "Aye."

The days passed erratically when measured against my own muddled sense of time. The Sun drifted away, flattening itself into a line and then squeezing itself behind the Earth, which became a round absence of stars, a drain into which starlight disappeared. Meanwhile, ahead, a red star grew brighter and brighter.

"We need to cross the next layer near Mars itself. It's the only place where the path through the labyrinth is known," Zip explained.

Mars was a featureless bulge the size of a large city that glowed a brilliant red. The Sphere that carried it consisted of the same latticework of girders and supports as the one that bore the Sun, but was far thinner, with larger gaps. The Solar Sphere had held back the celestial waters. Here, the waters above Mars floated on the Solar waters like oil above water. Zip navigated the ship through the complicated twists and turns of the lattice and we emerged at the edge of the dark side of Mars.

On this side, Mars was a jet-black disc, sealed beneath a blue transparent dome. A ring of posts around the dome's perimeter bore mirrors that reflected sunlight onto a medieval city of red bricks surrounded by fields of black dirt. I vaguely recalled hearing something about a Mars Colony years ago but had never given it another thought.

Forms moved among the buildings. There were people there!

"Zip, Zip, Zip. Look. People. Living people. We've got to go to them."

A light flared and died away on the far side of the city. It was then that I noticed the buildings were all in tatters, the fields barren. Another light blossomed, closer to us.

"What's happening down there?"

"The Mars Colony has been at war with itself since the Dire Comet appeared — fighting over limited resources. We can't risk them seeing us, Wren. They're dangerous."

"But humanity isn't dead. There's still hope. If there are other people —"

"The colony has no women, no children. It has no hope."

"No, no. I don't believe it. How do you know all this?"

"In the Venetian City there are machines that can see ... everywhere. There are only a few dozen men left here, and they will fight until there is nothing left."

"Maybe we can evacuate them down to Earth. Maybe the Tinkers sent us to rescue them."

A group of men spotted us and pointed in our direction as we rose past the dome. One of them typed into a keypad and something near the mirrors swiveled around and lined up with our ship.

"Watch out Zip, I think they're going to —"

Light flared from the turret and our ship rocked.

"Hang on," Zip said. He squeezed his eyes closed and we leapt upward, throwing me back in my seat. The dome shrank away from us while the turret kept barking light, joined by several others.

"I can't believe we're leaving the only people left alive in the Cosmos. Maybe if we came in from below, out of range of their guns we could start over, reason with them. If I ordered you to go back, would you?"

"Yes," Zip answered, his eyes still squeezed tight.

Guilt tested the door of my mind, shook the windows, trying to get in. Should I insist that we go back? Try to save them? From what? Themselves? If they would stop fighting and grow food, they could live just as long on Mars as on Earth. Could Zip and I be some sort of mediators and convince them to set down their arms? No. It was pointless. Finding a handful of survivors on Mars didn't change the fact that humanity had ended. It was a non-significant digit in the equation. I shook my head and sighed.

"It would have been nice to be around another person again," I said, surprised by my own words, having avoided people so thoroughly for so long. Then I looked at Zip. "No offense, buddy."

Zip opened his eyes and smiled at me. "None taken, Wren. This place," he motioned to the receding bubble of light that was the Mars Colony, "is not your destiny."

We rose, faster, through the frictionless waters above Mars, watching Earth and its attendant celestial bodies shrink away daily. I made playing cards out of some paper we found on board and taught Zip to play poker. He was pretty good at bluffing. We made up songs, and to my own surprise, I told him about Sammy.

I wondered if he already knew — about my great shame, my disgrace, the source of my endless guilt. He gave no sign of having known, listening intently with his head tilted in that way that meant he was reading my emotions. I cried and he waited, his face a portrait of patient compassion.

My dreams changed. The shame and horror of Sammy's death kept coming, as always, but instead of lying inert at the poolside, I found myself climbing a ladder into the heart of the sun. The effort of forcing my aching arms to release their rung in search of another before taking the next step made it hard to focus on my guilt, and the friends and family that despised me for what I had done were so far below that it was hard to see their judging eyes.

Jupiter bulged out from its sphere, as large as a continent, a clockwork monument of complex movement. Colored bands crossed its surface and great balls of light hovered around it like fireflies. It gave off a low mechanical hum of such intensity that I was afraid our little ship, dented by the Martian bullets, would fly apart. The Sphere that supported Jupiter was as formidable as the one that carried the Sun, full of crisscrossing struts and beams, but in constant motion, far more active than any of the other Spheres. I stared at it in awe. It was so clearly *doing* something. I could almost recognize it. It hung on the tip of my tongue like a forgotten word. It was making something. Destiny, I supposed.

"Buckle up," Zip said, "this is going to be tricky."

I attached my restraints and was glad to have them as we dashed and spun between the moving segments of the churning apparatus. I couldn't tell if the sub was a deft acrobat or a leaf in a stream. When we crossed the Sphere's outer edge, a giddy feeling rose in my stomach and my body rose up against the restraints. Suddenly the universe flipped. Jupiter spun from stern to aft and Earth, which had been a constant beneath our feet since the beginning, swung around to rest overhead. I flopped back into my seat, disoriented and dizzy.

"What just happened?" I asked.

"Gravity has reversed. The waters above Jupiter have that effect. We will no longer be floating upward through the celestial waters. To reach the stars, we must dive."

Somehow, the fact that our destination was beneath us, instead of above us, had a profound psychological effect. It made the stars seem more remote, as inaccessible as if we were heading to the bottom of a terribly deep ocean. And yet, our goal was far more distant and exotic than that.

Saturn was said to be the most beautiful of all the celestial bodies, but it was nowhere in sight when the Sphere that carried it emerged from the starry background as a rarified web, like filaments of starlight. We passed through it like birds through a cloud or a sleeper falling into dream. It faded back into the stars behind us as we continued our long fall.

Earth shrank to the size of my fist. The bright silver moon was its constant companion and even the Sun ventured no further than an arm's length from my old home. The sub groaned and creaked in disturbing ways. Even Zip started to have a worried frown on his face.

Finally, he spoke. "The submarine won't be able to withstand the pressure much longer. We have to abandon it before it crushes us and traps us within."

"What? Abandon it? You can't be serious? I'll drown. I —" I stopped myself. I didn't believe my own protests. Some part of me knew that I hadn't needed to breathe since I woke up in the Tinkers' City. I had no doubt that I would survive outside the sub.

Zip watched my protests die off.

"Ready?" he asked.

I nodded, and he concentrated for a moment, popping both latches. Cold water poured in and flooded the cabin quickly. We drifted from our seats and swam up and out into the darkness, watching as the dead, flooded sub fell away from us toward the depths of the starry ocean floor. It was terrifying, falling into the night sky, just the two of us, amidst such vastness.

We found we could still talk, in distorted voices.

"You can control the glass within you to change your form," Zip said, "just like when you controlled the rungs of the upper spire."

It took some effort, but eventually I learned how to reshape my legs into flippers. After some exploratory swimming, we were soon chasing each other and playing like infant otters that had discovered water for the first time. Eventually we grew tired and drifted down, side by side. The darkness deepened and I began to feel the weight of the waters above me. Zip felt it too — from time to time I caught him holding his head and grimacing. In the still silence, questions bubbled into my mind, creating a pressure of their own.

"Zip? Why did the Tinkers send you to me in the form of a dog?" I asked. "Why not like you are now?"

"I'm not sure. Would you have followed a talking automaton?" Zip answered.

"Hmm." I thought for a moment. "Good point."

My next question had been on the tip of my tongue since Mars, but I had dreaded asking it. I knew the answer and didn't want to hear it. But I had to ask.

"When you used the remote sensing equipment back in the Venetian City, did you look at Earth? You know, for survivors?"

"Yes."

"Did you find any?"

"No. None. Earth has been completely empty of animal life since you left it."

We fell in silence, holding hands, for a long time.

"What do you think will happen when we reach the stars?" I asked.

"I don't know. What do you think?"

I remembered my mother all those years ago. *Touch a star, baby, it'll make everything better.* What would that look like?

"I don't know. But it seems a shame," I said, looking up through the Spheres, "for all of this to be empty forever. For there to be all this beauty, with no one to appreciate it."

"Do you?"

I looked at Zip, illuminated as much by the Stars as the distant Sun. "Do I what?"

"Do you …" The delicate spinning flywheels behind his jaw had stopped moving. His chest plate was sunken, and he had a faraway look in his eyes.

"Do you …" he said.

"Zip, what's wrong?"

I held his shoulders and felt the creaking of his chest plate straining inward.

"Oh, no. No. The pressure. It's killing you. We have to go back. We have to go up! C'mon." I grabbed Zip under his arms and kicked furiously against our fall. I felt the water push back against my flippers and the strain of the effort in my legs, but had no way of knowing if I was making any progress.

His eyes swiveled to meet my own. "No. Wren. You must keep going." With a sickening shudder his skull plate crumpled and his eyes went dark.

I kicked against the water for a long time after that, begging Zip to answer. Eventually, there could be no doubt that he was gone, and I stopped.

"We were supposed to be together until the end," I said softly.

We fell together for a long time and I waited for the waters to crush me too, but the pressure had no effect on me. The glass was all through me, he had said. Suddenly I was furious. Why hadn't the Tinkers given the same protection to Zip? They must have known this would happen. Only one answer made sense. They wanted me to be alone. But why? Was I destined to be alone forever? A profound sadness settled over me as I fell toward my mysterious destiny among the Stars, clutching the husk of my friend.

Far overhead, the Earth was no larger than a marble; it was beautiful, serene. The silvery Moon kept close to its beloved Earth, while Mercury and Venus dashed playfully back and forth across the Sun. Earth cycled from crescent, to disc, to crescent, to blackness as the Sun swung around it, over and over. Achingly slow at first, the dance of the celestial Spheres gradually accelerated. I closed my eyes, letting their movements permeate my mind the way the glass permeated my body. From here, the connections between all its parts were obvious. The Cosmos was a living organism and humanity had given it consciousness. It was sleeping now.

A fluttering light caused me to open my eyes. The Sun was circling the Earth so quickly that its light flickered. It moved faster and faster until it became a fixed ring of light around the Earth. Years were passing between heartbeats. I remembered now — the waters above Saturn slowed time. The deeper I fell, the slower time passed for me. I would never reach the stars. Time would slow, and slow, and slow the closer I got. It wasn't possible to touch a star.

What did that mean? Had I failed at whatever the Tinkers wanted of me? Had they known I could never reach their goal? Did it mean that I could never heal?

But I had healed. Somewhere between Earth and here, I had forgiven myself. The wonders I had seen, the feeling of connection I felt, these had sapped the guilt of its strength and exposed it for the cruel madness that it was. Even when I was a child, the healing had never come from actually touching a star, it had been from the act of trying.

I squeezed Zip against me, closed my eyes again and felt the Spheres tugging me, each in its own way. All the parts of the Cosmos, connected, singing our song, together. Then I felt it. On Earth, but connected to me and everything else, as all things are. I felt something there, looking upon the Cosmos with the same awe I felt now. A new creature, not human, not even close, had risen from the ashes of the animal kingdom and was filling the world with self-awareness. It began as a flicker, then grew and grew.

The Cosmos was waking up again.

And the Firmament would be in danger again. It still hadn't healed from what we had done to it, and soon these new creatures would be at its gates. Maybe they'd behave more responsibly.

Maybe they'd be able to figure out what happened to us, learn from it, and avoid the same fate. Maybe. Or maybe the same cycle of destruction would go on forever without survivors of one era to warn those of the next.

If only they had someone to guide them. If only the Firmament had a defender. A voice. Someone to protect it until the new civilization was wise enough to take care of it properly. Could I do this? Could I face eternity alone? The alternative was clear; I knew the glass within me would obey if I told it to end my life. But the Tinkers had been right; I did not fear solitude. Loneliness was a familiar enemy, and it would feel good to have a purpose.

I held Zip's lifeless body at arm's length. "Thank you, my friend, for showing me these things. I understand, finally, why the Tinkers sent you." Gently releasing my grasp, I let him fall away from me. I watched as he grew smaller with distance until I could no longer see him against the starry background. Then I turned my gaze upward and started kicking my way back up.

When I arrived, the Venetian City was already humming with life. Everything — all the factories, sensors, monitors, and libraries — responded to my command. I could create whatever I needed and sent automatons out across the Spheres to make repairs. I hadn't been ready for this role the last time I was here, and Earth's new inhabitants had still been many millions of years away. My attempt to touch the stars had healed me and breathed new life into the Earth.

I discovered that Zip had uploaded his memories into the City on our way through, but they stopped then, before our climb. Our time together on the ladder, and beyond, were mine alone to remember. The Zip I lost beside the stars was irreplaceable, and would always be missed. Still, it was good to have the company.

On Earth, the new inhabitants had grown and expanded across the globe, forming a great civilization. They had invented steam power and it wouldn't be long before they were blowing holes in the bottom Sphere.

I reached down from the monitoring portal and patted the newly reconstructed Zip on the head, then I stood, stretched my back and unfurled my shimmering, rainbow-clad wings.

"Whatdya say, Zip? Are you up for a trip downward? I think it's about time we meet our new neighbors."

He did a little excited loop and sat on his haunches.

"I'll take that as a yes."

Daylight

L'Erin Ogle and David Gallay

him

The one time he went to the cemetery, he began digging. Just took his hands and started excavating mounds of dirt. He didn't plan it. He just wanted to be with them. The ground was cold and so they were cold; they needed his warmth. Hands pulled at him, taking him back, dragging him down. The ground was still, frozen. The only thing he could see was a glint of a blue sky. His hands were numb, nothing but meat.

Later, they told him he was crying. That he kept screaming that he heard them pleading with him. He kept saying his life was down there.

He doesn't remember any of that.

Daylight, flashing in strobe lights. Venetian blinds, rattling in the updraft of the vent, heat forced through metal ducts. Still goddamn cold in here. Raising gooseflesh on his skin, skin too young to feel so old and too elastic to stretch so tight and unforgiving over his skeleton. His head aches with the light, pushing against the sides of his skull. The drumbeat; unforgiving. Unforgiven. Unforgiveable.

Just out of reach, a bottle of vodka, lying on its side, no color to behold. His fingers, pale, trembling.

He can already hear the excuses he will make to his AA group. This was a slip. Just a slip. Look around this room. Don't you think it happens to all of us? They don't get it. He wants to slip. He needs to fall. To sink down into the earth.

It's the smell that finally gets him out of bed. He's poured out gallons of bleach. Closed and locked certain doors to contain the stink of scorched wallpaper. Pine trees hang from every hook. And yet, that smell lingers. It bites. It burns. He uncoils himself from the sheets knotted around him, remnants of a strangling dream. The soles of his feet sink uncomfortably into the cheap carpeting thrown across the hardwood ruined first by flame, then by water. The shag always feels damp. Mossy coldness soaking through socks and shoes.

Brushing his teeth, avoiding his reflection. Pale skin, dark bruised eyes, yellow teeth. Smiling mouth closed, because even if he doesn't smoke the shit anymore, it left his teeth stained. Spitting toothpaste. No blood anymore. Rinsing his hands. Leaving the bathroom, passing through another draft of ice cold. Sometimes the air itself here resists him. Tugs at his hair and clothes like little hands that used to grasp his as if they were holding on for dear life. Their tiny fingers swallowed up by his own. All he ever wanted was to be a better version of himself. Every day, he looked in the mirror and said, *Today's the day I'm going to be a better man.* Every day, he'd tell himself, *Just one more hit, just to get through.* He meant to do better, he was always going to do better, but today turned into tomorrow and the next day, and now ...

Maybe it's not cleaning the house needs. Maybe it's a cleansing.

Can a soul be cleansed? Can it be bleached to white?

Those fuckers in AA seem to think so. But they don't know. No fourth step is going to untie the knots he made. *Done, bun, can't be undone*, she used to say as her fingers worked the braids. It hurts to think of her. How she abandoned him to this ruination. He refuses to say her name, he even renamed the contact on his phone to just *her*, because to say that name summons a knife, serrated against the muscles of the heart. He couldn't just delete it. That felt like another betrayal.

her

Flicker-flicker, presses thumbs to closed eyelids, capillary afterimage washes to a black tide that drags her out from wherever she is, was, awareness spreading fragile moth wings even as she resists the urge to wake until strobing red and mounting panic collide, hammer to wire, minor key. Eyes squint open. Leaves of the overgrown maple tree outside the bedroom window sway in the watery sunlight, lifted by the wind and then released. Shadows of ever-present birds in the branches dance across her face. A trill of song just beyond the frame. *Beeed-ah. Beeeed-ah.*

Shut up! I'm awake!

How can it be morning already? She rolls over to check the time. No clock. Must have thrown it off the nightstand again. Must have been more sleep terrors. What does L call them? Summer storms. As in, fearsome to watch, but they always pass. After that first shattered screen, he forces her to leave her phone in the kitchen when they go to bed. It isn't worth arguing about.

Her descent back into sleep is interrupted by footsteps slapping across wooden floors. She winces at the familiar cadence. She's tired of it before even getting out of bed. They're up already? How can such small hearts contain so much energy? Too early. Not ready.

She calls out to him.

- L! L! Do you have it under control?

No answer. Oh, now she remembers, he split in the middle of the night. The long weekend was almost over and neither wanted to acknowledge the oncoming roar of real life. So, they had a little party. Locked the door. Closed the curtains. Set out the candles. Unpacked the pipe from its secret drawer, its velvet box. After, after, after, she was done but he wasn't. She heard him creep out like a fox from a henhouse. Click of the lock. Sneakers on the driveway. Leaving her behind, again.

Laughter. A piglet playfully scratches at the door, then runs away.

Fuck it. She's up, just ignore the pins and needles in her legs, in her back, that doubling sensation of exhaustion and too much sleep.

Their house balances on a fulcrum. On one side is their bedroom, haven from the noise and responsibility, a delicious secret in every drawer, preserving the carefree people they used to be, like an ecosystem sealed in a ball of glass. Beyond the door is the long hallway, the rest of the house, which is to say, the rest of the world.

She realizes that L must have returned. She can feel the weight of his presence. The little ones move differently around him. Excited piglets, two legs become four. Relieved he's taking a rare turn playing the good dad, the good shepherd, instead of the cop, the jailer, she steadies herself and swivels into the bathroom. Wait. It always takes a moment for the halogen bulb to tik-tik-tik to life. The light blinks on and she greets her mirror-self, still familiar, only slightly weathered by this strange new life they somehow conjured into existence, roughed up by the bulky furniture and the iPads and the corners of cheese crackers deep in the shag and the skinny warm bodies always bumping into her, always wanting, all little fingernails and little teeth.

Love, yes. Beautiful, yes.

As beautiful as the flame, the first sparkling inhale? Don't answer that.

Behind her, in the mirror, L silently slips in and out of the bedroom with unusual purpose.

She calls out to him, toothbrush in mouth.

- Good morning!

But he's already gone. She spits and scrunches her nose at the flecks of red.

Time to face the day. Breathe in, breathe out. Throughout the house, she can still smell them, sour and soap. Look, the couch is still unpuckering from their illicit jumps. L told them the floor is lava. The television is off, but she can hear the hum of resting electrons, gray warmth from a million sleeping diodes. The remote is abandoned on the floor. Dark handprints surround it like a worship of cave paintings.

Where is everyone?

Dishwasher is full; unfamiliar casserole pans, coffee cups, Tupperware. Rinse a few dishes clean. The garbage disposal eagerly gobbles up overcooked eggs. Wipe more handprints off the counter. A whole bottle of Windex and nothing. Did they get into the permanent markers? Probably. L would leave them out. Even with all his paranoid rules, he can still be careless.

Sleep pulls her back to the bedroom like a spring. No sense arguing with biology.

Pauses at the piglets' closed door. Maybe L camped out with them? That would be a relief. Another round from The Big Book of Fairy Tales. Good? Yes. Good. She could join them. They could be waiting for her.

She reaches for the doorknob. The keyhole shines in the darkness like the eye of a wolf.

Thinks better of it.

They can wait. She can't be what they need. Not yet.

him

Didn't drink enough last night. The dreams come, screams that scrape along his eardrums, and he arches awake. Sheet taut around his neck, his fingers digging underneath it, the homemade noose giving away. The screams, according to his strip-mall shrink, are internal. Inside his head. The sheets knotted around his neck a form of self-punishment created by his nightmares. Wishing he hadn't woken up. Wishing the screaming would stop. Stumbling out of bed, more of a cot really, army surplus dragged in by the old man from AA when he stopped by to check for beer in the toilet tank, whiskey in the peanut butter. Said he was fine sleeping on the floor, but the old man insisted. It's been like that. Since. People always want to help. He has that kind of face. Friendly. Trusting. Pitiable. A puppy's face. A harmless face. Funny how even his dealer cut him slack.

Sometimes he seems a little too friendly and they try to hug him. When they do, he stiffens like a board. He doesn't like to be touched. Even a clap on the shoulder or grip on his forearm, and he cringes, pulls away. His keeps his hands in his pockets. His fingers rub the sides of an old iron key, warming it to body temperature. If it weren't for the court-mandated meetings, he'd be tempted to stay home and never see another person at all. To tuck himself away and into a ball until he ceased to exist, became reabsorbed by the universe.

It would probably spit him right back out.

He almost slips twice on the short walk to the bathroom, goddamn carpet wet again. The headache sets in. Used to be could retreat to the comfort of a curved pipe of glass. They had a secret drawer full of them. The first thing he did, after, once they let him back in alone, was to pull them all out from the charred dresser and throw them down the storm drain. Those old days haunt the new ones, and now there's nothing but booze to hold it back.

What's that? Does he have it under control? How dare you even ask?

He retrieves the vodka from inside the bag of frozen peas, uncaps it, swallows it until his lungs scream and his eyes burn.

Burn.

That word.

He angles to the family room to sit alone. All the toys are gone. No more stepping on Legos, though he can still wedge his fingers between the cushions and finagle one out. He does that now, cheap plastic smooth and cold under the pads of his fingers. Rubbing it over and over, so he doesn't think. Count the circles. Drink. Numb, numb; numbness finally flooding through all his nerve endings.

The blackout begins as a curtain, dropping from the top of his head over his mind. Muffling the screaming, faint but still present. Past his eyes, which blur, darkening the room, down into his nose, no more smells, through his mouth and draining down his neck until his arms and legs are heavy and immobile.

Head falling back against the couch, eyes rolled down the hallway, and from here he can see the handprints, two sets of them, four total hands, twenty fingers pressing into the wall.

They won't be there tomorrow.

They never are.

He really needs to drink more, but his arm is too heavy, won't move to his mouth.

Pressure in his chest. Growing and pushing against his ribcage. Trying to pour out his mouth.

Smoke poured from the windows. The sounds the axes made in the roof. The blink of red, blue, red, blue. The night sky full of stars, like it didn't know they should be dulled out of respect.

Shadows on the lawn. Lined up in heavy, black plastic bags.

The pressure growing and twisting and something feels like it might burst out of his chest. The curtain at last dropping all the way down, and he's gone, baby, gone.

her

Even before the flicker comes the thirst, a trembling cramp that unwinds under her ribs like a serpent in a heap of dead leaves, forked tongue scraping against the back of her throat. Her fingers probe dry lips as the flashing shadows rake her eyes, red, black, red, black, until she turns away. The birds laugh at her. *Beeed-ah. Beeeed-ah.* She blindly feels the other side of the bed. He loves it when she wakes him up with a caress, the slightest skin against skin. But by the lopsided angle of the mattress she knows he's not there. He crept out again in the middle of the night, didn't even bother to try waking her up. So, she's just checking for warmth. Her fingers jump. The sheets are cold, moist, as if left outside in the dew. Presses her lips to his pillow. Sucks in cool air between her teeth. No slaking her terrible thirst.

Time? Searches for the fallen clock. No. Just little dark puddles of wax, votives burned down to stubs. Lines of used incense to hide the smell from piglets, who wouldn't recognize it anyways. Speaking of, playful footsteps approach the room and then they're running behind her, but it's just an illusion from the throbbing in her skull, the dry clench of dehydration.

L! L! Do you have it under control?

Scratches at the door.

Tik-tik-tik of the bathroom light. A faceless woman glares back at her through the unlit mirror, Ophelia in the reeds. Eye floaters drift down the glass like soft rain. She remembers the exact moment she became this woman. They were coming home from the grocery. One kid in the back, another on the way. She wanted to drive, but he had the keys. In the passenger window specked with yellow pollen, she stared through her half-reflection like a trapped animal through barbed wire.

Tired of waiting for the light to click on, she bends over to drink greedy from the tap. Behind her, in the mirror, L dashes down the hallway. The iron key dangles from his fingers. The house is quite old and has its quirks. Like the dirt basement. Like how the bedroom doors can be locked from both sides. If she feels one of her summer storms coming on, sometimes, she'll let him lock her in. Just in case. It's fine. She trusts him. And he loves that fucking key. The sense of control. How it slots perfectly into every keyhole with a satisfying metallic click.

She spits and spatters the sink with gobs of meat and blood. She twists the faucet on full blast until it's all drained. By habit, she sits to piss. Waits. Nothing happens. There are little handprints on the wall tiles. Dark. Chocolate, she assumes, and idly wipes at it with a bit of toilet paper. Won't come clean. She resists an overwhelming urge to lick it.

Where she usually finds chaos, the living room shimmers with emptiness. It's like stepping onto the moon. Stark. Airless. Her burning throat constricts by reflex. The wind picks up outside. Leafy shadows dapple then darken the room. The ropes of the swing set wind and unwind. The birds have followed her. They hop frantically from branch to branch. *Beeed-ah. Beeeed-ah.* More handprints smudge the glass. She can tell they won't wash off without something strong. Bleach. Acid. The image drives a screw into her thirst.

Spirals of angry red shine in the gloom of the kitchen. Fuck! L left the oven range on. She frantically flicks the dials. Eggs still in the pan, yolks burned to cinders. Charred bits of toast that disintegrate between her fingers. Whatever. Sure. Deal with it later.

A sound startles her. The familiar, heavy clink of a vodka bottle hitting the ground.

- L?

Throat is so dry. She gulps down water from the kitchen tap. It tastes like nothing. Why is it so dark? The shadows on the wall have coalesced into a solid block of darkness. The windows are obsidian. Is it night already? Maybe it always was. Maybe she woke up too early. Everyone is still asleep. That would make more sense.

Pauses at the halfway. At the piglets' door. Even in the dark, she can see the frame is filthy with handprints. Scuffling on the other side. Giggles. Delirious shrieking. Mommy? Mommy? Knock. Knock.

A twitch of panic. Then in the fish-eye reflection of the doorknob, she catches L glancing back as he bolts out the front door. He has that look. Oh, she knows that look. That need-another-fix look. Good. She could use one too. She chases him around the corner, following the untucked tail of his shirt, the fizzing molecules of sweat. She almost has him, reach out, *hey, hey, hold on*, then she's settling back into bed without recalling how she got there.

Dreams come, heavy, smothering. First, L on top of her, weighing her down. Then, the acrid taste of the pipe on his skin. The clink of metal against her teeth. The fairy-tale serpent winding around her throat, crushing the air out of her lungs. The deepest and purest black.

him

Bloodshot in the mirror, the whites mapped by crimson rivers. Up earlier this time, head pulsing. The faintest memory of a noose around his neck.

Sometimes he finds himself idly opening a web browser and searching for the keywords that Google refuses to autocomplete. The results scroll on for a while. Shotgun to the head, pistol to the head, self-incineration, and jumping from great distances statistically get the job done. Wrist cutting, pills, carbon monoxide poisoning — those carry the greatest risk of failure.

Other times, it's a fleeting thought. Driving down the road and getting the sudden urge to white knuckle that bitch off an overpass. A wish for cancer, the terminal kind, the one that comes with pain but also the kind of pills that only the dying get. Then even if the screams were real, he wouldn't hear them. He wouldn't be forced to care about them.

Over a basket of onion rings, the old man from AA says that two decades later he still picks phantom bits of bloody windshield glass out of his hair. He had to stop driving all together, give away his truck, move to a different state. Maybe you should consider ... selling the house?

That snaps him out from his stupor.

No. The house is *mine*.

A stink lingers in the kitchen, not just of smoke, but rot. He's left a carton of milk in the sink. He pours it down the drain, glug glug glug. Vodka doesn't smell and he's already thinking about that first drink. His stomach clenches in his abdomen, the light through the window stabs his eyes, each beam a needle moving in and out, in and out, in and out. And then the acid rises, bile stinging the back of his throat, and he retches in the sink, smelling the sour milk, unleashes a stream of thin watery vomit.

Stomach empty, he takes the vodka from the freezer. Thinks about how the first swallow will feel, stinging down his raw throat, stomach knotting up in protest. Thinks about the old man and the bloody windshield pieces. Thinks about the stench of burnt flesh, stomach now seizing in his gut, and pours it out — glug glug glug — and his headache worsens. But he pushes through it. The days ahead will be long and dark, a tunnel with no illumination. He has quit before and knows what to expect. Every moment stretched thin as his nerves, longer than the moment waiting for the dealer who says he's "just pulling up", so long it will seem infinite, but all things are finite. He'll travel that dark tunnel. He will hear things and see things that are not really there, he will not be able to tell the difference between what's real and what's a product of his scraped-out, overcooked brain.

Some neural pathways will fade and others will bloom. Like the house itself, only halfway destroyed. Enough left to salvage, maybe not restored to quite to what it was, but another reincarnation. Eventually, there will be a glimmer of hope. He will laugh at a joke. Hold the door for a pretty girl and smile back at her. Taste food, really taste it, again. Relishing a greasy bite of mozzarella stretched thin and bubbled brown.

Stop that giggling! Go to sleep!

Where? Oh. He's back in front of their door. He's been standing there for a long time.

The bottle slips from his fingers, bounces off the ground, empty save for a few drops clinging to the curved side. He reaches into his pocket for the key. Maybe it's time. After their room was scrubbed for evidence and the case closed as an ACCIDENT, maybe NEGLECT, but not MURDER, he must have locked it. Of course, he doesn't remember doing it. Just like he doesn't remember digging at their graves.

Before he can sink back into the dark, which has fingers and wraps around his ankles, he smells the same body spray J spritzed with after a hit. Like no one would see the moon-big pupils she wore. Every time he lets his mind wander down that path, it ends up back in the bottle; he unlocks the phone and scrolls through the numbers. Each one, a doorway to pity, sympathy, prayers. His finger briefly hovers over *her*.

You can't beat yourself up forever. You deserve to live.

He can't visit the cemetery anymore. He doesn't want to think about death. He also doesn't want to live like this anymore. It's the cumulation of so many days wanting to die but not finding the will to do so. He's just so damn tired of barely existing.

He is alive and she is dead. It's a small difference but an important one. A question of fairness. Of blame.

Scrolls past HER and taps the number of the old man.

her

Try to get up, can't. Her body refuses to move. Fuck. There's pain, yes, a dull beacon breaking through fogged nerves, but also, her body is exhausted, heavy as iron. She's sunk down through the sheets and the cheap mattress, caught in bedsprings like a snare, sharp metal coils scraping against bone.

The flicker bleeds from her eyes to the walls. The throb like a barely breathing thing, a dying animal. Birds flutter back and forth across the ceiling. Sharp beaks. Empty eyes. *Beeed-ah. Beeeed-ah.* She flinches as they dive at her, even though they must only be shadows.

In the end, the only way out is it to let gravity do all the work. Roll out of bed, throw herself to the ground. The carpet is moist, like rich soil, earthworms between the fibers. Bruises may come, but at least she's out. One final push, she stands up and everything tumbles like bricks down a well, all the blood, all the nightmares, all the fragments that remind her who she is. Her knees wobble. Why? She finds a memory snagged in her hair. Midnight. Piglets finally asleep. Candles. L offering her the spark. Breathing it in deep. Flesh to flesh.

Burn.

Slow lightning curls through her brain. Thoughts fragmented. Look. Look. No. Just dark. Must have been a shit batch. She knows the drill. She's been here before. *Done, bun, can't be undone.* Deep breaths, in, out, in out. The room keeps dimming, the eggshell paint spattered with spots, the floor weeping with stains. Her head vibrates in pain. Her joints creak like rusted hinges. Worse than any other hangover. Deep breaths, even though her lungs are full of thorns, in, out, in out.

No water from the tap. Brushes her teeth with the dry toothbrush. Takes effort to spit and all that spills out are rough little stones. Her mirror-self slaps a palm to the other side of the glass. From each fingertip, a small inky handprint blooms, then another, and another, multiplying. Little hands, little birds on a black, wet branch. *Beeed-ah. Beeeed-ah.* Behind her, L runs past. She tries to call out to him, but her larynx is a wasp nest, paper-thin, angry buzzing. She chases his reflection into the hallway, into the living room heavy with a thick miasma that marks the skin like blue chalk.

Beeed-ah. Beeeed-ah.

The birds keep trying to move her towards something.

She slaps a palm against the window. *Shut up!*

In the double-paned glass, something she doesn't understand.

On one side, her own face. No detail, sunken eyes, thin lips, frizzed hair. Not quite a reflection, because the colors are all wrong, inverted, and the longer she stares, the more oil slick wrongness she finds. Walls stained and warped. Electrical wire dangles from cracks in the ceiling. The carpet is torn ragged, clumps sheared away. On the other side stands the maple tree, burnt sun knifing between the leaves. L sits in the piglets' swing like a lonely little boy. His toes scrape against the dirt. She doesn't recognize his clothes. His hair is too short and too clean, slate at the temples. A new gold watch shines on his wrist.

She bangs the window. Wedding ring clinks against the glass.

He seems to see her. Or pretends to. Confusion on his face.

A flash of movement behind her. She watches a piglet crawl through the wreckage. Naked? No. There's the sheen of favorite pajamas. Footies, except, except, the skin is showing through black plastic, not just skin the beneath the what is that the muscle the meat but before she can sort it out L is running away across the lawn. *Get back here, you motherfucking coward thief liar, where the hell are you going, you shit, you useless thing?* Her throat is so dry and there's no way he can hear her furious whispers. Anger cracks her spine. She forces herself to look away and remember, remember, it's all just a bad trip, ignore the pain, ignore L. Focus on yourself.

At the halfway. The fulcrum.

Hesitates at the piglets' doorknob, the glowing keyhole which she wants to open, which she must open, but the bones in her hand lock up, fuse, scream in pain. Even if all that comes out are stygian wasps, she keeps going, she grabs it and the doorknob snarls with white-hot wolf jaws, clamps down on her, deep, all the way through, still she doesn't let go.

It won't turn.

The harder she tries, the more it pushes back. Her fingers blister. The nails break off.

Behind the door, they scratch. They knock. They laugh.

Screams float lazily out of the keyhole like feathers, like ash.

him

Two weeks in and he hasn't let a drop get past him. His lips aren't chapped and raw anymore. He can lick them and not peel away pieces with his sharp, dry tongue. No more headaches. He isn't waking up suffocated by his own sheets or soaked in cold sweat. Each breath goes in and out without a hitch. He's been reborn.

A new man.

He admits to the group that, occasionally, he still hears the screaming. Sober; it doesn't come from inside his head, either. He can lie underneath the laundered sheets that are much softer against his neck and still hear the screams, rising and falling. He can get up and walk around the house, trying to identify the place where they're coming from, but they are always changing, drifting this way and that, the way the ash drifted in the breeze that night and fell onto the snow. Big black footprints from the boots of the firefighters. Small black handprints on the window pane.

That's all part of the healing process, according to the therapist. You are finally allowing yourself to grieve. And what about the locked door? Have you opened it yet?

No.

That's fine. Take your time. Remember, that wasn't you, the therapist says. That was a different person, the broken one, the one who compartmentalized himself from his family. That man snuck out in the middle of the night to the dealer, left his wife passed out in their bed, candles lit. That man, that stranger, locked the bedroom doors in a fit of stoned paranoia. He, not you, was gone for too long. Halfway home, the sun breaking over soft suburban roofs, it was that man who stopped to do a blast on the side of the road and giggle at the sirens racing past. Understand?

The telling of it hurts in different parts, different amounts. There's a lot of bad. A lot of junkie moments. Not as many dad moments. Or husband moments. Can't mourn the person she was, but the one she used to be. Understanding they were both shells, hollowed out, all their heart squeezed into a tight little ball and boxed away. None of it was their fault. Or at least, not his.

The fourth step, the old man said, showing off a notebook full of scribblings. You got to write that shit down. Take a moral inventory.

So, he does. Or he tries. Several times. The problem is, he doesn't believe it. Like the house, those memories have grown colder. Every time he sits down to finally write it out, he gets restless. The ink in the pen won't flow. The house is frigid, like an icebox. He checks the thermostat; it's cranked way down. Like it's afraid of the heat, he thinks, and shakes away the wayward thought just as quickly.

Moral inventory. What does that even mean?

Cursing under his breath, he heads outside for some fresh air. Shake it off. He wanders over to the swing set. It feels like a lifetime ago when he was watching her through the window as *she* pushed them. How small their backs were. Wishing out loud they'd grow the fuck up and learn how to swing themselves. He never liked smoking by himself. He needed her to get to the right kind of high, mellowed out, pushing higher and higher, where everything was light as a feather, and nothing hurt.

He sits on one of the swings and it creaks. Sparrows burst from the trees. The house looms in front of him, rimmed in morning glow. He desperately tries to recall their faces. Can't. Already erased. Bleached away.

There's motion in the window. His breath catches in his throat.

She's screaming.

She's dead.

She bangs the window.

Something clinks or cracks and she is all fire and ash, red-skinned and red eyes and with bits of soot caught in her hair and floating like a halo.

He screams, a sharp, choking thing.

She's not there anymore.

She was.

He almost collapses. It's like his insides are being chewed up. His first instinct: a drink will fix this. That makes him turn and run. Or even scoring a quick hit. It would be ridiculously easy. No, no, no, he's almost through the tunnel. That joke he'll laugh at, that meal he'll enjoy, that new girl he'll kiss is right around the corner, almost there. If he gives up now, he might as well go ahead and kill himself. Choices, fanned out like tarot cards. Drink. Drug. Death.

He refuses them all.

Leave me alone. It wasn't my fault. You should have had more self-control. I'm not to blame. Fuck you.

Of course, he deserves to live. It's not even a question, is it?

He dashes inside, starts to write. Clean page, new story.

her

Easier this time.

Flickering sunsets into her bones. The meat comes clean. The sweet smell of marrow. The pain is still there, but only a blurry reflection in a furrow of rainwater, nothing that she recognizes in herself. Sit up in the bed. Bare mattress, bare walls, bare floor. A fine layer of charcoal dust. It covers her too. It sticks in the corners of her eyes. It paints the curve of her legs like delicate tattoos. Only her palms are clean, as if clenched for a long time. Birds swoop down from the exposed rafters, darting through the ragged hole in the ceiling, in and out, in and out. *Beeed-ah. Beeeed-ah. Come this way.*

L bangs on the door. He runs from room to room. She is tired of chasing him.

She holds herself together like a hit in her lungs. Her feet touch the ground and miss and she tries again and again until she feels the carpet under her heel, the dirt, the stones, until she has balance and can push herself into the bathroom. Cracked tiles, cracked mirrors, she presses her lips to the faucet and cracks her teeth. There goes L again, key in hand. She obediently follows. The hallway goes forever. It lurches ahead of her. The living room remains as far away as the bottom of the ocean. That's fine.

She arrives at the halfway. Cockroach handprints swarm around the locked door. The knob melts away in her hand. The keyhole gleams like a jewel. No. Don't look. Don't look. Eye to keyhole. Darkness collapses on her, it falls, it blinds, it crushes, it embraces, it tastes, it fucks, it begs, it demands, it rips, it shatters, it drowns, it chokes, it kisses, it promises, it is, it is, it is, it is. She runs back in the bedroom, into the bed, through the fog into the girl she used to be, the most herself she ever was, dancing in the woods behind the family barn of her childhood, tall winking trees heavy with black feathered bodies, the smell of recently plowed fields, of things being born and things being slaughtered, of blood flowing from slashed necks, of flesh on fire. She kneels beside her squealing piglets. I'm here. I'm not going anywhere.

him

He's replaying the conversation with the old man all the way back to the house. It had been a while since he had been to any meetings and they were all worried sick. He gently tried to explain to the old man that he was fine, that he hadn't fallen off the wagon or anything like that. It was just time to move on. Even his therapist thought so.

Confess, the old man demanded.

What?

He still feels the old man laying his hands on his. For once, he allows the touch. Warm, dry. Not awful. The kind of hand big enough to crawl into and disappear.

Step nine. Confess. Make amends. You have to. Please.

Confess? Confess what? I've done nothing wrong.

The old man is nervously tugging at his own hair, pulling at the roots.

But ... you told me ... it was your fault. That you locked them all in. That you left her asleep and the candles burning ...

What did he do then? One minute he is in the restaurant, wiping the grease off his lips with his sleeve, and the next he is speeding down the highway. Righteous fury boils through him. He just wants to move on. He wants to get to that next step and never look back again. He can't do anything about the past. It's gone.

At the house, he stomps in, makes a lot of noise. Calls out her name. His dare echoes down the hallway. Off the corners of the room. Hearing something — screaming and the shriek of fire alarms and smoke detectors. *Beeed-ah! Beeeed-ah!* Scratching, an odd sort of scratching. Smoke drifting around the corners. Starting to accumulate, thick at the ceilings. He knows it's not real. All in his head. Unresolved bullshit.

Clogs his nose. Fumbling down the hallway. Eyes stinging. This time, this time, this time.

Here it is. The door he never opened. The iron key cold in his pocket. Worn smooth as a river stone. Pulling it out, clamped in his right hand, the left fumbling for the knob. The taste of ozone. Something with him, a static charge, parting the smoke. Ignore it. Push on. He resists the urge to walk away, to run away, to cross off the final step undone, who would ever know. He could lie to the old man. It would be so easy. He's always been so good at it.

This house is mine.

Turning the key. The door opens.

Too dark to see anything.

A hand caresses his back. Pushes him towards the open door. He doesn't flinch at her touch.

Because finally, *finally*, he understands what is real and what is not.

"Oh, God. Forgive me."

her

The house is her. She is the house. Both contain the other. Lovers sealed in volcanic ash, interlocked in an eternal embrace. Waiting. For what? The sound of a heartbeat. The gentle touch of warm breath.

The bedroom. The bathroom. The hallway. The living room.

Her skull. Her teeth. Her hands. Her ribcage.

L comes and goes. She tries but can never catch him.

A thousand years pass in darkness. She lives a thousand lives, all unseen as albino fish in an underground lake.

Until.

Pressure of footsteps. A familiar scent.

L is shouting *her* name this time. L is looking for *her*. Chasing after *her* shadow.

Eyes open. Just for a moment. Long enough to see the fire roaring up the walls. A tide of blue smoke rippling along the ceiling. Bits of charred drywall flutter on currents of hot air. Somewhere in the house, an alarm bleats for attention. Closer by, the pounding of little fists. The scratching of little nails. Wailing. Screaming. She wills herself to move. Her brain soaks with adrenaline, her teeth grind against each other, her stomach tightens and clenches, but her body is trapped in the evergreen of the needle, the rush, the crystal coffin. She keeps pushing, thrashing against the waves, even as the chemical sleep overtakes her, even as she sinks into the black.

Thunder shudders in the night, no flash of lightning, only a distant rumble. Wind rattles the leaves. From the empty, cloudless sky, the summer storm erupts in a birth of violent reckoning. It picks up sticks and dust and insects and grains of bone and bits of wax and broken glass. Charged with negative electricity, it seeks the iron key in his hand, the crackling thoughts of his despair. It scrapes together a shape with dry lips, a buzzing throat that rattles. He stops running. He becomes still. He listens to the storm. It whispers. The darkness is here. That's it. The darkness. I see it in me. I see you, in me. Let me take your hands and hold you to me. I know you are there. That's it. Feel you. Feel me. Small wings. Dark. Let me take your hand. I know it's your fault. It's my fault. Let me hold you. This whole night is your fault. My fault. I've been lying to you. I've been lying to you for years. I've loved you. I need you to see. I've hated you. We've been waiting for you. You. Dark. Dark. Hear them scratching? Unlock the door. Look. See. Dark. There. There.

Look at them, waiting for daddy.
Your skin, your spine. Warm. Clean.
What?
It's hard to hear over these screaming birds.
What are you saying? What are you asking me?
Ah. I'm sorry, my love.
"NO."

Infernal® Policies and Procedures Have Changed

Douglas Anstruther and J. Tynan Burke

General Sargon,

We here at Infernal® are excited to announce that we've finished our hostile acquisition of Beelzebub Corp., making us the largest corporation in the underworld. We recognize you have several options for managing your afterlife needs, and appreciate that you have chosen Infernal®, even as we cause you to have fewer choices than ever before.

Beelzebub Corp. was a leader in the pro-disease movement, and as such had extensive dealings with social media in the mortal realm. This means that Infernal® is now subject to terrestrial data-protection regulations such as GDPR and CCPA. As such, please find below the new privacy policy for our Hell line of services. At your earliest convenience, please log in and accept this policy on infernal.hell, as well as every subsidiary website we own, including:

I squeezed hard on my smartphone, which remained stubbornly uncrushed. The message wasn't just a reminder of my old boss's recent capitulation; it was also part of a never-ending torrent of annoyances and petty tasks driven by wave after wave of new regulations. Only the living could have devised such an elaborate torture. The hellions I'd come to tolerate lacked such nuance, preferring an eternity of pointless, cyclical brutality. I adjusted my tie, shifting uncomfortably in my pinstripe suit. Another ingenious torment stolen from the living. It was the Infernal® dress code, and I was now subject to it. My discomfort was lessened only by the sword hanging at my side. The accessory was Lucifer's twist on the standard corporate uniform; it was in honor of Hell's martial past, according to the new-hire handbook.

"Lucifer will see you now, General," a disembodied secretarial voice said. I stilled the fury in my heart, tucked my phone into my pocket, and drew myself up ramrod-straight. A sense of decorum always put kings at ease. I'd learned that old trick during a youth spent approaching thrones, and confirmed it during a life spent occupying them.

Lucifer's throne room was lined with the worst sorts of demonic courtiers. Charred chimps jumped up and down, shrieking; razor golems thrashed around, shredding inattentive creatures that got too close; pig-headed succubi moved through the crowds, doing whatever they did. The disgusting spectacle seemed to go on forever. Over the cacophony, I could barely hear the tapping of my oxfords as I moved towards the throne.

The King of Hell was draped over his obsidian seat, dripping with arrogant disdain. His face was illuminated by his smartphone. The fallen angel's elegance was timeless, but the ugliness of his personality shone through his features. It was enough to sour my stomach; in Hell, even the beauty was vile. With clacking claws, he scrolled through screen after screen. I stopped ten paces away, moved my sword aside, and bent into a deep kneel. A hush spread through the crowd.

"Sargon the Great of Akkadia, First Emperor of Earth, at your service, my lord."

Tap. Drag.

Lucifer's claws clattered against his screen.

Tap, drag. Tap, drag.

I risked a glance up to see if he'd noticed me. There was no way to know. His casual disrespect was expected, but irksome all the same.

Tap, drag.

Then ... screams? No, meows, things falling over, a shout, Lucifer chuckling. This continued for some time and my mind began to wander — back to the discovery I'd made, and how I hoped to use it.

"Sar-gon," he finally said, drawing the name out disapprovingly. "The Great, you say? I'm not surprised that Beelzebub allowed you to keep that title. There's little of greatness about him. But in comparison to myself, you are nothing but a boil on the ass of a rat. Do not style yourself thus again."

I kept my head bowed, studying my silhouette, which was reflected on the floor's glossy black marble. The pose let the expression of rage consume my face unseen. I forced it down. I had not been a patient man in life, but I'd survived far worse humiliations in the millennia following my death. What was one more? So I convinced myself that this was fine. *For now*, whispered that old restlessness, simmering in the back of my mind now that my moment was near.

"Yes, my lord."

"Rise," Lucifer said, and I did. He put his phone into his breast pocket. The light fled his face as if afraid to illuminate his next expression. He tilted his head to study me. "Tell me," he said, "did you like working for Beelzebub?"

I chose my words carefully; surely any falsehood I uttered would be detected by this Prince of Lies. "I found him disgusting, but admired his ruthlessness in battle," I said, honestly enough to get me through this visitation. The truth was, had my former master been a soldier in the Akkadian army, his senseless cruelty would have found him imprisoned. I expected no different from Lucifer, but he didn't need to know.

"Yes, he was formidable with battle plans ... but not so good at forming a business plan, am I right?" A leathery, bat-like courtier hurried over to give Lucifer's fist a bump. "Where is the gibbering Archdemon now, anyway?"

A pause confirmed that he was asking me. "I heard he was retiring. To spend more time with his ravenous spawn, my lord. And binge-watch all of Netflix."

"*Netflix*." Lucifer rolled his eyes. "Beelzebub always was such a Philistine." The waiting courtier fist-bumped him again. "Get it? Anyway." A bored sigh escaped Lucifer's blood-red lips. He waved the back of his hand at me. "So you were in charge of his Realm Expansion and Addition Project, which is now *my* project. And your excavations have uncovered something so *terribly interesting*, I must be shown in person. Is that about right?"

Terribly interesting. I couldn't have put it better myself. "Yes, my lord. I'm here to lead you below, as I arranged with your assistant."

Lucifer met my eyes and held my gaze with a hungry look. Did he know what I'd found? How much of my soul could he see? I almost let a moment of panic wash over me. But then he smiled, flashing his formidable teeth, and said, "Excellent. Let's see this, then. And I understand you've installed my new punishments — let's go by those on the way. I'm told their inventor is a genius." He grinned at the crowd, which tittered appreciatively.

"Yes, my lord." I bowed. "This way." I turned and left the way I'd entered. His footsteps followed a few paces back, loud enough to fill up the massive chamber, which was still deferentially silent. Though he was only a hand's width taller than me, his footfalls boomed wherever he went, one of his many conceits. The raucous courtiers resumed their shrill posturing as soon as we exited the chamber.

I wasn't sure how much Lucifer knew about the 'discovery'. Very little, hopefully; I certainly hadn't told anybody the details. My construction crew had found it several days ago, not long after the merger, while excavating space for the Realm Expansion and Addition Project. Our goal was tunneling through the limitless stone that surrounded the Boiling Abyss; we would then plant explosives in the tunnels to clear large areas at once. "Hell may be infinite, but we're still out of real estate," Beelzebub had said; Lucifer had been all too happy to agree, following the takeover.

On that fateful day, my crew and I had been following behind a tunneling firewyrm when it halted and began to shriek. The monstrous creatures were famously unflappable; something very strange indeed must have happened. My workers had frozen in place, then slowly backed away. Simpletons and weaklings, they wanted nothing to do with any irregularities, and refused to investigate when I asked for volunteers. I dismissed them with a scowl, but not before I snatched a Lamp of Eternal Light from one of their trembling hands. Down here, as above, if you wanted something done right, you had to do it yourself. With the lamp hanging at my belt, I squeezed between the firewyrm's rough scales and the still-cooling tunnel walls, half-flaying myself in the process.

I reached the head of the terrible animal and calmed it with a hand on its snout. The poor thing was too simple to know it was letting us down, and thus deserved more sympathy than my underlings. I sent it back the way it had come. Ahead, a new passageway led away at a right angle, its irregular surfaces indicating a naturally occurring pocket in the stone. A strange green light filled the tunnel from beyond a bend. It grew more intense as I rounded the corner. I hardly noticed when my Lamp blinked out, even though they were dependable to a fault — the green glow so firmly held my attention, the thrill of novelty so enraptured me.

Novelty — *discovery*. A lost passion. It had been easy to satiate while building an empire that reached beyond the borders of my known world. New peoples, new lands, new foods — these were the natural spoils of a conqueror. I had even written celebrated poetry about my journeys, as befit a great ruler. But novelty was difficult to find as a subordinate fighting an endless war over the same plots of land in Hell, or as a cog in a corporate machine. I'd all but forgotten the sway it could hold over me, having had only a vague sense that something was missing. But it seemed that the hunger had merely been dormant.

The passageway opened into a dripping cave, its stalactites slick with condensation. The green light, as well as a strange ululating trill, poured into the cave from a vertical gash as wide as my outstretched arm, and twice again as high. I crept around sulfurous pools to the cave entrance, not wanting to disturb whatever was making the sounds. Singing? Chanting? Screaming hellions? The opening overlooked a wide plain below. Above it, something I hadn't seen in over four millennia: the sky. But it wasn't my sky, or any other human's, for in it burned three emerald suns.

Lucifer and I walked in silence through the gloomy caverns of his palace, and into the service corridors. Ordinarily the only light came from guttering torches, fueled with the fat of bad tippers. Right now, Lucifer himself provided most of the illumination, beaming like the morning star.

"You have been with us a long time, Sar-gon."

Simple answers; do not give anything away. "Yes, my lord." *Longer than you*, I did not add.

"What was it that your people called this place?"

"The Great Below," I said. Except that the Great Below had been a place of shades and spirits that wandered unmolested like the echoes of the living that they had been. It hadn't been so bad, at first. With nothing to mark the passage of time, the years had gone by quickly. Then Lucifer and his demons had arrived. They replaced our chilly caverns with the Boiling Abyss, and the place had filled up with fallen Christians, as well as those who'd worshipped toppled gods. Said gods even arrived themselves on occasion, like my former boss Beelzebub.

"'The Great Below'," Lucifer said as if tasting the words. "How quaint."

The service elevator arrived, and I slid open the grille and held a hand out for Lucifer, who brushed past. I joined him in the small space, closed the grille, and selected the bottom floor. The cage began its rattly descent.

"I've studied you, Sar-gon," Lucifer said with affected weariness.

"Oh?" I struggled to look at his face from my too-close position. The evil was visible in every perfect pore of his skin. "I trust you are satisfied, my lord?"

"You killed many people while alive," he said, nodding. "Slaughtered villages, starved cities. Terrible, terrible things."

"My —" I closed my mouth when I noticed the approval in his voice. He was testing me. Lucifer came across as petty and cruel to the point of being insipid, but there could be traps within his words. And he'd almost goaded me into telling the truth, here: that my cruelty had been necessary to bring order to a chaotic and lawless land, to free the scattered and divided city-states from petty and reckless rulers and unite them for a greater good. Yes, I had slaughtered villages, but only so the next would yield without a fight. I had starved cities so the next would bend their knee. I had discovered and assimilated entire civilizations, that we might all benefit from the bounty of their farmland and knowledge. All my cruelty had served a greater purpose. Unlike here.

I settled for another simple answer. "Yes."

"And yet." Lucifer half-frowned. "For several thousand years, you served as a general under several Archdemons. And not once has word of your exploits reached me. You're competent, but, how shall I say? Lackluster."

My blood boiled at the slight, and my face burned. He wasn't *wrong* — the futility of it all had worn me a bit dull this last millennium or two, like an overused blade — but if there'd been a war worth fighting, I'd have been the greatest general ever to grace Earth or Hell. On Earth, war had been a means to an end. Here, nothing was accomplished but suffering. Like everything in this place, Hell's wars were pointless, a form of organized cruelty for cruelty's sake.

Lucifer looked down on my stifled discomfort and smiled broadly. "Perhaps it was easier to make a name for yourself when there were so few humans. Don't worry, I'm sure you make a fine foreman."

My fist clenched at my side, hidden, I hoped, behind the pommel of my sword. The elevator dinged and I released my grip, reaching out to pull the grille open again. We'd arrived at an area my team had excavated several months earlier. Lucifer's minions had made quick work of his request to install his new punishments, and the excavation's vast gulf was now filled with a sea of gray-walled cubicles.

Lucifer's smile beamed. "My torments," he purred.

We passed by workstation after workstation. Each held two unhappy souls typing furiously, slumped in front of decrepit CRT monitors. Once more I slipped into the role of a soldier, a persona I wore effortlessly after all that time. "Per your instructions, my lord, all futility-based torments have been moved here, in the form of endless arguments on Facebook and Twitter."

"And the Sisyphean Hills?" Lucifer said.

"We've already broken ground on the new resort you requested."

Still beaming, Lucifer made a show of looking around at the damned souls. "No demons are making them do this?"

"No, my lord, they do this willingly."

"Self-sustaining torture," he said, clearly pleased with himself. "Brilliant, wouldn't you say?"

Just another idea you stole from the mortals. "Yes, my lord."

"It's this sort of innovation that's putting Infernal® ahead of the others," Lucifer said. Theft or no, I had to admit it truly was ingenious; my old Head of Torturers could never have designed something so elegant.

Ahead, intense flashes of light interrupted the dull glow of the failing fluorescent tubes that flickered above this simulacrum of an office. As we walked by, scattered souls were bursting into flame. They writhed and wailed in their seats before collapsing onto their keyboards. After a pause, they brushed the soot off their burned skin and went back to typing.

"These must be the 'flamers'," Lucifer said, making air quotes with his claws. "People that would never say a mean word in person, but transform into terrible bullies online, pulling every discussion down to a name-calling contest, doing more harm than they care to realize." His face took an expression of dreamy admiration. "It's a terrible sin, you know. Admirable, if not quite up to our hiring standards."

The final group of cramped cubicles we passed were stuffed full of souls slowly working their way through mandatory training videos. Words like 'HIPAA' and 'tolerance' wafted from innumerable speakers. The victims exuded a level of boredom that was difficult to behold. "A good general-purpose torment," Lucifer explained, to no one in particular.

"I was one of the first, you know," he said as we left the vast department of computer-based torments behind, "to see the tremendous potential of computers to cause misery."

We continued through areas still under construction to a massive steel hatch. All the unfinished excavations lay behind it, sealed to keep the rabble away from the explosives and the powerful firewyrms. I unfolded a nearby tablet and entered my password.

<Your password has expired. Create a new password now.>

"The damn sysadmin makes me change this every time I come down here," I explained. "I must have gone through ten thousand passwords by now."

Lucifer chuckled. "I like you, Sar-gon. I shall punish this sysadmin for you." He snapped his fingers and the enormous hatch swung open. It was a reminder that Lucifer had power over all things in his domain. We continued through the portal to the new excavations, and to the destiny that awaited us there.

I wasn't the same man that had died in Akkadia forty-three hundred years ago. I wondered about that sometimes. Would I have ended up here if this version of me had lived on Earth? If I had been born at a different time? The arbitrariness of it all drove me mad.

Since Lucifer's invasion of The Great Below, I'd learned a lot from talking with those that came after me. Many were, like myself, not worshipers of Lucifer's former Lord. These so-called 'heathens' tended to arrive in batches, sometimes even accompanied by their pantheon; but they told of other faiths whose adherents were nowhere to be seen. Eventually I formed a theory — Christianity was a conquering religion, and the civilizations that fell to it found their own afterlives absorbed into this place, the victors' Hell.

Did I recognize something of myself in this? Of course. But like everything else in Hell, it was reflected through a twisted mirror. My empire would never have assigned its new subjects a fate of eternal torment. If nothing else, it would have encouraged slave rebellions.

There was much more to learn as the years passed. My horizons expanded — literally. I learned that the world was not confined by the sea to the West and mountains to the East. I heard stories that the Earth was round, which I rejected utterly for a thousand years after the deceased began insisting it was so. I learned that the Sun was an immense burning ball of gas, no different than the distant stars, that other worlds could exist there like our own and that intelligent life, utterly different than us, might live there. I learned that many in heaven perhaps thought otherwise, and that they were best ignored.

The day of my discovery, when I looked down onto the emerald-lit plain for the first time, I saw tens of thousands of creatures pinned to the rocky ground. They were globular, pulsing things, like clusters of veins, ringed with an outline of delicate tentacles. I'd never seen a demon or man like them, and I'd been to every corner of Hell. The creatures were squirming and straining against their bonds, without effect. *Not just creatures. Aliens.*

But what I saw from that cave mouth was not an alien *world*. I recognized it for what it was instantly. Implicitly. Perfectly. It was Hell. A Hell. An alien Hell.

I had sunk to the ground on failing knees when I'd realized this, worried that in my shock I might stumble out of the cave and join them. It was the discovery of a lifetime, of many lifetimes. The implications were overwhelming. It meant that there was *more*, just as I had always suspected. The Hell I was in had never felt right. Ill-fitting, like the suits I was forced to wear during meetings. And now I knew that something else was out there. The world was wide again. There was more to see, more to explore. No longer was I trapped in a demons' playground.

I hadn't felt so invigorated since before I'd died. My passions hadn't been lost, merely abandoned. It made me wonder: what other parts of the human heart could be reclaimed from this land without hope or dreams?

Hungry to learn the entirety of what I'd found, I walked this strange new cavern with one hand against the porous right wall, to ensure I saw everything. In dark recesses I found rough passages leading off in innumerable directions. For the next day I fumbled through them, until I was satisfied I knew enough to act on. I returned to the cave and collected the lifeless Lamp of Eternal Light that I'd left there. As I crossed back into the smooth firewyrm tunnels, the Lamp stayed dead. I looked at it for a long while before continuing.

Lucifer and I moved past the messy staging area, littered with firewyrm pens and the camps of demonic and human laborers. The work was on hold pending Lucifer's visit, and in their boredom, the hellions were improvising new ways to torture their workers. Screams rose from the camp like a morning fog.

Lucifer turned to stare at me like a curious bird. "You don't like it here, in Hell, do you?"

I avoided his gaze. *Simple and honest; you're so close.* "No, my lord. But I believe that is ... as intended."

"Yes, yes. Of course." He stopped to admire a nearby disemboweling before continuing. "But *why* don't you like it here?"

The truth was that I hated its arbitrary and pointless cruelty. Eternal life, squandered. But this was not something I could say. I just needed a few more minutes without triggering his wrath, or his suspicion. I would only have this one chance.

"Nothing here lasts," I said. "Victory and defeat are fleeting."

This elicited a sneering chuckle from Lucifer. "You think things are so different among the living? All that remains of your great empire is a few crumbling statues, and they will be gone and forgotten soon enough."

He was right, of course. The crucial difference was that for the living, history had a direction. And although Hell adopted the trappings and fashions of the living, it was only ever a poor mockery. Conquest, but of the already conquered. Competition, but without goals. It was why I'd volunteered to lead the excavations. It was as close as I would ever get to leaving a mark on this place, to creating something new and perhaps lasting.

"Yes, my lord. Of course, my lord." I bowed my head in not entirely mock humility. *Just a little further.*

We reached the mouth of the firewyrm tunnels. I picked up a Lamp from a rack and led him down the tunnel in question. As we walked, I held myself at attention, using long-practiced discipline to avoid betraying my fluttering heart.

"That's what I find most pathetic about you humans," Lucifer mused to the darkness ahead of us. "You always think you're a bigger part of things than you are."

I let him cross into the cave ahead of me. His arrogance faded to the slack stance of the utterly baffled. "What is this place?" he whispered, stepping through to the gash on the far wall, where he stopped to look out over the emerald field.

I followed behind him, setting the Lamp down when it blinked out. "It appears to be an alien Hell."

"How is it possible?" He turned to face me, with an expression utterly foreign to the face that wore it. *Fear.* "How could I not know such a place existed?"

A flash of green illuminated his face, the light of the alien suns reflected from my sword as it arced down onto his alabaster neck with all the force of my being. His head separated from his body with ease, the fear shifting to astonishment as it toppled to the ground.

"Perhaps you're a smaller part of things than you think," I said, and spat on his corpse.

The branching passageways of the cavern led to other afterlives. She'ol, Jahannam, Rarohenga, and others, with innumerable alien hells as well. These other realms must have surrounded the only one I had ever known, embedded in the limitless rock like geodes in sandstone, like the city-states of Mesopotamia. It turned out I'd been right about worshippers from surviving faiths: they had different places to go.

I stood over Lucifer's body for several minutes, my sword pointed at his neck. He remained dead. I was pleased, but not surprised. The place where the firewyrm became spooked and the Lamp of Eternal Light went out were the limits of his Realm. He had no power beyond. I had taken a great gamble and won. Now to claim the winnings.

I returned to the labor camp and climbed a mound of limbs that had been torn from the workers. Lucifer's lifeless head was tucked under my arm. There, I waited. Slowly, the screams of the tortured and the laughter of the demons dissipated. A crowd gathered. I took a deep breath and spoke with all the gravitas of my mortal station.

"I, Sargon the Great of Akkadia, First Emperor of Earth, The Raging Flood-Wave That Destroys Even Stone, have slain Lucifer." I held his head up by its perfect hair. A muffled hush went through the throng of demons and their victims. "From here on out, we are no longer in the business of torture." A gasp of incredulity rose from the crowd. "Nor are we in the business of business." The gathered demons and humans looked from one to another in puzzled silence. Somebody in the back coughed.

I threw Lucifer's head to the ground. With my bloodied sword, I cut the tie from my neck, and cast it down onto his face. "We are in the business," I shouted, "of conquering!" A great roar of excitement erupted in response.

I didn't know if we would succeed, but the immortal souls of the dead deserved better than stagnation and suffering. Humans were not creatures of hopelessness; we were creatures that dreamed. Call it what you will — hubris, ambition, destiny — it was what I would return to my people.

The Writing Process

Evan Marcroft

As a relatively new writer, this anthology was my first collaborative experience. I didn't come in with any kind of plan, and as such, I had to discover what model worked best for me. In doing so, I quickly found that there was no one perfect model, but rather that I would have to tailor my approach to each writing partner.

With Tynan and David, I found that our writing styles were similar enough that we could write alternate scenes, taking turns to lay down our vision for where the story would go, and building off of what had come before. It was a fairly easy process from there to retroactively edit for consistency of voice. The challenge, I found, came from getting to a unified vision of what the story would be. Everyone involved had strong ideas that we were passionate about, and there was more than a little argument. What we found though was that this bickering was productive; an idea that couldn't withstand the crucible ultimately wasn't suited for the story. The final products were stronger for it.

Working with L'Erin and Douglas was a vastly different experience. Here, the story's core concept was more or less my own, but L'Erin was invaluable in providing a unique interpretation of one of the two principal characters, creating a vastly more powerful character than I could have written myself, and her take on that figure drastically reshaped my vision of the other. Though we in-theory divided the two perspectives between us, ultimately, the complete narrative was more a product of the both of us than I expected it would be, and better for it.

My greatest challenge of this product was "Snakeheart", with Doug Anstruther. It was here that I encountered the greatest clash of perspectives and styles. We both had radically different visions for what this story would be, and we both fought mightily for them, producing many different concepts. Much as with my projects with Tynan and David, however, this months-long struggle produced many great ideas, and the breakthrough came when we realized we could take only those good ideas and compact them into a streamlined piece that achieved what both of us wanted from it. All in all, this project drastically changed the writing that came after it. Each piece forced me to take a different approach, try something new, and exposed me to styles and techniques different than my own.

About Evan Marcroft

Evan Marcroft is a speculative fiction writer from California currently residing in Chicago with his wife. Evan uses his expensive degree in literary criticism to do menial data entry, and dreams of writing for video games, but will settle for literature instead. His works of science fiction, fantasy, and spine-curdling horror can be found in a variety of venues across the internet, such as *Strange Horizons, Asimov's*, and multiple times in *Metaphorosis*.

evan-marcroft.squarespace.com, @Evan_Marcroft

David Gallay

Thinking about writing, that is, everything that comes before the first scratch of ink on paper or pixel on a blank white screen, is an intensely solitary experience. Insubstantial as a dream, whole universes are born, live, and die trapped entirely inside our head. No one else can see those epiphanies of connective themes and plot pacing back and forth like a holographic tiger in a cage of mirrors. So much of the work happens inside the mind that it's natural to assume that the actual act of writing will be the same, a raw extension of the self into the physical world, a thought, a clenched hand, a lonely candle in the dark.

Every writer knows that's not quite what happens.

As soon as the first word appears on the page, the work is already something apart. It exists. It can be read. That once-singular viewpoint cannot help but go bicameral; writer and reader in a constant feedback loop. So, that's already a collaboration of two. Add in the fact that we are not the same person today as we were yesterday (never stepping in the same stream twice and all that), the historical and sociological forces in our lives, the influence of every book we've loved or loathed, the omnipresent drone of media, and, well, every story ends up written by a crowd of millions we have no control over.

There, we've killed the idea of the virgin genius author!

How about another way to think about collaboration?

A universe in our head, a tiger in a cage. Why not start with two universes? Two tigers? Infinity plus infinity equals infinity but it's not quite the same as it was before. We all came into this project with our own perfect ideas and none of them survived. All were transformed into something new and absolutely unexpected:

Musings on religious conflict blossomed an entire mythology of death-metal kaiju.

Prosaic technology frustrations were reborn into a tale of algorithmic demonic incursion.

A scientific article on hydrothermal vents grew to an odyssey of war and friendship.

A strange dream of playing tag became something much, much scarier.

I hope you enjoy reading these stories as much as we did watching them come to life.

About David Gallay

David Gallay is a writer of speculative fiction and horror. After receiving a B.A in Creative Writing from Binghamton University, he currently resides in Wisconsin where he leads a double life as an IT SysAdmin.

J. Tynan Burke

For me, writing alone is all about answering questions, whole piles of them, loosely in this order: Are any of these ideas good? Should I outline this one? Do I know any arborists? What's the best way to get a hold of somebody at NASA? Is this story bad? How can I tell the difference between a flawed plan and a flawed implementation? As I iterate on this — sometimes 'flail around' better describes the sensation — the characters, settings, and plot can change drastically.

Everybody's process is different. While ones like mine certainly aren't uncommon, I was concerned that it wouldn't work so well for collaboration. Fortunately this was not the case.

I could write a note this length about the process for each story. About how I helped flesh out the world of "Boro Boro" by leveraging my time in exurban California, as well as a certain breakup. Or how many versions of the starship's personality we went through in "The Relic". Or the evolution of a gag into a story, as happened with "Infernal® Policies and Procedures Have Changed". But I find the process behind "Project Blackbook" to be most worthy.

The parallels between software development and writing have always fascinated me. They're both processes of iterative improvement, where you learn about the problem even as you are solving it. The direction of your project can turn on a dime if a reviewer provides a new insight, or points out a glaring hole. It is not uncommon, while reading code, to mutter *What idiot wrote this*, only to check and find out it was you last month. And so on.

As for the last example: code changes are usually tracked using a tool called 'git'. Every changed character is recorded, along with a (hopefully) explanatory message, signed by the author of the change. The website GitHub provides a convenient interface for managing this, which lets users suggest code changes to be merged in, and comment on them.

I'd long wondered what it would be like to write a story this way. David was all too happy to humor me when I suggested it to him. And what do you know — writing a story about git, using git, was a total blast. Things turned out pretty well for us — or at least, much better than they did for our characters.

In the end, each collaboration produced a great story, no matter our methods. I'd like to think that the result, which you hold in your hands, speaks for itself.

About J. Tynan Burke

J. Tynan Burke is a software engineer and writer. He lives in New York City with his husband and their enormous cat, Samwise. He hopes to someday be an old man futzing around in the garden.

www.tynanburke.com, @tynanpants

L'Erin Ogle

The Relic

"The Relic" was one of the two stories that really pushed me out of my comfort zone. Science fiction and world-building are probably two of my biggest weaknesses as a writer. I think spaceships and outer space are cool. My knowledge of science is pretty limited on anything that isn't medical knowledge, and a lot of my initial attempts at sci-fi were pretty laughable, as in: this is not a thing that could ever work in real life.

Which is why Tynan was an excellent partner. We both tossed around ideas and then settled on a sort of hybrid idea about madness and isolation in space. Having an alien presence driven mad by jealousy, and showing that in the flashbacks, was a neat twist. We alternated scenes, with me primarily focusing on the flashbacks and the tragic end to the love triangle with the ship and the two aliens, and Tynan did the heavy lifting with the descriptions of the actual ship and the world around it.

It was a difficult story to write, mostly wrapping my head around the logistics of what could and couldn't work in deep space, but I'm so glad I did step out of the horror/light fantasy niche I like to hang out in and I actually learned quite a bit! Tynan was very patient and helpful with the narrative throughout,

Third Chamber on the Left

Doug and I both work in the medical field, and one of the first things he e-mailed was along the lines of, *Hey, I've always sort of* toyed with the idea of zombies in a medical clinic, and I was immediately like *YES*. Pretty easy story, like Daylight. We emailed scenes back and forth. Both of us wanted to keep the setting mostly in a clinic setting with the zombies and creepy robotic nurses. But why were our narrators going to be in the clinic?

Addiction is ever present in the medical field — it has so many physical as well as mental costs. It was such a cool premise. I really enjoyed the breakdown at the end when my character begins to turn into a zombie, the stuttering thought process and disconnect from emotion. Another dark ending, but I liked it.

Doug was very easy to work with, with a pretty similar writing style, and it all flowed together fairly easily and neatly. I really enjoyed his ideas and willingness to collaborate. Plus I'm a sucker for a good zombie story, movie, show, anything!

The Blood Dance of Ape and Mouse

"The Blood Dance of Ape and Mouse" was not easy to write! I loved the idea of both Ape and Mouse being from the wrong side of the tracks, fighting over a woman they both loved, but like sci-fi, worldbuilding is not a strength for me. Evan had the coolest idea about the world being in the treetops, with the lowest of classes surviving on the scraps dropped down by the lofty upper class.

I love Mouse as a character, her ferocity, her unwillingness to change, her at any cost attitude. The fight scenes were a blast to write. Evan usually drafted the first portion, because I also lack knowledge about fighting styles. Where I come from, you just start throwing fists. It was such a cool story to write and Evan has these huge ideas I never would have come up with on my own.

One of my favorite endings, to be sure. I tend to overwrite, and overdramatize, as the editor of this collection can attest, but I love the language and the flow of this piece, even if I had to tone it down a smidge. I really enjoy Evan's writing style and his enthusiasm. He really pushed me to a new level in creative worldbuilding and I'm glad there are writers who do this so well!

Daylight

"Daylight" was a story that mostly seemed to write itself. David and I corresponded and threw some ideas around, settling on a story about trauma, addiction, and ghosts. He wrote a scene, then I would write a scene, and it all came together pretty easily. Out of all the collaborations, I think our writing styles and use of language and imagery are the most similar. It would have been easy for me to the write the vengeful, mad, female ghost, a pretty familiar territory for me, but David suggested writing the opposite part and I think it turned out great.

I've always loved a dark ending. It's easy to wrap up a story about addiction and remorse in a neat little package tied up with forgiveness and absolution, but that's not how these things work. Maybe if our man had sobered up and moved out of the house, maybe the ending would have been different. The world is full of maybes, and I was glad David thought the same way.

The birds were a great touch. Creepy as hell. Loved them. All in all, this story took the least time to write, as it could fit right into one of my own collections, should I ever make one. I'm really happy with the end result.

About L'Erin Ogle

L'Erin is a writer, mother, and ER/Trauma Nurse from Lawrence, Kansas. She loves all dark fiction and rarely writes happy endings, but is excited about them in real life. She has stories at *Metaphorosis, Syntax&Salt,* and *Pseudopod*. She's hard at work saving lives, writing a novel, writing more stories, and resisting the Trump administration and all that it stands for. She can be found online at lerinogle.com

@Lerinjo

Douglas Anstruther

At the start of the project, none of us had collaborated before and no one had a strong sense of how to proceed, so the methods used to collaborate coalesced out of nothingness, taking entirely different forms in each case.

For "Snakeheart", we had extensive discussions and abundant outlining beforehand, then Evan did an amazing single take on what we had discussed and I added some edits. It was sort of the "college project" model, where one person actually does most of the heavy lifting (to be clear, it was Evan).

For "The Third Chamber from the Left", we came up with the story idea together, then each of us wrote one character's perspective. This became challenging when it turned out that we had slightly different ideas about where the story was headed, and the two versions had to be reconciled. Although I didn't try to match L'Erin's wonderful writing style entirely, I did venture into the previously unfamiliar and exotic territory of first-person present. And I liked it!

"Children of a Winedark World" was the result of some initial collaborative planning followed by David's beautiful initial take. I added scenes and tweaked the overall story a bit, followed by a good amount of back and forth. I feel like a lot of this story could mean different things to different people, and its authors are no exception. The story's name is an example. David liked the 'wine dark' reference because of its use in the *Odyssey*. I liked it because of the idea that ancient cultures had no concept of the color blue, just as the characters in that story had no concept of the larger universe around them.

Typically, my collaborators and I decided on a story idea very quickly, but Tynan and I had so many ideas that we struggled to settle on one. Even after we knew that we wanted to do a modernized, semi-humorous Dantesque story, the details were unclear so the actual writing of "Infernal® Policies and Procedures Have Changed" started out as an 'exquisite corpse' with each of us writing a few paragraphs, then turning it over to the other. At the end of that process, the story was still lacking and it took several back-and-forth overhauls of the entire thing to make it work.

It's hard to say which method was best. The universal constraint, as is so often the case, was time. Everyone is busy, always. So a lot of the methods used were a product of one person briefly having a shred more time than the other.

Compared to solo writing, I found that the collaborations made me venture out of my usual routine and helped drain some of my insecurities. I felt braver, writing with another. But there were frustrations, as well. Many times, things I had written that I thought were pretty cool were changed or deleted by my collaborator. There was wording that I didn't like and changes to the story that I thought made it worse, rather than better. But I had decided early on that I'd need to set a pretty high threshold for complaining — to keep the peace, to keep things moving, and with the understanding that the street went both ways. I had to pick and choose carefully which things to keep harping on and which darlings to let die.

The final products, I believe, represent not only a melding of different author voices, but are also the result of different methods that were born by the particular circumstances of the moment.

About Douglas Anstruther

Douglas Anstruther was raised among the long cold winters of Minnesota. At age seven he discovered that there were other worlds beyond our own and was astonished, and frankly disappointed, that no one had thought this important enough to mention earlier – a sentiment he still holds today. At some point he married his lovely wife, Dana, went to medical school, had three very nearly perfect children, and moved to Wilmington, North Carolina. When not tending to people's kidneys, Douglas likes to read, write, and talk about history, linguistics, space, AIs, the singularity, and everything in between. He particularly enjoys writing stories that will rattle around in the readers' head for a while after the last page has been turned.

www.facebook.com/douglasanstruther, @DouglsAnstruthr

Copyright

Title information

Reading 5X5 x2: Duets

ISBN: 978-1-64076-044-8 (e-book)
ISBN: 978-1-64076-045-5 (paperback)
ISBN: 978-1-64076-046-2 (hardcover)

Copyright

Copyright ©2020, Metaphorosis Publishing.

Woman and tree icons by Michael Tenebrae

"Children of a Wine-Dark World" © 2020, David Gallay & Douglas Anstruther
"The Relic" © 2020, J. Tynan Burke & L'Erin Ogle
"Lambs Fight to Die" © 2020, Evan Marcroft
"The Third Chamber From the Left" © 2020, Douglas Anstruther & L'Erin Ogle
"Boro Boro" © 2020, Evan Marcroft & J. Tynan Burke
"Instar" © 2020, David Gallay
"Snakeheart" © 2020, Douglas Anstruther & Evan Marcroft
"Sudden Oak Death" © 2020, J. Tynan Burke
"Titanotheosis" © 2020, David Gallay & Evan Marcroft
"Memories Written in Scars" © 2020, L'Erin Ogle
"Project Blackbook" © 2020, J. Tynan Burke & David Gallay
"The Blood Dance of Ape and Mouse" © 2020, Evan Marcroft & L'Erin Ogle
"The Firmament" © 2020, Douglas Anstruther
"Daylight" © 2020, L'Erin Ogle & David Gallay
"Infernal Policies and Procedures Have Changed" © 2020, Douglas Anstruther & J. Tynan Burke

Authors also retain copyrights to all other material in the anthology.

Works of fiction

This book contains works of fiction. Characters, dialogue, places, organizations, incidents, and events portrayed in the works are fictional and are products of the author's imagination or used fictitiously. Any resemblance to actual persons, places, organizations, or events is coincidental.

All rights reserved

All rights reserved. With the exception of brief quotations embedded in critical reviews, no part of this publication may be reproduced, distributed, stored, or transmitted in any form or by any means – including all electronic and mechanical means – without written permission from the publisher.

The authors and artists worked hard to create this work for your enjoyment. Please respect their work and their rights by using only authorized copies. If you would like to share this material with others, please buy them a copy.

Moral rights asserted

Each author whose work is included in this book has asserted their moral rights, including the right to be identified as the author of their respective work(s).

Publisher

Verdage

Verdage is an imprint of
Metaphorosis Publishing
Neskowin, OR, USA

www.metaphorosis.com

"Metaphorosis" is a registered trademark.

Discounts available

Substantial discounts are available for educational institutions, including writing workshops. Discounts are also available for quantity purchases. For details, contact Metaphorosis at metaphorosis.com/about

Metaphorosis Publishing

Metaphorosis offers beautifully written science fiction and fantasy. Our imprints include:

Metaphorosis Magazine

Plant Based Press

Verdage

Help keep Metaphorosis running at Patreon.com/metaphorosis

See more about some of our books on the following pages.

Metaphorosis Magazine

Metaphorosis
a magazine of speculative fiction

Metaphorosis is an online speculative fiction magazine dedicated to quality writing. We publish an original story every week, along with author bios, interviews, and notes on story origins. Come and see us online at magazine.Metaphorosis.com

You can also find us at:
Twitter: @MetaphorosisMag, @MetaphorosisRev, @Metaphorosis
Facebook: www.facebook.com/metaphorosis

We publish monthly print and e-book issues, as well as yearly Best of and Complete anthologies.

Metaphorosis: Best of 2019

The best science fiction and fantasy stories from *Metaphorosis* magazine's fourth year.

Complete Metaphorosis 2019

All the stories from *Metaphorosis* magazine's fourth year. Fifty-two great SFF stories.

**Metaphorosis:
Best of 2018**

The best science fiction and fantasy stories from *Metaphorosis* magazine's third year.

Complete Metaphorosis 2018

All the stories from *Metaphorosis* magazine's third year. Fifty-two great SFF stories.

**Metaphorosis:
Best of 2017**

The best science fiction and fantasy stories from *Metaphorosis* magazine's *second* year.

Complete Metaphorosis 2017

All the stories from *Metaphorosis* magazine's second year. Fifty-three great SFF stories.

**Metaphorosis:
Best of 2016**

The best science fiction and fantasy stories from *Metaphorosis* magazine's first year.

Complete Metaphorosis 2016

Almost all the stories from *Metaphorosis* magazine's first year.

Plant Based Press

plant based press

Vegan-friendly science fiction and fantasy, including an annual anthology of the year's best SFF stories.

Best Vegan SFF of 2019

The best vegan-friendly science fiction and fantasy stories of 2019!

Best Vegan SFF of 2018

The best vegan-friendly science fiction and fantasy stories of 2018!

Best Vegan SFF of 2017

The best vegan-friendly science fiction and fantasy stories of 2017!

Best Vegan SFF of 2016

The best vegan-friendly science fiction and fantasy stories of 2016!

Susurrus

A darkly romantic story of magic, love, and suffering.

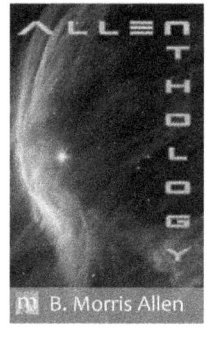

Allenthology: Volume I

A quarter century of SFF, including the full contents of the collections *Tocsin, Start with Stones,* and *Metaphorosis.*

Verdage

Science fiction and fantasy books for writers – full of great stories, but with an additional focus on the craft of speculative fiction writing.

Score
an SFF symphony

What if stories were written like music? *Score* is an anthology of varied stories arranged to follow an emotional score from the heights of joy to the depths of despair – but always with a little hope shining through.

Reading 5X5
Five stories, five times

Twenty-five SFF authors, five base stories, five versions of each – see how different writers take on the same material, with stories in contemporary and high fantasy, soft and hard SF, and a mysterious 'other' category.

Reading 5X5
Writers' Edition

All the stories from the regular, readers' edition, plus two extra stories, the story seed, and authors' notes on writing. Over 100 pages of additional material specifically aimed at writers.